The Artisans

JULIE REECE

Month9Books

Month9Books

For Blake
Fierce defender of those she loves

"The boundaries which divide Life from Death are at best shadowy and vague. Who shall say where the one ends, and where the other begins?" ~ Edgar Allan Poe

The Artisans

JULIE REECE

The Before

The winter of two thousand nine brought influenza, taking twenty-seven souls from Colleton County, South Carolina. The good people of Sales Hollow deposited their corpses in the ground. The following spring, Hurricane Isaac hit the coast, and the earth gave them back.

Scandal covered the news. It seemed the proprietors of Coffee Funeral Home took money from several grieving families to cremate their loved ones, including my late mother, Ida Elizabeth Weathersby. They buried the bodies in their own backyard. Granted, the Coffee family plantation consisted of sixty acres. Still, the urn filled with pasty white sand was a poor substitute for my mother's actual remains, and the undoing of my stepfather, Ben.

While the sheriff handcuffed Wade, Jerry, and Thomas Coffee and led them away, the deceased, who had resided up until that point in shallow graves behind the crumbling Coffee family tennis courts, were identified through their dental records.

Some things you never see coming. Like Ben's attempt to smuggle a gun into the courthouse at the Coffee brothers' arraignment, his subsequent arrest, release, and emotional breakdown.

Other things are glaringly obvious. Like the crippling pain of someone you care for. Dreams wither and waste away much the same as an apple core curls under the hot southern sun.

What sacrifice is too great when you love someone?

I decided there was none—the day I gave my freedom away.

The Middle
Chapter One

Sweat drips from my temple as I push a needle through my friend's torn flesh. Years of sewing custom clothing enable me to make tiny sutures in his skin, close the three-inch gash in his shoulder. I hope it won't leave another scar.

Dane sits on the closed toilet seat in my bathroom. The space is too tight, the air between us close and cloying. I toss my head, shaking damp hair away from my eyes. Blood trickles down his bicep as I pierce him again. Today makes the third time I've sewn him up. He doesn't complain about the pain. I don't ask what pissed his father off this time.

Dane Adams introduced himself in my English Literature class a year ago when he first moved to Sales Hollow from Nashville. He missed the drama concerning the Coffee brothers, my mother's corpse, and Ben's trial. After Ben got out of the psyche ward, my name became synonymous with social pariah. People don't look me in the eye anymore. Pity, guilt, fear ... whatever the reason, I make them uncomfortable.

Dane doesn't treat me that way.

Angry and incessant buzzing breaks my concentration. I scowl at the window where a fly is trapped between the screen and the world outside. I can't set him free. The windows are painted shut. Refocusing on my task, I complete two more stitches, tie them off, and cut the thread. Not bad. I tape gauze loosely over the angry wound and straighten. He grabs my fingers, giving them a tender squeeze.

Sorrow mixed with gratitude shines from his dark brown eyes. I clear the knot from my throat. "All fixed up, bro."

I take a step back allowing Dane to stand. The guy dwarfs the little space. He leans around me, lifting a white cotton tee from its place on the sink countertop.

"Wait, you'll tear your stitches." I help him stretch the fabric over his head and cover his impressive torso.

When he showed up earlier, he was wearing the new, camel-colored leather jacket I made him. Double lapel over a red button up paired with dark stonewashed jeans and boots. Sharp. He can't afford to pay me for the clothes I make him. I wouldn't take his money if he could. The dumb guy spent ten minutes hanging out, bleeding, until finally admitting he needed stitching up.

I glance at my wrist for the hundredth time. The watch is my own design, fashioned from discarded parts into a silver, steampunk beetle. The wings slide to reveal a clock face. Two forty-five AM.

"How long has he been gone?"

The 'he' referred to is my stepfather Ben. I raise my eyes to find Dane studying me. He lifts an eyebrow, waiting. My shrug is my only answer.

A heavy breath leaks out as my friend leans against the wall. "You should have called me when he went missing."

Hoping to avoid an interrogation, I head out of the bathroom and into the storage area of our leather repair shop. The lease doesn't cover our living here, of course, but since we lost our apartment two months ago, we had no place else to go.

Dane follows and I face him. "It's not your job to protect us all the time. You've got your own problems. I can handle this."

"As if." He snorts. "Don't I always find him? You need me. Besides, I'm scary as hell."

I can't help my smile. He *is* scary as hell. Severe facial bone structure makes him look perpetually pissed off. He's tall and skinny but in a wiry, muscular sort of way. The boy can bend metal pipes with his bare hands. I've seen him.

Our rent is overdue. I glance at the fabric piled on the work counter. Resentment sprouts like weeds in my chest. "I have a clothing order to finish ..."

"I know you're broke, but can you sew while you're worried about him?" Dane tosses his long, rust-colored dreads over his shoulder revealing the fresh bruise on his neck.

Anger burns a hole in my gut, but there's nothing I can do to help him. Or anyone else it seems. "I can't always drop everything and go looking for Ben!" I slink to my sleeping bag on the floor. I don't know why I'm yelling. The people I'm angry at aren't in the room to hear. "Sorry. I'm sorry."

"Don't be sorry, Rae. I get it." He scratches his chin. "Leave him be for one night. He'll turn up."

What I haven't told him is that I've already been looking.

All night long, I searched Ben's usual haunts—the liquor stores, card games, and bars he frequents—with no sign. Jacob, who owns the pawnshop Ben visits, said the hot game in town was one held near the docks at Maddox Industries, a textile warehouse district turned seedy clubs and bars. The name Maddox is like a shadow over our town, drawing a collective shudder. Everyone has heard the rumors: money, crime ... bodies in the river.

Surely Ben knows better.

I meet Dane's gaze. "I'm lucky to have you looking out for me."

He grins. "Yes you are. Should we go find Ben?"

"Do you mind if we just chill here for a while first?" The truth is, between school, work, my earlier search, and treating Dane's wound, I'm exhausted.

"Whatever you need."

Gratitude pours out in the form of a sigh. I lean my head

back against the concrete block wall to rest. Edgar, my twenty-five pound Maine Coon, climbs around in my lap and lies down. He's too big to fit, but that doesn't stop him from trying.

Shirt and shoes discarded, Dane flops on top of Ben's sleeping bag a few feet away. His long dreads spill across his brown, tatted shoulders. From this angle, he looks like the monster from the movie *Predator*. The thought makes me smile.

He's snoring in minutes. I've lost count how many nights he's slept over. Though his father owns a physical house, the fact he prefers our storeroom floor says everything about his home life. The unforgiving linoleum digs into my tailbone through my thin sleeping bag, and I shift, exacting a complaint from Edgar, whose weight puts my legs to sleep.

My cat purrs, his whiskers vibrating with the contented sound as I stroke his black fur. I wish I were as unconcerned, but honestly, I'm too keyed up over Ben's prolonged absence to think of much else. Anytime he's missing longer than forty-eight hours, bad things happen. A grueling night of searching turned up nothing, so we wait here. School starts in a few hours, but I won't sleep.

Pounding on the back door sends Edgar scrambling for the corner. Dane's up in seconds, chest heaving, my baseball bat clenched in his hand. I hold up a palm and slowly step to the back door. The one leading to the alley reserved for loading and deliveries. "Who's there?" I ask.

"Jacob. Let me in!"

Fingers tangle as I unbolt the lock and push the door wide. Jacob stands in the sickly orange glow of a buzzing street lamp in a rumpled trench coat. His green Cutlass idles in the background. Hanging limp at his side is Ben. "Come inside," I whisper.

Dane drops the bat and rushes forward. His stitches might rip, but there's no use trying to stop him. He lifts my unconscious stepfather like he's a small child and lays him on the other sleeping bag. His body is too thin, wasting from addiction and despair. His clothes are covered in black smears. A purple bruise blooms like an inkblot across his forehead. His nose and lip are busted.

"Is he okay?" Dane asks what I can't. I rub my forehead where an ache starts, weary of this scene. Jacob hitches his broad shoulders, stretching his fleshy neck to one side. I feel for him. As my stepfather's oldest friend, I've lost count of the times he's brought Ben home.

"Took a beating, but yeah, he'll be okay."

I stare at Ben's listless form on the floor. He stinks of cheap booze and body odor. It's hard to get really clean in the little sink in our half bath, not that he tries.

"Raven?"

My head snaps up. I have no idea how long Jacob has been calling my name. "Sorry, what?"

"There's more." He rubs his neck and stretches again. "I hate to tell you this kiddo, but Ben hawked your mother's wedding ring last night." My chin drops. "Well, you don't think I'd let him pawn it in my shop, do you? Don't you look at me like that!"

"Sorry, I just—"

"I know, sweetie. Lost every dime in a poker game." He shakes his head, stroking a hand down his ample belly. "I never thought he'd give up your momma's ring, never that." My heart cramps with every word. "He left the casino but showed up again an hour later, begging for a chance to win his money back. When they told him to get out, he went wild, tore the place up. He was so drunk, he … started a fire. It was an accident, but the place went up like a match. Thousands in damage. I can't see any way out for him this time."

An arm comes around my shoulder, and I lean into it. The next thing I know I'm sitting Indian-style on the floor, staring at Ben. How did I get here? My cheeks are wet. My chest tightens in a vise grip of fear, and I release a sob. I'm so tired. All I want is to curl up and sleep. Forget.

"It's okay, Jacob, I'll stay with her."

Dane? His voice is distorted, as if he's floating somewhere above me. Wouldn't that be nice? All of us floating away together, like puffy clouds on a summer's day.

"Will they arrest him now?" Dane asks.

"These people don't arrest you, boy. They make you disappear, you know that. Best to get him out of town. Oh, Ben had a letter with him ..."

I glance up at Jacob. Our old friend pulls a thin, white envelope from his coat pocket. "Give it to me," I say.

He hesitates, gaze darting from Dane to me and back.

"It's all right, guys. I need to know." Dane nods to Jacob, and the letter finds its way into my hand. I'm not sure how long I sit there. Shoes scuff the dull linoleum. I'm vaguely aware when the door clicks shut behind Jacob as he leaves. Outside, his motor revs, and then fades as he drives away. The letter still waits in my shaking hand.

"Give it here, little Rae." Dane pries the envelope from my tightly clenched fingers. "We'll read it together, want to?"

Edgar curls up next to Ben still crumpled on the floor. I don't speak. I can't.

Mr. Benjamin Edward Weathersby,

This letter is an attempt to collect a debt. Please meet me in my office at 11:00 AM Friday morning on September 21st to discuss my terms for your restitution. The judgment has been recorded and documented in my ledger and needs to be paid.

Come alone. Do not contact the authorities, do not sign the payment arrangement attached to this letter, and do not respond to this communication in any way other than to meet me in person. If you fail to appear, I will take whatever action necessary to collect the debt owed me.

Sincerely,
G. N. Maddox

Blood turns to slush in my veins, thick, barely moving, slowing my ability to hear, or breathe, or think. *The* Mr. G. N. Maddox. Are the rumors true? Crime boss, ruthless killer, an evil beast incapable of compassion or mercy. Of all the people Ben could owe ... I stare at my hands. My fingers quake, but I can't feel them. Everything's gone numb.

Ben. I can't lose him.

"What is today?" I ask. My voice is quiet but hard as an ice pick. Every sacrifice I've made to hold on to what's left of my family seems in vain.

"September 21st. That meeting's four hours away." Dane drops down on my sleeping bag. "There's no way Ben can make it, Raven. Look at him."

"It doesn't matter, bro. Can you check on him after school today? I'm going to skip."

"Why?" He props himself up on his elbows. "I'm almost afraid to ask what you're planning in that stupid, stubborn head of yours."

"Ben's not going to make the meeting at Mr. Maddox's house this morning."

Dane scowls as if he knows what's coming, and I think he does.

"I am."

Chapter Two

When I pull up to the curb at number seven Wormwood Road, my insides curl up. Who knows why it's numbered seven; it's the only house for miles around. Nothing could prepare me for the Victorian monstrosity that looms beyond a heavy wrought iron gate. Who are they hiding back there, King Kong?

I put my vintage red Beetle in park and step onto the street. The only reason I still own this car is that I hide the title from Ben. Dane keeps it for me at his house.

Built in brick and cream sandstone, more than a dozen grouped chimneys rise like spires over a slate roof. I know because my ninth-grade history teacher had us build scale models of European castles for midterm exams. My preoccupation with Edgar Allen Poe doesn't hurt my knowledge of all things Goth, either. Mother knew what she was doing when she named me Raven.

The windows range in shape from pointy arches to clover-shaped, the third story encasing colorful leaded glass with decorative tracery. Battlements, parapets, and Oriel balconies set this joint off as your basic vampirism party house—deluxe.

Whatever. Determination (and maybe a solid dose of desperation) spurs me on toward the sidewalk. My three-inch heels click across the concrete. A knife is tucked just inside the knee-high laces of my right boot, just in case. My fingers run over the ornate leaves, gargoyles, and iron scrollwork that make up the front gate. The entrance seems more suited to a creepy old graveyard than bayside southern mansion, but I think the artwork is beautiful in a disturbing, retro sort of way. The scene calls to the dark poet in me.

Warm winds blow off the salt water, filling my nose with the scent of brine, and marsh, and forest. The breeze sends my long, razor-cut hair across my eyes. I shake the dark strands back, pulling the gate open with a clank. Above me, the word Maddox stands out in arched relief over the door—the name of my nemesis.

My vision clouds as I stare. Eyes watering, I rub them as the letters on the gate appear to stretch and bend in front of me. The font drips iron like black wax melting off a candle. I shudder as the metal morphs into something cryptic and sinister. Unsure of what I'm seeing, I squint at the newly forming word *Vigilis.* I stumble back. When I blink, the odd lettering is gone. Everything is as it was.

Vigilis. What the hell?

Body racing with adrenaline, I draw a deep breath. I can't afford to freak out. Ben has no one else, so I slough off the strange vision as nerves, square my shoulders, and march toward the double-arched front door. If the bell chimes the beginning of Beethoven's Fifth Symphony, I'm coming back with a cross and some Holy water.

I don't find out what the doorbell sounds like because some old guy in a black coat opens the door. "May I help you?"

Plastering a big smile on my face, there's little need to fake my out-of-breath speech. "Hi! Oh, am I late? I'm so sorry. Half the time those GPS instructions are wrong, you know?" I hold my breath, hoping he'll fall for my act as I blow past Maddox's gatekeeper into the foyer.

Mr. Butler Guy, or whoever he is, spins to follow me.

"Excuse me … just a moment … Miss!"

Okay, so he's no dummy. Too bad, but no one is stopping this meeting. "I apologize again," I say with my best, faux perky voice. I'm making myself gag here with my imitation of a ditzy schoolgirl, but oh well. "I'm aware Mr. Maddox doesn't like to be kept waiting." I glance at my wrist for the time. "Oops. Watch stopped. Silly me, no wonder I'm late. Ha, ha, ha. Could you tell the gentleman his eleven o'clock appointment is here? I'd be so grateful, thanks bunches."

Apparently, batting your eyelashes only works in the movies, because Mr. Butler Guy straightens himself to his full height—which is shorter than my five-foot-seven. He's got to be seventy. Thin, frail, the man is nearly bald, and his scalp is covered in dark liver spots. Black spectacles slide down an impressive nose stuffed with white hairs. They match his eyebrows, as though all the hair on this guy's body migrated to those two areas. Attractive.

He glares at me, but I pretend not to notice.

"Nice place. Very …" Ominous, spooky, chilling. "Imposing," I finally manage. The interior of the house matches every expectation based on its shell. Asymmetrical floor plan, the massive mahogany staircase curves left with a thinner stair breaking off and winding right to what must be the third floor. Everything is dark wood, red carpeting, crusty, dusty, and haunted looking. You gotta be kidding me. All the place lacks is a suit of armor and *The Addams Family.*

"Young woman, you are not expected. Now if you will be so kind as to leave the prem—"

"Jamis? It's all right. I will see her." A disembodied voice floats down the hall. It's a nice voice, young, low, and well, hot.

A muscle in the old man's jaw flexes as he glances from me to the long hallway on our right.

I drop the sugar-and-spice routine now that I've been admitted. I am many things but sweet isn't one of them. My arms fold over my chest. I'm enjoying my victory over the snotty butler just a little too much, but I'm building my confidence for what's ahead. "He'll see me now, Jamis."

The butler ignores me and faces the empty hall. "Very good, sir."

I follow as he heads in the direction of the mysterious voice. My fingers twine together. I glance at the oil paintings on the walls, exotic vases on the credenzas lining the wide hallway. Despite my bold plan, I'm full of crap, so full my eyes should be brown and not gray. I'm scared to death of what might happen if I fail to convince this guy to leave my stepfather alone.

"Madam." The old man bows at the entrance to the last door at the hall's end.

From miss to madam, huh? I wink and he rewards me with a look of shocked disdain. Maybe I shouldn't be so hard on the poor old guy. How nice could he be, though, working for a skeeze like Maddox? *Ladies respect their elders, the position of age, no matter their behavior.* My mother's prim voice echoes in my mind. Fine. "Thank you," I mumble. That's all he's getting.

His eyes widen ever so slightly as I breeze past him. Floor to ceiling bookshelves cover the walls between rich, dark paneling inside. I breathe in dust, and age, and something sweet. A bowl of red cherries sits on a green blotter atop the desk, an open deck of playing cards scattered beside them. There's an ancient looking camera resting on a wooden tripod that takes center stage in the middle of the floor. It's oddly placed, the lens aimed directly at the doorway I stand in.

"Why have you come?"

I don't see anyone at first as I shuffle forward. Heavy brocade curtains block the windows, keeping the room dark. One lamp burns on the desktop flooding the surface with light but leaving the rest of the space dim. My gaze darts around the room until movement pulls my attention to a silhouette behind the desk. I swallow hard, my heart hammering. "I'm Raven Weathersby, here on behalf of my stepfather Benjamin Weathersby. He's too sick to meet with you today."

"Raven?" I still can't see him. My name rolls off his tongue slowly. His pronunciation is deliberate, as if he tastes the sound it makes. "Will you sit?"

"I'll stand." My refusal is meant to appear tough, but I immediately regret my words. Nerves are multiplying and my knees rattle beneath me. I guess he keeps to the shadows to intimidate me and it's working. Why won't he show himself? It's pissing me off.

"Then let's get to it, shall we? Your stepfather's gambling debts are extreme, not to mention his drunk stumbling into a display of candles in the foyer set my club on fire. Regardless of his health, your stepfather will have to keep his appointment. He's caused me more than enough trouble."

The shadow sounds too young to own a club, or anything else, for that matter. Not yet a man's voice, but not a boy's either, his speech is prep-school snark or tutored, home-school formal. "I understand your frustration, *sir*," I say. "But it was an accident. That 'club' was a hundred-year-old warehouse. A pile of kindling used for illegal gambling. Insurance will pay for physical losses, anyway. I know you're covered."

I did, too. I spent the hours before my meeting in Jacob's shop on his laptop. Google helped me check up on the illustrious Maddox Enterprises, their textiles and manufacturing ... Between Jacob, Ben's bookie, Michael Botts, and a few others, I'd gotten quite an education this morning.

Maddox didn't corner the market on connections. Sure, some of mine were less than reputable, but Ben grew up in this town. Everyone knew my mother and the story of her ... unearthing. I wasn't above using their pity to save the only father I'd ever known. When you're down and out, you do what you must to survive. It might not be pretty, but I couldn't afford the luxury of pride. "I will pay what he owes. There must be something we can ..."

It's too quiet. All I hear is the sound of faint breathing. Footsteps brush the red, Persian rug beneath us. The light from the desk lamp illuminates handsome male features as the figure steps closer.

A boy stands in the center of the room. Boy? Guy. He's six feet, at least. Messy, blond hair falls in an appealing way over his brow. He casually rests a hip against the giant walnut desk. He's wearing tan leather pants, a white cotton tunic, and a green, duck canvas overcoat that hangs to his knees, complete with faux fur collar. His clothes are good. Not as good as mine, but custom, and quite nice. I make my observations in seconds, ticking off the particulars. This guy oozes more electrical sex appeal than the Las Vegas Strip.

When he shifts his weight, I notice his cane for the first time. The dark wood and gold, lion-head grip makes it the most beautiful walking stick I have ever seen. I'd kill to own one like it. Well, maybe not kill, but maim? Definitely. I feel my brow creasing. This isn't the infamous Nathan Maddox. He's too young. "Who are you?"

He leans over, twisting the lamp switch from low to high. Light brightens the entire room. "Gideon Maddox, at your service," he replies.

Maddox has a son? I guess I'd heard that, but few have ever seen him. Always away at boarding school or something. I wonder if the square-jawed, GQ model standing in front of me knows his father's plan. "What do you want with Ben?"

"Restitution. Isn't it obvious?" He stares like I'm a puzzle that needs solving. "Only, I wasn't expecting you …" He shifts and glances at the camera in the center of the room. "This is quite a surprise." A line forms between his eyebrows. "So, what do I do with you? What to do …"

My feet tingle. Before I know what's happening, I pace. If I stand in one spot any longer, I'll crack. "Let me speak with your father. I'm sure we can work something out."

His expression hardens to granite, eyes flashing dark and dangerous. "The correspondence was from me. I handle these matters now, not my father." His voice is careful, calculating. Plotting against Ben as if he's planning his next move on a chessboard.

He shifts, leaning on his cane. The guy is stunning from a physical standpoint. I hate myself for noticing, but it's actually hard not to stare. He said he's taken over. Does that mean the son continues his father's ruthless practices? I detect no compassion in his stony expression.

"Let him go," I say, trying to keep the pleading to a minimum. "Talk to your dad or whoever. Ban Ben from your clubs, your game tables. He's been through a lot, more than you could possibly understand. He's old and sick, not that you care. I'll pay whatever he owes if you'll just give me some time."

His chin lifts ever so slightly, giving the impression he's unused to being questioned. "That's not how things work with our family. Rules must be followed; justice served."

What 'things' is he talking about? Is he with some sort of gang, the mob? "I'm talking about a payment plan, not a pardon. Can't you change the rules?"

His jaw stiffens as he shakes his head. "No." He watches me carefully before continuing. "You're on dangerous ground here, Raven. We are very powerful people. You have no idea who you're dealing with."

There are two kinds of arrogance in boys. The first is when a kid is all bluff and brag without the skill to back it up. The second is a guy who knows he can deliver, there's a quiet confidence in his eyes, a deadly grace to his movements. Gideon belongs in group two. I'm not sure it's wise to argue, but I don't want him thinking I'm afraid.

"Why, because you have money? That doesn't make anyone noble, or worthy, or good ..." Gideon's eyes narrow. I know I should shut up, but I can't. Anger builds in me as I speak, years of pain and loss, boiling up my throat like acid. "Parasites, that's all you are. Cruel and manipulative, preying on—"

"Enough!" Gideon growls. "How dare you talk about my family like that, challenge our reputation?"

"Your reputation is nothing compared with Ben's life. He's the only family I have left." I hate the weakness in my voice, but I can't control it. "I'll do anything to protect him."

He pauses, gaze darting again to the camera in the center of the room. A frown pulls at his perfectly shaped lips as he exhales. "*Anything* is a big word, Raven."

My swallow is more of a gulp. At first, this guy came off

wary but cool, a little mysterious. After listening to him talk, I'm suspecting the real story. The boy's got some damage, enough to make him a monster. No one reasons with this level of pride.

"Yes, fine, take it out on me instead. Whatever you want, just leave Ben alone." I'm offering myself up like a lamb. God help me, I'm really doing it. Gideon's going to kill me, or someone is.

His eyebrows spike. "You'd do that? Give up your freedom?"

My freedom? Wait a min—"What do you want?"

"You." He clears his throat. "Your designs, rather. The Maddox clothing lines are weak and suffering losses. You create for me unconditionally, give me production rights, and at the end of a year, I will stamp your stepfather's debt paid in full."

"My designs ... ? How do you know about my clothes?"

"Good strategists study their opponents, Raven. I know more about you than you might think. Now, what do you say? You for your father."

I step toward the old camera, stalling. His offer whirls in my brain. This morning, I discovered that Maddox Enterprises had changed their name from Maddox Textiles forty years ago. Once cotton moguls, the company diversified when production overseas killed their domestic markets.

They still manufacture a struggling fashion line that supports half a dozen designers. Any one of them stands to make money if he or she hits the right clothing chord with America. The idea Gideon wants my work is flattering, or would be, if I didn't want to choke him to death with my bare hands.

A pretty, red velvet ball hangs from the side of the camera lens. Lost in my thoughts, I reach out a hand.

"Don't!" Somehow, Gideon is beside me. He tugs me against him, holding my wrist in his iron grip. I lift my face to his. Blond curls fall over his forehead, obscuring one eye. The other is brilliant blue. "Didn't your father teach you not to touch what isn't yours?"

I snatch my hand from his grasp. "Didn't yours?" Ragged breaths pump from my lungs as I back away. "What's your problem? Have you got a gun hiding in there?" I'm half-joking, but he doesn't look amused. In fact, his face pales. My heart stutters in response, wondering if I was right after all.

"Decide, Ms. Weathersby. You may remain here. Work in my house—for a year—and your father goes free. Those are my terms."

"Stay here? You can't be serious. That's impossible." I've got Ben to look after, school, the shop. Maybe dying is better than being tortured over a year. Who knows what this guy might try? But then, who would care for Ben? "That's illegal. It's kidnapping, extortion, blackmail—"

"Don't be ridiculous. As far as anyone else is concerned, I'm simply a family friend offering to help with your career, providing you with a place to stay while your father gets the help he desperately needs." He walks back to his desk, the hitch in his step barely noticeable. His tone takes on a cheerful note, as if he really sees himself as my benefactor. "You're still a minor, aren't you? One anonymous call to Child Services informing them you live in a storage room with a drunk ought to do the trick. I think there are child endangerment laws that apply here. Which of us do you suppose they'll believe?"

No. This can*not* be happening.

"You will not get another offer."

You were willing to die for Ben a minute ago. The voice inside my head is barely a whisper, and I sound like a hypocrite, but this is falling on a different kind of sword. I've learned some things are worse than death. *What did you think would happen coming here*, I ask myself. Ruthless people don't say 'Oh sure hon, my mistake. I forgive your father. Go have a nice life.'

"I can't."

"That was a quick turn-around. You said *anything*. Not as committed to dear old dad as you thought?" The words stab like barbs.

He's right, but dying is different than selling your soul.

"No. Yes. I mean, what about school? It's my senior year, and what about Ben, my cat, my clients? I can't just move in here with you."

A wicked half-smile escapes. "You can, and you will, or no deal. Your clients are irrelevant. Tell them you found an investor and cancel their orders. I am your world now."

My world.

I was a happy, carefree kid once but since mom died? No dating, no sleepovers with friends, or school dances. My world has been part-time jobs, picking my stepfather up from whatever bar he's passed out in, and dragging him home. Five years on that hamster wheel, the routine is automatic. I can't save Ben, or fix all our problems, but I can't stop trying. God, what do I do? The temptation to feel sorry for myself is too great. The room smears as my eyes fill with unshed tears.

Gideon won't meet my gaze. Instead, he lifts his chin, squinting at a spot above my head. "Move in. Bring the damn cat. Ben wins an all-expense paid trip to a rehab facility. Based on the sketches I've seen in your portfolio, by the time my people finish marketing your new line of clothing, the profits will more than reimburse me. As for school, you're not on house arrest. Continue to go, or I'll hire a tutor. I'll decide later." His eyes narrow. "Don't attempt to contact the authorities about our true arrangement. For those that ask, explain that I'm helping you launch a product line and you're working for me. You figure out how best to convince your friends this is a good thing, but remember, one slip and Ben is finished. Understand?"

He has my portfolio? Had one of his thugs steal it from our storeroom, I'll wager. I can't believe this is happening, or how this jerk thinks he can get away with his proposal. It's like something off one of those nighttime news shows where girls are found chained to sewing machines or computers in the basement. Slave labor, child labor, I don't know—something. Then I think of Ben. What wouldn't I do to save his life? My answer is swift. Nothing.

"I'll do it."

"I know you will." The guy exudes confidence, and I realize he never had a moment's doubt I would agree. "Take a few days and get your affairs in order. Terminate your lease, and if you have any problems with your landlord ... Never mind, you won't have any trouble." Gideon paces as he speaks. He's focused, intense. "I will prepare your workspace. Make a list of the materials you'll need to get started and give it to Jenny, the housekeeper. I will make your father's travel arrangements to enter a rehab facility." He stops, scowling at me as if I insulted him. "Don't you have any questions?"

Only a hundred, but my mouth is as dry as sawdust. How will I endure a year under the same roof with his cruelty? I won't. The guy is dangerous. Like a golden lion that enjoys toying with his victims before he ends them. Then one of his statements jumps out and slaps me in the face.

"You said travel arrangements. For my stepfather ..." Is Gideon lying? Telling me what he thinks I want to hear? That my father is going to rehab when in truth he'll wind up missing, dead in some ditch somewhere. Gideon will use me until he gets what he wants and then put me down next to Ben.

"Raven." His voice is steady, quiet, a snake rearing before the strike.

A tear breaks free and rolls down my cheek. My gaze locks on my adversary, wishing I could burn a hole through his forehead. How can I fight you, I wonder? Everything about him is relaxed, from his proud stance to his barely-there smile. My hands curl to fists at my sides. My teeth clench. How can I save my dad and save myself? There must be a way. "It doesn't make any sense. Why do all this? Why trap me here?"

"You're an investment. A valuable one that I intend to keep my eye on."

Thoughts of planting the heel of my boot in his groin keep me busy. My wish must be obvious because Gideon smiles wider. He stands there, staring me down. In fact, we eye each other like Cobra and Mongoose.

"Try not to struggle, Raven. I assure you, no one escapes from me."

Chapter Three

"What the hell?" Dane asks. A wisp of smoke leaves his mouth as he takes the last drag off his cigarette. He tosses the butt to the ground and gives me his trademark scowl. "You can't seriously be considering this deal with Maddox."

Me, Dane, and Maggie Wilson, my only other real friend, lounge on the hood of her Toyota Camry in the parking lot in front of Harry's Shoe and Leather Repair Shop. The Sales Hollow Plaza hosts a total of four shops: the shoe shop we manage, Maxim Liquor (a favorite of Ben's until they cut off his credit), Zany's Thrift, and Real Quick Pawn where Jacob works. The strip mall is a thing of beauty, really.

"Quit it." Maggie shoves his formidable shoulder. "Don't make her feel worse. What are her options?"

When I returned from Gideon's house to the shop, Ben was asleep on the storeroom floor. I woke him up, filled him in, and waited for a response. Lifting his head, he stared up at me for a minute. Then he drooled on himself before his eyes glazed over and he face-planted on his pillow. He's been there ever since. Beat up and drying out, he needs the rest.

I needed to talk to someone, and so despite Gideon's

warnings, I phoned the only two people in the world I trust. Both would endure being flayed alive before they'd tell anyone my secrets.

Maggie faces me. "I'm sorry, Raven. I'd be scared to death if I had to live in that creepy old house with total strangers."

"Yeah, thanks for that." My wry smile is meant to convey two things: I'll face this decision better with my cynicism intact, and I know she loves me.

Dane's palm casually covers the spot where Maggie touched him. She's five-foot-two and curvy. Okay, plump, but despite her lack of stature, the girl packs a wallop. Dane's eyes harden, his jaw clenches. She's killing him, has been since they met a year ago, and it's a sweet, slow, torturous thing. He'd die for her and she has no idea, stupid girl. I can't tell her either since he's convinced her dad's middle-class income makes her too good for him. That and he promises never to speak to me again if I do. The sad thing is he means it.

"No, but really," Maggie goes on, "Suppose Maddox sticks to his word? He's greedy, but that doesn't mean he'd hurt Raven. He said she could go to school, where she'll be expected and seen every day. Ben gets the expensive counseling needed to get sober, and Rae gets experience designing for a huge corporation."

All the girl needs is a set of pom-poms. She's delusional, but I love her. Maggie frowns when I pat her hand.

"What? I'm serious."

Dane opens his mouth, but I cut him off. "I know you are, Mags."

She looks from me to Dane, as if convincing us is her life's ambition. "All right, think of it like an internship you don't get paid for. Maybe Rae's name starts popping up in magazines or on runways. Once the year is over, Maddox might write her a recommendation, even give her some recognition. It might actually work out okay."

Dane stares at Mags, mouth agape. "Sure, if he doesn't rape or kill her first. Maybe he'll make her president of Maddox Enterprises. Even better, they'll get married and have five kids. Are you insane?"

I cringe, and Maggie's hand shoots out. Her arm braces against my chest as though I'm a passenger in her car and she's slamming on her brakes. "Shut up, Dane. I'm trying to be optimistic. It's not like she has any choice."

She's right about that.

"I'm sorry," Dane says, without an ounce of sincerity. "But I've done some checking, heard some creepy ass shit about that house—ghosts, disappearances, a drowning ... ghosts. You want her to sleep there for a year?"

"Still not helping." I roll my eyes heavenward and silently ask for help.

"Cut it out," Maggie orders.

"No. He's stealing her designs, pure and simple," Dane tosses his hands in the air. The movement highlights the intricate tattoos on his mahogany skin. "That rich asshole sees her talent. He'll rob her blind, make millions off her skill, and she'll get the shaft. Raven has to finish high school, leave Sales Hollow, and go to college." He crosses his arms, like he's some Persian King and his opinion makes a difference.

Only Dane would put the words 'Rae' and 'college' in the same sentence. He ought to know better, but the kid never gives up on anyone but himself. The truth is my dreams for a solid future died with my mother. I just didn't know it then.

Sales Hollow High has a graduating class of one hundred students, the largest in years. Few will stay, though. They'll go to college at UGA or 'Bama, anywhere but here. Design school in New York? I wish. It's out of reach even to dream about SCAD right here in Savannah. Bringing me again to my current, hopeless situation.

Maggie's cheeks flush. "What's your solution, Dane? Put them on a bus? Where would they go, they've got no money." Her short, blond bob bounces with her head shake. The single pink stripe in front swishes like a ribbon.

"At least the bus is a chance. Look, I'm not trying to be a jerk, but Ben made his choices. How long does Rae have to keep paying for them?"

Maggie tucks a lock of platinum hair behind her ear as she

does whenever she's frustrated, and with Dane, that's pretty much all the time. "She'll get there. She's seventeen years old, for crying out loud. A lot could still happen to her. *For her*, I meant *for* her ..." Maggie's expression twists into an apologetic frown.

My stomach lurches, inviting my breakfast to reappear. "No offense, but all this cheering up is making me ill." I slide off the hood of Maggie's car and head toward the shop's front door. "I need to talk to Ben." No use putting this off any longer. "I'll see you guys later, okay? Since I only have a few days left of freedom, please don't fight."

Dane and Maggie's spines straighten. They send stiff smiles my way, and Dane raises a hand. I acknowledge the try, but as I head inside to find Ben, I hear their argument rekindling.

The bell clangs as I push the door open. Edgar comes running like a dog, greeting me with his silly, high-pitched meow. I bend, lifting the oaf into my arms and yell, "Ben?"

"Yep." His voice travels from somewhere deeper in the store.

When I glance in the storeroom, he's sitting on his sleeping bag. The man from my childhood was kind, and strong, and handsome. Only a shadow of that man rests bruised and beaten before me. Left eye swollen shut, he peers at me with his right. His cheeks are sunken, skin sallow and paper-thin. Dark veins fork over his red, swollen nose.

"You hungry?" I ask, noting the tremor in his hands. He shakes his head. With his injuries so severe, I'm guessing he drank what booze he had stashed at the shop and hasn't been able to get out for more. I ease onto the floor across from him and adjust Edgar on my lap. "Decision time, Ben. We've got to choose what to do. I leave for Maddox's place at the end of the week. What about you?"

I love my stepfather, no question, but I ready myself for the lies I assume are coming. The excuses as to why he can't go to rehab. Empty promises, the apologies, pleading, anger, defensiveness, and tears loom on the horizon of all our talks. My responses always follow. I apply a thick layer of guilt, manipulation, fear, exhaustion, resentment, and false hope that if we do the same things one more time—something will magically change. Ladies and gentlemen, please choose your partners. It's time for the spotlight dance between alcoholic and enabler.

Ben lifts his chin. "I'm going to Maddox."

I stiffen. His response is a dance step I don't know. "He'll hurt you, Ben, maybe worse."

"So, I should let you take that risk?" I open my mouth, but Ben raises a quaking palm effectively silencing me. "Hear me out, okay?" I nod, unwilling to entertain any idea having to do with him meeting Maddox. "I'm not a young man, anymore. When your mother died, anything good inside me did, too. For her sake, I deluded myself into thinking I'd stay, take care of you, but it's all been a lie." He runs his hands through his greasy hair and squeezes. "I failed you, and I failed her, and the more I fail the more I drink." He lifts his head, his hands dropping to his lap. "You're better off without me."

"No." Even if it was true, what he's missing is the hope that he and I could still be a normal father and daughter. This is our chance.

"Let me do this," he says. "For once in my life let me do the honorable thing. Let me go to be at peace, to rest with your mama. It's what I want."

Anger boils in my gut like a pot on the stove. "What *you* want?" I bite my lip to curb my tongue and choose my words carefully. "You want to talk about honor? Doing the right thing? What is that exactly, Ben, and right for who?" The roil of bubbling fury in my stomach simmers barely below the surface. "If you want to be a hero, then make your decision based on me this time. What *I* want, because it's always been about you, hasn't it?"

He winces, but I'm just getting started. "Did it ever occur to you that just because I can survive and feed myself doesn't mean that I want to? I don't enjoy being alone, Ben. I've had enough of that. You're the family I have left and the only link to my mother. Your memories of her are precious to me. I remember our life in the before, when you were my Poppa."

I don't know what causes me to use the old title. Perhaps on principle because I haven't called him that in years. "*You* matter to me! Don't you understand?" Tears slip down my face. Old wounds reopen as I try and explain what he means to me. Exasperation swamps my lungs, and I heave a breath.

"I'm sorry."

My shoulders slump. "Don't be sorry. Be brave. Go to rehab." My eyes implore him to simply try.

"What if rehab don't work?"

My mind screams, but I fight to keep my voice steady. "One of two things will happen to us now, Ben. If Maddox is full of shit, we both die. You said yourself that's what you want anyway, but if you're getting help at a rehab that we could never afford otherwise, it's worth the risk to me." I lean against the stock shelf behind me with a long sigh. "Truthfully, the reason I'm going is because I honestly believe Maddox wants my designs to rejuvenate his clothing business, and not my life. I really do. I have something he wants, and that's why he won't hurt me."

My stepfather rubs his hand over the sprouting silver whiskers on his chin.

I have no idea if my theory about Gideon is right, but I have to convince Ben. It's my best attempt at bluffing, and I learned from a pro. "And here's the million dollar question, Pops. What if rehab does work?"

He glances at me and shrugs. A tentative smile pulls at his lips while tears still shimmer on his lashes. "It's a gamble."

"I'm willing to bet on you."

"Always did like the long odds."

"A hundred to one, but think of the payout." I'm done coaxing. The cheese factor is climbing, and I'm running out of gambling euphemisms. "What'll it be, Pops?" He's squirming, rubbing his gnarled hands together. I can almost see the gears in his head turning. Thinking, scamming, plotting a way out; he's searching for another option. One that will bring his next drink, his next fix, but we both know that isn't going to work. Not this time.

"What the hell." He finally says, "I'll go."

Chapter Four

A heartbeat later and the week is gone. The night's sky is inky and calm. It's as if someone drew a black sheet between the earth and sun, then poked holes in the fabric with a pin to let dots of light shine through.

All I have in the world fits inside two duffle bags. They sit like a bad omen on the backseat of my car. Earlier, I refused Dane and Maggie's offer to come with me, but promised I'd call tonight once I'm situated. I'll keep that promise, if only to keep Dane from showing up and tearing the front door off its hinges to check on me.

At eleven thirty today, a stretch limo pulled up to our little storefront and collected Ben. Swallowed up behind a big, black door of opulence, he's heading to Belle Meade, a rehab center in Savannah, forty-seven miles away. What will come of all this I can't say, but a tiny wing-beat of hope flutters in my chest.

"Might as well get this over with, old man," I say to Edgar, as I heft the strap of his carrier over my right shoulder. My purse and two duffle bag straps hang at awkward angles over my other arm as I make my way to the front door. Heavier than anticipated, the weight of my luggage affects my balance. Good thing I'm in my black, military boots. I waddle to the front stoop and drop all but Edgar in a heap at my feet.

The door swings open while my finger is poised at the bell. A stout woman in a conservative blue dress greets me. "Mercy me, child. Why didn't you ring for help?" Her cheeks are bright pink. Scratch that, her whole face is pink, arms too, like she's allergic to air. She's huffing and puffing as though she ran to the door, and her eyes match the color of her dress. "I'd have sent Mr. Jamis down to fetch your bags straightaway. We're all so excited you've come to stay."

Yeah, I'll bet, though her smile is genuine enough. "It's no bother," I say. "I've got it." Perhaps I will have one ally here, after all.

"Miss Weathersby, I presume. So nice to meet you, my girl, I'm Jenny. And who's this little nugget?" She squeaks, bending to peer inside the pet carrier. "Oh, well I never. What a little lamb you are. Hello, pussycat."

Never mind she just referred to Edgar as a lamb, she's nice to my cat. It's official. I like her. She motions me inside with instructions to bring Edgar and leave my bags. I obey. My heart pounds as I step through the doorway. Dark, hollow, the foyer swallows us like a great throat. The place seems different somehow, now that I'm to stay instead of confronting Gideon and leaving like the last time.

"This way, dearie," Jenny says. "You have quite a walk, but I dare say you will manage the distance far better than I will." I follow her plump form up the creepy stairs I viewed during my first visit, to the smaller, creepier stairway veering to the right. "You're on the third floor."

My brow creases with my confusion. "Up there? But I thought—"

"What? That you'd sleep in the servants' quarters with 'ole Jamis and me downstairs?" Not exactly, I'm thinking more like a damp basement or freezing dungeon. "Master Maddox gave detailed instructions concerning you. Your rooms, work area, and study are all together in the eastern part of the house.

No one will bother you there."

I'm not worried. Okay I am, but presently, I'm more curious. My status is prisoner. I don't care what other name Gideon is claiming to hide his indecent proposal under. We pass no one on our way. I'm wondering where everyone else is in this enormous house, and I say as much.

"Oh, there's no one else stays here but me and Mr. Jamis, now. There was a time, of course, before the Master passed away ... Well, never mind about that. Mr. Maddox keeps to the west wing for the most part. You'll not be going over there, mind you. Don't forget. And the cellar, under no circumstances should you go into the cellar, nor the attic. If you need anything ask me."

She peers over her shoulder, searching my face for a response, I guess, so I nod. The last place I want to be is near Gideon or in some dreary cellar. Hell, I didn't even know anyone had a cellar in the lowlands. Any basement would be underwater, wouldn't it?

My breathing increases with my steps. The panting coming from Jenny up ahead reminds me of a freight train. How she goes up and down these stairs every day without keeling over, I don't know. Maybe she doesn't.

The older woman turns lights on as we pass. The elegant furniture lining the hallway is covered in dust, and cobwebs connect the arms of crystal chandeliers dangling from molded ceilings above.

I glance at huge black and white photos in walnut frames. People I assume are ancestors of the Maddox family adorn the walls. They're placed intermittently between various oil paintings and gilded mirrors. In one, an older gentleman stands in the yard outside next to a big white horse, in another a middle-aged man poses with his gun and black and white hound.

As I pass one of a young boy with dark hair, his handsome face engages my imagination. *Who were you?* I wonder. Something about the image gives me an eerie feeling. Big and sorrowful, his life-like eyes seem to follow me. In most of the old photos I've seen, the subjects look stern or bored, but most of these people appear startled, even shocked. Edgar's meow is deep and guttural, setting me more on edge. Oh yeah, we'll sleep like babies in this museum of nasty curiosities.

At the end of one hallway, I stop dead. This frame is larger than the others. The woman in the photo is young and very beautiful with curling hair, a full mouth, and large, expressive eyes. Though the picture is done in black and white, her chenille halter dress is modern, chic—and looks expensive.

"Ah me," says Jenny. "Did I lose you, dearie?"

I glance up. "I'm sorry. A lot to take in, I guess."

"Of course, I understand. There will be plenty of time for that later." She follows my line of sight back up to the photograph. "Mrs. Maddox, before she left us."

"Gideon," I clear my throat, "Mr. Maddox was married?" I thought him way too young, but who knows with these freaky people.

She purses her lips. "I'm referring to Mr. Maddox senior, Nathan. The woman in the picture was my mistress, his second wife, Desiree." Her eyes narrow and her lips pull back in a sneer. The idea the housekeeper didn't care for her former mistress seems an understatement.

Mistress? I can't believe she just said the word mistress. Good Lord, I'm stuck in an episode of Downton Abby. Though more sophisticated, Desiree doesn't appear a whole lot older than me.

"Mr. Maddox was a hard man, but we all grieve his passing. Oh, but pardon me, it's wrong to speak so of the dead. You'll forgive the musings of an old woman."

"Mr. Maddox is dead, too?" When Gideon said he 'ran things,' I should have put it together. No wonder he thinks it's no big deal that I move in here with him. No daddy around to monkey with his decisions.

"To be sure, miss. Gone four years last August, and broke his son's heart, poor lad. Shall we press on? There's much to do before dinner."

"Yeah, sorry. I got distracted, I guess." Why hadn't his

father's obituary shown up on my Google search? Dane hadn't mentioned it. Maybe he didn't know. So, Gideon is an orphan, like me. Well, sort of. I do have Ben. What would Gideon have done to Ben had he come for the meeting instead of me? How can someone as young as Gideon already be so ruthless, so full of hate? The housekeeper's description of 'poor lad' confused me. It hardly fit with my opinion.

"Don't be silly, my dear. Curiosity is natural in young people. But you are here to work, are you not? The rest will come in time, at least I pray so." I'm not sure what she means by the last comment, but I let it pass.

On we walk until she stops at an arched oak door at the end of the last hall. It looks like eight others we passed on our way here, but who's counting. I'm never going to find my way back downstairs. If a fire breaks out in this tinderbox, color me crispy fried bacon.

Raven ...

I slow. Glancing over my shoulder, I'm sure someone called my name from the stair. "Hello?"

"What is it, dearie?"

"I'm sorry, did you call me?"

"Why no, miss."

My head swivels behind me once more and back to Jenny. "I swore I heard someone calling."

The old maid clears her throat. "Old houses make all sorts of odd noises. Not to worry. Come and see your room." Jenny fiddles with a heavy-looking ring of keys. "I did the best I could on short notice. Mr. Maddox says I'm to expect a list of supplies from you. Once you get settled, you can give it to me, and we'll get you started. Dinner is downstairs every night promptly at eight. Remember, stay out of the west wing, the rest is yours to explore, only don't leave the grounds without informing someone." Jenny stops trying keys, giving me her pointed 'I mean it' look again. "Mr. Maddox is quite adamant."

I'll bet he is. "Got it. No leaving the grounds without permission." Does she find my moving here as weird as I do? She gives no hint if she does. Maybe working for arrogant killers makes a person numb to strange circumstances. I have no idea. Sweet as she seems, I doubt she knows all her employer is up to.

"Found it!" Jenny opens the door to a suite of rooms, one opening to the left and one to the right off the larger main.

New carpet smell wafts off the plush cream shag beneath my feet. Light, airy bedclothes cover a queen-sized bed in the center of the main room—white on white on cream on white. The maple furniture is sparse but tasteful. A few steps forward and I notice a theme. Feathers. Massive wings are carved, one folded over another, to make up the four posters of the bed. The design is echoed in the pattern on the quilt and again in the ironwork over the brick fireplace. Cream, fur throws, and pillows sit on a chair and ottoman. They have the carefree look of careful placement by someone with exquisite taste. I stand dumbfounded at the view.

"Is the room to your liking, miss?" Jenny asks.

"It's the most beautiful room I've ever seen." As confounded as I am, I'm thankful not to be chained to a cot in the basement.

"Excellent. Mr. Maddox will be pleased."

Will he? I wouldn't think Mr. Maddox gave a damn.

Jenny points. "Through there is your work area with two sewing machines. That way is the bath and dressing area. Eight o'clock sharp for dinner, please. I'll leave you now ... unless there's anything else I can get you?" Her face looks frantic. If it's just she and Jamis waiting on Mr. High and Mighty for dinner, I imagine she has better things to do than stand here and hold my hand.

"No, you're fine, go, go." I wave her off. "Thanks for showing me around."

She smiles. Her lips part as if she intends to say more but thinks better of it. She bows with her retreat.

I stare at the lavish room, flabbergasted, until a soft mew snaps me out of my stupor. "Edgar!" I open his crate and lift him out hugging the breath from his tiny little lungs. He meows again, annoyed with me. Too bad.

Strange surroundings, sounds and smells, the idea I will be here, all alone, for the next twelve months runs me over like a Mack Truck. Who cares how fancy my room is if I'm cut off from everyone and everything familiar to me. My knees shake, and I slide to the floor still cradling my cat.

Ben. I miss him. I miss my friends. How can I explain my fear, and how I'd rather be curled up in my sleeping bag on a hard storeroom floor than in this gigantic house?

My breathing comes hard and fast. I fear I'm hyperventilating as I bury my face in Edgar's soft fur. Oh, God, you have to help me. Get us out of here.

But God doesn't answer as the first of my tears hits the back of my hand.

Chapter Five

A knock on the door has me bolting upright. Perfect. I guess I fell asleep. Edgar slides off my back to the floor and glares at me. Sorry, boy. "Come in?"

The door opens with a creak and Jamis pokes his head inside. His eyes bug. The old guy works quickly to regain his composure, but I saw him. I'm guessing he's not used to teen girls, that, or I'm witch-scary after my nap on the carpet. Wiping the drool off the side of my mouth, I say, "Can I help you?"

"Dinner is served, miss."

Right. "Listen, as you can see, I'm not ready. Do you think I could eat in my room? Actually, I'm not even hungry. I think I'll just pass tonight."

"That is ill-advised, Miss Weathersby. You are expected."

I don't care if I am or not, until I think of Jenny. The trouble she's probably gone to in preparing a meal for my first night. She's the only one who's nice to me. I don't want to lose that. "Yeah, all right, just a sec."

With no time to change, I fly into the bathroom and gasp, both at the size of the joint and my image in the mirror. Wavy, black hair juts out all over my head. My lanky body, pale skin, and tear-stained eyes make me look like an old store manikin that's past her prime. The jeans are fine. I tug the back of my sable jacket down with one hand while pulling my new burgundy corset up with the other.

My fingers smooth my wild hair into place, then rub across my cheeks in an effort to erase the layers of smudged eyeliner that stain my face. Whatever, good enough. I doubt Jenny cares. I whirl, nearly hitting the copper, claw-foot tub to my rear.

Jamis stands like a toy soldier in the doorframe. If he entertains any thoughts about my post-meltdown appearance, he doesn't voice them. On the way downstairs, we pass the old photographs. The eyes in every picture seem to follow me down the hall. The butler offers no conversation as we make our way to the dining room. Good, I don't want to talk to the old prune anyway.

Room after room, I follow him through parts of the house I've not yet seen. I'm certain I'll never find my way back when we enter a last set of heavily carved, wooden doors. Though clean and free of a moldy wedding cake, the dining room reminds me of Miss Havisham's from the description in Dickens' book *Great Expectations*. I read the novel in English last year. Loved it, actually. The old maid in the story wore her wedding dress every day for years until it disintegrated. She wouldn't clear the wedding decorations after she was jilted at the altar, and eventually, she lit herself on fire and burned to death. There's something terrible and hypnotic about that sort of crazy.

'Course, I never thought I'd live my own version either.

Without a word, Jamis pulls out a chair at the end of the table. I sit. He bows and leaves me alone. The stuffed lynx staring at me from the mantle puts me on weirdness overload. Nothing is what I expect, and I don't know how to act or what's coming next.

Cosmic forces in the universe must think they're pretty funny though because the door on the other side of the dining hall opens and in walks Gideon.

Black slacks, ruby dress shirt, and a black velvet vest with ornate silver buttons down the front. He's stunning with his short blond curls falling in perfect messy rings around his face. His compelling beauty makes me hate him all the more.

"Miss Weathersby." He greets me with a stiff nod as he slides his chair away from the table.

Why is he here? Never did I think Gideon would show up wanting to eat in the same room with me. Does he think I'll be his friend, eat with him every night like he hasn't stolen my life? Well, he better think again. I jump to my feet nearly knocking my chair over in the process.

"Calm down. You're being rather dramatic, don't you think?" He stands by his chair. The amused expression on his face unnerves me.

My fingers weave together until the knuckles show white. "You never mentioned anything about meals, or ..." My hand flaps back and forth between us. "How my living here was going to work. I don't know what you're expecting, but maybe we should get some boundaries in place. I'm not here for, uh ... to be your ... er ..." I stop my mind before it wanders into an ugly episode of *Law and Order: SVU*. My cheeks heat like two stove burners.

His grin spreads wide in the most sincere show of mirth I've seen from him yet. He actually laughs. I glare so hard I think I'll damage my sight. "Oh, Raven. Did you think I brought you here to seduce you?"

Yes. No. "Maybe." I sit with a huff and Gideon sits. I throw my napkin on the table and stand. Gideon stands. "Stop that!"

"What?" His eyebrows lift.

"Would you stop copying everything I do, it's making me nervous."

"Manners first." The smile is gone and his icy stare is firmly in place. "Let's talk a while, preferably without you throwing anything heavier than that dinner napkin. All right?"

I lower my butt to the seat beneath me. My gaze never wavers from his. I'm all suspicion and fear, but I concede we need to talk through the logistics of my stay here. If he's not lying, which I doubt, why on earth does he want to eat in this fancy-schmancy hall together? With my nerves threatening my cool, I glance at the chandelier above the table, anywhere but Gideon's eyes. The fixture is a gorgeous thing, granted, but as big as Ben's old recliner. I feel so out of place.

Gideon sits across from me and folds his hands on the table, fingers threading. "Concerning your stay at present, Raven, I hope you'll consider our arrangement a short-term business agreement." A year doesn't sound short-term to me, but okay. "With any merger or acquisition of properties, meetings, conferences, and ongoing negotiations are necessary. Don't you see? We will not share every meal, quite the contrary, but on occasion, you will report to me of your progress. I will have input, and you may have questions or concerns that need attention."

I press my lips together. Doubtful, dirt bag.

"There are few electronics in this house. No television, no video games, or computers. You're here to work. The logistics are in place for you to complete your senior year. There is a landline in the kitchen if you must phone someone. When I require a meeting, you will come without question and without attitude. Do you understand?"

I fantasize about plunging my fork through his manicured hand. First off, no one is allowed input into my work. No one. I work alone, always have. Ben says my creations are a gift from God. That I have a genius. I don't know, maybe it's true. I've always been able to create beautiful things from the time I was very young. At this moment, however, I feel like an idiot savant because sewing trendy leather boots is all well and good, but they can't help me here. I can't create a way to get Ben and me out of this mess. Gideon is winning in a game of high stakes poker, and I have everything I love on the table. He may have strong-armed me into moving in, blackmailed me into giving up a year's worth of designs, but I'm not his dog to come when called, and he's going to understand that right now.

"You don't own me, Gideon. No one will ever own me.

I'm here to protect Ben. So, I will give up graduation with my friends, put off my ambitions, and design for you. Allow you to steal from me for a year because I have no choice, but you get nothing else."

A muscle in his jaw twitches. Challenge fills his eyes. "You misunderstand me entirely. For our arrangement to be profitable, you and I must communicate on a regular basis. You will bend to the requests I've made, and you will do so with a professional attitude. This is not open for debate. One call and Ben is on the street. Tonight. How long do you think he will wait before there is a bottle in his hand? Another call to Child Services and you are a ward of the state until your eighteenth birthday." His eyes narrow to slits. "Are we clear?"

My birthday is June 2, seven months away. Ben's got no money, nowhere to go. Gideon is just mean enough to give him fifty bucks as he leaves the rehab facility, enough for a couple bottles of scotch.

"I hate you." My shaky response is barely a whisper.

He pulls a large gold coin from his pocket and rolls it with practiced grace between his nimble fingers. "I'm counting on it." He must see me balk because he adds, "Artists are their most productive when their souls are in a tortured state, did you know? The loveliest music ever written, the most profound poetry, satisfying paintings, beautiful novels all are born from exquisite suffering. There is great power in pain. My father said affliction produces a like-minded bond between spirits with a commonality in experience. Like precious metal refined by fire, those of us who understand the path are drawn to the end product of such agony. We understand and admire it."

I'm not sure he's even talking to me anymore. Gideon's words seem to target someone else, something in his own experience, far beyond the room we occupy. Fear blooms in my chest. The guy is a sadist, or maybe he's just broken. His bitterness is a sharp, jagged thing, slicing anyone who gets too close. I blink back the tears gathering in my eyes because as warped as he is, I've experienced the truth in what he says for myself.

An idea nags at my mind, a thought or feeling asking for acknowledgment. I numb my brain and shove all emotion aside. I'm here for Ben. Nothing else matters.

"You are here first because of your designs," Gideon says. "I've never seen their equal. The innovation, craftsmanship, attention to detail—all of it, your talent is remarkable." There is no false flattery in his tone. Why would there be? The fact we loathe one another is clear, so he must mean what he says. "What you're wearing now, in fact, the corset, the jacket, every detail is perfect."

"Right." Every clothing item on my body I made with my own two hands, down to my boots. My clothes are cut from antique fabrics. Even my underwear is from vintage lace and disassembled silk nightgowns.

"A subsidiary of Maddox Enterprises took a hit in the last two years with sagging clothing sales. I intend to release a new product line next year with a show both in Paris and New York, renaming the brand Raedoxx Apparel."

An invisible noose tightens around my neck. "You're stealing my name, too?" I can't control the quiver in my bottom lip. Somehow, combining his name with mine is an intimate insult, worse than the loss of my designs. I can't breathe.

"Part of it."

"That's an unnecessarily low blow." My voice cracks.

"Be that as it may, the name stays. I'm fond of the sound."

"I'll hate you 'til I die."

"Not that long, surely." His gaze remains hard, despite his small smile. "And my requests?"

Ben, think of Ben. Whole, free of addictions. You can do this. "I'll do as you ask."

He tosses the coin high in the air, catches and replaces it in his pocket. "Perfect," he says. "Excellent."

Chapter Six

With my room dark as pitch tar, I blink again, tilting my head and listening as hard as I can.

Nothing. No sound at all other than Edgar's soft purring. Since my cat shows zero concern that an ax murderer waits outside my door, or Gideon, I guess I'm safe enough from attack. Of course, I have no idea how reliable kitties are about watching out for their owners. The fatty would probably beat me out the door at the first sign of trouble, but I pretend the opposite is true for the sake of my sanity.

I ease out of bed and head for the double hung window of my room. The curtains are filmy white sheets of fabric, but they hide light blocking panels that I push aside. Moonlight floods the room. I draw comfort from the full shining orb in the sky, inspiration for so many writers. Poets like my beloved E. A. Poe, though I decide it's not the smartest to dwell on *The Tell-Tale Heart* right now.

A shudder overtakes me as I stand at the window. There's enough light on the yard to highlight the mighty oak trees outside. Spanish moss sways in the breeze. The draping of foliage waves as though gray banshees dance a warning to stay indoors. Heat lightning flashes in the sky revealing a small building next to a charming little pond amid the trees. If my warden will let me out, maybe I'll investigate the gardens tomorrow.

A familiar thud signals Edgar has jumped off the bed and is on his way over. "Come here, boy." I scoop him into my arms and continue watching the yard. Ben's face pops into my mind. What's rehab like? Is he in pain, lonely, does he miss me like I miss him? I wish so hard for him that I accidentally squeeze Edgar. I whisper a prayer, begging God to help him and me. Dane, Maggie, and Sales Hollow High assault my thoughts next. Maddox assured me I'd finish school, but how? The thought makes me crazy. He probably lied just to shut me up. I scratch Edgar's chin and he purrs his brains out. No matter what, I'd always kept my grades up. "What happens now?" I ask my cat. He squints his kitty eyes, ignoring me. All those lessons will remain undone. My seat in each classroom will stay empty. And my teachers, what will they think as they a draw a line through my name on the role, obliterating the memory of my ever having attended at all.

I know I'm feeling sorry for myself, but no one's here to watch. No one but Edgar. Whoa and the guy outside!

Another flash of lightning shows a boy streaking across the lawn beneath my window. I didn't get a good look, but he was young, a brunette in a white shirt and black pants. What the heck? Edgar growls, freaking me out more, and I put him down. Peering outside for another glimpse of the stranger, I can't see a thing.

Help me ...

With my heart stuttering in my chest, I whirl around, but no one's there. I swear I heard a voice behind me. That's enough scaring myself for one night. I bounce back into bed and pull the covers over me, adhering to the unwritten law of all girls everywhere. If all extremities are well beneath the covers, the boogeyman cannot get you.

Edgar releases another growl as I hunker down deeper in my blankets. My cat doesn't make that sound for no reason, so I know something's up. My fingers wrap the sheets in tight balls. My heart gallops, my legs are trembling, and I feel like the biggest scaredy-cat ever. Wasn't that me last year trying to convince Mags that horror movies were so fake they made me laugh? I'm sorry, Maggie. I'm an idiot.

Help me ...

"Who's there?" I demand, like ghosts usually come out and introduce themselves. My lungs constrict to the point I think I'll pass out. The skin on the back of my neck prickles. "Gideon? This isn't funny. Knock it off!" I don't like the thin quality of my voice. I clear my throat. "Jamis, are you okay?" My thoughts move from Gideon being a jerk, to Jamis. I picture him lying on the floor in the hallway hurt, having a heart attack. The man is old, and I'm cowering under the blanket while he might need help. "I'm coming, Jamis."

I leap out of bed. My feet tangle in the sheets and my knees hit the ground hard. Way to go, *Grace*. "Hang on. I'm ... just a second." I kick the sheet off my legs, bolt for the door, and throw it open. When I stumble into the hallway, Edgar saunters out behind me, nosey as ever. My head snaps back and forth as I glare down the shadowy hall. No one is here. Not a soul. "Hello?" Cripes, this place is getting to me. My imagination and Jenny's rich cooking is a bad combo. "Come on Edgar, here kitty, kitty."

My cat ignores me, moving down the hall, sniffing everything in sight.

"Bad cat!" I chase him, not happy to deal with a disobedient feline in the wee hours of the morning. Edgar spits as I lift him over my shoulder. "Tough noogies." I scold him to cover the fact that his hiss frightens me. "You're with me, big boy." Whatever is spooking my cat affects me, too. Usually too sotted with an overindulgence of kitty chow and excess weight to care, his skittish behavior is the last straw. "We're going to bed, old man. You can chase mice tomorrow."

Inside the room, I drop Edgar, lock the door, and scramble into bed. Flopping my head against a sea of pillows, I let out a breath, determined to sleep. "This is ridiculous. You're seventeen years old." Resentment burns a hole in my gut. Exactly. Not an adult, not a teacher, or a fifty-year-old man with drinking problem, and not a mother. Where are the people meant to protect me? How long do I have to be strong? *Help me ...*

As I sit up, a boy faces me from the foot of my bed. He's thin with dark hair and pale, blue skin except for the shadows lurking under his black eyes. Water streams off his hair, down his white shirt, molding to the planes of his body. His image strikes a familiar chord. His eyes widen until the whites show bright around a black iris. The boy's mouth opens, a perfect black maw of terror with no sound. My scream sticks in my throat, strangling me.

Legs shuffling, I scramble back until my spine smacks the headboard. When I glance up, ready to meet my doom, the boy disappears. I blink and rub my eyes. Still gone. Mother Mary and Joseph, what was that?

I swear I know the scary face from somewhere. Then it hits me. The photo in the hall of the kid with sad eyes—the dead one—is the same boy who stood in my room just seconds ago. Holy freaking ... I cover my face with the blanket and breathe deeply, trying to slow my heartbeats. When I raise my head, there's no one there. Clutching a pillow to my chest, I sit still, barely breathing, afraid the ... whatever *it* is will come back.

How long I wait there I can't say. My eyelids droop, and I snap them open, terror demanding I keep watch. After a while, Edgar reappears. He curls into a ball and snoozes peacefully at my feet. His steady purr tugs at my weary brain inviting me to sleep.

Once the soft, pink glow of morning colors the windows, I give in, falling on my side, sliding into a world of peace and dreamless slumber.

***

For several days I sketch and stare at the fabric scraps I've pinned to the three manikins in my sewing room. I don't sleep, or at least not much. Convincing myself that I hallucinated the poltergeist standing in my room the other night isn't working, but what other explanation is there? On a positive note, the ghost hasn't made a reappearance, and I haven't seen Gideon all week, thank all that's holy. I know it's only a matter of time.

I glance at the clock on the wall and check the time. Seven minutes after four. My stomach growls. I can't remember when I last ate, nor do I care.

A sigh slips out as my gaze roams the work area for the hundredth time. Will Gideon get angry when he notices how little I've accomplished? I never struggle with creating. Never get sewing block or whatever people call it. Not until now. Tossing my charcoal pencil across the table disturbs Edgar who meows and stretches. "You're no help," I complain.

A faint knock on the door draws my attention.

"Miss Weathersby?" Jenny's voice rings out, chipper as ever. I've asked her to call me Rae but she smiles and ignores me. "You have visitors."

My tummy cramps. Gideon? Who else can it be, but she said visitors with an s. "Come on back." Soft tread brushes the carpet from my bedroom door to the workroom. Dane's huge form fills the doorway followed by Maggie and Jenny. My heart goes from zero to fifty in one second. Yes!

I jump from my seat and race for Dane. As I tackle him, my hand reaches out, finding Maggie, and I pull her in for a group hug. I'm so past acting cool, I couldn't care less who's watching this sloppy display of affection. When we step back, questions pour from me. "How are you guys? Why did you come? What's happening at school?" I'm a little surprised they're allowed in, but I can't stop grinning.

"We have so much to tell you!" Maggie gushes. She's changed her stripe in front from pink to purple. I smile as my friend gestures wildly to the housekeeper. "We just got here and met, uh—"

"Name's Mrs. Jennings, dearie, but everyone calls me

Jenny." Who knew? Jenny pauses. "Shall I bring beverages up here, or would you like to visit in the drawing room? I can make a few sandwiches, if you like."

"Yes, thanks," I say, suddenly hungry. "That'd be awesome. We can eat in my workroom, if that's allowed."

"Of course," she nods to my friends and retreats.

"This place is legit," Dane says once Jenny shuts the door. He sits in my chair at the worktable and ogles my sketches. "I thought you'd be dressed in rags and chained to a tree outside or something."

I shudder.

"It's true." Maggie adds. "I'm glad Maddox didn't answer the door. Dane might have killed him. And Jenny, is it? She's like someone's grandmother. Nothing is what I thought it would be like for you here."

You and me both, I think.

Maggie picks her way around my room, hands gliding over everything she sees. I know the feeling. The room is so beautiful, I doubt it's real myself. "Okay, so let me fill you in on what happened at school yesterday."

"Rae?" A moment of annoyance pings through me at Dane's interruption. I'm starving for information beyond these prison walls. "Your sketches? They're shit."

"Well, thanks." I know they are, and the idea that even Dane recognizes the truth makes me crazy and frustrated. Time to face facts: maybe jail time is killing my creative mojo. "I'm having some trouble, but I'm still adjusting to everything. I'll figure it out."

"Of course you will," says Maggie, pinning Dane with an evil glare. "Let me see." Dane holds a dozen sketches in the air with a petulant expression. Maggie snatches them, pursing her lips as she peruses my pitiful ideas. "They're not so bad, and she'll fix them." She leans over, lowering her voice, but I totally hear her. "Can you just *try* to be encouraging?" Dane's Adam's apple bobs as she whispers against his ear. I hide my smile.

I doubt he hears a word she says because the next thing out of his mouth is, "Are you eating, Rae? Are you sleeping or sleep*walking* again, because you look like one of the zombie scarecrows from that movie *Midwestern Apocalypse*." Maggie smacks him with my sketchbook. "Ow."

"Really?" Maggie asks, "Did your mama drop you on your head?"

Dane shrugs. "May-be."

Maggie slides my drawings onto the worktable, and then walks toward me. She takes my hand and stretches out on the carpeting of my bedroom floor, pulling me down alongside her. "You do look tired, sweetie. What's up?"

They won't quit until I spill, so I don't hold back. Dane makes his way to join us as I relay all the events since my arrival. I tell them Gideon's dad is dead, about my shock at the living quarters not being a six-foot square cell, my argument with Gideon and his demands. I end with the freaky dream of the ghost boy standing at the foot of my bed, the same, dark haired guy from the photo in the hall.

No one speaks for a minute. Then Dane says, "Can I see it?"

"Oh, you mean the scary photo I've been avoiding since the night the kid showed up in my room? The one that makes me stare at my feet as I pass by, so I don't have to view his creepy, realistic eyes? Sure."

Maggie puts a hand on my arm. "You don't have to, Rae." Dane nods his agreement. "We get to go home. You have to stay here tonight, so don't do anything you don't want to."

"No, it's fine," I say, getting to my feet. "You can tell me about school on the way."

"Done," my friends say at once.

"And Dane, can you find out more about Gideon's parents?" He shrugs. "I guess so, but why?"

"Curiosity, mostly." I'm not sure what I'm looking for, maybe some insight into Gideon's twisted mind. "It might be good to learn more about them." Dane and Maggie lounge on the carpet, apparently in no hurry, but I am. The pictures give me serious heebie-jeebies. I want this over with. "Come on people, quick like bunnies, I want to get back before Jenny brings the snacks."

Food is usually enough to motivate Dane. He stands, leans

over, and drags Maggie to her feet.

As the three of us plod down the hall, Maggie does most of the talking. "So, you know how my mom volunteers in the front office twice a week?" Her question is rhetorical, so I wait. "Well she was in there yesterday when none other than Gideon Maddox himself shows up asking to see Principal Myers. You never told me how incredibly hot the guy is." I glare. "For a loser," she adds, and then continues. "He's in there for about a half hour and the pair comes out all smiles and handshakes and thank-yous. A regular mutual-admiration-society going on or something." Her hands flail as she talks. "Mom found out Maddox made some arrangements. About you."

"Me?" My pulse picks up, unsure where her story is heading.

"Yeah, get this, Maddox tells Myers you've been chosen for some sort of fashion designing honor." Dane snorts and Maggie shushes him with a look. "The whole school is talking about it. He makes your absence sound like you're a contestant on one of those talent shows for singing or sewing that allows minors to compete. Except this contest isn't televised, it's funded by independent clothing manufacturers looking for new talent. Clever, right? He says his company is backing you. It's a once in a lifetime chance, and if you win, the publicity and prize money will pay for college, change your whole life."

The guy is good. I almost wish it were true.

"So by the time he's done explaining all of this to Myers, Maddox has our principal eating out of his hand. That and Mom said he made a generous donation to the art department."

I stop walking. "What? Why? Why do all that? I don't understand."

"Hang on. I'm getting to that part. Maddox persuaded Myers to allow you to finish school at Sales Hollow without actually attending class. Once a week, you get all your assignments and exchange your completed pages for the next week's work. The teachers will grade your stuff and so on until the end of the year. You'll graduate. With us!"

"And guess who's bringing you your assignments?" Dane adds.

"My mom knew I would want the job and volunteered me on the spot." She beams. "Dane is my unofficial escort."

"So I can smash Maddox in the face if he hurts you."

Maggie elbows Dane in the gut. "So we can check on you every week and make sure you're doing okay."

Stupid with shock, I stand in the center of the hall. Gideon mentioned he was making arrangements for my last year of school. I guess he did. There's no need to say how relieved I am, my friends know me well enough by now, but Dane picks me up anyway, crushing the air from my lungs before setting me down again. In a rare moment of approval, Maggie wraps her arm around Dane's waist and gives him a squeeze. My eyes burn with unshed tears, my throat closes on the gratitude I can't express.

I shake my hair back and notice the photo of a dark-haired boy on the wall. "We're here." I point, eager to get the focus off me for a change. "I swear that's the guy who showed up in my room." Something about the photograph seems different, but I can't put my finger on why.

Mags steps to the wall, studying the famed subject. "Whoa. Boy's got it going on."

Dane's eyebrows form a sharp V.

I cross my arms, ready to take back all the nice things I just thought about my friend. "Seriously?" It's usually Dane with the sensitivity issues. Maybe he's rubbing off on her.

She laughs. "No, I'm sorry. But if you have to have someone haunting your dreams … young Mr. Hot and Mysterious here isn't half bad, if you're into the cougar thing."

Dane's nostrils flare like a pissed off bull.

"Okay, bestie, you can shut up now." I tilt my head, studying the picture. "I could have sworn it was his left hand that was raised, not his right." Weird.

At the sound of a rattling tray, our three heads turn. Jenny frowns as she finds us milling around the hallway. "What's all this then?"

Dane points. "Rae's having nightmares about the dead guy in that picture."

Awesome, thanks Dane.

Jenny's eyebrows arch toward her hairline. "Is that so?" The dishes, laden with food, jiggle on the tray. Without a word, Dane reaches out and lifts the heavy burden from the older woman's arms.

"Thank you, my how polite."

Maggie's smile is radiant and more reward for Dane's thoughtful gesture than if she had handed him twenty bucks. "Who is he?" she asks.

Jenny's hand flutters to her chest. Her frown stays, her eyes dart everywhere but at the picture, or us. She seems guilty or upset, but I can't see why. "His name is Cole Wynter, an old acquaintance of the young master, I believe."

Not a relative? Does anyone else think it's bizarre that old man Maddox took a picture of some random kid, and hung it on the wall in his house? I don't get these people. At all.

"*Is* Cole Wynter?" Maggie asks, voicing my next question. "Then he's still alive? I assumed he lived, like, a hundred years ago or something."

Jenny examines a spot on the floor. "No, not that long ago, dearie."

Her answer doesn't seem to satisfy my friend who presses for more. "Do you know where he is now? How old he is? When this photo was taken?"

"So many questions. You young people are such curious creatures. Perhaps we should—" Somewhere, a door slams shut. I jolt as the noise echoes throughout the mansion. Picture frames clatter against the walls, the chandelier above us bounces, crystals jingling as they settle back into place. "Oh, well my goodness." Jenny's words are breathy, as though she's been running. "Old houses are so drafty. What a nuisance. Shall we go back to your room now, Miss Weathersby?"

She's clearly bothered. My friends and I exchange tentative glances at the housekeeper's thin explanation. The air is as still and heavy as the calm before a storm.

There is no wind in the hallway. No wind at all.

Chapter Seven

Creepy old houses, ghosts, and cranky-ass butlers are all great reasons not to go traipsing around at night in my jammies, yet that's exactly what I'm doing. Earlier, I couldn't shut my mind off from worrying about Ben and design ideas for Maddox. I skipped dinner, and now all I can think about are Jenny's peanut butter and chocolate chip cookies. Maybe if I raid the fridge and fill my stomach, I'll sleep.

I tiptoe across the creaky floorboards in my black and white tennis shoes, laces dragging behind. From the hall into the kitchen, Edgar follows close at my heels. Nothing gives a body courage like the company of another beating heart, even if it's small and feline.

As I slink across the smooth floor, my eyes scan the countertops. Refusing to turn on the light, I smile, thinking how dumb it is I'm acting like a criminal when all I'm sneaking is dessert. Jenny's queen of her domain. She scolds me whenever I enter this room, but I actually love it in here. Though the lovable housekeeper seems to live for serving others, I hate the idea she has to wait on me. I'm used to doing for myself.

I grab a handful of cookies and peek in the cabinet under

the sink for a paper towel.

"Those are a lot better with milk, you know."

My heart ricochets through my chest ending in my throat. Cookies fly from my hand as I jolt upright, stumbling on my shoelaces.

"Gideon?"

"None other." He flips a switch on the wall, flooding the room with light.

"Oh, let's not do that." I let my hair fall across my face. Wearing a clingy black tank and thin, drawstring pants, I'm grossly underdressed compared to Gideon. The last thing I need is *more* visibility. He leans his cane against the counter and steps forward. His acid-washed jeans are perfect with the gray thermal shirt hugging his form in all the right places. To avoid him, I kneel and gather my broken cookies.

"Crap, sorry."

He crouches near me, gaze fixed on my eyes. Edgar rubs his thigh, and Gideon runs his fingers over my cat's dark fur. "I didn't mean to startle you," he says.

"Don't worry about it." I glance down, scooping up the last of the crumbs before standing. "I shouldn't be in here. We were just leaving anyway ... "

"There's no reason you shouldn't be in here, Raven. It's not my intention you starve."

I jump when he presses his fingers on the toe of my shoe. "Hey, what are you—"

"Wait." He holds a hand up, giving me that infuriating look of his—the smug one that hints he finds something I've done funny. "Just relax. I'm not going to hurt you." Gideon leans on one knee before me like he's going to pop the question. The only thing I want to pop is his inflated ego. As I peer down, he tugs my shoelaces tight and begins tying neat bows. "There, isn't that better?"

"I can tie my own shoelaces, thanks."

"Yes. I'm sure it's just one of your many amazing talents, Raven."

My face heats as I bend to retrieve my cat. I can't believe

the guy just tied my shoelaces. And I let him. Cookie-less, I brush past my captor and return to my room, flustered, and embarrassed, and worst of all, surprised.

***

The next morning, three peanut butter and chocolate chip cookies decorate a tiny, china plate on my nightstand. Very funny, Gideon.

Jenny had better be the one who left them.

I get up, dress, and head for my workroom. After my friends' visit (and my unfortunate meeting with Gideon), I'm as creatively dry as ever. Frustration builds as I sew sections of fabric together and rip out the seams an hour later. Nothing I try works, so I decide to take a walk in the yard.

There are eleventy-hundred doors in and out of this house, but I choose to go through the kitchen. Different in the daylight, the room is bright, cheerful. Warm sugar and vanilla scents the air. It's an enormous space with rows of sunny, small paned windows running down the length of one side over a long, industrial sink. From this angle, the same beautiful oaks I see from my bedroom window are visible, alive and fresh, and green. White tile runs up three-quarters of the wall where they meet plaster painted a soft yellow. Silver pots hang above the island in the center of the room over a wood floor.

I tell Jenny where I'm going so Jamis won't get his nose out of joint. Edgar wraps himself around her legs mewing, and is rewarded for his pestering with a pat and small treat. She informs me in a lengthy speech that the Maddox property is over one hundred acres of fenced, South Carolina lowland, including waterfront access to Coosaw River, which then dumps into St. Helena Sound.

Yippee for the Maddox empire.

I have no intention of exploring all that today. My goal is a short walk around the garden, but I listen. Jenny means well and is nice, so I open the door to the commercial-sized fridge and grab a water bottle, stuffing my impatience.

"Tsk," Jenny bumps me with her hip, pulling the refrigerator door wider. "If you want something to drink, ask me. I'm more than happy to get if for you."

"Thank you, but I'm standing right here. You don't have to wait on me." I twist the cap off and down half the contents.

She ignores me, peering at something on the second shelf. "Now how did you get in there?"

"What?" I bend over, our heads side by side, and look with her.

Jenny reaches for a brown bottle of ale stuck all the way in the back. "This one escaped my notice." When she straightens, I follow, jumping clear as she swings the door closed. "Westvleteren 12, the master's favorite beer. He ordered all the liquor out of the house before your arrival."

What? I almost spew the water in my mouth. "What? Why would he do that?" Other than the fact he's underage?

She shrugs, her expression turning thoughtful. "In truth, I worried you might have a taste for the stuff." She smiles. "Then the master explained you're just the opposite. That you don't approve of drinking, and you are everything a well brought up lady ought to be. He had no wish to offend his star pupil and protégé."

Well brought up lady? Ha! Protégé? Is that what he's telling people? "That was very ..." Unnecessary, theatrical, condescending. "Considerate."

"Wasn't it?" She pours the bottle's contents down the drain. "I quite approve your choice. Too many young people ruin themselves on drink and what-have-you. The only alcohol left is Mr. Maddox senior's wine collection. A whole room of old labels in the cellar, locked up, of course." She pats her pocket, rattling what I assume are keys. "Considering Gideon's, Mr. Maddox, I mean. Considering his past, it gives me hope to see him so—" She chokes on the next word. Her face reddens. "Well, the master is very thoughtful of late, to be sure."

I don't contradict her and, as much as I'd like to press

her on what Gideon's 'past' means, I drop the subject. She's clearly worried she overstepped her place sharing, or almost sharing, personal information. "I appreciate you working so hard to make me feel at home here, Jenny." And I do. She's very sweet, so I won't pry. Though I still wonder what she thinks of Gideon inviting an underage girl to move in with him.

I down the last of my water and toss the empty bottle in the trash can.

"Don't go near the old mill behind the greenhouse," she warns. "It's an ancient building, dangerous, and there's black mud around the pond that'll suck you down and bury you alive." I think she's exaggerating until she adds, "Lost a lawn care worker back there two years ago. Shame, he was only twenty-six."

Whoa. Millpond. Bad news. Got it. "I'll only be gone an hour or two," I assure her. "I need to clear my head."

"Then a walk's the best thing for you, poor dear. Wait a minute ..." She rushes to the double stove and back, clucking her tongue like a chicken. "Here, take these with you." She deposits two warm sugar cookies in my hand. Without another word, she scoots me out the back, letting the screen door slam shut as though I'm a cat put out for the night. I can't help my smile. I think the old girl likes fussing over me, and I can't pretend I don't enjoy the attention.

I wander the grounds, eating my cookies and letting the soft breeze caress my skin. The air smells salty, and I know the river isn't far off. A crow on the branch of a tree is joined by several more. A rhyme from my childhood comes to mind.

One for sorrow
Two for mirth
Three for a funeral
Four for a birth
Five for heaven
Six for hell
Seven's the devil his own self ...

That's all I remember. I always get stuck after the seventh

crow.

Under the oak, a wooden swing hangs from a massive tree branch, and I can't resist. When I plop my butt on the wide seat, my hands wrap the thick ropes on either side. I rear back and pump with my legs. My mom was with me the last time I did this. A lump forms in my throat.

Her memory is worn and fading, but I can still picture her in my mind, her dark curling hair falling over her shoulder as she taught me to thread a needle, or the way she bit her lip in concentration piecing a pattern together. Mom took me with her shopping. We scoured antique stores for vintage fabrics. Thrift stores and flea markets provided the occasional treasure, as well.

I smile remembering her frustration while at the sewing machine. She wasn't a very good seamstress, never able to accurately produce the visions she dreamed in her mind, but she knew about quality and craftsmanship. Mom said I got my talent from my father, a tailor who worked for my mother's parents in their shop and died in a car accident before I was born.

Then in walks Mr. Weathersby, an apprentice her folks hired out of necessity after my dad passed away. He fell for mom instantly, never mind she carried another man's child. Me. Ben didn't care. A smile tugged at mother's full mouth as she explained her feelings for him came a bit slower. Married young, I think she must have loved my dad a whole lot, and didn't want to let go. With her pregnancy advancing and few prospects, mom was continuously thrown in the path of their handsome new employee. Ben was more than willing to fill in as husband and father, and his patience paid off when she finally said yes.

I never knew any father but Ben. He was kind and gentle and we were happy, until we weren't.

All the romantic movies in the world won't convince me to commit to any one person. I wanted to, once, back in middle school. Then I got smart. Sure mom cared about Ben, but I don't think he ever took the place of my dad in her heart.

That had to hurt. I saw what love did to Ben after she got sick and died. I know what love did to me as I watched my stepfather slowly pickle himself to join her. The agony Dane goes through believing Maggie is too good for him, suffering through her indifference. No thanks.

Suddenly angry, I leap from the swing and land in the soft grass with a thud. I'm marching through the trees but with no idea where I'm headed. There's nowhere to go. A pretty jail is still a jail. I've been imprisoned in one form or another for a long time with no end in sight. I could let that break me. It might be easier to quit. But that's what Ben did, so instead I let the anger fuel my resolve. I'm not giving up.

The greenhouse comes into view, and I angle toward the gabled, glass building. A white blur runs around the far side of the structure. A dog? It moves so fast I'm not sure. I hope he's friendly. A pang of worry fills my chest for Edgar, should he wander out here. No one mentioned other pets. I file my questions away until I can ask Jenny.

I don't see the animal as I near the greenhouse, not when I push the door open to enter, and not when I peer through the long, glass windows to the other side. Beyond the pond out back, the mill house looms through the oaks and moss in the distance. A shudder runs over me as I think of the man that died out there. Drowning. Suffocation. What a horrible death. I rub my arms against an imaginary chill as my gaze sweeps the little hothouse.

Three gardening tables sit here and there piled with clay pots filled with dirt. Tools are scattered around the floor, half buried in dust and dead leaves. No one appears to use the place. Sad, because it's pretty cool, or could be. Plastic containers are bunched in one corner filled with dead plants. On closer inspection, the spiny thorns reveal they used to be roses. My favorite. I imagine the lush bushes they once were, bursting with color instead of the skeletal remains they are now. And just like that, inspiration hits. I'm picturing scads of designs, dresses, separates, and accessories based on the slick bark and black thorns. Yes!

Frustrated, I curse myself for leaving my sketchbook in my room. I make for the door, anxious to get started. I'll grab my book, a pencil, maybe pack a lunch, and come back here to draw. In my defense, I've been so empty artistically, it's no surprise I'm unprepared. Easily fixed, but as I turn to shut the door of the greenhouse, my gaze rests on the hazy image of the mill house through the dirty panes. If a few withered rose bushes spark so many ideas, what might a gloomy old mill do?

Ignoring the tape of Jenny's voice warning me away from the rickety building, I pivot toward the pond. My plan is simple: check out the mill, steer clear of the black muck of death, and use my head. What can go wrong?

I choose not to answer my own stupid question as I make my way toward the crumbling mill house steps. Clouds thicken in the sky casting long shadows over the pond. The wind ripples the water. In the center, something moves under the surface. With no desire to meet an alligator, I hope the pond water is brackish. The ground under my feet gives, and I cut a wider berth from the water's soggy border.

The mill is dark wood with a few holes in need of patching. A huge wheel on the side of the structure no longer turns. Lime green algae clogs the base. The slate roof is still intact, though it sags in the middle. Rafters poke through in places like broken teeth. The round handle on the front door spins, apparently unlocked, but the old door is swollen and stuck. I hit it twice with my shoulder, and it shudders open. Light pours through the opening.

The building stands empty, aside from a few barrels, sawhorses and the mill gears themselves. Birds flutter in the rafters, at least I hope they're birds and not bats. I hate bats. Making a slow circle, my feet brush the gritty floor as I view my surroundings. Dust motes dance like waltzing couples in shafts of sunlight. Another bird takes flight causing my heart to skip a beat. My hand involuntarily flies to my chest. "Stupid bird." My voice echoes in the empty room.

Then I see him.

The boy from my room. The ghost from my nightmares.

He stands next to a wooden wheel fixed between two poles, part of the machinery that ran the mill at some point. Cole, I think that's what Jenny called him. He isn't blue, just pale as paper. And though I know he must be dead, he looks real enough. Solid. Not all shimmery and see-through like the ghosts in a movie.

My glance shifts to the door and back. I should probably run, but my feet are cement blocks. Fear sends prickles up the back of my neck. Adrenalin lights the veins in my arms on fire. Screaming won't help. Even if I could unlock my jaw to do that, no one would hear me out here.

Help me ...

He's English, or the accent is. I didn't notice it the first time he spoke.

Can ghosts really kill people? Or do they just follow you around until your brain melts down, and psychiatrists put you in a rubber room with coloring books and crayons. "Are you real?" I'm an idiot. Trying to communicate with my own hallucination must mean something in the world of shrinks, right? Psychosis, a psychotic break, schizophrenia—something. I have no idea what any of those are, but I'm starting to believe it doesn't matter because Cole raises his hand. Not in a 'Hey, how are you doing' sort of way, but in a 'Hey, I know I'm freaky, don't run' sort of way.

"Cole?" The word echoes inside my head. Pressure builds in my ears, affecting my hearing.

He nods, the movement slow and robotic.

A shudder wracks my frame. You're not real, you're not real, you're not—

Help us ...

Us? When did things go from helping you to helping *us?* Plural ghosts ... meaning more than one. Are they coming? My legs shake and the inside of my mouth floods with a metallic taste. I think I'm peeing, am I peeing? If I faint will he kill me or go away?

I do what I always do: pretend I'm tougher than I am. My chin comes up. "What do you want?" The pressure in my head grows, as if I'm on a plane or underwater. I need my ears to pop, relieve the build. I wiggle my jaw, but nothing happens. The acting tough thing isn't working. Uncomfortable escalates to painful. I need to keep an eye on Cole, but the dull pounding in my brain turns sharp and stabbing. The strain overwhelms me. My hands move to my ears as I double over, sink to my knees. I cry out, unable to withstand the torture in my head.

Everything stops ... the pressure, my screams. All goes quiet.

My gaze darts to the place where Cole stood, now empty. "Where'd you go? Hey!" I snap my head around looking for him, even checking dark corners and the ceiling. Nothing. I try the direct approach. "If you're real, and I'm not crazy, you're freaking me out. If you want my help, stop scaring the hell out of me and say so."

No one answers. I really didn't think they would, but that means I'm bat-shit crazy and for that reason alone, I wish my old buddy Cole would make an appearance. Brilliant. Either I talk to dead people or I'm certifiable. I'm going with the latter. First the loss of my mom, Ben's addictions, the stress of moving here, the pressure to create, naturally I cracked. I heave a breath and rise. All I want is to hug my cat. I need to feel something warm, someone who needs me and loves me. I stifle a sob at how pathetic I am. Then a new thought whacks me. Oh, God! What if I have a brain tumor? A big fat hairy mass is pushing on the parts of my brain that affect my reasoning. The pain, the hallucinations, my total lack of creativity, of course! The whole thing makes perfect sense if I'm dying.

A strange calm washes over me. My theory is weak, but makes more sense than a real live ghost. I'm at peace, almost numb. I snort. After all my fighting, the awesomeness that is Raven Weathersby will be taken out by a brain tumor.

Well, I'll be darned.

Chapter Eight

S nick, snick, snick.

Soft tapping wakes me. I sit up in bed, wondering if Cole is back. The drapes are drawn leaving the room black. I forgot to open them before crawling under the covers, but I didn't think I'd fall asleep, not that I'm afraid anymore. I understand the visions aren't real. They belong either to a crazy girl or to a big tumorous mass in my head.

"Cole? Is that you?" More tapping, faint scraping shushes throughout my room. Like an army of tiny mice. Ugh, I haven't seen one yet, but I dearly hope it's not mice *or rats!* My skin breaks out in gooseflesh. "Edgar, are you here, sweetheart?"

I reach for him, feeling across the quilt. While I can't find my cat, my fingers slide across something smooth and slick. Gross. Whatever it is, it's wriggling. I lurch for the lamp on my bedside table and pull the chain. Light blinds me. I blink to adjust my vision, trying to focus on my covers. There's nothing there. When I glance to the foot of my bed, there's no Cole either. Fear chews on my nerve endings. "Edgar! Darn cat, where are you when I need you?"

The tapping continues. I push my tangled hair off my face,

still working on where the sound is coming from. A shadow moves on the wall across from me. As I squint, the dark spot glides in a wide arc over the wall. Tap, tap, tap. It's moving fast. They're bugs. Cockroaches. Thousands of them scurry over the far wall. My fingers clutch at my sheets until the knuckles are white. I'm not phobic. One or two bugs I can handle. It's not like they weren't plentiful at the shop, but not like this. These suckers are massing for full-scale Armageddon.

I lean over the bed's edge, looking for my shoes. I'll crush every one of the nasty things if it takes all night. The carpet's dark. I gasp as the floor writhes with the bodies of a million insects. Brown, shiny wings flutter as they climb over one another, their tiny legs skittering against the carpet like salmon swimming upstream. "Edgar!" My voice cracks. Roaches can't hurt him, can they? They aren't venomous or anything, but still, there are so many. Another wave rises on the wall next to the window. How are they getting in? My breathing stalls. My lungs constrict as panic grips my chest.

The room crawls. My skin crawls. I have to get out, get help, but I hesitate. The thought of running across a floor ankle-deep in bug guts brings a gag to my throat, even if it means freedom. I imagine the feel of their shells crunching under my bare feet, their slimy insides smearing against my skin. A wail peels from my mouth as a tickle starts on my legs beneath the covers.

When I throw back the blankets, hundreds of brown, shiny insects shake out of my sheets. They flit across my mattress, up my legs toward my torso. I scream, jumping to my feet as the creatures continue scurrying up my body. With a leap, I'm on the floor dashing for the door.

I can feel them now, on my neck, my back, tunneling into my hair. They bite my skin. Scratch and claw at my flesh with their spiny legs. Hysterical, I stamp my feet. My hands wave in a flurry of movement trying to brush them from my face. I squeeze my eyes shut, but their bodies burrow into the corners, which are wet with tears, or blood. With what feels like needle sticks, they gnaw at my flesh, eating, consuming. One tunnels deep into my ear canal, then another. When I shriek, more pour into my mouth.

I vomit insects, but others press in on me, digging with their filthy legs until I'm engulfed in a sea of wiggling pestilence. I pray it's over soon. My knees buckle, and I sink to the floor, covered in carnivores. The room spins, darkens.

Then there's nothing.

Snick, snick, snick.

Soft tapping wakes me, and I sit up in bed. A dream? I lunge for the light on my bedside table and pull the chain. A glow fills my room, and I blink to focus. I raise my arm, searching for bugs. My skin itches. I scratch everywhere. Dig and claw until I break the skin, but there's nothing there. Edgar meows at the end of my bed, complaining as my squirming disrupts his sleep. I throw my sheets back just to assure myself the attack was a nightmare. No bugs. Not on the wall, the carpet, not a single, nasty cockroach in sight.

"Oh, Edgar." I bend, reaching for my beloved cat. He meows as I pull him into my arms. He hates it when I'm all needy with him but too bad. He's all I've got. I'm tired of being alone and way tired of my stupid hallucinations. Okay, this was a dream, but still, it felt real enough.

I'm sleeping with the light on.

Gently, I ease Edgar down on the mattress and freeze. There *is* a noise. The sound is coming not from my room, but from the hallway outside. And it's not a snick; it's a tap, like the sound Edgar's claws make when he walks across a tile floor.

My dream provided enough drama for one night, but the sound doesn't stop. I know myself well enough to accept that I won't sleep until I solve the mystery … though the idea of big brown cockroaches flooding the hall does give me pause.

Whatever. I put my big girl panties on and slip out of bed. With as much stealth as I'm capable, I tiptoe across the carpet, double back for my shoes, and then heave a breath before opening the door. My head peeps out. There's a Tiffany-style lamp burning at the end of the hall. Jenny calls it my night-light, so I don't kill myself if I need something after bedtime.

A shadow moves under a long credenza with more clicking and sniffing. It's a dog. His tail wags back and forth with his snuffling as though he's found something of interest. Edgar growls, and I bend to gather him in my arms. I don't need any showdowns between my cat and this mutt.

Too late. The dog lifts his head, and I assume he's heard Edgar. Big mouth. It's the same black and white dog I saw outside today. Before I can get Edgar into my room, the dog bounds down the hall straight for us. He bays like a hound after a rabbit ... or a cat! My heart jumps to my throat. "No! Bad dog. Down!" Poor Edgar jolts with every ear-piercing bark.

I'm yelling, but at the same time, notice there's definitely something off with this dog. He doesn't look right. The white of his fur has a bluish tint, and his eyes are red. Not the red sheen from a camera flash either. They're glowing. At the last minute he veers away from us and races down the hall, barking nonstop.

A fine mist rolls across the floor. Appearing from nowhere, it gathers in a dense fog around my ankles. The hound brakes at the arched window near the end of the hallway and peers over his shoulder. Not at us, but to the opposite end by the stair banister. He barks, once, twice, and waits.

As though in answer, thunder echoes overhead. Pounding and rolling, it isn't thunder at all. It's the hooves of a horse, and they sound like they're in the next room. Edgar's claws pierce the skin on my chest as he tries to free himself. Pain rips through my tearing flesh. My eyes and nose sting with unshed tears, but I won't let him go.

Opposite the dog, a massive head appears. A great, white stallion plows right through the wall like a vapor. He snorts and whinnies, dripping silver foam from his mouth. Riderless, the animal's reins slap his neck as he throws his head, and paws the air. Eyes burn like red flame as he gallops over the rugs and hardwood floor after the hound.

I feel the vibrations through my bare feet. Edgar squirms in my arms. Scratches so hard, I cry out and he breaks free. Once on the ground, his back bows. With his hair standing on end, he hisses and spits, but the other animals ignore him.

The neck of the blue-white horse arches as he canters toward his companion. His ivory teeth are bared, ears flat against his head. My mind says move, but I'm stuck, cemented in place. When the horse hurtles past, I watch his nostrils flare, his eyes widen in terror. My blood chills, stinging my veins. The animal charges, sideswipes me. I see his skeleton glowing hot and orange under his white coat as I'm thrown to the floor. My hip and elbow crack against the wood. Stings radiate up both limbs. The stallion screams, a sound of horror, and fear, and rage that grips my senses, binding me to his torment.

The dog jumps and barks in answer. When the stallion reaches him, they leap through the window and into the night together. No glass breaks. The animals don't fall to their deaths. They're ghosts I realize, more hallucinations.

Just like Cole.

* * *

For the next few days, I do nothing but sketch, try to stay awake, and ignore Cole as he wanders around my bedroom or shows up at the greenhouse, staring at me while I draw.

Occasionally, he asks for help but doesn't explain why or what he expects me to do. I guess he doesn't expect anything seeing as how he's a figment of my imagination. Perhaps his plea is my subconscious, warning there is something terribly wrong with my mind. Everything's changed now that I know I'm either crazy or dying. Poor Ben, my death might finish him off, but I hold out the hope if he can get clean, he'll survive this last shock without relapsing.

I could make it my dying wish, but that's pretty manipulative. I learned that word in group counseling two years ago for teens at risk. The school psychologist, and practically everyone else in Sales Hollow, knew enough about my past to recommend me for the after school program called Wholeness for Life. She made the meetings mandatory, in fact, despite my good grades.

All I want now is to stay sane long enough to give Ben a chance to get healthy. That and to create a line of spectacular clothes as a last legacy. A tribute to my father and his talent, to my mother and her sacrifice, and Ben, who did the best he could with what he had. Pretty lofty for a Steampunk princess in a Goth dress, but oh well.

Cole sits near the containers of dead roses. I set my sketchbook aside and rise. While I never get used to them, my hallucinations grow tiresome. I meander over to the utility sink, turn on the faucet, and run water over my graphite-covered hands. Caught without a glass, I cup my hands under the flow and drink. My throat is dry, and my back aches from leaning over my sketchbook too long.

My reflection in the large mirror opposite is alarming. The tone of my skin is paler than usual. I'm all sunken eyes, and severe angles, and sharp bones. Last spring, I cut my thick hair in long layers. They look great with a flat or curling iron, but not when they stick out all over my head, like they do now. Black eyeliner rings my eyes, smears where I've rubbed it, giving me a vampire vibe, especially over the red stain that I use on my lips. I'm a pretty girl, at least, so I've been told. Maybe that was true once but not anymore. The girl in the mirror is a haggard, worn shadow of someone once vibrant who's long gone.

Cole slides into view behind my image.

"What do you want, ghost boy?" He doesn't scare me anymore. I don't know why I talk to him at all, except I've come to that level of acceptance with my insanity.

"My freedom."

I turn and face him. Well, that's new. He's lost that whole, spooky talk-without-moving-his-mouth trick. "Me too."

Cole lifts his hand and touches my arm. There's sensation, not as strong as an actual person's touch, but as if someone runs a feather over my skin.

The black and white hound from the other day jogs neatly through the wall and heels next to Cole's leg. Cole grins revealing a pretty set of white teeth. He's attractive. Well, if the guy were alive, and a couple of years older. "Hello Rex," he says.

My heart skips a beat as I scan the walls, waiting for the glowing stallion to gallop through the room. "That horse," I ask, though I don't know what I think Cole can do. "It's not coming, is it?"

Cole smiles without his pretty teeth, and shakes his head. His dark bangs fall across his forehead—downright sexy, for a ghost. The dog bumps Cole's hand and he pats the hound's head. When Cole raises his gaze to mine, his expression sobers. "We're ... trapped here." He chokes and coughs. "All of us. We need your help, Raven. Please."

A shiver wraps me. "I don't understand. Who is all of us?" This is as much as he's ever spoken. Maybe my tumor is further along than I thought. The dog barks, and I jump it's so loud. He yips again and again.

With a sharp jut of his chin, Cole motions out the window. Shoulder to shoulder, a dozen people stand together just outside. An older man with a frosty white goatee anchors the group in the middle. I swear he's wearing a Confederate uniform. I've studied fashion and uniform trends long enough to recognize the gray fabric and gold trim. To his right, another man wears a pinstripe double-breasted suit and fedora straight out of a 1940s gangster movie.

"What's going on?"

"Trapped."

Rex, I think that's what Cole called the dog, continues his ear-piercing barking. I back away until my butt hits the sink. "Hush, dog!"

My throat tightens. A headache begins over my eyes and small wonder. Overwhelmed by confusion and noise, I whirl away from them, facing the mirror again. The same gaunt girl stares me down. My gaze lowers to my chest. The red furrows in my skin where Edgar scratched me are still raw and angry.

The sight evokes a new thought. Edgar scratched me because the *dog* frightened him—a dog from my imagination that only I can see. If that's true, how does a fictitious hound scare a cat with no brain tumor? He doesn't.

"You're real?"

Cole's reflection isn't there when I glance up. I spin around, searching the room for the boy or the dog, or the people outside the window. They're gone again. Holy freaking cow …

I don't know what to believe.

***

Two days later, as I lean over my worktable, I hear the door to my bedroom click. "Who's there?" I call.

Soft footfalls brush across the carpet. I tense, fearing its Gideon until Jamis rounds the corner. He's carrying a small cardboard box that he tips slightly my direction.

I shake the hair back from my eyes. "What's this?"

His brow withers into deeper wrinkles. "I believe you left a list with Jenny? I did my best to procure the items you requested, miss. Where shall I put them?"

You did? "On the table." He takes a step then hesitates. The table is covered with fabric and sewing crap. Jamis seems at a loss. "Anywhere is great, thanks." The old man places the box over one of my patterns and backs away. "Shall we see what you found me?" I ease around the corner of the table and grab for the box. I'm curious as hell to know what he did with my odd shopping list.

His watery blue eyes dart toward the exit. "Must I?"

"I'm afraid you must." I'm teasing now, seeing if I can break the ice a little with the stiff old geezer. I pull the flaps open and peer inside. On top sits a pair of old spectacles, underneath is a black crow feather nestled among several skeins of ribbon in blues and grays and soft browns. When I glance over, Jamis inches nearer. In spite of his protests, he leans his skinny frame over the box and peeks inside. Like a child at a friend's birthday party, his lips purse, and I imagine he's wondering if I am pleased with the gifts he brought. I lift the ribbon. My fingers thread through a tangle of otter brown velvet. "This is beautiful." I swear I detect the hint of a smile. "Aren't you going to ask why I want this stuff?"

"I wasn't planning to, no, miss."

"They're for my inspiration board." I can't help my squeal as I pull a pair of leather aviator goggles from the box. "Oh my gosh!" Jamis winces. "How did you find these? They're perfect!" I find two more pairs in the box along with a pocket watch, old wristwatch, Bakelite jewelry, lace, and rhinestones. I grab his arm, and he stiffens like a cadaver. "You did just awesome, Jamis." He nods, eyes widening a smidge. "See, what happens now is I tack all these things up on a corkboard, over there on the wall."

He stares at me as though I have a rhino horn instead of a nose. "Indeed."

"Yeah. You know, for inspiration. And when I look at this stuff, I have a color palette and a theme. See?" He glances at the box again. When he says nothing, I add, "You've never heard of an inspiration board? I'll bet you think it's a dumb idea."

"Not quite, Miss Weathersby, but then, it is not I that need be inspired."

"Oh, come on, Jamis, we're all motivated by something."

"Not necessarily."

With his eyes fixed squarely on his clasped hands, his silence prompts another question. "You think I'm crazy?"

"Madness, and its varying forms, is something I'm quite accustomed to, miss."

I think of the house he works in, its ghosts and inhabitants, and I have to concede that one. "Truth." I shift my weight. "Do you have a hobby, a passion, or pastime?" I don't know why I'm trying so hard. I feel like Edgar, or any other cat I can think of, for that matter. They zero in on the one person in the room who hates them most and stare or try to sit in their lap.

Or maybe I try because I miss Ben so much I can't breathe.

"None, miss."

"Reading, gardening, cooking … photography?"

"No." His tone is as crusty as dry toast. "Decidedly not. If the young lady needs nothing else, I have work to do."

My lungs deflate. Of course you do. "That's it from me. Go." The last word is a sigh. My gaze returns to the box and its treasures. The old guy really outdid himself. I love everything he found. "Thanks again, Jamis," I say, without looking up.

"Music."

What? "What?"

"I prefer the cello, but the violin is pleasant also."

I smile and lift my head. "Vivaldi was my mother's favorite."

Jamis makes a slight bow and leaves me to my sewing.

Chapter Nine

It's ten o'clock in the evening on Friday night. After catching my friends up on my week, including my various nightmares, insanity, and brain tumor theories, I sit in the kitchen with Maggie watching Dane ingest his seventh maple-walnut fudge square. His display of gluttony is as fascinating as it is disgusting, but Jenny beams, pouring him another glass of ice-cold milk.

Staring down at her matronly black shoes, I frown. My cat is absent from his usual duty of begging while wrapping himself around her chubby ankles. That animal never misses a meal. I slough off my worry as an overprotective mother and face Maggie. "So, I'll call you to see how I did on the test, okay?"

She shrugs, and I watch her stifle a yawn. "Righto, but I don't know why you're so nervous. You ace anything having to do with poetry. It's nauseating. The only interesting poem is one a gorgeous European guy whispers in my ear to get me hot. And it had better rhyme."

Dane chokes. His eyes water, and I'm waiting for milk to shoot out his nose.

Something clatters behind us, and I twist in my chair. Jenny is fumbling with a dish in her arms, her cheeks a brighter pink than usual. "Pardon me, children. I think I left something upstairs. I'll be back in a few minutes."

"Mags," I hiss. "Cut it out. You embarrassed her."

She grins, tossing her hair. "Pfft. It's good for the old girl. Besides, now that she's gone, we can talk about whatever we want. Like when does Gideon get back into town?"

I shrug. "I don't know." I rarely see him. Thank all that's good and merciful.

"When do you visit Ben?" Dane asks, changing the subject. Maggie and I reach for the last maple square at the same time. Dane beats us both to the treat and tosses it to Mags. I huff my protest, but he only smirks at me, crossing his arms. "Oh, come on! Jenny cooks for you every day. We just eat here once a week."

He's got me, there. "True enough."

Maggie smiles and winks at him. His eyes soften, and I think his small gesture is repaid fifty times over.

I wrap my arms around my waist as my gaze bounces between the pair. "Next weekend is one month. If nothing goes wrong, Jamis is supposed to drive me over to see Ben." If nothing goes wrong … Despite the fact I'm next of kin, no one calls or reports anything to me, his daughter. Gideon pays the bills, insisted Ben sign legal forms allowing access to his medical information. *That* pisses me off to the nth degree. Of all the people in the world, I have to rely on my jailor for news of my own stepfather? My blood boils.

Dane seems to sense my mood because he scoots his chair over, wraps his arm around my shoulder, and pulls me close. Our foreheads touch. "We have to go, soon." I nod. "If it gets to be too much here, we can figure something else out. You don't have to stay. You don't." The last two words grind out of his mouth like ice in a blender. He means well, but we've been all through this.

Maggie drags her chair closer on the other side of me. Her arm snakes around my shoulder in the opposite direction, overlapping with Dane's. "Ben is being helped. It's normal to be anxious, but it's going to be fine." When she pats my arm, Dane shivers. "The hallucinations are stress related. That's all. It makes sense, doesn't it? Anyone would have nightmares going through what you have. So shut up about the tumor crap, okay? It's ridiculous. You're suffering from nerves, and maybe post traumatical, that's a thing, right?"

"Absolutely a thing," Dane says, voice gentling.

His gaze captures hers, eyes light as though a candle burns behind each sable iris. He accidentally brushes my skin as he rubs her shoulder. Why can't she see how wild he is about her? I'm almost jealous. Not of Dane, he's the brother I should have had. It's more the idea of security, constancy, or devotion. Hell, I don't know—something.

"I'm okay," I lie. "Things will get better. I can do a year. Anyone can do anything for a year."

"Exactly." Maggie pulls away and settles back in her chair. "The new sketches you've come up with are amazing. That ought to keep Gideon off your case for a long while. I'll admit when you first came here, Dane and I almost went to the cops." I give her a sharp look, but she meets my glare head on. "Twice."

Shock keeps me mute.

"What? We did." Maggie holds her thumb and first finger up in the air. "I came *that* close to asking my parents if they could apply for temporary custody and have you move in with me."

Dane eases back into his seat, threading his long fingers over the linen tablecloth.

"Until the braniac that is Dane explained that it was too late. That anything having to do with the government and red tape takes time, that you wouldn't agree, that we couldn't protect or help Ben. The state might screw up and you could wind up living anywhere ..."

"I'm smart like that," Dane agrees with a smug smile.

"Good thing, too." Maggie sweeps her new, green hair stripe aside. "Dane was ready to go all *Red Dawn* on Maddox's ass." She lifts her chin daring Dane to argue. "Anyway, point is once we came here and saw you in that palatial room of yours, we felt a little better. That and the fact Mary Poppins is baking for you. You don't seem in any real danger."

Sure, none except for the ghosts, and the imprisonment, and the blackmail. My hair falls in my face. I rake my fingers through the thick mass, twisting it back and out of my vision.

"Here." Maggie scoops a ponytail holder from her purse and hands it to me. The purse is worn and unimaginative. I make a mental note to sew her a new one. "Girl, you have enough hair for three people. I sort of hate that about you," she whines.

With a smile, I take the band from her and secure my hair in a messy bun.

"All I'm saying is you can always create more designs, better ones. You're just getting started. And Ben will get sober, and you'll be famous, and live in hotels and drive a Maserati." She straightens her back and grins like she just delivered the pep talk of the century. Her gaze zooms in on my face and her smile dims. "Try to get some sleep, will ya? You look tired." She stands, "I wish I didn't, but I really have to go. I'm grounded with an eleven o'clock curfew all month."

"For?" I prod.

"Being out past my twelve o'clock curfew." She gives me a sheepish grin.

I push her shoulder. "Dummy." I'm envious and happy for her at once. What's it like to have two parents looking out for you like that? Maybe my mother would have watched out for me, but Dane and I don't have what Maggie has. "It's okay. Thanks for everything. I'd be lost without you guys. If I ever do get famous, I'm buying you both Ferraris."

"Done," they answer together.

As my friends wind their way through the house, I tag along behind. The place is library quiet. Two old servants, a Goth girl, her cat, and some ghosts don't make as much noise as one might think. "Oh! Did you find out anything about Gideon's parents?"

Maggie shoots me a smirk over her shoulder. "It's still weird hearing you call the Maddox tycoon Gideon."

I ignore her. "Did you?"

When we reach the foyer, Dane makes an about face and walks to the staircase. He squats, settling his lean frame on the second step and waits. I sigh and follow with Mags trailing after. "There's not much to tell, Rae. It's not like we sit around reading Fortune 500 or watching CNN, but most of it is public record. The story is Nathan Maddox committed suicide three or four years ago when Gideon was around fifteen. Poison."

"Whoa."

"Right? Pretty intense." Maggie slides around me and takes a seat next to Dane. The staircase is widest at the bottom, but she sits so close their thighs touch. He's big and dark, and she's fair and petite. They're quite the pair. Her head droops. She leans against him, stifling another yawn.

I'm sorry she's tired, but I really need to hear this. "What else?"

Dane glances at the top of Maggie's head every so often as he speaks. "There was some epic legal battle. Stepmom contested the will that leaves everything to Gideon on his twenty-fifth birthday. She lost. Board of directors runs the company until then. Gideon is just the face with no real power, though it sounds like he's required to be involved, attend their meetings and shit. When she didn't get her money, old lady Maddox disappeared. Gold digger, I guess, 'cause no one's heard from her since. They were only married five years."

"What about Gideon's real mom?"

"Died. When he was little, I think, I don't remember." When Mags readjusts her head on Dane's shoulder, he wraps his arm around her, pulling her close. "I asked around for more than what's common knowledge. Nathan Maddox was a judge for a while and a lot of their ancestors were, too. Guess that's where they got all their money."

That's a lot of death for one little boy. I refuse to feel sorry for him, though. A lot of people suffer. Not everyone turns bitter enough to inflict their pain on others.

"And now I've got to get her home before her parents ground her again." Dane stands, hauling my weary friend up with him. Maggie's elbow pushes Dane's sleeve up, and I gasp. As he steers her toward the door, I stop him with a hand to his wrist.

"Bro?" I glance from the ugly black and purple bruises on his bicep to his face.

He shakes his head, and mouths. *Don't.*

I feel the frown covering my face. My lungs fill with the air to argue. Dane's father cannot be allowed to get away with abusing his son.

"Later." His eyes plead, glancing from Maggie to me. One look at the terror in his eyes and I give in, like always.

Oblivious to our exchange, Maggie grins at me like a drunkard over Dane's chiseled arm. "Do you think I could spend the night sometime? When I'm not on lockdown anymore?" Dane stops and angles around so we face each other again.

"You want to?" My heart lifts at the thought. "You wouldn't be scared, you sure?"

"For a brilliant girl, sometimes you're so stupid."

I grin. "I'll ask."

***

"Edgar!"

It feels wrong to yell in a house that's more museum than home, but it can't be helped. I haven't seen my cat in almost twenty-four hours, and I'm nearing panic mode. I've been everywhere, from the mill to greenhouse, in and out of drawing rooms and bedrooms, and any other kind of room you can think of. As of eleven-thirty, there were only four places I hadn't checked, and as I leave Gideon's study, I've just marked another off my list.

That leaves the attic, cellar, and west wing. Awesome. The thought of dealing with ghosts in the attic is too much tonight, same with the cellar. When Jenny mentioned those places, her voice was severe with warning. Either will be my absolute last resort. Idiotic cat. Probably curled up on some chair in a room I'd recently searched, laughing his kitty heart out. No way could I assume that, though. He's my baby.

That leaves me with one choice.

Ding, ding, ding. We have a winner! The west wing it is. I head up the stairs as quietly as possible. Not that I can't go days without seeing Jamis, but the one time you hope to avoid Mr. Crabby Pants ... bang! There he'll be.

Other than our 'moment' in my workroom, the guy has barely spoken to me since I got here. He glowers at me with his beady little eyes through a couple of slits in his face. Jerk wad. I picture him as Gideon's snooping little stoolie, watching me, reporting back to his master. Jenny keeps telling me what an honorable, loyal little stoolie he is, but other than the time he brought me cool stuff, I haven't seen anything admirable. At all.

I veer to the left and sneak into the west wing through double mahogany doors. The air inside the vast hallway feels bristling and eager with no lights on. "Edgar! Come here, sweetheart. You're scaring mommy."

No meow answers from the black. I feel along the wall for a light switch finding nothing. The lamp I bump into on a buffet, however, makes a great substitute. My fingers twist the knob under the shade and glorious, if dim, light shines forth, enough to see by. "Okay. Operation: Where's My Damn Cat is a go." The hall is ridiculously long, with doors to the left and right that go on forever. The task of finding one silly feline inside is daunting.

"One room at a time, Weathersby, let's go."

The first three doors lead to elaborately decorated bedrooms. They appear neat, but dusty, as though no one's used them in years. There's a distinct smell in this wing of the house: pleasant, woodsy, though none of the fireplaces are in use, and tart, like black licorice. Edgar's not in any closet or under the furniture. Where is that darn cat? In the fourth room, I flip on a small table lamp. It's a sitting room, or maybe a library. There is a truckload of books in here.

An old camera sits on a tripod in the center of the room near an ornate armoire. The camera's middle looks like a leather accordion with two wooden boxes on either end. A big brass lens sticks out the front. I wonder if it's the same camera I saw downstairs on my first visit. I think it is.

Maybe Gideon collects them. Dozens of pictures fill small silver frames all over the shelves. The same little boy with blond curly hair smiles out from most of them. He grins from a bed or wheelchair in some. In others, he's older, leaning on a pair of crutches. My mind wanders to the lion-head cane Gideon holds. The idea it's just for show seems doubtful now.

I lift another framed picture. A young Gideon sits in a high back chair with a book in his lap. There's a crow on his shoulder with sleek, glossy wings, a childhood pet perhaps? How cool is that? Standing with Gideon in the photo is a tall man. Dark hair flows to just above his shoulders, but the same beautiful features make his identity unmistakable. Nathan Maddox, Gideon's father. I replace the photo on the shelf.

A quick sweep of the room produces no cat. I do however spy a painting over the large fireplace. This is clearly not a photo but a portrait of Nathan's dad with a woman. Not the blond beauty on the wall in the east wing, this woman is a redhead. She lacks the coldness and severity of Nathan's second wife's features, and has a sweet expression with laughing eyes. I doubt Gideon was born bitter and ruthless and he learned it from someone. Of the two people in the portrait above me, I'm going with his father.

The room is flooded with pictures, trophies, and plaques dedicated to Judge Nathan Maddox, honors from other businessmen, awards for this and that. Daddy issues, much? I glance back up at the painting. Nathan is leaning toward his pretty young wife, his hands clasping hers in a possessive hold. How could she be happy married to a guy like that? She's smiling, face radiating joy and contentment. I think I might have liked her. Maybe. She's the only Maddox I can say that about.

On the far wall are four more family portraits. Under each one is a title, name, and date. All judges starting with Judge Mathias Maddox 1863 to Magistrate A. K. Maddox 1948. They stare out with stern expressions on their handsome faces. I get the feeling the Maddox men have never been the warm fuzzy types.

Who cares? I chastise myself. Find Edgar.

The last place I look is beneath the desk. I don't find him, but I didn't really think I would. As I rise, my hands grasp the top of the desk for balance. The surface is covered with books. Correction: green, leather ledgers with rows and rows of names, amounts owed, dates. Some are marked paid, a few are highlighted or starred or both. Who uses actual books to do this stuff anymore? Bookies? I thought everyone kept their records on computer programs. Of course, we don't. Ben and I are small time and can't afford a laptop, but Gideon is practically King Midas, isn't he?

Curious, I open the desk drawer. Sweat breaks out across my brow as I pick amongst the items inside. Stacks of bank statements, bills, I'm no longer looking for my cat. I'm openly prying into someone else's private affairs. An envelope is stuck under the blotter on the desktop. It's worn and stained. The handwriting is small and neat, addressed to Judge Nathan Maddox from S. Allen Gamble, Malcolm College, Wiltshire, England.

Footsteps in the hall send my heart rocketing to my throat. I stuff the letter inside my blouse, and shove the drawer closed.

"What are you doing in here?"

My head snaps up. Crap. Gideon stands in the doorway, glaring. I straighten, stall by pretending to smooth my skirt. "I, uh ..."

"Weren't you given strict instructions never to come to this part of the house?" He takes a step, his hand tightening on his beautiful cane.

"Yes. I was, but—"

"And because I leave for a few days, you think you can just disregard my rules and do whatever the hell you please?"

Another step, and another, he moves slow and purposefully, like a tiger.

"No, I—"

"And of all the rooms to find you in, here you are, in my—"

"Shrine?"

He stops two feet from me, his brow in deep furrows. "Private office."

He hits the light switch on the wall next to us, shedding more light on his features. Obviously furious, I wish I didn't notice the condescending arch of his golden eyebrows, or how the quick toss of his head flips his curls back in a way that's both confident and sexy. With both eyes visible—one bright blue, the other sea green—they hypnotize me, but nobody would miss his commanding presence, despite his awful behavior.

Gideon gazes at his desktop. A noisy breath escapes his nose, before he faces me again. "What are you doing in here?" His voice is steely calm.

"Snooping." Damn. "Searching, searching, I'm looking for Edgar. My cat. I can't find him. I've been all over the house." My heart pounds, and my hands are clammy, but I resist the urge to wipe them on my skirt. First rule of battle: never let them see you sweat.

I swallow thickly as he moves closer. "I don't think Edgar is hiding in my paperwork, do you?" He slams the ledger on his desktop shut. His bloodless face is less than a foot from mine. "In the future, should you need something, inform Jamis or Jenny. *They* have permission to be here. You do not. Now get out!"

"Hey! I—"

"Get the hell out!" He swipes the lamp from his desktop, and it shatters on the floor.

Anger swells my chest. He angles as if he'll walk away, but my finger juts out. I poke his chest, stopping him. "Quit bossing me around, Gideon."

His gaze drops to my finger and back to my face as if I've lost my mind.

"Look, I'm sorry. Do you think I wanted to come in here?

I said I would play your game your way, but don't talk to me like I'm nothing. I almost pissed myself a dozen times living in your stupid, ghost-filled, nightmare-inducing, creep show of a house." My throat constricts. Tears burn, threaten to fall. "And I want my cat!" He could be sick, hurt, chased by a poltergeist in the shape of a dog. I *have* to know he's okay. "He's all I have."

Gideon straightens to his full height. I swear the corner of his mouth twitches.

Is he laughing at me? More water collects in my eyes, threatening to spill over the rim. He's not going to make me cry again. At least, he's not going to see it. I whirl and run around the far side of his desk.

I leap aside as he lunges for me. "Raven, wait."

Wait? Nothing doing, pal. It's too late for talking. "Go, stay, come, fetch, beg ..." I'm muttering like a loon as I break for the door, but I don't care anymore.

"Raven, you're out of control."

Seriously? And smashing a lamp isn't? I'm stressed. I'm female. I'm an artist. That's pretty much the trifecta of emotion. When I hear a thud, I fly out the door and down the hall. Footsteps echo behind me. He's moving pretty fast for a guy who needs a cane. Maybe I was wrong about that.

Thunder crashes outside, as I reach the stairs. My heart stutters the boom is so loud. When I glance behind me, there's no sign of Gideon. Maybe he gave up. I skip down the steps, anxious and unhappy. The confrontation rattled me more than I want to admit. No, I shouldn't have gone into his office, but I didn't know it was his office or that he'd come home. So that happened.

And my cat is still missing.

What next?

Chapter Ten

In my room, I stuff the stolen letter in a poetry book and make one last search for Edgar. No luck. I flop on the bed. Exhaustion weighs me down as though there's an anchor parked on my stomach. Lightning flashes outside, thunder follows in its wake. The clock on the wall reads two in the morning, if it can be trusted. There's something odd about the clocks in this house. They're old, and stop and start when they feel like it. Maybe they need winding. I raise my head, reading the clock again to make sure. Yep, two o'clock.

I lift a boot to my hand and unlace one, then the other. They fall in consecutive thuds on the carpet. The cool air feels great on my sore feet. Gideon's face drifts into my mind. I can't believe I straight up confessed I'd been snooping in his office. I'd been so embarrassed when he found me; I went on the defensive immediately. Boy's got quite a temper, ordering me out of the room like a naughty child, which didn't help. Still, when he'd tried to stop my leaving, his voice was, well, not apologetic or anything, but sincere. Sort of. Maybe earnest is a better word. I get the feeling he actually wanted to talk, but I was too mad to care. And now? Am I still mad? Hell yeah, but I'm curious, too.

Shame he's a jerk, that's all.

I force myself up and change into my black tank top and drawstring pants. Kneeling to gather my dirty clothes, I consider searching the attic next for Edgar. A soft knock against my bedroom window has my neck twisting around. Another flash shows the silhouette of a person there.

Raven ...

"Cole?" I'm up and padding toward the multi-paned window remembering I'm three stories up. It *is* Cole. I drop my clothes and unlatch the lock in the center before pushing on the sash. The window opens out on iron hinges. Rain splatters the sill, my clothes, and face. Cole levitates between a giant oak in the dark and me.

"Come with me, Raven."

What, outside? I'm about to ask my hallucination if he's insane when I stop myself. His mouth moves and he's speaking out loud, more than just a voice in my head. "Cole, are you real, or am I dreaming?" The question is absurd, but I want to understand what's happening to me.

He nods vigorously. "I'm very real."

"You're louder, more clear when you speak, now."

"I'm learning. Follow me." He peeks over his shoulder and back. "Hurry, please. It's important."

Learning? His tone is pleading. I hesitate a moment more. Trailing a ghost outside in the middle of a rainy night won't make it onto my 'brightest moves' list, but I already know I'm going. "I'll be right out."

My boots are too time consuming to put on, so I leave them and slip out of my room. I doubt anyone is up at this hour, but I creep down the steps anyway. Cringing with each squeak and groan of the stairs, I make it to the front door and into the side yard.

My heart thuds. The grass is cold and slick. Water pelts my face, and my cotton pants and tank cling to my skin. I start as thunder crashes and rolls overhead. This better be worth the trouble, Cole. Ha! *Cole.* I probably made the whole thing up and coaxed myself out here, or better yet, I'm dreaming again and will wake up any minute nice and dry in my own bed.

When I reach my window on the east side of the house, I don't see him. I pace, my gaze following the roofline of the house for a glimpse of the boy. "Cole! Where are you?" The longer I stand there, the stupider I feel. Maggie's right, I'm reacting to traumatic events. Until tonight, I called my visions by what they were, hallucinations. A healthy normal response to what was occurring. Not now. Now, I'm standing in the rain because I asked my psychotic break if he was real, and he said yes, and I believed him.

I trusted that the attractive boy in a photograph is haunting me in my captor's house and wants to be friends. In a thunderstorm. At two in the morning. And I'm barefoot, and freezing, and stupid! Ugh! *I already said that!* When I stomp off toward the front door, Cole appears, blocking my path. "What the ... ?"

"Follow me," he says. His big, dark eyes do the pleading thing again. Thin but not gaunt, Cole is tall and classically handsome. Not as beautiful as Gideon, but he's compelling with an unmistakable sorrow in his eyes.

I stiffen. "No." I'm over it, this house, my promise to stay, the hot pair of guys making my life a living hell.

"The black cat is in danger."

Forget everything I just said.

"Show me," I say. Cole walks, or I should say glides, over the grass, past the greenhouse toward the mill. Of course he does. Sticks and briars dig into my bare feet. I stumble and trip. Cole doesn't slow, and I fall behind watching his white shirt growing dimmer with distance. "Wait!" Just like that he pops up in front of me again. My breath catches and my racing heart threatens to stop. I want to tell him to never *ever* scare me like that again, but I did call him, and maybe he can't help it. I struggle to stand. "Can we go a little slower?"

He nods. When I glance down, I notice he has no feet. His body smears and fades where his knees should be. Oo-kay. "Follow me," he repeats. I get that part, but I say nothing and pick my way through the brush behind him

As we near the mill house I hear a soft cry. "Edgar?" He answers with a meow, weak and piteous. "Oh, God. Please take care of my cat."

Cole waits at the foot of a huge oak and points up. The tree is thirty feet high and at least that wide. Perfect. Edgar cries again and snaps me out of my stupor. I bolt to the base of the trunk and peer into the massive branches. I can't see him. "Edgar. Come here, sweetie! Can you come down, baby?" His yowling doesn't sound any nearer.

Considering how long my cat's been gone, I decide he's stuck or too afraid to climb down. Either way, my choices are few. I rule out the fire department. Gideon might go into cardiac arrest if I brought them out here. Too many questions from the authorities and Ben is back on the street. Not to mention I heard firemen don't rescue cats anymore, so I cross that off the list. Cole is useless to me as a ghost. Gideon would probably rant or laugh if I asked for his help. Jenny is out of the question, and Jamis is way too old.

I face Cole. "Ladder?" He lifts his arm, finger directing me toward the greenhouse. "Right." As I race back to the greenhouse I call over my shoulder, "Hang on, Edgar." Careful to avoid the muck at the pond, I push through the bushes and dart across a small yard. Along the backside of the greenhouse wall, an old ladder is propped up amid a hose, dead leaves, and other junk. I frown, the thing is awkward and heavy looking but my cat needs me. Grabbing the first rung at one end, I haul the ladder behind me. My progress is slow, the weight and bushes make formidable obstacles, but I won't quit. My pride keeps me from seeking Gideon.

Hard to see in the dark, I wander too close to the pond. The mud surrounding the little pool sucks at my bare feet. Keeping the muck from pulling my ladder or me underground is a Herculean task. My thigh muscles burn. Both hands and every finger ache from gripping the slick wood. It's dangerous so near the water, but the most direct path. Falling twice, I decide to drop the ladder to rest and catch my breath. At least the rain is slacking off. The moon appears, revealing the clouds above in misty outline.

I lean over, grasping my knees. Air saws in and out of my chest when a gleam flashes in my peripheral vision. I glance up spying a large spider web nestled in the fork of a branch overhead. Moonlight glints off the wet strands. Leaves quiver, and the threads thicken, clustering together. At first I assume it's the spider, or a breeze, but no, the silken threads jerk and tighten as though being manipulated by an invisible needle. I squint, unsure of what I'm seeing. Letters. Words form in the webbing, like some sort of wicked message out of *Charlotte's Web.*

Get out!

Stumbling back, I try not to shriek. I kneel, groping the leafy forest floor for my ladder. My fingers clutch the first rung. I shove the cold wood under one arm and speed as fast as I'm able away from the hideous web.

Cole waits beneath the oak. His white shirt glows in the distance. When I reach the tree, I call again and Edgar meows. I picture him shivering and frightened, and it's the motivation I need to keep moving. My teeth clench as I force the awkward ladder against the trunk of the oak. I step on the lowest rung, testing the steadiness at the base. My arms are like noodles. I have no idea how I will climb, let alone rescue my cat and get us down again.

Before I can think anymore I'm moving, climbing the ladder, and then pulling up on the thick branches. One after another, I make my way higher amidst the foliage, doing my best not to look down and freak myself out. "Edgar, where are you, hon?" A faint cry is my answer. I talk, and he yowls, until I see the faint outline of my friend. He's soaked and afraid but unhurt.

"Hey, buddy."

I situate myself on a wide branch and take stock. We're maybe halfway to two-thirds up the tree. Cole materializes near the end of the branch I'm sitting on, and I jump a foot. My hands scramble for purchase on the slick bark until I steady

myself. "Cole! You idiot, never do that again!" A sigh leaks
from me at his crestfallen expression. "Sorry, but you almost
gave me a heart attack. I'm not used to people vaporizing out
of thin air, okay?"

"Okay," he says. A pause. "How will you get down?"

"Good question, Einstein." He blanches, and I instantly
regret snapping at him. I can't take the seriously wounded look
on his face. It's not his fault. I'm worried about the same thing,
and though he's scared the crap out of me a half dozen times,
he did help me find my cat. "Cole? I'm sorry. I'm not like
you. I can fall or drop my cat and kill us both. I'm tired and
bleeding and afraid. Do you understand?"

His face softens. "Of course, I do."

"Good. Thanks." I stare at the tangle of branches on the way
down. Trying to plot a pathway to the ground, my mind does
the mental calisthenics of holding my cat while attempting my
descent. It's not looking too promising.

"Your cat can climb," Cole says.

"Hmm, yes I know," I answer without looking. I'm thinking
that's how he got us into this big fat mess, but I don't say so.
I'm trying to be nice.

"No, I mean he can climb down, he just doesn't know it.
He's too frightened. He needs a start."

Hmm. I lift my gaze to Edgar, crouching on the branch
above.

"I tried to scare him, but he won't let go. He needs a push."

Not bad, spooky boy. I balance both feet on the trunk
below me and pull to a stand. If Cole's plan doesn't work, I'm
no worse off for giving this a shot. I stretch until my fingers
reach Edgar. He meows then purrs as my hand pets his back.
"My poor baby," I croon. "If we get out of this alive I will kill
you, dumb cat." He purrs louder, and I can't help my smile.
When I try to lift him, his nails grip the branch. He's dug in
like an Alabama tick. When I yank him from his perch, bits
of bark come off with him. He clings to me, but surprisingly
leaves his claws sheathed.

"Okay, sweetie, let's get down." I toss him over my

shoulder like a baby and start my decent. Edgar growls in my ear, and I assume he's seen Cole. It's my cat's reaction that first got me thinking Cole might be real. I still don't know what to think, but I doubt my subconscious knew my cat was stuck in a tree by the millpond. The reality of spirits is gaining more credence.

Climbing down a tree isn't easy. Attempting the act on a dark rainy night while balancing an overweight cat with one arm is suicide, yet that's what I'm doing. My pace is painstakingly slow, but I focus on one branch at a time. Cole is quiet. I don't see him, and I wonder if he left. Why did he help me? He wants something, my mind whispers. He's been asking for my help since we met, maybe he thinks I'll—

"Whoa."

I slip and totter on the edge of a branch. Edgar meows as I squeeze his tummy. My other arm wraps the trunk of the tree. The rough bark scrapes the skin on my cheek. "Sorry. We're okay, we're okay ..." I'm going to kill us. My heart's wild beating echoes in my ears, the rhythm a warning the poor thing will dive into pulmonary failure any minute if I keep this up. Carefully, I kneel, setting my cat on the branch. "Help me out, bud. Can you get down on your own from here?"

I give his hips a tiny nudge, then another. Edgar jumps to the next branch smooth as a jaguar in a jungle. Stinker. Cole was right. He could have done that at any time. I'd like to maim him, but I'm too happy. Now all I have to do is get myself on the ground.

The rain stops completely, encouraging me. As I peer down the trunk, I lose track of Edgar. I need to get down there before he decides to climb something else. What I wouldn't give for a nice set of wings right now. I scramble down several more branches. When I'm fifteen feet from the ground, I pivot around a dip in the oak's trunk.

"No. Don't!"

Cole? "What's going—?"

A firm shove against my back propels me forward. Too surprised to cry out, the image of me lying on the ground with a broken neck flits through my mind. Unable to stop myself, I crash against the limbs below me. My ribs scream. Stars burst from behind my eyelids when I whack the side of my head on a branch. Sticks scratch my arms and legs. Several more limbs block my path and my body smashes through like a boulder. My arms scramble as I try and grab onto something, anything, but my momentum is too fast. I free-fall until I hit the earth with a thud. Lungs on lockdown, I can't breathe. When I try to adjust my legs, they're numb and won't respond.

I lose track of how long I lie there, trying to absorb the pain, process what happened. My ribs and head ache, but my fingers move. Below my chest, my muscles tingle painfully with pins and needles. Whether that's good or bad, I can't say. Air trickles down my throat as my lungs slowly reopen.

"Raven?" Cole stands at the base of the tree a few feet from me.

"I fell." What a stupid thing to say. He can see that for himself, can't he? I need help. I'm formulating the words when someone steps out from behind him. It's a woman in a white, chenille dress. The fabric flutters in the breeze behind her. She's beautiful, blond. Even in the dim light, I see enough of her features to recognize her.

Desiree. Gideon's stepmother.

Chapter Eleven

Cole and Desiree stare down at me from their lofty positions at my feet. If Desiree is here, wearing the same dress I'd seen her wearing in the photo in the east wing of the Maddox mansion, she's a ghost. Not missing as Dane suggested, but dead.

A scowl darkens Cole's face, but it's not directed at me. He's staring at her. I've never seen him angry before, and I'm confused. Their verbal exchange takes place in harsh whispers. I can't hear what they're saying, but the stiff body language and sharp hissing suggests an argument.

"Raven ..."

My name floats across the grounds. I crane my neck around. "Here!" My answer is a hoarse croak. The effort drains the air from my lungs. I pant, suck up more oxygen, and cry out again. "Hello?"

"I'm coming."

Gideon. Thank God. Three words I never thought to use together. My body goes limp with relief, knowing he's on his way. My gaze flits over the ground in front of me. The two ghosts are gone, but I hardly care. The static of snapping twigs and brush tells me Gideon's close.

"Almost there." I feel the thud of his boots on the ground through my back. He's running.

"Raven, good God what's happened to you?" He kneels, glides his hands all over my body with definite purpose. His touch on my face is feather light yet filled with an electric charge. I start to protest and stop. The panic in his tone surprises me. "Can you move your feet? What about here, can you feel this?" He squeezes my toes, pushes behind my knee, on the inside of my thigh.

Another shiver runs through me and not from the cold. "I don't know. I think I'm okay."

"You're not okay. You are a damn fool." His fingers press against the pulse at my neck. "Do you mind telling me what you were doing out here?"

Edgar! "My cat," I say. "I found him."

"*I* found him. He came racing into the house, soaking wet and screeching like a monkey. When I went to your room to inform you his highness had returned, you were missing. I've been looking for you for the past half hour."

I'm speechless. For a second, I'm shocked he bothered trying to find me. "He was stuck in the tree," I offer lamely.

"So you thought you'd shimmy up and cart him down all on your own, did you?"

Well, yeah, sort of. I didn't say it was a smart plan. His expression is stormy as his face hovers over mine. I don't like his tone. He's scolding me like I'm a little kid. He continues to work ascertaining my injuries with his strong hands, which I try and fail to ignore. "You don't understand."

"I understand a lot more than you think I do, woman."

"Edgar is important to me."

"You're important to me!"

That shuts me up.

"Are you aware how dangerous this part of the property is? The pond is treacherous, and that tree is forty feet tall. You might have been killed." I swallow as he grinds out the last word between clenched teeth. His head hangs a moment, eyes closing with his exhale. "Let's get you home." His arms slide beneath me. He stands, lifting my body against his chest.

Cradled in Gideon's arms, I feel a definite limp in his step. My head hurts and my side throbs, but I'm acutely aware of him. His warmth, the firm muscles beneath his dark T-shirt. He smells woodsy, with a hint of spice, like autumn. "I'm good to walk," I say.

He adjusts me in his arms. I like the way his biceps roll and harden against me, though I'd sooner die than admit it.

"I like a positive, if delusional, attitude in my patients," he says. I can't see his face, but I hear the smile in his voice. "It makes their recovery time so much faster."

"What?" My gaze travels upward to Gideon's strong jawline.

"I appreciate your offer, but I'm afraid it's out of the question."

"Oh."

I say no more as he carries me across the lawn and through the front door, but as he nears the stairs, his limp becomes increasingly pronounced. When I open my mouth again to protest, he silences me with a ferocious glare. My guilt is only surpassed by my weariness. It's comforting being held like this, even if it's Gideon that's doing the holding, and I really do feel like crap.

By the time we cross the threshold of my room, the only sign of Gideon's exertion is his accelerated breathing. He lays me gently on my bed with strict instructions not to move or argue. Next he pulls out his cell and dials.

"Dave? It's Gideon. Yes, I know what time it is, but I've got a situation here. No. A guest, no broken bones, but I'm concerned about a concussion or internal bleeding. Yes. What? Fell from a tree. Seventeen. Female. We'll be there in twenty minutes, and Dave? Keep it quiet."

***

Soft purring wakes me. When I crack my eyelids open, Edgar's lounging on a pillow near my head, warm and dry. My heart lifts. His whiskers shoot out on either side of his nose, a white spray of fireworks against the black backdrop of his fur. "Little brat," I croak.

"How do you feel?" Gideon's smooth voice greets me. My heartbeat catapults.

I roll to face him. My back screams with pain. Neck muscles are stiff, but thankfully, I can move. The x-rays Doctor Dave ordered during my secret exam last night proved I'll live. We didn't go to the hospital like normal people. We went to some emergency walk-in clinic—through the back door. No nurses, no paperwork, everything as abnormal as can be. That's what comes of practically kidnapping a person. Gideon couldn't exactly get me help through normal channels, could he? Good thing he's connected. The guy even has a doctor is his pocket.

My host has pulled a stuffed chair to the edge of my bed. His ankles are crossed on the mattress next to me. I shiver as he shifts, bare feet brushing my leg over the blanket. He wears a sexy, sleepy half-smile. His eyes are hooded, hair disheveled in an underwear model photo shoot sort of way that's making my pulse race. No one should wake up looking so effortlessly hot.

I hate his guts.

"I feel awesome, thanks for asking. You?" Sarcasm drips from my words, but I'm not crazy about his close proximity. While thankful for his help, if he hadn't blackmailed me, my cat wouldn't have been stuck up that tree, and I wouldn't have been forced to rescue him and, and, and … "You didn't need to stay."

"I disagree. Since you have a slight concussion, I'm not taking any chances with your health."

I rise up on both elbows, testing my mobility. Everything hurts. "Where've you been, anyway? I haven't seen you in days and then you pop up out of nowhere—first to shout at me and then come to my rescue." Again, I was glad when he discovered Edgar, but it's not something I'd planned to say.

"Rescue you? I did, didn't I? You can thank me later."

I wish my eyes were flamethrowers.

"I was in Katunayake."

"Where?"

"Sri Lanka."

And …? I'm hoping my blank stare will help.

"We deal with a clothing manufacturer there."

"Ah."

"Did you miss me?" The stiff smile is back. I answer with an incredulous stare. "I can ring Jenny when you're ready to eat. Dave said you should try to move around a bit and work the soreness out of your muscles, but don't overdo it. Your ribs are badly bruised."

Who is this guy? And when did he become so chatty? He lowers his feet to the floor, stands, and stretches his arms toward the ten-foot ceilings. I'm envious. He makes it look so easy, and pain free. His T-shirt rises above his navel while his jeans sink lower revealing smooth hip bones that disappear below the denim waistline. Taut muscles ripple under his golden skin. I glance away, but not before he notices me noticing him. Damn.

He winks. "Glad to see all the neurons are still clicking. That's a very good sign."

I blush, then groan. I still hate him. There are little trolls in my head with sharp objects poking at my cerebral cortex. "Are you always this chipper in the mornings?"

He lifts a brow. "Only when I do good deeds the night before, now get up. I want to talk about the sketches I found." He rises from his chair and saunters off toward my work area.

I imagine my face, my hair, good Lord, and my breath are all varying shades of humiliating. Self-conscious, I ask for a minute.

"Sure, sure," he yells from my sewing room. "Did you know you talk in your sleep?"

"I do?" Dang it. I know I do, and sleepwalk, too.

"Hope you don't mind, I showered in your bathroom, brushed my teeth about an hour ago. I thought it unwise to leave you for too long."

"Ugh, gross!"

"Not with *your* toothbrush. Be serious."

"Whatever." I ease out of bed and gimp my way to the bathroom. As I wait for the water to heat, I strip down and glance at myself in the mirror. My hair is a riot of black waves, falling to my elbows. I'm pale without a scrap of makeup. Nights of broken sleep make my wide eyes wider, my cheekbones sharper. If my body is a crossword puzzle, the answers are one down, 'bruises', and two across 'cuts and scrapes'. Lovely.

I'm sure a shower will help, and it does. Getting clean always perks me up, and the hot water is a balm to my battered muscles. "Edgar," I say to the cat-shaped outline waiting on the other side of the steaming shower door. "If I didn't love you so much, you'd be roasting on a spit right now."

"Raven?" Gideon calls through the door.

"Gah! Shower. I'm in the shower!"

"So?"

"So, get the hell out! I'll be another minute." Pervert.

"It's nothing I haven't seen before, stop overreacting. I need to ask you about these designs."

"Well, you haven't seen mine!" Crap, have you? "Gideon, get out," I order. "I'm not kidding." I'm trying to remember how I got in the T-shirt and shorts I woke up in with growing alarm.

I peek out the door. No one's there but Edgar. Fifteen minutes later, I'm brushed, dried, and dressed in a pair of black yoga pants paired with a red, chenille sweater. Not so much my style, but it's about all I can stand next to my tortured skin.

When I hobble into my workroom, Gideon's already reclining in my desk chair. Okay, technically I guess it's his chair, and he's examining my drawings. He makes even holey jeans and a white T-shirt look hot.

"Finally." His tone's impatient. When he rolls his mismatched eyes, my temper flares. Maybe he can be nonchalant about walking in on me in the nude, but I'm not that girl. "Can you—"

"Don't you *ever* invade my personal space again or I'll ..."
Panic seizes me, my mouth stops working. I'll what? Too angry
to think through my threat, I know better than to make one I
can't keep.

"Yes?" His eyes flash a challenge. A smile plays at the
corner of his mouth. He appears anything but worried about
my warning, and my hesitation makes it seem like I'm bluffing.
His smirk gives me an epiphany. "I'll set Dane on you."

"That won't be necessary, Raven." He leans forward. "As
delightful as ravaging your body sounds, I like my victims less
ready for the ICU. I have no intentions toward you, at present,
other than to pick your mind clean of more of this ..." He
raises my sketchbook in the air. "Can we talk now, or would
you like to punch me first?"

I consider it. "Fine, so long as we understand each other."

His lashes shield his eyes, and he's all business again.
"What was your inspiration? It appears you did absolutely
nothing for nearly three weeks and then ..." He flips through
several pages. "Here, you began designing and didn't stop."

My eyes narrow. "How do you know all that?"

He taps the bottom right corner of my notebook. "You date
your drawings, Ms. Weathersby."

Oh. I blow out a breath.

"Sit." He rises, vacating his seat, and takes the chair on the
far side of the table.

He barks orders like a marine expecting obedience, and
I'm too sore to quibble. "I discovered your greenhouse. The
place has a kind of magic to it. Honestly, I love the time
I've spent in there, and I don't know ..." I click a nail on
the tabletop. "Outside the windows, it's green and lush and
alive, but inside, the place is forgotten, withered. I liked the
contrast—the idea of sleeping or dead things being brought
back to life. Rejuvenation. Redemption."

My fingers move to one of my designs, and I pull the page
closer. Using a palette of charcoals, browns, plum, dove gray,
and black, my gaze scans the colored pencil drawings. Coats
lined in fur, pants that button or lace up the front, brocade

vests, and tall boots. Top hats in suede fashioned to mimic smooth bark grace the heads of my male models. In one of my favorites, a girl wears a corseted dress in dusky rose. Its skirt spreads helped by the blooming gray crinoline underneath, giving the impression of a dying flower. The cuff at her wrist loops around her first and third finger in thorny spikes. After a time, I lift my chin. Gideon's gaze stays fixed on mine. A crease between his eyes makes me pause. "Sorry, but you *did* ask. I get carried away."

"Wait, is that a smile?"

My cheeks burn. It is. I didn't realize.

He stands. Gideon peruses my work as he strolls about the room, the manikins with their patterns and scraps of cloth pinned here and there. He stops at my inspiration board. Somehow his staring at my art makes me feel naked and exposed. I wonder what he thinks. Not that I care.

"You work quickly."

"Mostly." Always have, even to the point of sleepwalk-sewing, but I don't see the point in sharing that particular weirdness.

"You can tell a lot about a person through their tastes, wouldn't you agree?"

Yes. "I guess so."

"I know a great deal more about you than I did last night, Raven Weathersby." Voice smooth as a cello, the way he says my name sends a shiver through me. He lifts the new pocket watch I've transformed into an insect with moving parts from the table. The jewelry soldering iron Jamis bought worked perfectly, splitting the cover in half to form two wings.

"The gears won't run." Why I feel the need to explain to him, I have no idea.

"Pardon?"

"My Steampunk-beetle-watch ideas are a series I started before coming here. I don't have the parts to complete that one."

He places the half-finished project on the table. "You're quite brilliant, so much passion, and excellence, and maturity for someone self-taught. You're amazing."

All of the sudden, I'm staring at my fingers in my lap. Lacing them together seems like the most important thing I'll do all day.

"I'm going to make a great deal of money with these ideas." And just like that, the moment is gone, and I want to kick him in his nether regions. "Get me the final list of materials you'll need. I want to order immediately and start production."

"I'm not finished. There's not enough here yet to—"

"Now that I know what turns you on, I've got something I want to show you."

My mouth pops open.

"Get your mind out of the gutter, girl." His lips curve. "It's a place. I'm going out of town, but when I get back, we'll go. I have a feeling it will ..." He runs a finger along the black feather pinned to my corkboard. "Produce some interesting results."

What? "You're leaving again?"

"Ah, see? You *did* miss me." He smiles and shakes his head. "You should be well enough upon my return for our outing, I think."

That reminds me. "Can my friend, Maggie, spend the night? Can I have friends ... stay?"

"I'd prefer you did not."

Um, let's be clear. "Prefer or forbid?"

"The answer is no. Short visits from the pair who deliver your schoolwork is all I'll permit.

No apology. No regrets. No nonsense. The same controlling, arrogant guy he's always been stands in front of me. I don't know why I bothered asking. I push my drawings away and lean back. My side throbs where my ribs smacked the tree last night, and the trolls in my head are hard at work with their pickaxes.

The misery must show up on my face because Gideon says, "There are pain meds next to your bed. Make sure you take them on time. If you never let them wear off, the pain won't get so bad."

A frown tugs at my mouth. "I'm not a fan of drugs."

"No, of course, how could you be. Your stepfather's illness made sure of that." I glare at him, but his expression is as innocent as a baby fawn's. He lifts my diary from the desk.

"Hey! That's private."

"I already read it. Last night, while you were sleeping."

Well, shit. "Isn't there anything of mine you recognize as off limits?" I'd scream but my head hurts too much.

"Not really, no."

"You're such a jerk."

"So you've said." He opens the book. I stiffen. Terrified he's going to read my own poetry to me. Out loud. "You're a fan of Poe. I didn't understand the reference to your cat's name until last night. I learned we both like Frost, and Keats, and Whitman as well."

He likes poetry? "Look, if you don't mind, I'll try again to explain how some things are personal. Per-son-al. You understand?" I hold out my hand. "Give me my book."

He ignores me, turning a page or two. "Ah, this one here …"

Just shoot me.

"When we two parted in silence and tears, half broken-hearted to sever the years, pale grew thy cheek and colder, thy kiss; truly that hour foretold sorrow to this. In secret we met in silence I grieve that thy heart could forget, thy spirit deceive. If I should meet thee after long years, how should I greet thee? With silence and tears."

He snaps the diary shut. "Lord Byron?"

My eyes widen, shocked he knows the author. "Yes."

"Hmm." He shutters his gaze. "Where did you hear this?"

"English Lit?"

"My mother wrote it in one of her journals."

His story trumps mine. "That's nice. Can I have the book now, please?" He places my diary on the table where I can't reach it without getting up. His long fingers tap the top cover in a possessive gesture. Jerk face.

"You wrote this again in your own hand. Under the clipping

you taped here, you took the trouble to copy this one poem. Why?"

Because of the poet's passion, the longing and desperation in his words, and how, in the quiet, secret places, deep in my heart of hearts, I want to know what that kind of love and devotion feels like. That's why. But Mr. Sensitivity isn't going to get that out of me. "There isn't always a why, Gideon."

"Sure there is. Do you believe him, the poet, or is he speaking of an ideal? Are you a believer in love?"

"Yes." Of sorts. There are different kinds of love. "Can't you hear his honesty? The poem came out of his experience. That can't be faked."

"No, but … "

"But what?" I'm curious now. I guessed at his father-worship from the trinkets I saw in his office, but that doesn't mean Gideon loved him. True, he's known loss, a lot of it. Maybe that's what's left him so unfeeling and ambitious. A guy like that reading poetry seems an off mix, though.

Gideon rubs the dark gold stubble on his jaw. "I think people confuse the idea of romantic love with lust and desire. My father said love is a fantasy, a fleeting dream that destroys your soul. He believed in passion, justice, and in what you can consume, control, and discard with your own two hands."

"I don't believe people are disposable." I bite my lip. He's drowning in a vat of acid cynicism and doesn't even know it. I'm almost sorry for him. How'd he get so jaded at nineteen? *Love is a fleeting dream that destroys your soul.* Did love destroy Ben? My hypocrisy pokes me in the chest, accusing. Isn't that why I've never wanted to do more than date a boy once or twice and move on?

My mother believed in magic. She told me once that magic is seductive, smooth going down but leaves a bitter taste in your mouth long after the spell wears off. I wonder if magic was her code word for love, and if her view affected mine. I lift my gaze and find Gideon watching me. Handsome, and rich, and smart, maybe the only one keeping his heart locked in a cell of bitterness is him, right? Or does his father's memory and poisonous words bleed through to stain his son? I have to admit I don't know Gideon well enough to guess.

Who cares? He's over my head, and his issues are none of my business anyway.

"What are you thinking?" Gideon's curls fall across his forehead and he whips them back exposing both eyes, green and blue. A girl could get lost in there if she wasn't careful. His fingers stroke the cover of my little book of poetry. The third finger on the right bears a gold and onyx ring.

I shrug. The motion hurts and stops me short. "Don't judge others unless you're prepared to be judged yourself." I cross my arms over my chest, as if that protects me from his penetrating stare. "That's from the Bible, you know."

"Is it?" His lips hitch up on the ends. "Clever, even true. Now why don't you tell me what you were really thinking?"

Stubborn, tenacious, he won't stop asking until he hears what he wants, so I tell him straight out. "I was thinking that it's hard not to judge you. But what you said, about your father and love ... it's the loneliest thing I've ever heard."

***

When I wake the next morning, a basket tied with an enormous black bow sits on my worktable. Attached to the bow is a playing card, the Queen of Hearts, with the words 'For Raven' penned in black marker on the back. Under that are at least twenty pocket watches and parts in all shapes and sizes.

Chapter Twelve

I'm resting on a chair Jamis refers to as a *chaise,* on a porch Jenny calls a *veranda.* She has fussed, scolded, and petted me since she learned I fell rescuing my cat from a tree.

That was three days ago. The woman won't let me do anything, and I'm so bored, I called Mags and Dane and asked them to come over and keep me company. I don't have to beg hard. While I know they love me, they also love Jenny's snacks. The three of us recline, stuffing our faces with chocolate-raspberry torte. I've never eaten a torte before, and I know I speak for all of us when I say we could get used to this part of captivity.

"Fallout is in two weeks," Maggie says. "I don't suppose the warden will let you out of your cage to go with us?"

While I'm not the most social of creatures, nor have I had much time, I do like to dance. Fallout is the first of three annual dances our high school throws, the others being homecoming and prom.

"Doubtful," I answer. "He gave me a resounding no when I asked if you could spend the night."

"What if we ask him?" she counters. "He can't keep you

locked up here for the entire year can he? It's indecent."

Dane lights a cigarette. "Are we ever going to meet the guy?"

"I don't know. He said he was going out of town again." Dane is the single most intense person I know—until I met Gideon, that is. Aggressive, opinionated, masculine the two of them in a room together could be a real dogfight. "Dane, if you do meet him, be cool, okay? For my sake ... and for Ben's."

He grimaces. "I won't like it, but I will. What I'd like is to rip his head off and shove it up his ass."

"Dane!"

His grin is terrifying. "Those are my *thoughts*. On the surface, I'm frickin' Mother Theresa." He takes a long drag, releasing the smoke through his nostrils like a dragon.

"Mother Teresa. That's exactly the image of you I carry with me," Maggie says, her sarcasm at full throttle. "In other news, I'm not seeing Joseph Pate anymore."

I watch two leaves chase each other across the flagstone flooring. "I didn't realize you were seeing Joseph Pate at all?"

"I'm not. Well, one date. He was late, texted while I talked, and he smokes. His loss."

I try not to look at Dane, but I can't help it. "I didn't think you cared about smoking."

"Meh, I didn't either. Then I decided while it looks cool, I don't really like how it tastes. Might as well fall in love with a non-future lung cancer patient as not, right?"

"Your logic is stunning," I say. Maggie gives me a goofy smile. Meanwhile Dane's crushing his cigarette butt under his boot with a vengeance. I want to strangle the pair of them. "So, who are you going to take to the dance instead?"

"You?"

I snort. "It's a Sadie Hawkins dance, hon, though we would make a cute couple."

"Oooh, tongues will wag," she giggles. "Okay, I forgot about the part where girls ask the guys out." She peeks at Dane. "What about you, handsome? You want to be my date?"

"Suu-rep." Dane's face turns an uncomfortable shade of

purple. I'm guessing his answer is an equally unfortunate combination of 'sure' and 'yep.' "Yes. Sure, that would be good," he stammers.

Poor guy. If I owned a katana, I'd loan it to him so he could slit his guts and end his suffering right here and now.

"Uh huh." Maggie faces me and says, "Got my date, now what are *you* going to do?" Behind her, Dane's wide-eyed, open-mouthed look of shocked euphoria is priceless.

"My epic plan is to miss the dance. I'll sew, maybe argue with Gideon a while, and if I'm really lucky, a couple dozen ghosts will meet up in my room for the Harlem Shake."

"I love that dance!" Maggie swivels to face Dane. "Don't you love that dance?"

He comes out of his stupor enough to answer quietly. "I love it."

Maggie pauses. Her pink lips part as if she's going to say something, but she presses them together again.

"I love it, too." My grin is huge. I'm enjoying this far too much.

"Speaking of ghosts, Rae," Dane says, deftly changing the subject. "The claw marks on your chest, finding Edgar in the tree. I'm thinking maybe I was wrong about them. There's definitely something sketchy going on in this house."

Of course something's going on. I just don't know what.

"There is no such thing as ghosts," Maggie says. "Don't fill her head with more crap she'll be scared of. She already believes she's seeing things."

Dane shakes his head. "Think about it, a 'ghost' tells her that her cat is in a tree, and she finds her cat ... In. A. Tree. What's your explanation?"

"She was sleepwalking and saw her cat run up the tree. She dreamed the rest, perfectly plausible. She dreamed she saw a horse in the hall while holding Edgar and squeezed too tight. He scratched her. Case closed."

It's not a bad theory, but something in my gut doubts her.

Dane rubs his hands together in a helpless gesture. "I don't know ... "

Maggie shoots him her best 'shut up now' look.

The wheels in my head turn as they bicker. "We could test it," I say. Both heads swivel my direction. "I could sneak you in. You two spend the night, and we'll see if we can get them to show up."

"Brilliant," they answer in unison.

"What's brilliant?"

Gideon's unexpected voice makes me fumble my glass of iced tea. "Uh, hey. I didn't know … aren't you out of town?"

Maggie snorts. Dane shoots to his feet, and Gideon ignores my stupidity. "How are you feeling?"

"Good. Fine." I push to a sit. My jailor stands in all his glory wearing ripped, stonewashed jeans and a flimsy brown T-shirt. Casually leaning on his cane, when the wind blows, the fabric hugs his lean torso, revealing the long lines of his waist. He's got an inch or two on Dane, who waits with his chest out and shoulders squared. "Mr. Maddox these are my friends Maggie and Dane."

"Just Gideon," he corrects, with a smile that in no way reaches his eyes. "What's brilliant?"

"Right, sorry." I say, though no one appears to listen. I don't know why I'm being so formal. Mr. Maddox? I sound like an idiot.

Dane's eyes fix on our host. "Nice stick."

"Like it?" Too fast to track, Gideon pulls the lion's head from the shaft, separating his cane into two pieces. Attached to the handle is a six-inch blade. "This is my favorite feature."

As if reading my mind, Maggie rises. She leans into Dane. Her hand comes up, knuckles resting softly against his straining pectorals. Her slightest touch works like an iron stay. "Impressive." When she steps in front, Dane visibly relaxes, settling his chin on her head. "It's nice to meet you, Gideon. We've heard a lot about you." Her gaze cuts to mine and back. "We were discussing Fallout. It's a dance at Sales Hollow High. I invited Rae to come with us."

With a swish, Gideon slides the knife inside his cane. The rubber heel pounds the floor and he rests against the lion grip once more. "I see." His gaze roams my face before dropping further down. My cheeks heat annoyingly under his scrutiny. "Unfortunately, she's injured, as well as busy with work for me."

"All the more reason for her to get out," Maggie asserts. I've got to give it to my friend; she's tenacious when she wants something. "Recharge her battery, and get her creative juices flowing, you know? The dance isn't for two more weeks. It'll be fun. A Sadie Hawkins dance." Maggie hooks her arm with Dane's. "I've already got my date, and Raven can tag along with us. Plenty of time to heal up, right Rae?"

"Rae?" Gideon gives me his elusive half-smile. "Do you wish to go?" His eyes glitter with some secret amusement. A warning bell goes off in my head, and I wonder what he's up to.

Sore muscles aside, I struggle to a stand. "Sure. I mean, it would be nice to get out for a while and have some time with my friends."

He glances at the thick silver watch on his wrist, and then to me. "It's getting late. Let's you and I talk about it some more later, all right?"

Maggie takes the cue to leave. "Rest," she orders and kisses my cheek. "I liked your *other* idea a lot, too." Her tone is heavy with meaning. "We'll talk soon. Tell Jenny thanks for the dessert." She turns to Dane. "Ready handsome?"

Dane stops glowering at Gideon long enough to kiss the top of my head. "If you need *anything*, little Rae, I'm here for you."

I lift my chin, searching his coffee-brown eyes. They're severe with the worry and protectiveness I've come to recognize. I run my fingers down his cheek. "Thanks, bro. I'm okay." What else can I say? We both know short of Gideon physically torturing me, I'm stuck here for Ben's sake. Still, it feels good to know my friends care. I'm less alone.

Gideon shifts against the doorframe. His gaze tracks Dane with an expression not unlike a powder keg waiting to explode. What the hell? Maggie smiles, waves, and tugs Dane out the door past Gideon who's still fuming.

He leans his cane against his leg and pulls the gold coin from his pocket, rolling it through his slender fingers and back. His expression relaxes as his eyes follow the gold piece. "While you work for me, I'm responsible for your safety, but I'm not a tyrant." The words 'work for me' stick in my brain. He's delusional. Hot but delusional. Slave is a better term. Tyrant on the other hand fits Gideon very well, I think. "I have no problem with you attending the dance," he goes on. "There would, of course, be certain conditions."

"What, like a curfew?"

"Not exactly. Your friend Dane, he's very ... loyal."

"Yeah. So?" My ribs and back ache. I sink onto the cushion beneath me, relieving the pressure.

Watching Gideon juggle the coin between his fingers is mesmerizing. I want him to go, and oddly, I want him to stay. The loneliness must be getting to me. My friends just left. After seeing them every day, once a week is nothing. And poor Ben. What must he be going through? Is he hurting, making friends, does he miss me like I miss him?

Gideon strolls the distance between us. "You care for him? Dane?"

"Very much."

I assume he's heading for the chair Maggie vacated until he sits on the end of my chaise, right smack next to me. His thigh brushes mine sending a funny quiver through me. Personal space alert! There are only a handful of people I allow breathing space within my private air bubble, and Gideon isn't one of them. Not that he seems to care.

His gaze drifts over my face, pausing at my mouth, rising again to my eyes. "The Fallout dance. What could be an enjoyable evening becomes a predicament for us."

Us? Another breeze dances across the porch, teasing the curls around his face. I sketch his profile with my eyes. Though his forehead is hidden by a curtain of blond hair, he sports a straight Greek nose. His lashes are light disappearing against hooded lids that obscure his odd eyes. There's discoloration around his right orbital bone. I never noticed it before, but the bright sun makes the burn scars faintly visible. A strong chin ends with a curving line to his smooth throat. I imagine what it might be like to run my lips along his jaw, down the flashing pulse in his neck. Gah, snap out of it. The guy practically kidnapped you!

"Predicament how?" I know I'm going to regret this.

"If I let you go, you might get it in your head to say more than you should to the wrong person or attempt to run away. Your friends might decide you need saving or protection. From me. That would be disastrous for Ben."

Yep, I regret it. His veiled threats against Ben fuel my resentment. My palms itch to slap him silly.

"There's only one solution." The sparkle is back in his eyes.

I think he's enjoying dragging out his answer, perhaps to punish me for asking in the first place, which means I'm officially over him and any momentary insanity his hotness caused. I push to my feet. "Don't strain yourself, Gideon. I withdraw my request."

"On the contrary, Raven. You will go. And I will escort you—as your date."

Chapter Thirteen

It takes exactly sixty minutes for us to get from the Maddox mansion on the Coosaw River to Belle Meade, Ben's rehab facility in Savannah, Georgia.

South Carolina low country is beautiful with its lime-green marshlands, gray water, and spooky oaks, jutting out with knotty fingers toward a pale blue sky. I try to lose myself in the haunting landscape, but my nerves twitch with adrenaline. After weeks of waiting, I will see Ben today.

If I'm truthful, that's not the only thing affecting my pulse. I'm still unsure whether I've seen ghosts, but since I did, in fact, find my cat up a tree as Cole predicted, the mother of all tumors theory has lost some steam. While I spent half the night hatching a plot to get my friends in the house for my 'are they real' poltergeist experiment, the other half was spent thinking of Gideon. The suggestion of his taking me to a high school dance is outrageous. Really? What hardcore drugs do you have to be on to propose such a thing to the girl you're blackmailing? The girl whose stepfather you're ... helping? No, no, threatening. Gideon couldn't care less about Ben's health. He's leverage, pure and simple, and I'm a hostage.

Surprisingly, when I called Maggie, she didn't see the big deal. I might have screamed, except I'd been waiting a whole hour for Jenny to leave the kitchen so I could use the phone in private. The last thing I needed was to draw more attention to our conversation, so I stage-whispered into the phone telling her what she could do with her opinion. Maggie said I could ignore Gideon once we got to the dance (Erm, sorry, but no one ignores a guy like Gideon). She said I'd be with them all night so who cares if Maddox tags along, and the lowest blow? She mentioned how incredibly edible my scuzzball of an extortionist is, and how great we would look in the clothes she wanted me to sew everyone for the dance, *including* my extortionist.

Shallow much?

Then she pointed out how my room is cooler than something Duchess Kate sleeps in. How Jenny is practically my private cook, maid, and caregiver, and how, so far, Ben is getting the help he needs, which is what I always wanted. It's like she sees this as some sort of reality game show instead of my real, jacked-up life. I flip her off in my mind, and then send her a mental hug. Because she's not all wrong, is she? Maybe I should go. Goodness knows I could use a distraction, but attending a dance with Gideon has an icky-squick factor of ten, like sleeping, or in this case dancing, with the enemy.

I sigh and squirm in my seat. My gaze meets Jamis' in the rearview mirror. What does he think of his boss, I wonder. He's not one to show his hand. The guy is old-school loyal. Even if he thought Gideon was a spoiled brat or worse, these old-fashioned servants have a code, don't they? Don't ask, don't tell or something. Maybe I've seen too many episodes of Masterpiece Theatre at school.

We pull into the parking lot in front of a cream stucco building complete with a red Spanish tile roof. The structure is surrounded by acres of green lawn and several matching buildings that resemble three story hotels. The joint looks more like a golf resort than any rehab facility I've ever heard of.

"Jamis?" I ask. "Are you sure we're in the right place?"

"Quite sure, miss. You may ask for your stepfather at the front desk. You are expected. I'll wait for you in the car until your appointment is finished."

"Okay." My voice sounds thin, even to me. I was nervous, but now I'm terrified. All of this is really happening. I should be used to difficult situations by now. But no, this time it's different. This is the first and maybe only chance Ben will have to get sober. We could never have afforded a place this nice with its top notch staff and resources, but will he take advantage?

"Jamis?"

"Yes, miss?"

"Uh. Never mind." I don't know what I thought I'd ask him. To walk in with me, hold my hand. Read me a story. Grow up, Rae. "I'll see you in a little while."

"Very good, miss."

I scoot out of the car, walk up the steps, and push through one of the double front doors. Thick glass makes them heavy. I'm sore from my fall, but I manage. If wild horses and some bruising couldn't keep me from seeing Ben today, neither will this dang door.

The lobby is tastefully decorated in rattan furniture. I could do without the tropical tone of prints and colors, but maybe their patients do better pretending they're on vacation—for a minute, that is—until reality hits. I've thought a hundred times about how hard it must be for Ben here. I know they have drugs to help ease patients off the physical side effects, but that's just the start. The mental, memory addiction sounds worse, harder to overcome.

"May I help you?" The woman behind the counter even looks like a hotel clerk with her gray suit, tight brown bun, and pleasant smile.

"Raven Weathersby to see Benjamin Weathersby, please."

She checks the paperwork on her desk. "Welcome to Belle Meade." Her smile widens as she points with her pen. "You will conduct your visit in the Palm Room today. Through that hallway, first door on your left."

I frown. She's nice but sterile, mechanical. Whatever it takes, I remind myself. They're the professionals. "Thanks." I make my way down the hall and find my way to the Palm Room, so named I assume, from the frothy potted plants clustered in every corner. It's like Hawaii in here.

From the doorway, I see someone sitting in a wingback chair, facing the opposite direction. "Ben?" His khaki-colored pant leg sticks out. An elbow clad in starched blue cotton hangs over the armrest. He stands. Turns. "Ben!"

I race toward him. His arms stretch to envelop me. My stepfather smells of soap and fabric softener, a very nice change. "I missed you so much," he says.

As I step back, his hands fall away. "Sure you did," I tease. "Pretty nurses, sun, and an Olympic sized pool ... are you kidding me? When can I move in?"

"You don't want to be stuck in here, trust the old man." His serious tone stings my heart for his sake. So much for keeping things light.

I search his face for clues as to how he's doing. Something's wrong. His expression is too serious. He's still rail thin and his skin's sallow.

"Sit and talk with me, Rae. I want to hear all about you. How is school, your life ... is Maddox treating you right?"

Ah, he's worrying about me. This I can handle. We recline in facing wingbacks, and I start. "It's not bad at all. I have a friend, well sort of a friend. She's the cook, Jenny, and she's doing her best to make me chubby."

He smiles revealing tobacco stained teeth. "Impossible."

"I have my own bedroom and sewing area with the fanciest machines I've ever seen, all the bells and whistles. He supplies me with gorgeous fabrics and a huge budget. And I have Edgar, though I fell out of an oak rescuing the dumb cat."

"Is that where those bruises came from? I was worried ..."

Right, my bruises. I forgot. No wonder he's freaking.

I laugh to show him how fine I am. "It's my own doing. They took me to the doctors for x-rays. Nothing broken. Dane and Maggie come over, too. I'm pampered. The chauffeur

drove me today, in fact. It's really nice there. I actually like it."
I lift a finger and cross my heart. "I promise." Dang, I'm good.
I almost believe me.

He rubs his chin with his bony fingers. Spidery veins tangle
and knot under his skin. "But he's taking advantage, stealing
from you."

I tilt my head, deciding to inject some truth or he'll see
through my happy act. "Yes he is. I think of it more as a trade,
though. You are getting help. I'm getting experience, maybe
some exposure in the end, who knows." Exposure to ghosts,
exposure to hot, arrogant guys ... no need to mention every
tiny detail. "It's not as bad there as I had pictured." That is the
truth.

"You look tired."

I smile again. "I am. I'm working hard, sleepwalking a lot.
Sleep sewing!" I force a giggle that threatens to turn into a sob.
"You wouldn't believe it, Ben. I cut out all my patterns during
the day and the next morning, poof, complete outfits sit on
my manikins and workbench. I have no memory of the night
before. It's crazy."

He stares at his feet. A frown tugs the wrinkles around
his mouth down. I panic he's catching on, and that I'm not as
carefree as I sound. "Rae, we should talk. I need to tell you
about—"

"No, enough about me." I lean forward. "How is it here?
You look really good. How do you feel? Are you eating? Do
you like your doctors?"

"Whoa." It's his turn to smile, but he mangles it. Pain
flashes in his eyes. He rubs his hands together, twisting his
fingers into a tight weave. We sit in silence a long while. I
don't want to force him, and it's nice to just sit awhile together.
Outside the plate glass windows, the wind moves tree branches
up and down in a gentle sway, like they're cheering us on,
doing the wave.

We rest so long I think Ben might fall asleep. If he does,
I'm happy just to sit here and watch over him. Finally, Ben
straightens in his chair. "No point in lying, I guess. I want to

come home. I know that can't happen ..." He pauses. A hopeful expression lifts his features, and then fades with my continued silence. Pity swamps my heart. He can't come home. I can't give in to him, no matter how much I want to.

"The first week was the worst. They gave me pills, and stuck me with needles to help with the sickness. I did go to the hospital the second day." When I open my mouth, his palms rise. "Got me some help, and I feel much better now." His head dips. "It's been thirty days, but I'm a pretty bad case of it, Rae. Doctors say I have a bad liver. Without the drink and my gambling, I'm nothing but memories, darlin'." His gaze drifts to the windows. "I can't bear to think of another sixty days in here."

"Any change is hard at first," I say, trying to encourage him. "You'll get there. Don't pressure yourself. Everyone says it gets easier. Keep trying, okay?"

His fingers stretch to pat my hand. "I will, gal, don't fret. This bunch has me taking walks and something called mesmerizing ... no, meditation therapy or some such foolishness. Had me a wild dream or two since I come here. Might be them pills."

"Did you?" I figure as long as we're sharing, I'll spill about my nightmares, too. "I've had a few dreams myself in the past couple of weeks."

"Saw your mother, Rae," he says, as if I didn't speak. "Standing like an angel at the end of my bed at Mercy General. She's so beautiful. Like you." He winks. "She told me things, Raven, about me and about you, too." His hazel eyes are wide and excited above his sunken cheeks. Though his silver hair is still thick and full, the rest of him seems closer to the spirits he talks about than flesh. I fear I'm losing him. "Do the dead speak to us?"

"I don't know."

"What do you believe?"

"I'm working on that." Whether or not spirits *can* talk, I'd rather trust to God. That's what Mother taught me, and the rest totally wigs me out to consider anyway. "I believe there are things beyond our ability to understand. Maybe we're dreaming, Pops. Seeing what we want to see or what we're afraid of. I've seen some things, too, at the Maddox mansion, but ghosts?" I shrug. No way am I mentioning my tumor versus insanity theories today.

As Ben leans back, a breath hisses from his mouth as though his lungs are deflating inner tubes. "Maybe so, darlin'. There are other things we should talk about before … "

The pause is so long I prompt him. "Before what, Ben?"

"Your mama wanted me to tell you when you was old enough. I'm not getting any younger, and I think it's time you knew more about your father."

What? "You're my father."

"Your birth father."

Oh. *Oh!* "What about—"

The far door swings open, stealing our attention. A portly, bald man and young Asian woman walk through.

"Mr. Weathersby, how did you enjoy your visit today with Raven?"

My stepfather stands, but I take his hand, determined to maintain contact, finish our conversation. The bald man's use of my first name catches me off guard, but of course they would know who I am here.

Bald Guy's gaze travels from our clasped hands to my face. I rise and take my place beside Ben. "I'm Dr. Tom Wilson, this is Dr. Lee. We're so pleased to formally meet you, Raven. We've heard a lot of wonderful things about you." He extends his hand and I shake first his, then hers.

"Hi." I glance around the room and find no wall clocks.

As if she can read my mind, Dr. Lee raises her arm revealing the wristwatch below her sleeve. Five minutes to three."

"Already? How is that possible?" I ask, leaning into Ben.

"Everyone says the same thing. Especially on their first visit, but provided your stepfather continues to improve, we will increase the visit lengths and add calls home in between."

Dr. Wilson peeks at the clipboard in his hand. A slight frown crosses his face. It's gone in a moment, but I saw it. "Time for roundtable, Ben." I lift an eyebrow. "Group therapy," he explains. "We don't want to be late."

"Miss Weathersby?" Dr. Lee says. "I can escort you out."

I'm sure you can, but I don't want to go. One hour is too soon. We didn't finish our talk and Ben had been about to tell me something about my birth father. His weighted tone makes me believe it's important. I didn't get a chance to tell him about the *A* I received for my paper in poetry, or the dance, or my new design for a pump with mechanical heels.

Ben squeezes my hand. "Next time?"

I weave my arms around his neck. "Yes, next time." I breathe in his clean scent. "I have so much to tell you. I'm very proud of you, Pops, and how hard you're trying. You're doing great."

"Time to go," Dr. Wilson states behind us.

The doctor is only doing his job. It's what's best for Ben, and what I want too, but seeing him and leaving again so soon makes goodbye ten times harder. Ben pulls away. The weight of my empty arms is heavier than hundred pound dumbbells. He pats my cheek and gives me the saddest thumbs up I've ever seen.

Courage, Rae. I smile, and wave, and pretend this is anything other than what it is—

A desperate, hopeful shot in the dark.

Chapter Fourteen

The ride home is quiet for two reasons: Jamis doesn't talk unless spoken to, and I can't open my mouth for fear of crying. I stare out the window, but it's not like I really see anything. My head rests against the glass. The subtle vibration is a soothing distraction against the pain clawing my gut.

My visit with Ben left me uneasy. He's sober for the first time in years. Somehow, I thought that would fix everything, but I was a fool. He's abused his body for years. No one bounces back from that in a month. His appearance is frail. He seems weak and tired. God, what was I thinking? What was it Ben said? *I did go to the hospital the second day. I'm a pretty bad case of it, Rae.*

By the time Jamis parks in front of Maddox mansion, it's all I can do to keep it together. The fetal position is calling, that and some serious weeping. I'm not talking the poetic shedding of a few tears. No. I'm ready to rock the ugly, red-faced, snot-producing bawling that a good dose of self-pity includes.

I hurry through the door and dart across the foyer. Taking the steps two at a time, I've hardly begun when I hear my name. The soft, sultry tone can mean only one thing. "Not a good time, Gideon."

"Wait, please?"

I don't. If anything, I move faster, but his footsteps thud on the stair behind me and continue all the way up to the second floor. For the tenth time, I consider how agile he is for a guy with a cane. I *feel* him coming up behind me, his pace quickening. "Leave me alone."

Fingers, gentle, but unyielding, encircle my arm. Without quite knowing how, I'm whirling around until I'm chest to chest with one Gideon Maddox. The contact sends a parade of tingles throughout my body. I stand there like I'm the victim of a freeze ray gun, staring into his gorgeous, mismatched eyes.

He drops his hand and takes a step back. His expression is open, unguarded for once. "Damn." The word comes out froggy, and he clears his throat. "I wanted to … damn." His fingers comb his bangs. I'm guessing he's done that a few times today because his hair is disheveled in the most charming, tangled mess possible. "How is Ben, your stepfather … Mr. Weathersby?"

I scowl. "What do you care?" I've never seen Gideon with such a lack of, well, cool. His fingers alternately grip and release the top of his cane. His shoulders hunch, head ducks even lower. What the hell?

His gaze searches mine out and locks on. "I'd hoped … that is, I …" He curses under his breath. "I meant to ask about his health. Did you have a good visit?"

Good? Ten different emotions inside my head pick up AK-47s and point them at each other. They're all wearing T-shirts that read: rage, confusion, exhaustion, fear, and yeah, one even reads gratitude. Ben's unlikely benefactor stands in front of me in all his awkward glory asking if Ben is okay, and I don't know how to handle that. My stepfather is in the nicest rehab I've ever heard of and Gideon arranged, and is paying for, the whole shebang. Yet, I'm also here against my will, and he's taking supreme advantage of our pain. Do I hug or punch him?

I decide rage holds the biggest gun.

"It was good to see Ben. A relief." I answer truthfully, keeping my voice steady and matter-of-fact. "He's suffering, so I'm suffering. That should make you happy." Gideon blanches, but I'm not stupid enough to think anything I say can wound him. "Imagine all the beautiful designs my misery will create for your company." I turn the words he used on me my first night here around and throw them back in his face. "Art born from exquisite suffering, remember? You said there is great power in pain. Well, congratulations, Gideon. I'm incredibly powerful tonight." His image smears behind the wall of tears gathering in my eyes.

"Raven ... don't." My name—uttered so softly by the one I want to hear from the least. It sounds like a caress, and unnerves me as little else does. I don't know why.

"Oh, don't trouble yourself, Gideon." Something between a laugh and sob erupts from the back of my throat. "We made a bargain, didn't we? We're both getting something we wanted. No one gets it all though, not even you. One day, you'll learn that, too." I wipe the back of my hands across my wet cheeks. My gaze rises to the ceiling as I run my soggy hands over my blouse. I can't take his infernal staring another minute.

When I look down, Gideon takes a step toward me. He's practically on top of me. He exhales, breath cool against the moisture on my skin. I breathe him in. The scent is tart, fresh. What is he doing? "What do you want, Gideon?" Lord, I hate him. My gaze flits to the hall leading to my room and back. "Let me go." My demand is all but a whisper.

His eyebrows slam down; shoulders straighten. I don't know what he might have said, but it doesn't matter. With his emotional walls firmly in place, he takes a step back and places both hands on top of his cane. A hiss escapes through his teeth as his head jerks toward the hall leading to my room. "Go."

Two steps away and I break into a run. There's no stopping me until I hit my bed. Throwing myself down on the soft quilt, the tears come freely. I curl into a ball and weep until long after dark.

***

When I wake, three things are immediately clear. First, it's tough to sleep with a really tubby feline on your chest. Second, I'm wearing flannel jammies and a tank top without a bra. Last, and maybe most important, a solid, long leg is propped up next to mine, and it's connected to the body of Gideon, who takes up residence in the chair next to my bed. The same way he did the night I fell from the tree.

Perfect.

I shove Edgar off of me and roll to my feet. Moonlight floods the room, enough to see by, so I don't bother with the light. With what little stealth I have, I tiptoe across the room to my dresser and slide the top drawer out. Pulling my favorite gray sweater on over my head, I sigh, wondering what the heck Gideon is doing in my room. Keeping me company, watching me sleep? Glad that's not creepy or anything.

When I pivot toward the bed, Edgar meows in happy cat talk. "Shh," I whisper.

"I'm not asleep," answers a smoother more seductive voice.

I climb onto the bed and push the mass of black hair from my face. "What are you doing in here?"

"Of course you're glad to see me. I would be, most everyone is. Why yes, my chair is very comfortable, thank you. And no, I don't mind staying here with you and making sure you don't kill yourself or someone else."

Huh? "What?"

"Riddle me this, Batgirl. Who runs around snooping in the west wing, makes herself a peanut butter and jelly sandwich at three AM, and sews like a demon half the night with no idea that she's doing said things?"

Gulp.

"I'm sorry, your time is up. The answer is: Raven Weathersby."

"I did? I mean, I do, yes. Sleepwalk. Sometimes, but ..." I didn't know to what extent. I do, however, realize I'm rambling, and that I sound like a complete and blithering idiot. "I'm sorry." A rustle precedes my bedside light switching on. I'm acutely aware of how hideous I must look having fallen asleep after a long, hard cry. I picture a puffy face and scag-witchy hair. That thought is immediately followed by the fact Gideon must have trailed me all night to know so much about my nocturnal activities. "How did I get into these clothes?"

His grin is his answer.

"No you didn't!"

"Sadly, no, I cannot take credit for your stunning sleepwear ensemble. Though dressing you does sound like fun. You were wearing that at midnight when you climbed into bed with me."

What? Shit. "I did no such thing!"

"You did, snuggled right up next to me like a lost little kitten." The grin fades to that tantalizing half-smile he owns, wicked and super-hot. "Every guy's dream actually, waking up to a beautiful girl in his bed. Imagine my shock—and disappointment—upon the realization you had no idea what you were doing. Of course, it also occurred to me you planned to slit my throat as I slept." I gasp, and he chuckles. "I've heard it's dangerous to wake a sleepwalker. I thought you'd break your neck on the stairs, jump out a window, cook and eat your cat. Tsk, tsk, tsk." He shakes his head. "Can't have that now, can we?"

Oh my gosh. I fall back in a dramatic slump on the bed. The muscles in my legs burn, my back aches. The way they did sometimes when I— "Did you say I was sewing?"

"I did, though I'd rather talk about the part of your subconscious that wanted in my bed—and why."

"Shut up, Gideon." Jerk. I force myself up and wander into my office. The sight takes my breath. There are brand new outfits on each of my three manikins and another three lying on the tables. The clothing is finished, perfect down to the last buttonhole, shoelace, and hemline. I've outdone myself, and I have no idea how. "Did you watch me do this, Gideon, the actual sewing part?" It hurts me to ask Gideon for anything, but I've always wondered about my sleepwalking. I've never dug too far into *how* I accomplish so much in a night, and I've never sewn this much at once before. My curiosity overcomes my pride. "Can you tell me what you saw?"

"Come here." Gideon's voice is low and husky. It frightens and excites me at once.

When I turn, he's sitting on my bed. He's wearing navy, drawstring pants, and a gray T-shirt that hugs his body in all the right places. His hair is a perfect mess of corkscrew curls falling around his face. He's all confidence, and ease, and grace.

As if in another dream, I walk toward him, afraid of what he'll say, yet needing to know. When I sit on the bed, he slides nearer. I stiffen as he lifts his hand. "I'm going to touch you, Raven, because I want to, and you're going to let me. Do you understand?"

No. I nod. He takes my hand in his and gently rubs it with the other. So not what I had pictured happening between us right now and the letdown surprises me.

He shakes his hair from his eyes and smiles. "I knew you were different, special, but I had no idea ..." His fingers give mine a squeeze. "When you work, sew, you ... damn, I don't even know how to explain it. You speed up."

"Speed up?"

"Yes." His hand continues to hold mine and the electricity shooting up my arm is exquisite. "Not when you came to me in the night, or created the biggest mess I've ever seen erecting your triple-decker PB&J. It's when you sew." When his voice softens, my stomach flutters. "You are robotic, the 'times two' fast-forward on a TV remote control, Raven. The shutter on a camera lens, so fast it's hard to imagine."

I'd accuse him of lying but it's clear he isn't. "How is that possible?"

He lifts his head, eyes hooded. "I've already learned there are things in this world beyond explanation." His voice has a hard edge. "Some good we must exalt and some bad that must be punished." Gideon releases my hand. Placing a finger beneath my chin, he lifts my face. "*You* are good."

We're inches apart. I continue to allow his touch, I can't help myself. "Only God is good, Gideon. I merely have a talent." Albeit one that is freaking me out right now, but it's just a talent. "It doesn't make me better, only different." He slides his finger along the line of my cheek. The space between our bodies crackles with energy.

When he drops his hand I'm almost sorry. "No," he says, head shaking.

"Yes. Any gifts we have, any good thing, that all comes from God."

"The Bible was full of judges, Raven. There's a whole chapter devoted to them. Someone has to keep a balance between good and evil."

I remember the long line of judges in his family tree. "I don't think that's the same as—"

"Yes it is. Wrong must be dealt with."

I cross my arms. "So stubborn."

His eyebrows wing up. "Me?"

"Uh huh." I lean forward and poke him in the chest with my finger, impressed by how firm his muscles are. "You."

"Obnoxious, is what you are." He shakes his head, but there's a small smile. He slaps his thighs, then stands suddenly. "There's another reason you are graced with my presence."

I stare, waiting.

"Yesterday, when you came home, you were … Well, understandably, you were very, uh … "

My eyes narrow. "Upset?"

He thrusts a hand out pointing. "Exactly! Yes, upset. So, I've made a decision, or amended one, actually. Call your friend, Maggie is it? I'll leave a form on the kitchen table for her parents to sign."

I lift a brow, suspicious. "Because … "

"Because I've reconsidered your request to have her spend the night."

I feel my eyes bug. "You have?"

He's smiling again, a cat with a canary smile. I sort of like it when he does that. "Indeed, but not here, in New York. That's what the consent form is for. I'm flying the pair of you to the city for a fashion show."

"When?" My heart is racing. A tiny voice in my head warns I'm selling out. Seduced by the lure of my first airplane ride, my first real fashion show, my first a lot of things, makes all my lofty principles paper-thin. I stomp on the tiny voice with my five-inch stiletto heel and grind it to dust. Who said I had principles? Not me.

"Tomorrow night." His eyes dance. The smile he displays is panty dropping.

He seems almost happy. For Gideon. A warning bell goes off. "Wait, why?" Why would he do all this for me?

"Oh, well ..." His eyes widen as though he got caught with his fingers in the cookie jar. His jaw squares and his expression hardens. "It's not ... uh, that is, in your case, you seem more productive when you're less stressed. And I don't want you reverting to that useless state I found you in a few weeks ago, that's all."

Ah, there's the Gideon I know, always an ulterior motive.

A loose string on the hem of his shirt ensnares his full attention. He fiddles with it, without looking up. "You have something to wear, I assume?"

My smile is slow. "I think I can figure it out."

Chapter Fifteen

The show we're attending isn't Fashion Week in Lincoln Center. It's an invitation only, private collection at Saks Fifth Avenue. Ask me if I care.

There might be people taking pictures for magazines, so I pack a pretty pink dress for Maggie with a cuff bracelet and nude heels for height. For me, a white blouse, short black skirt, leather jacket, and wicked, red patent pumps. We'll look so chic. While I love my designs, I'm flying under the radar for this show, in what apparel I wear at least. It's not the time, place, or venue to make that kind of bold statement. My time will come.

Eat your heart out, New York. Here we go.

Actually, Dane *is* eating his heart out a little as he's been effectively excluded. Not that he cares about attending some glitzy show in New York. He just doesn't want us (Maggie) out of his sight, or more to the point, in Gideon's. I was surprised and thrilled Maggie's mother agreed, but once Mags started working on her, the poor woman was done for.

I stand in front of the bathroom mirror, applying the finishing touches to my makeup, while Maggie oohs and ahhs over the latest sewing creations in my workroom. The girl is good for my ego.

"Do you think these black stretch pants are okay for the plane ride?" she yells. "My clothes never look as good on my body as they do on the hanger or lying out on my bed." Her voice lowers to a mumble, but I hear her. "My bubble butt gets in the way."

"Don't be ridiculous," I answer. "You're adorable. You look great and you never care what people think. That's why I like you. Don't change that because we're flying to a fashion show, and you're worried you'll be amongst the swank and snobbish. They're just people, Mags. I bet they're all really nice."

"How much crack you been smokin'? Don't you watch *Next Top Model?* Besides, I wasn't fishing for compliments. I know I'm cute. Sometimes a girl wants to be more, though. Sometimes she wants … sophisticated, dazzling … "

I roll my eyes as I replace the top on my mascara bottle and grab the water glass next to the sink. "You're dazzling enough already, trust me. Dane thinks so, anyway."

"What?"

I check my tongue. "Nothing. I'll be out in a second. I still need to brush my teeth!" When I glance into the mirror a white flash catches my eye, followed by a hiss.

Free me …

My eyes focus on the space to my rear. Desiree's perfect, bloodless face hovers above my left shoulder. She presses against my back, jogging a memory. When her red lips pull back from her face in a snarl, her breath is as dank and foul as mold. "Free me, or you're as good as dead."

She lifts a hand and scrapes her nails over my bare arm. I think of the night I fell from the tree. Or was I pushed? The pressure on my skin is light, but enough I sense the hate dripping from her slow-moving, one-inch talons. Her eyes arc black and lifeless. A doll's eyes. As I gaze into their depths, my lungs compress. I feel the weight of her stare as I'm drawn inside. Helpless, I fall into Desiree, into her mind.

There's a room inside her memory with a low ceiling and dirt floor. A chill snakes up my spine. Fear prickles the skin on the back of my neck. There's a sense of evil here, a smell, something dark and oppressive. Or someone.

My gaze drifts over the clammy, sweating walls to a dozen crates stacked on the far side of the room. When I try to extract myself from the vision, my body won't obey. I will my legs to step back and they move forward. Electrical impulses seem to have lost the connection between my brain and limbs. As I near the wooden boxes, I find they're long and thin. Coffins.

Icy perspiration drips from my temples. My hands jut out without permission toward the first box. Stiff and mechanical, my rebellious fingers pry at the first lid, though I'm terrified of what's inside. A fingernail bends and peels away exposing the soft, pink flesh beneath, then another until they are all gone. Blood seeps from the raw nail beds, spattering the wood and my feet.

Since my voice is silenced, my brain screams. I gasp and pant, pleading with the powers that be to stop my torment. Splinters puncture and slice my skin, tearing at the flesh until my hands are warm and slick with blood. There's no reprieve from the agony, yet I work like a robot, a puppet at the mercy of whoever pulls my strings.

On and on, my hands scrape at the rough wood. Bones break through the ends of my shredded fingertips. Flesh, in the form of bloody pulp, still clings to the tendons. I yearn to faint, escape my torture, but I don't. I work on and on and on. One last yank and the coffin lid jerks free. My lids won't shut, nor can I look away. My heart hammers sharply against my ribs. Sweat trickles down my back as I peer inside.

A body in a white dress lies within, tucked into a straw bed. Her skin is smooth, undamaged, and blue. Desiree.

Her eyes open. She stares straight ahead until the socket stretches on the inside corner of one eye. The pupil dilates. Her gaze snaps to the side, focusing on me. Mucous membranes swell and rise into a thin bubble until the skin under the socket tears away, excrete a milky white substance. The dark, oval head of a worm pokes through. Fluid runs from her tear duct, following the dip beside her nose to her lip. Like a twisted birth, the larva writhes, chewing and clawing its way free of the flesh that incubated it.

Vomit climbs my throat. Fighting against the force that holds me is useless. The grub convulses and rolls free, but there are more. They push from her nostrils, the edge of her lip. A scream smothers in my mouth that won't open. Desiree's head twitches unnaturally, jerks to face me. Her hands grip my shoulders, nails penetrating deep into my skin.

Release me!

The glass in my hand shatters, cutting my fingers. I cry out and jump away from the splintering shards nearly plunging headfirst into the toilet.

"What the hell?" Maggie says. I whirl around. Desiree is gone, but Maggie appears in the doorframe. She glances to the tile floor and back to my face. "What happened in here?"

I'm breathing like I just ran a fifty-yard dash. My gaze darts all over the bathroom, but the specter is gone. "It slipped?" There's no controlling the tremor in my voice, but I try. I'm not sure what I saw, but there's no use frightening Maggie. Today is special. I'm not ruining our time together with talk of rotting bodies, or mausoleums inside my head.

She reaches for my hand. "Your fingers are bleeding. And here, too ..." She points to my arm where bright red scratches mar the skin. "Geez, they're deep. All this from one little glass?"

I doubt that but can't exactly explain.

"Do you have any Band-Aids?"

Stepping out of the broken glass, I shake my head. "I-I don't know. I don't think so. Maybe in a drawer."

"Calm down, Rae. Why are you shaking? It was an accident." Maggie rummages through the cabinets without success. She grimaces as she peeks at me again. "Don't worry, honey, it's just a glass. No one's going to be angry. I'm going to find Jenny. Stay here, okay?"

Where else would I go? "Okay."

Maggie heads for the door. "Watch you don't cut yourself more. Sit down. I'll bring a broom."

My knees tremble as I ease down on the toilet seat and wait. I'm not in pain. I'm freaked out. Was Desiree really here, trying to hurt me? Why would my mind make something like that up? Free her, she said. How and from what? I'd love to get rid of her. She's like the echo of a cast member from *Rich Housewives of Atlanta,* only the nasty, dead kind. Drops of blood fall from my fingers to the white floor forming a puddle. There's a thin trail from my elbow to wrist. I tear some toilet paper off the roll and wrap my throbbing fingers. The cuts aren't too deep, but they bleed nonetheless.

Raven …

Cole's image wavers in the doorframe and solidifies. I jolt and half fall off the potty. "Geez will you *not* do that!" I right myself and attempt to slow my heartbeat. "What's going on?"

He glides nearer until he's a foot away and kneels before me. "She's newer, stronger than the rest of us."

"Who?"

"Desiree."

"Oh."

He glances over his shoulder. "She's angry and dangerous. She wants you to release us."

Yeah, I sort of got that. "What does that mean, release you?"

His mouth opens but nothing comes out. He shakes his dark head. "Go to the attic. The answer is in the attic."

That's pretty vague, and I've had enough of creepy dark spaces for one day. "Why? What's up there?"

"We're bound—" His body convulses and he can't finish. "Trapped. Punished …"

"Punished?" I repeat.

He nods. "Maddox." His body seizes. He grips his throat. "Enemies."

"Okay, okay." I reach out to console him, but my hand passes straight through his image. "That's enough, I get it." I don't, but he acts like he's suffocating. Can a ghost hurt? "Do you feel pain?"

"Not …" Cole chokes and falls to his hands and knees. A long pause follows before he lifts his head. He searches my face with his dark eyes, presses his lips to form a line. His head tilts and his eyes plead for understanding that I'm willing to give but can't.

"What? What is it?" I can't figure out what's wrong with him. If certain words bring him pain, perhaps he's searching for the ones that don't.

He reaches for me, but I pull away. I hate the wounded look in his eyes, but I don't know who to trust. "We feel through our memories, and through the life inside of you, though some of us grow weaker with time."

"Rae?" Maggie calls to me from the bedroom.

Cole leans forward, speaking into my ear. "The attic. Don't forget. And Raven, be careful."

"I'm here." My ghost fades and disappears. I shudder. Whenever he does that, it's disconcerting to say the least.

"Goodness gracious," Jenny says. "Had we an accident, my dear?" She's carrying a broom in one hand and a dustpan in the other. Maggie is loaded down with a bottle of peroxide and enough gauze and tape to treat an army.

While Jenny gets to work on the broken glass, my best friend rests her bum opposite me on the narrow rim of my bathtub. She unwinds the blood-soaked toilet paper from my finger and tends my cuts. "Aw, it's not so bad. Fingers and facial cuts always bleed like a mother but amount to nothing. Rae?" I raise my chin and meet her gaze. "You okay? You look weird."

"I'm fine. Just a dumb accident is all."

"Nothing embarrassing about that, dearie," Jenny tuts.

I'm not embarrassed. Dazed, terrified, and curious as hell about what may be hiding upstairs, but they don't need to hear that. With less than an hour before we leave for the airport, there's no time to visit the attic. I'll have to wait until we return from New York. Maggie lifts her eyebrows, giving me a doubtful expression that suggests she knows I'm holding out on her.

Ignoring her, I lean around my friend. "Thanks, Jenny. I could've cleaned up my own mess, though. You don't have to wait on me."

"Not a bit of it. What am I paid for then, to twiddle my thumbs all day, and see? It's all done. There's a good girl. Now you two finish up and get downstairs. Jamis is fit to be tied when he gets behind schedule."

"You're too good to us," Maggie says as she stands.

"You are helping the master, and nothing is too good for that boy. Any friend of his is a friend of mine."

Maggie glances at me. Her pleasant expression hiding whatever thoughts she's having. "Absolutely," she says. "I couldn't agree more."

***

Jamis drives us forty minutes to the airport in Hilton Head where we board a commercial flight to LaGuardia in New York City. Three and a half hours. In the air. With Gideon. That's as much time as I've ever spent with the guy all at once, well consciously anyway. I'm grateful Maggie is here as a buffer.

The plane is full. I don't know what I expected; maybe daydreaming with Maggie as we both crane our heads out the same little window for a peek at the distant earth. We'd whisper about school, gossip about boys, get caught up. I expected a lot of things, but being sandwiched between Mags and Gideon wasn't one of them.

I squirm in my seat. Gideon bumps me with his knee. His thigh occasionally rubs mine, or his elbow brushes my sleeve. The curve of his tricep slides against my arm in an annoyingly provocative way. Every time he touches me, a tiny cluster of moths take flight in my stomach. When his hand meets mine on our shared armrest, I shift away. His lips curl in the slanted smile I've identified as mild amusement—usually directed at me. I swear he's doing it on purpose to upset me. I glance up. Smooth yet defined, I follow the line of his cheekbone to his jaw with my eyes. I'm hyperaware of the fact that I'm hyperaware of *him*. Somebody slap me, please.

When I lean once more toward Maggie's seat, she blows. "I love you Rae, but you can't get in my lap, all right?"

I straighten. "Sorry."

"Are you scared?"

"No."

"Sick?"

"No."

"Nervous."

"No! It's nothing. I'm sorry." I pantomime using two fingers, and outline the space around me. "I'll stay within my designated area." Next to me, Gideon's chuckle unsettles the moths and they flutter again. I'm ridiculous.

"Freak," Maggie whispers. Her gaze rests on me a little too long, then she shrugs and goes back to reading her fashionzine. Thirty minutes later, however, she puts the magazine down and curls into a ball, or as much of a ball as our cramped seating allows. Her head lolls onto my shoulder and she whimpers.

"What's wrong?" I ask.

"Car sick. Plane sick." She wriggles adjusting her head. "Motion sick, I don't know." My poor friend's skin is olive green and a light sheen of perspiration covers her forehead. "Oh no." She bolts upright and crawls over Gideon and me to the aisle.

"You going to puke?"

"Mount Vesuvius." She stumbles over Gideon's feet, but he catches her. Helping her to a stand, he walks behind my friend, escorting her to the bathroom.

He hesitates at the door a few minutes before returning to his seat. "She won't let me in."

"No," I say, surprised he's willing to help her. "I imagine not." There are people who share toilet moments and people who don't. Maggie and I, we're members of the hurl alone club. Sure, I've read in romance novels where the cute guy holds the pretty blonde's hair back for her while she retches.

Afterward, she's so grateful, they end up making out. In real life, I think that's bull. No guy wants to help a girl vomit, I don't care how hot she is, and he sure as hell isn't going to kiss her sewer mouth afterward.

After an uncomfortable amount of time, in which I imagined Maggie flushing herself out of the plane's belly, she staggers back to her seat. She's pasty-skinned and sweating. I pat her arm, but she says nothing. Once the plane lands, all I can think about is getting Mags to our hotel so she can wish she were dead in peace.

Gideon's firm chest presses against my back as we exit the plane. His muscular leg pushes my much smaller one on the long taxi ride to our hotel. I glare at him, but he's oblivious, or pretending to be. He smells clean and inviting, like fresh sheets and faint cologne, and I hate that, too. By the time Maggie and I reach our room, it's ten o'clock at night. The show is twelve hours away, and I'm as tense as any tightrope walker hovering above the Grand Canyon. No big.

In our hotel, Maggie throws herself down on one of the two queen-sized beds and groans. I climb on the bed next to her and flop.

"What's eating you?" Maggie mumbles into the bedspread. I can hardly hear her. She rolls to her side and yawns. "Nice undies, by the way. I love black."

I smooth my skirt down in a half attempt at modesty. "Glad you've kept your sense of humor." She grunts, and I can't help my small smile. "Keyed up, I guess. First time out of the state, on a plane, to a fashion show … a lot of firsts today."

"Mm hmm."

"I'm worried about Ben, school, graduation. And Gideon annoyed the crap out of me all the way here."

Maggie opens one eye. "Not shy, is he?"

"Not even—"

A knock has us both jolting. I force myself up, walk ten steps across the room, and open the door.

"Always ask who's there before you open the door, Raven. We're not in Kansas anymore." Gideon hovers in a pair of dark jeans, distressed bomber jacket, and heavy boots. A chunky silver bracelet hangs at his wrist, the onyx ring on one finger. Towering over me is an audacious display of knee-weakening masculinity. He steals my breath and enough brain cells to render me speechless. "Get your coats, ladies. Let's explore New York City."

Chapter Sixteen

October in New York can be chilly, yet as I sip my coffee on my way to the eighty-sixth floor of the Empire State Building, I'm impervious to cooler temperatures. I am *that* girl. The green, wide-eyed tourist running from one viewpoint to another in awe of the epicness that is Manhattan.

A group of sightseers stand together in the elevator heading up. Gideon leans on his cane between a pretty redhead to his right and me. She's wearing a cheaply made, ruby-colored cocktail dress, so tight I wonder how she breathes, so short she tempts hyperthermia. Another young couple waits behind us.

The ride is long, silent, and awkward. When the redhead sends a flirty smile Gideon's way, my hackles go up. She's got a lot of nerve. He's not mine, but she can't know that. A bell dings. The doors open, and the redhead exits first. Her shapely bottom jiggles under the clingy fabric of her dress.

In the midst of wondering if the redhead is Gideon's type, or if he's staring at her butt, feet scuffle behind me.

"Ow!" When I glance over my shoulder, the guy behind us shies away from his girlfriend. "You hit me."

"Damn right I did," his girlfriend admits. "I can't believe

you bring me up here for a romantic evening just to ogle another girl!"

"No, I didn't." His face colors ten shades of guilty. He's in the doghouse for sure.

"Don't deny it. I saw you! Take me home." She crosses her arms and steps off to the side. Clearly she doesn't want to go home. If she did, she'd be in the elevator stabbing 'down' buttons with her angry little fingers. My guess is Pissed Off Girlfriend is looking for some major sucking up. Girlfriend's voice fades as she continues to berate Doghouse Guy.

I face Gideon and scrunch my face into my best 'Yikes!' expression. He laughs as we drift toward the terrace. He has a nice laugh.

A man with a silver goatee plays the saxophone. I've never been much for jazz, but it sounds nice and helps cover the rising voices of the bickering couple. I stare at the lights through the metal bars on the observation deck. There must be thousands, maybe millions of lights. Each one represents a life. Someone's cramming for a test, eating take-out, falling asleep—are they happy, are their dreams coming true? They could just as easily be insects, striving together like ants trying to fix a broken mound.

Dreams and struggle. Maybe life is both.

"What are you thinking?" Gideon leans with his back against the wall, facing me. His body is relaxed, ankles crossed. His cane leans against one leg. The wind stirs his golden hair, blowing a curl across his forehead. I resist the urge to brush it aside. I've had to resist a lot of urges with Gideon today.

I didn't want to be here. Alone. With *him*. What sort of friend abandons her bestie when she's ill? My resolve melted like cotton candy on a hot tongue, however, when Maggie warned she wouldn't be well enough to attend the fashion show tomorrow if I didn't shut up and let her sleep. Just like that, I'm thrown out on my rear. I swear it's a conspiracy.

"Humanity."

He chuckles. "No light reading for you, is there?"

I shrug. "Guess I don't do small talk very well."

The crooked smile appears. "I see. And what about all the humanity out there, Raven Weathersby?"

My gaze shifts from the scenic view to his face and back. Something about the way he stares at my mouth unnerves me. The moths are alive and well in my stomach. "The world is bigger than I imagined. Intellectually, I know there are billions of people on the earth, but to see proof of them is blowing my mind, more or less. I was wondering if they're happy or unhappy or whatever."

"Happiness is an illusion, Raven. No one is happy, at least not all the time. There has to be balance. Ambition, power, satisfaction, self-control, that's what's real. People have to be managed because most of the time, they don't know what they want or how to get it. Me? I take what I want."

I bet that's his father talking. I think of the long line of family portraits hanging in his office. Portraits of ancestral judges—ending with one of his father. "That sounds exactly like what one of the criminals appearing before your relatives might have said."

His eyes narrow. "That's different."

I'm starting to enjoy our conversation. I get the idea he's not used to people disagreeing with him, speaking their mind. I'd love to rattle his cage for a change. When I think of rattling other things belonging to him I mentally punch myself. "Yeah, how? Who manages you?" A sudden shout has me peering around Gideon's formidable shoulder. I don't mean to spy, but the couple we rode up on the elevator with is in a full-blown spat. I pull my 'Yikes!' face again.

"No one. I don't need managing ..." He follows my gaze to the pair behind us.

I feel the scowl coating my features. "Ah. Well, forgive the rest of us great and unwashed multitudes who need a Maddox to tell us what to do." When he faces me again, his lips press to form a thin line. "No one wants to be managed, Gideon."

"You think so?" Arrogance and a sort of dark humor oozes from every pore, he's sexy and charismatic in the most obnoxious way possible. "Observe."

"What?"

Gideon makes a slight bow, pivots, and heads straight for Doghouse Guy. I follow, more curious than anything, but I cringe when my companion interrupts the sparring couple. "Hey, man, I'm sorry to bother you, but I noticed that you were admiring my cane."

What?

"What?" Doghouse Guy asks.

"My cane, I saw you eyeing it in the elevator and again just now."

Girlfriend faces her date as if waiting for an explanation. "Peter?"

Peter's mouth gapes before he answers. "Er ... listen dude, I—"

Gideon holds the cane out, handle first, forcing his experiment on the unsuspecting man. "It's okay, don't be shy. It happens everywhere I go, and I love to brag on it." He nods to the cane. "Check it out. I swear it gets me more attention than dating a beautiful woman." Gideon pauses, looks with meaning into Peter's face. "I saw you staring earlier as we rode up in the elevator together. Staring and *staring* ..."

I may die of embarrassment, for Gideon and for me.

A dim light brightens over Peter's head. "Right. Right! Your cane! It's a beaut. I wasn't trying to be obvious about all that gawking, but I guess I didn't do too good of a job."

"No brother, you didn't." He laughs. "My father had this commissioned for me by a man in Ireland. That walking stick is handcrafted. One of a kind." Gideon points to the lion's head. "There's a dagger under the handle. I'd show you, but then the security guards would wrestle me to the ground and arrest me, so you'll just have to take my word for it."

The guys share a phony laugh.

They're so obvious. Pissed Off Girl will never believe this. But as I glance at her, her shoulders relax. *You're not buying this. Please tell me you're not buying this!* Gideon and Peter banter another moment or two until a small smile emerges from Girlfriend.

No way!

"Okay, well it's nice to meet you." Gideon accepts the cane back from his new buddy. "I hope the two of you enjoy the rest of this beautiful evening."

"No, listen, thank you so much." There is a little too much emphasis on Peter's 'thank you' and my stomach sours.

As we step away, Gideon leans into me and lowers his head. "I think my work here is finished."

Gideon's sultry voice in my ear gives me chills. I like it, which makes me mad, so I shrug him off. "That doesn't prove a thing."

His grin is smug. "It proves reasonable doubt, and I think the young lady would agree with me."

"Why do you—" I follow the line from his jutting thumb over his shoulder. The arguing couple is now wrapped tighter than a croissant. Peter has his tongue down Pissed Off Girl's throat, and she is anything but complaining.

"I'm Batman."

"You're ridiculous."

"I saved their evening."

"Maybe. But if he was 'looking', he'll do it again, and she'll dump him for disrespecting her."

"And so she should, but my point is proved. People believe what they want to believe."

I don't disagree, but I'm not about to admit it. I'm committed to my side of the debate. As if to rev myself up, I toss a hand in the air. "Oh, come on, Gideon. Just because people make mistakes, doesn't mean they want to be controlled. How would you like that? Have you never been dishonest in any of your business dealings?"

"No. The people I deal with are well aware of what they're getting into."

Damn. He has me on a technicality. I knew what I was giving up when I made my deal with him. And Ben *is* getting something from our bargain. "No one is all good, dude. We rebel. We are selfish. Have you never let a girl think you felt more for her than you really did just to get ...?" The minute the words are out, I regret them. Heat swamps my cheeks. I cough and take a sip of my lukewarm coffee. His silence is answer enough, I guess, and my cheeks burn again.

Gideon's shoulders straighten as he readjusts himself against the wall. He cocks his head as if considering.

When his focus on me doesn't waver, I cave under the pressure. "Okay, you win."

"My three favorite words."

"But let it be known, I have lied and cheated and stolen to survive. I'm not proud of it, but I won't be a hypocrite."

His eyebrows crash down, and his eyes darken with a pained expression. "Don't confess to me, Raven. I'm not your priest."

"Good thing I don't seek absolution from you then, isn't it? We're just two people having a discussion. You're not my judge ... unless you choose to judge me."

He shakes his head. "The way you talk." The anger in his tone is gone. If anything, I'd say he sounds surprised. "You have a queer perspective."

"And you speak like a forty-year-old professor ... or that guy who hosts the classic movie channel."

"Be nice." He smiles. "My speech is my father's influence I suppose, that and too many boarding schools."

Okay. "Well, did you mean my perspective's odd or—"

"Different. Quick to see the good in people, quick to forgive. You're unlike anyone I've ever known."

I don't know what to say to that. He doesn't know who I am, but I'm shocked at how accurate his guesses are. How observant he's been in the short time we've known each other. I face the skyline again, marveling at the incredible sight. Pressure on my coat sleeve draws my attention. As Gideon stands next to me, I'm aware the chill running the length of my spine has nothing to do with the wind.

Leaning on his cane, he gazes out on the same scene I do, but I imagine we'll never see it the same way. His heart is closed, maybe more than mine. I still believe in loyalty and friendship and love. Maybe not the romantic kind, but Gideon is alone in a way I've never been. As I study his face, something hammers at the hardness in my heart and I give a little. How different would I be if I'd grown up as he had?

"Raven?"

"Yes, Gideon."

"I've never told a girl I loved her in order to sleep with her."

"That's good."

"I've never said those words to anyone before. Ever."

That's not so good. What do I say? Anyone includes his parents, right? He's never loved a pet, a great uncle enough to tell them, or did words of affection simply go unspoken in his family? 'Anyone' includes everyone. "I'm sorry."

"Are you?"

"Very."

"Thank you. I think." He grazes my shoulder with his arm producing another shiver. The warming effects of my coffee are long gone.

We're quiet a while, then he says, "I never thought I'd meet anyone I'd care enough about to say those words to. Didn't think I'd want to hear them back." As though he remembers who he's talking to, his scowl returns. The grooves in his skin so deep, I fear he'll make them permanent. He grips the railing as he blasts the skyline with his glare.

"I understand," I say. And I do, though why he's telling me is anyone's guess. I take it back. I know why. Because sometimes it's easier confessing something to a stranger, someone who will pass out of your life and never tell a soul. There's also the hope they might take a little of your pain with them. Like a sin-eater.

He doesn't say so, but I'm curious, based on our conversation, if Gideon feels as superior as he claims. Does he have a guilty conscience? Most people do about one thing or another. If so, maybe I'm his scapegoat. It also explains why my blackmailer has been thoughtful at times. I'm making a lot of assumptions, but they ring true, regardless. "I get it, Gideon. More than you might guess."

***

As I slip into my hotel room, I'm pleased to see Maggie awake and watching TV. She's propped up against some pillows. Her color is less pea soup green which is decidedly better.

"Hey."

"Hey yourself."

"How are you feeling?"

She shrugs. "My soup is staying down, so I'm thinking that's a good sign."

"You ordered room service?" To her right sits a silver tray supporting an empty bowl, some crackers, a glass of water, and a yellow rose in a crystal vase.

"Not exactly." She leans over picking a folded note card from the bedside table and tosses it to me.

Dear Margaret,

I'm very sorry you are ill this evening. Your company will be missed.

Perhaps this will help. Feel better.

G. Maddox

Slowly, I lower my butt until it hits the mattress beneath me. "I'll be darned."

"Rae," Mags shifts to her side. "I know this whole scenario with you pseudo-kidnapped and Ben in rehab is weird and all, but still. I think Gideon is ..." She bites her lip.

"What?"

"Nice."

Chapter Seventeen

The fashion show is a wild success. I don't care what the critics think, or what the reviewers will say in tomorrow's papers. Ashley Mackee's designs are freaking genius and a great way to end a show that featured three new designers. Plus Ashley smiled at me. Okay, maybe she smiled at Gideon, but I'm pretending it was me.

Seated between a much-improved Maggie and our benefactor, I squirm and squeal and fangirl until Gideon bursts out laughing and Maggie threatens to bodily remove me. The show ends to the crowd rising in a standing O. How awesome to have people react like that to what you create. My dream is to experience that. Maybe one day.

After the show, we're escorted into a posh reception room. Tables are covered with white bone china and crystal. The menu lists an appetizer of jumbo shrimp, displayed over ice with cocktail sauce and lemon. Asian glazed Chilean sea bass, farfalle pasta with baby spinach, sun-dried tomatoes, and garlic serve as the main fare. As delicious as it looks, I'm too keyed up to eat a bite.

Attendees mill around the room in groups. Executives

network, models flirt, and waiters rush around with heavy trays. Maggie and I try not to gawk and look as intimidated as we feel. A pretty brunette ignores us completely as she grabs Gideon by the arm with a 'Hey baby' and drags him across the room. I'd like to object, but on what basis? We're business associates, here to work.

He stands talking with a crowd of impeccably dressed people. I'm amazed how relaxed he appears for someone so young. Then I remember he's been exposed, even groomed for his position in this world his entire life.

A waiter passes carrying a large tray of drinks. Maggie snags a flute of champagne. I shake my head as she offers one to me. "Delicious," she chirps. "Where are the strawberries?"

I don't know. I can't take my eyes off the scene before me.

The brunette drapes her arm over Gideon's. I recognize her as one of Ashley Mackee's runway models from the show. She might be six feet tall, but she can't be more than eighteen. Her tinkling laughter bubbles up, grating on my nerves as she rubs herself against Gideon like a cat in heat.

My palms are sweaty, and my feet are cold. Maggie's saying something, but I hardly hear her over the blood pounding in my ears. I hope I'm not coming down with her stomach bug.

"Raven," Maggie says. "Try one of these shrimps. They're fantastic. I swear I'm going to gain five pounds on this trip."

"Hello, ladies." Maggie's eyes light up as we face the guy addressing us. He's young, early twenty-something with light brown hair and amber eyes. He strikes me as someone who just stepped out of a movie trailer. "I'm Stephen." I'm not great with accents, but I think he's Italian. "You are here for a model?"

I sneak a quick glance at Gideon. My stomach churns as the brunette brushes her hand down his arm. His smile proves he doesn't mind. Why should he, she's gorgeous.

Maggie giggles, fluttering her false eyelashes at the swarthy-skinned guy before us. "We could be."

"I think he's asking us if *we're* models. Not if we came for one." Though I answer Maggie, my gaze fixes on the stranger.

"I also think Stephen is being a flirt, as neither of us are the model type."

The smile he flashes is toothpaste commercial material. "Ah, and what is model type, please?" He leans in so close I take a step back.

"Pretty, vain, shallow, you know how they are." I'm smiling too, having a little fun at his expense.

Stephen throws his head back and laughs. His hand covers his heart. "Siren. You hurt me already, uh ... your name is, please?"

"Raven."

Another step closer. "*Sei molto bella!*" He stoops, taking my hand in his. I can't keep the heat from my cheeks as he lifts my fingers and drops a kiss on my knuckles. He doesn't hurry.

"Maybe I should just leave," Maggie jokes. She taps her bottom lip, perusing the hors d'oeuvres on the table nearby. "Or you two should get a room ..."

I'm about to elbow her in the gut when Stephen wraps his arm around my waist and tugs me against him. Champagne flavors his breath. His nose grazes my cheek. Personal space alert. My elbow redirects itself toward Stephen's rib cage when we're jostled from behind.

"Stephen, *salve*. How are you?" Gideon interposes himself between the guy I'm getting to know and me, breaking our contact.

"Mad Dog, you are timed to save me. Raven and her friend are *da solo*. We should welcome them properly, you and I, eh?"

Mad Dog?

"Actually, they are with me." Gideon's tone is deliberate. He pins Stephen with a cold stare and his warning is clear. Hands off. I shiver, and rub my shoulder against the chill. Gideon's hand slides down my arm, stopping at my wrist. When I try to pull away, he holds me tighter.

My hackles go up. The idea he might feel responsible for us is swallowed up by his presumption. I can handle party-guy interested in some harmless banter. I'm caught up in the day, the glamour. Stephen made me feel a part of this world, pretty, glamorous—for a minute. Of course, when the female equivalent mauls Gideon it's perfectly fine. Ugh! Hypocrite.

Gideon releases my wrist and stands feet apart. Both hands rest quietly on the head of his cane, yet there is nothing relaxed about the tense lines of his body. His broad back momentarily blocks my view.

Stephen clears his throat. "My apologies, I did not—"

"No, you did not." Gideon's shoulders align. His smile is tight as he tilts his head toward a gathering of people nearby. "I understand Mae is here. Have you seen her yet?"

"Ass," Stephen says.

That word I know.

Stephen glances at me once more. A sheepish grin spreads his lips. "*Che vergogna.*" With a last nod, he saunters off and disappears into the crowd.

Gideon whirls on me. His fingers press my arm. "Stay here," he orders. "We're leaving, but I need to thank our hosts first, I'll only be a moment." His fingers trail down my sleeve before he retreats.

"Wow," Maggie says, popping a shrimp between her plump lips. She chases her food with more champagne. "That was telling ..."

"What, jerk boy?"

"Which one?"

The tension in my neck eases with my laugh. "Gideon's ridiculous."

"Is he?"

"Yeah. Wait, which one did you mean?"

"I mean I've been watching the two of you all afternoon. I see you, Rae. Undressing him with your eyes when you think no one's paying attention. Your claws were showing when that skanky model was all over him." I open my mouth, but she points her finger, effectively shushing me. "Don't even say it. Your reaction was that of a very pissed off girlfriend who caught her man getting too friendly with another chick."

Pissed Off Girl! Me? Oh, no. "No. No and no. It's not like that."

"Sometimes you can be so blind, Rae." She downs the last of her champagne.

"Me blind? What about you!"

"What does that mean?"

Shut up, Raven. I almost spilled about Dane, and I can*not* go there. "Nothing, you just don't see everything either. Gideon and I loathe each other. We will never be more than civil enemies."

"Sure, hon, keep telling yourself that." Maggie calmly shoves another shrimp in her mouth and then talks around it. "What you may not realize is that the cool and collected Gideon Maddox almost unzipped and stepped out of his skin when he saw Stephen slobbering all over you."

I nod at her empty glass. "How many of those have you had?"

Her lips purse. "Two. Three. No more than four."

"Uh huh. I'm cutting you off."

"You're not the boss of me! And that's not why I think Gideon likes you."

"He's a control freak. The guy has barely spoken a word to me half the day and spent the rest glaring at me like I ran over his dog. He always talks about protecting me as his 'investment.' That's all I am to him."

"Hmm." She glances at Gideon and the brunette again at his side. "Seems more like plain old jealousy to me."

She's wrong. "Maybe he thinks I'm going to make a side deal for my designs, undercut him, or cut him out altogether. Network for future jobs, hire Stephen to model for me, stab him in his big, fat back. Trust me. He's not jealous of Stephen."

"Nope. He definitely was, but when I mentioned jealousy just now, I was talking about you."

Chapter Eighteen

The sun sets, leaving a legacy of darkness. Maggie snores softly in the bed next to mine but as usual, I can't sleep. Her accusation earlier plagues me. Am I jealous of Gideon? I'm attracted to him, that's clear. Infatuated, under some spell he cast. I have been since the first day I walked into his house and my watch stopped—my heart along with it.

Okay, maybe that was just an odd coincidence, but there's something dark and frightening that surrounds him and his home. As hard as it is to imagine, say Gideon was interested in me for more than my creative bent. Interested in what? A one-night stand, a fling? I can't imagine someone as gun-shy as me entering into a full-on relationship with someone as calculating as Gideon. He told me he takes what he wants, does that mean *who* he wants, too? His father taught him that love is a fantasy, a fleeting dream that destroys your soul. I wonder if the son holds the same view. Based on his actions, I fear he does.

But the guy has these moments of generosity that confuse and confound me. My beautiful room. Ben's rehab facility. Gideon could have met the requirements of our deal with far less luxurious accommodations, but he didn't. The night I fell, he was looking for me to tell me he'd found my cat. When I was injured, he got me help and stayed with me all night. Then there's the fact he allowed Mags to come to New York with me. He even had chicken soup sent up with a note.

Maybe Maggie is right. Maybe he's not the beast I thought he was. I mean, yes, the way he's collecting Ben's debt is skeevy, and he's said some troubling things, but … maybe I misjudged him on the whole.

I slip out of bed and pad to the bathroom. Sure it's one in the morning, but this is important. I need to talk to Gideon. There are questions that need answers, and they won't wait. I brush my teeth, run a comb through my hair, and apply a touch of lip gloss. Not bad. I'm still thin but the circles under my eyes have faded and my cheeks are pink with excitement.

Maggie snorts and rolls over in bed. I freeze until she settles, and then I creep toward the door. Easing it open a crack, I hear muffled voices filling the hallway. A low, silky tone I recognize as Gideon follows a higher, feminine pitch.

"I've missed you, baby."

I can't resist and peer far enough out my door to see into the corridor. The brunette model from the reception earlier faces Gideon whose back is against the closed door of his hotel room. Her hand is on his chest and her red lips are in full-on pout mode.

My mouth goes dry. My chest constricts until I can't breathe. Me jealous? Check. The sight of her so close to him makes me more than a little ill. She presses herself against him. I can't hear what they're saying anymore, but her tone sounds seductive, almost pleading.

I take what I want. He'd said. How about what's thrown at him in a six-foot package wrapped in fishnet stockings?

Fingers wrap my arm, drawing me back, and I jump.

"Shhhh. Rae, come away, sweetheart." Maggie? Caught up in the scene outside, I never even heard her approach. She closes the door with a click. "Shit. I'm sorry, Rae. This is all my fault. Come back to bed."

I lay down feeling raw, and stupid, and insanely

disappointed. "Nothing is your fault, Mags."

Maggie crawls in beside me and pets my head. A sigh leaks out of her. "You never would have thought about Gideon as a possibility if I hadn't brought him up."

"You saw him ... with her?"

"Yeah." Her voice is chock-full of pity, and I bristle.

"Well, don't worry about it. I wasn't *thinking* anything about Gideon Maddox."

"You forget. I know you. You thought he was an evil, mean, jerk face until I started talking about how he might like you, how you might like him, and what a poor misunderstood millionaire he might be."

Truth. "No, I wasn't."

"Where were you going when I dragged you back in here, Rae?"

Ack. Busted. "To talk."

"To talk. To his royal hotness. At one in the morning?"

"Uh huh."

"About ..."

"Okay, you got me."

"Thought so. It sucks being right only ninety percent of the time. Clearly, I was wrong about him being decent boyfriend material."

"Boyfriend? Whoa, slow down."

"Point is, if he was as into you as I thought he was, he wouldn't be—"

"Got that part, thanks." I shrink into a ball. "Go to sleep."

A pause. "I'm sorry. I really thought ... I mean he acted like—"

"Don't be sorry. I dodged a bullet." Gideon's passion was like an inferno. He'd burn you down and leave the ash behind without ever getting scorched himself. Heaven help the girl who actually falls for him. "I must have been crazy, but it's fine. I'm better off alone."

Maggie strokes my hair. Strangely, the old excuses don't satisfy anymore. I must be lonelier than I thought. Maybe if I say them long enough, I'll believe myself again.

Chapter Nineteen

The clock on the wall ticks. The second hand mocks me, sucking time into a black hole as I sit at my worktable and groan. I shuffle through stacks of paperwork but can't focus. The three days back from New York seem more like three weeks.

Edgar winds around my feet, and I lean down to scratch his ears. His purr is my reward. With a sigh, I abandon the waiting sketches and open my book of Edgar Allan Poe poetry.

"Yes, I now feel that it was then on that evening of sweet dreams—that the very first dawn of human love burst upon the icy night of my spirit. Since that period I have never seen nor heard your name without a shiver, half of delight, half of anxiety ..."

Gideon's face floats around in my head. The image of him in my chair the morning after I fell from the tree haunts me, looking all mysterious and *smexy* and stupid. I slam my book shut. Gah! "Loser." I have Stockholm disease, syndrome, whatever. That must be it, right? It's a thing, as Maggie would say.

As I toss the book down on the table, the corner of an envelope sticks out. The letter I'd stolen from Gideon's desk.

How on earth could I have forgotten? I cut myself some slack. The fall from the tree, insomnia, worry over Ben, not to mention all the general, ghostly weirdness in this house is reason enough, I suppose. Still, I'm surprised I forgot.

With no small amount of guilt, I slip the envelope from between the pages and withdraw the letter inside.

Dear Mr. Maddox, esquire,

Please accept the school's deepest regrets and our most sincere apologies for the incident occurring last Tuesday. The four boys responsible for locking Gideon in the cafeteria freezer have confessed and received one week's suspension each.

I quite understand your workload and inability to fly here to oversee your son's hospitalization, but the doctors confirm he is doing very well. Thank you for allowing Gideon to remain enrolled for another semester. He is intelligent, well mannered, and a favorite among our educators. As I stated on the telephone, all tuition fees are waived from last term. We assure you that hazing new students is not a common problem at Malcolm College.

To ensure that this will not be a repeat occurrence, we are adding new security measures to the campus and heightening the supervision of our student body as a whole to prevent this ever happening again.

If you have any questions or concerns regarding this matter, please feel free to discuss them with me.

Yours respectfully,
S. Allen Gamble, Headmaster

The letter flutters to my lap like a dying leaf from a tree. Oh, Gideon. What must you have gone through? The anger I felt toward myself a moment ago for my attraction to him, shifts to the boys that hurt him, and to his selfish father.

No matter what Gideon's done to me, I can't ignore the pain he must have suffered as a child. He's still suffering. The reasons Gideon Maddox became who he is are becoming clearer, but he still had a choice. I can't call him blameless. I don't know what to call him. Why does he tug on my emotions this way?

Edgar jumps to the table. I survey all the work waiting there for me, though I feel less like working now than before. My heart is a stone in the pit of my stomach.

Gideon ...

I stare at the piles of work on my desk. The trademark for my new clothing line is in place and registered, logo done and demographic targeted. I say *my* line but it isn't, it's Gideon's. He had his lawyers construct a subsidiary company, Raedoxx Apparel, under the name Maddox Properties as an LLC. Business plans, production run costs, advertising, and marketing. I had no idea so much went into launching a clothing line. I'm creative but not so much into finance. It's overwhelming but exciting, too. I won't lie. I'm getting a crash course in business, and I'm hoping I'll be graded on a heavy curve.

I check over the list Gideon's given me. In the next several weeks, I'm to create the following:

1. Computerized and technical sketches that the apparel manufacturers require for accuracy, and to use for catalogs, investors, and buyers.
2. Spec Sheets
3. Line Sheets for clothing retailers
4. Garment quality checklist

Everything has to be ready before the debut showing of my work in Paris this spring. I repeat that sentence three or four times over in my head just to feel the rush of adrenaline it brings. My clothes and Paris in the same breath. Maybe I can get Dane and Maggie a pass.

All that in addition to my regular schoolwork. I'm in over my head, and truthfully, I am pretty much waiting for my brain to explode. I need help, but I've been avoiding Gideon since New York. Thankfully, he's been distracted. We haven't talked much other than necessary conversations for business. He's not busy enough to leave town, though. I'm jonesing for that because I still want to sneak my friends in and go ghost hunting. Plagued with too many tasks and interruptions, I haven't been to the attic either, but I'm going and soon. For today, the poltergeist quandary remains last on the list.

The Fallout dance is two days away. After the 'episode,' as Mags terms it, in the hotel hallway between Gideon and his sexy model gal-pal, I no longer want to go with him. Not that I ever did. Hoping Gideon had forgotten all about the stupid dance, I gave the clothes I'd made for Dane and Maggie to them yesterday when they dropped off my schoolwork. Told them to go without me and have fun. I had to bite my tongue, literally, not to warn Maggie of Dane's feelings. I don't want to see him hurt, but I can't protect him either.

Another glance at the clock shows 4 PM. Time to phone Ben. I head for the kitchen to make my call. Rehab gave the go ahead allowing us to talk briefly twice a week. I'm hoping the conversations will encourage us both.

"Rae?"

"Hey, Ben, it's great to hear your voice."

"Yours too, honey."

"Any more dreams?"

"No. But it's funny. I can feel her, Rae. Your mama's spirit calls to mine. I think … I think she's proud of me … since I came here."

I don't tell him he's crazy. If it comforts him to think of my mother like this, I won't take it from him. "I know she's proud, Ben. So am I." I pause. "How are you doing? How's the recovery going?" I'm not sure I want to hear what's coming, but Ben needs my support.

He lets out a deep breath. "It's hard. Maybe the hardest thing I've ever done. The doctor says my body doesn't need the booze anymore, but my head still wants it."

"Every day?"

"Every minute."

Oh. My heart sinks.

"I don't know which voice is louder your mother's or the Scotch."

All the cliché answers I might give at this moment fight for top billing and in the end, I say, "I can't imagine. I'm sorry this is so hard on you."

"Don't. Don't apologize to me, honey. Listen can you come visit me next weekend? The doctors have given us permission."

My pulse kicks up. "Why? What's wrong? Should I come this weekend instead?"

"No need to get riled. I have some doctor's appointments this week. These people stick me like a pincushion. No, next week is better. I just want to talk, face-to-face."

I shift my feet.

"See, in our daily meetings here, we talk about something called amends. There are some things need sayin' and it's past time to say 'em."

I feel the tension leave my neck and shoulders. This has to do with his therapy. Good. "I'd like that."

"Since I'm working on my honesty, there's something else you ought to know."

I swallow, uncomfortable with the hesitant tone of his voice. "Okay ..."

"The sober thing happens in stages, they say. When the fog of drunkenness first lifted, I started thinking with a clear head. I was so full of rage, I wanted to hate God for taking your mother, hate you for sending me here, and hate that Maddox fella for stealing you away from me. I thought of ways to break out of here, buy a gun, and blow that boy's head clean off."

"Er, Ben, that doesn't sound clear-headed, like, at all."

"I know it. It's them stages they talk about. Once I got out of the hospital, more fog went away. The doctors said I should talk to the boy, so I did. Thought you should know." He finishes with flair, like he just won first prize in a truth-telling contest.

"You spoke with Gideon?"

"Yeah. Came down here twice to see me when I asked him."

"Twice?" Holy crow ... I'd only seen Ben once. What the hell. Anger, resentment, jealousy all mix together in my gut making a volatile cocktail.

"Point is, he ain't what I thought. Point is, I done enough that caused you and me to be in the fix we're in without blaming everyone else. A lot of what's happened is my doing, Rae, and I'm sorry."

I can't answer. Ben is apologizing because it's good and right for him to do so, but I feel cut out of all that's going on. Like my puppet master has more to do with Ben than I do. Fury builds a fire in my veins. I squeeze my eyes shut and try to remain calm. "Why did you need to talk to Gideon twice?"

"The first or second time?"

"Both. Stop stalling. Why are you talking to him, Ben? What's going on?" I hear a muffled voice in the background. "Ben?"

"Sorry. The nurse is here. I have to go, Rae. We'll talk more when you come. I love you, gal. Everything's going to be all right, hear?"

He repeats the words I've said to him back to me, and I put my frustration in neutral. "I know. I can't wait to see you. Good night, Ben."

Jenny rushes into the kitchen as I hang up. I wonder if she's been eavesdropping but doubt that's her style. "Master Maddox is dinning in his office this evening. He's neck deep in paperwork. I imagine it has everything to do with your joint venture." She frowns, moving a large stainless bowl to the sink. "I wish he'd tell me these things sooner, I've set the table for naught."

I run my hand over the back of a chair, my mind still on Ben. "I'm sorry, Jenny. Can I help?"

"No, thank you, miss. What a suggestion. Mr. Maddox would toss me out on my ear, and rightly so." She stops fussing and wipes her hands on a dishtowel. "Is everything all right?"

"What? Yeah, he's fine. I mean I'm fine." Edgar trots into the kitchen, yowling for his dinner.

Her head tilts and eyes narrow. "Hmm. Well, anyway, I'm to tell you Mr. Maddox will collect you at seven o'clock for your outing tomorrow."

"What outing?" A shiver snakes it way under my skin.

"Such a tease. Why the dance, of course. He seems quite excited, had me press his clothes and Jamis has washed the car. Will he drive your friends, too, or do they have their own transportation?"

I shut my open mouth. Gideon hadn't said a single word about the dance. I assumed he forgot, or decided against going. "Jenny …" What can I say? She worships her boss. How do I explain to her, or Gideon, or anyone else how a week ago the thought of dancing close to my jailor had an almost irresistible pull? The visual reminder of his man-whore status in the hotel hallway had worked better than a hose on my raging hormones. "Are you sure?" I pause as her brow bunches. "I was under the impression Mr. Maddox is too busy. I mean I think he, we, changed our minds."

"About what?" Gideon strolls into the kitchen, cane in hand, and heads for the fridge.

Crap. I can't tell him what a horn dog I think he is in front of Jenny. I won't hurt her that way. "Uh, well. I was explaining to Jenny we are too snowed under with work to make the dance tomorrow. It's not important considering all we have to do. I'm not a big dance girl anyway." Lie. "And I'm sure you have way more important things to do than attend a cheesy high school dance." As in, paw your sexy, model hook-up. Truth.

Gideon takes a water bottle from the refrigerator door, twists the cap off, and turns it up. Dark jeans hang on his narrow hips beneath a tight, navy T-shirt. I watch, trying not to salivate as his golden throat bobs with each swallow. How can anyone doing something so pedestrian look so enticing? I need that hose again.

When he lowers his head, our eyes meet. "Nonsense. This is your senior year, Raven. Events like this are important. I don't want you missing out on anything because you work for me." His words come out polite and purposeful. They are for Jenny's sake, I realize. Gideon's gaze, however, is all about me. He scrutinizes my face, as though I'm a Sudoku he wants to solve.

Fine. I'll play. "You're right, I guess. But there's absolutely no reason for you to waste your time with something so mundane. You're an important, busy guy. Places to go, people to see." And do. "I appreciate the offer, but I'll just go with Dane and Maggie like we originally planned. No big deal. You can even set my curfew and Jamis can drive."

There. Deal with it.

His lips crook in that dangerous smile he loves to unsettle me with. "Raven, I'm nineteen not twenty-seven. A high school dance is not beyond the pale for me to attend. Besides, I'm not the sort of guy to go back on my word once I've offered to escort a beautiful woman somewhere." He takes a step nearer. "Nor am I used to that word being contradicted."

I peek at Jenny who watches us with a bewildered expression. When I glance back, Gideon is a foot in front of me.

"It is my pleasure to go with you tomorrow. End of debate." His eyes flare, colors intensifying. "Do we understand one another?"

The boy deals it back, and I'm in up to my keister. I shrug. "Have it your own way."

His smile is devastating. "I usually do."

Chapter Twenty

Maggie glides into my bathroom in the tight, brown leather corset, complete with green, satin lace-up ties that I designed for her. She wears it over a cream peasant blouse and a short, peach tulle skirt with brown ankle boots. I can tell by the spring in her step she feels good in my clothes. She even dyed the strip in her hair peach to match. Her obvious happiness is the only good thing about tonight so far.

"Your hair is to die for done up like that."

"Thanks," I say with a flat tone. Maggie frowns. Always so good with hair and makeup, my friend outdid herself curling my hair into corkscrews. She pinned it up, allowing a few tendrils to fall down my neck in the back. "No, you did great, it's just …"

"What?"

I toss my eyeliner in the sink as though it offends me and glare at myself in the mirror. "I don't know if I can do this anymore."

Maggie stands behind me, staring at my reflection, daring me to meet her eyes. "What's wrong?"

"Look, I don't want to be Debbie Downer to your plans

tonight, but the last thing I want to do is go to a dance with Gideon."

"He really got to you in New York, didn't he?"

Yes. "No."

"I'm sorry." Maggie's voice is sympathetic. I don't want her pity, and I can't stand the thought he got the better of me. That his charisma had worn through my armor, and I'd actually thought about him as ... as what? A hook-up, my boyfriend? I'm beyond lame.

"I know I agreed to all of this. To be civil, play a part, and pretend I'm happy about his supposed offer of help, but it's way harder than I ever imagined. And I can imagine a lot."

Maggie puts her hand on my shoulder. "Sorry. I really thought getting out tonight might be good for you. You don't have to go if you don't want to."

"Thanks Mags, I know you understand, but now I have to go. Gideon made it pretty clear last night. You didn't see him. He intimidates the crap out of me when he gets like that."

"I've seen him in action, remember? Poor Stephen, I thought he might wet himself. Gideon has that whole animal magnetism thing going on. Exciting and yet sort of dangerous, too."

"Dangerous, yes. I don't know how exciting he is," I lie. He's unpredictable and exhilarating, the kind of attitude that makes girls all stupid and swoony. Even me. "I can't be in 'like' with a guy like him."

"Then we'll go and make the best of the night. Ignore him and dance with us, okay? Besides, you look amazing. The boys will bust something over this outfit you're wearing."

That sounds about right. My dress is red, bustier style with a sweetheart neckline. I covered the push-up bust in pleated black damask netting with light padding for shape. The skirt flares from the waist to an uneven petal hem, and I added two layers of netting underneath for body. My clothes are what have value, not me as a person. Who was I kidding? It has always been about what I can do, not who I am. But whatever.

We head downstairs and find Dane waiting at the foot of

the stairs. He stops pacing. His eyes rivet onto Maggie. She looks hot in my designs, if I do say so myself. I consider rolling Dane's tongue off the floor and shoving it back in his mouth when he clears his throat. "Hi." The crack in his voice is the cutest darn thing I've ever heard.

Dane wears tan, canvas duck pants with a white button-down and brown tweed waistcoat and boots. He's gathered his gorgeous dreads in a leather tie at his nape. They cascade down his back in a dramatic statement. I dusted his jacket with chalk to make him look like a Steampunk cowboy who's just ridden into town. He's billboard worthy. If Maggie doesn't *see* him tonight, she never will.

"Oh, you're fantastic!" Maggie squeaks. Her cheeks color. "I mean, Rae's clothes are. Fantastic. You look great."

I hide a smile. *Vera nice* ... maybe there is hope.

Jenny waddles into the room, bosoms jiggling. "Ooh, here you are. All my little lambs." Dane's brows lower as he glances my way. I'm not sure he's okay with Jenny's description. I wink, a signal to humor the old woman, but it's hardly necessary. Dane adores her. "Now let me see you all together." We obey and she clasps her hands beneath her chin. "Lovely. But where is the master? Jamis has gone for the car. You know how he hates to be tardy."

"I'm here, and Jamis will survive, Jenny." Cane in hand, Gideon descends the staircase like royalty. He's all poise and unhurried ease wearing the clothes I'd sewn specifically for him last week. I'd given them to Jamis this morning, unsure if Gideon would even want to wear them, and *voilà*, he appears. A small masterpiece. I'd covered his long legs in slim, black pants under a coat with tails. A black leather vest with copper buckles and accents cinched over a button-down shirt. The fabric is thin and faded, with an old world map print design in the background and ruffled cuffs.

"Damn my eyes," Mag's whispers.

I take a deep breath.

Gideon nods to my friends, but doesn't stop until he's standing in front of me. "Raven."

"Gideon." My eyes narrow to slits.

A pause as we size each other up. "You are breathtaking."

I nod. "You, too."

"Will you take our picture with my phone, Jenny?" Mag's asks the question, but neither Gideon nor I move a muscle.

"Oh, my goodness. I couldn't. I wouldn't know how!"

"It's easy, Jen. Here, I'll show you …"

A ghost of a smile plays at the corner of Gideon's lips. He lowers his head, eyes glinting with humor. "I get the distinct impression, Miss Weathersby, that you are angry with me." Another pause and he chuckles. "More angry than usual, and here I thought we were making some headway."

I lift my chin, but that only brings his face closer. "You thought wrong."

"Did I?" He's smiling now. The insufferable, egotistical smile that turns my bones to jelly. His eyes flash as though I just challenged him to a duel. "We'll see about that."

***

We arrive at nine to a dance that started at seven. Perfect. Only two hours to endure until the end. We choose our seats, deposit our things on a cloth-covered table, and survey our surroundings.

The theme of this year's dance appears to be the Zombie Apocalypse. Tattered sheets hang from the ceiling in strips. Bloodied manikins are strewn over the bleachers and hang from the rafters. Chaperones with white painted faces and blackened eyes line the walls of my school. Several rub their temples, as if the throbbing strobe lights threaten them with seizures.

A mob in the center of the basketball court dances to pounding music. "I love this song!" Maggie shrieks. She tugs on Dane's hand. "Let's dance." His grin proves she won't have to ask twice. Any fool can see it's all he wants.

As they disappear into the throng, I wring my hands together. Dane's happy expression scares me. I can't control Maggie's feelings, but if she knew how Dane felt, she might be more careful. I ease into my chair at our table and glance at my watch. Damn thing's stopped again. My 'date' sits beside me, extending his long legs out in front of him, crossing them at the ankles.

A giggle pulls my attention back to my friends on the dance floor. Dane's been through so much already. A small voice reminds me that I can't protect him from pain or life. Shut up, voice. I swore I'd never tell Mags that Dane loves her, but I'm not sure it's a promise I can keep. My desire to break promises is becoming a theme.

"Raven?" I shift, meeting Gideon's eyes. He's so close I can feel his breath on my skin. Uncharacteristic concern covers his attractive features. His gaze darts to Maggie and Dane on the dance floor and back. "You care for him, don't you?"

Fear must be written all over my face for someone as self-absorbed as Gideon to notice. There's no use denying the truth. "I'd do anything for Dane."

Gideon scowls in answer. One hand covers mine, and he lifts me to my feet. The other hand props his cane against his chair, and we're off. "Dance with me."

"Dance? But I thought …"

"What?" he snarls. "That a cripple can't dance?"

What? "No!"

He doesn't seem to care what I think, because he tows me onto the dance floor. A slower song starts as I'm enveloped within his arms. His chin rests on my head, and I breathe him in. The intoxicating scent of male and spice fills my nose as his arms tighten about me. Though he's slim, his chest is solid, and warm. I lean into him. I know it's loneliness on my part, but I hate admitting how good his body feels next to mine. Good thing I don't have to, at least, not out loud.

"Raven." His tone is rough. He clears his throat but says no more. My skin erupts in gooseflesh as his fingers slide down my neck and across my collarbone. Gideon's lips brush feather light across my forehead. My skin feels hot, yet his touch sends shivers over me. The air is suddenly close. I wish my body wouldn't respond this way, but he's so good at what he does. When he moves us around the dance floor, his limp is barely discernible, but it's there. I recall the framed pictures in his office, him in bed, in a wheelchair, on crutches. I wonder what happened.

I can't allow him to believe I didn't want to dance with him because of his disability. No matter what he's done to me, or who he is, I'm not *that* girl. I lift my lashes. "Gideon?" His eyes are veiled by shadow. I can't gauge his emotions. "What I said back there? I don't judge people like that. I only meant you don't have to dance with *me* tonight. There's no obligation. I wasn't implying anything or making assumptions about your dancing prowess."

His hands press against me more firmly, crushing me, and his smile is like the sun. "My prowess?" He laughs. "Raven, you and I haven't begun to explore the inexhaustible possibilities of my prowess."

I roll my eyes. "All very impressive, I'm sure."

His grin is sexy and sends my pulse skipping. "I've been trying for weeks to impress you, but I'm not sure it's working. You're exhausting, actually."

My eyes bug. "Me?" I step back. "Please. I know you're here to schmooze and cover your tracks with Principal Myers. And to prove a point to anyone paying attention that our ... *arrangement* is all business and above board. I'm not stupid. I don't have any illusions about you."

When a faster song begins, Gideon leads me off the floor. His limp is more pronounced without his cane, but he moves easily enough, navigating through the other dancers. He cranes his neck over his shoulder, shouts over the music. "You have a lot of illusions about me. Initially, those I wanted you to have, but I've changed my mind."

"That so?" My curiosity is off the charts.

My arm threatens to come out of the socket the way he's tugging. He maneuvers me into a dark corner behind the punch table. My back presses against the painted concrete blocks. Cool against my skin, they offset the fever building in me at Gideon's nearness. "Before we left for New York, we were talking in your workroom. I told you there is a place I wanted to show you. A place that's special to me. Do you remember?"

I did. I wondered if he'd bring it back up.

"Tomorrow. Will you go there with me?" His voice gains volume and momentum as he speaks. "I'll ask Jenny to pack a lunch. We'll spend the day. There are some things I want to say to you, Raven. Important things."

I swallow, try to stay calm. "Are you asking me or telling?"

"Asking." The intensity in his eyes suggests he's serious. When he leans closer, I catch my breath. My heart thrums a crazy beat against my ribs. He runs his thumb pad over my lower lip, dropping to trace the line of my neck to the hollow of my throat. As he glances down, his thick lashes fan his cheekbones. "So beautiful."

Right back atcha'.

Gideon stares at my mouth. The kind of staring that makes a girl so uncomfortable, she wants to do cliché things—things like bite her lip, or play with her hair, or sigh, or faint. Crap! His head arches. I think he wants to kiss me, and if he does, I'm going to let him. "Say yes," he orders.

"Excuse me, are you Gideon Maddox?"

I manage my disappointment as he straightens. When he pivots, I take in three men dressed in spiffy blue uniforms. Cops.

"I'm Sergeant Andrews with the Sales Hollow Police Department. We need to speak with you on the whereabouts of a delinquent teen."

Chapter Twenty-One

"Raven Weathersby?" says the policeman in front. He glances at a photo in his hand. "We received a call at six forty-five yesterday evening reporting you as a runaway." Sergeant Andrews is around five feet ten with a paunch and crew cut.

"This is a mistake," Gideon whispers over my head. "Don't worry."

I'm not worried.

Sergeant Andrews squares his shoulders and his buddies take a step forward. That's when I notice the tiny Hispanic woman with them. She's wearing tan slacks, a blue cardigan, and glasses. "This is Mrs. Rodriquez with DSS," Andrews says. I tilt my head. "Child Protective Services. She's going to take you outside now where you two can talk. Mr. Maddox will accompany us to answer a few questions."

Okay, now I'm worried.

Gideon puts his arm out, blocking the police from approaching me. "Temporary guardianship has been granted to my family by Benjamin Weathersby, her stepfather who is in the hospital. I have every legal document to prove that."

Hospital? He's in rehab. Maybe the hospital sounds more dramatic, less dysfunctional, which Gideon thinks will play better with the cops.

"Come with us please, Mr. Maddox," Andrews repeats. "We'll talk about the details at the station."

The station? None of this sounds good.

Mrs. Rodriquez gives me a tentative smile. "Raven? If you will follow me. My car is out front where we can discuss your current situation."

The woman doesn't want to talk. Okay, maybe she does, but she also wants to stick me in foster care. I'm sure she's doing her job. She might even care if she thinks I'm in trouble, but I know how this works. Explaining takes time. Time I don't have. Provided Gideon has the documents he claims, documents I've never heard of before, by the way, straightening out this mess could take days … weeks.

"I don't want to go with you."

People are gathering around us. Gideon scans the crowd until his eyes lock with Dane's. As if guys have some secret code, they exchange a hard look. Dane gently eases Maggie behind him. She clutches at him as he leans forward, but Gideon shakes his head no.

"I understand this might be confusing," Ms. Rodriguez says. Might be? Try definitely. Her voice is soothing, but I'm not buying into her tired sympathy routine. "For the time being, you will have to come with me."

"No." I inch away. "I'm staying with Gideon. My stepdad knows where I am, so does the school. If you move me, he won't be able to find me. I can't get my homework." I find Principal Myers amongst the other bystanders. "Can't you explain?" I ask him. "Make them leave us alone."

Before he can answer, a tall skinny cop with red hair holds his hand out, indicating Gideon should follow. He hesitates, glancing at me. "It'll be okay, Rae. Don't resist them. My lawyers will clear this up in a few hours."

I'm sure he means what he says, but I've seen the sort of justice the law doles out. The court let the Coffee brothers off easy for what they'd done to my mother, and Ben was arrested for defending her. The state will send me to live with strangers. Boxed in and trapped by someone else this time.

The space feels close and tight, like all the oxygen is being sucked out of the room. My breathing escalates. Blood rushes to my head, pounds in my ears. When I put my hand inside Gideon's, his fingers grip mine like a vise.

"Rae? It will be all right." His sure, steady voice filters through the noise.

Thick hands close around both my arms, pulling me away. I'm bookended by a bad polyester blend of navy blue fabric. "Please, come with us, Miss Weathersby." My feet scrape the shiny wood floor as I'm carted away. Panic engulfs me. "Gideon?" I call, breathless. "Gideon!"

I hear him, but I can't make out what he's saying. Dane bursts through the crowd around us, Maggie close behind. He tosses Gideon's cane in the air. A hand rises over the heads of everyone, catching it.

Laughter rains down over the room. The sound is eerie, turning the blood in my veins to freezing sludge. "Did you hear that?" I ask Officer Andrews.

As I lean back, he nudges me forward. "Hear what, exactly, Miss Weathersby?"

Consecutive peals of haunting laughter echo off the walls, so loud I think someone's stolen the microphone and is playing a prank. *Raven* ... Holy freaking crap in a basket! My gaze darts everywhere and then finally up. A flash of white chiffon flies from one end of the rafters to the other. I gasp and point. "Don't you see her? Over there!"

A blast rocks the gymnasium. Debris flies in every direction.

A girl screams. Another crash and an orange glow spreads in one corner of the bleachers. Black smoke billows from the flames. "Fire!" Someone yells followed by more screaming. A crush of freaked-out students pushes against us, knocking me from the policemen's hold. Fabric rips as I fall on my hands and knees. Pain shoots up my thighs to my hips. Pins rain from my hair as half my up-do tumbles down my back.

When I glance up, I see her. Desiree. Her ghostly image shimmers near the ceiling. Trails of dank smoke snake their way upward, tangling themselves in a cloud around her delicate feet like silver ivy. She's giggling as we run for our lives. Did she cause that explosion; start the fire? Our eyes meet, and I know she sees me, too. What on earth?

Cole said they couldn't leave the grounds. Well, he was wrong. A truth clicks in place inside my brain once and for all. Desiree was never a figment of my imagination. She's real. An actual ghost, and while I'm not sure what that means, she's a nasty piece, not a romantic idea or harmless vapor.

The heel of someone's shoe stabs my hand, and something crunches. A cry tears from my throat as a steady arm wraps my waist, righting me. I'm drawn against a rock hard wall. "I've got you." Gideon, thank goodness. "Let's get out of here." Another explosion blasts from the same spot, rocking the room and raining ash down on us. A girl stumbles past. Soot covers her face, blood drains down her temple.

"No! Wait." I cough on the smoke filling the room. "We have to get Dane and Maggie out."

"I need to get *you* out." Gideon tucks me under his arm as he leads me on, but I fight him. He stops. His hands grip my arms and he gives me a shake. "Dane took Maggie through the emergency door, but I came back for you."

I came back for you ...

"What about the cops, Child Services? They'll be waiting for us out there."

"The cops have their hands full with the fire. Besides, I have a plan. Stick with me."

Always the guy with a plan, Gideon pulls his phone from his pocket as we run for the door. We stumble into the hall where other students run for multiple exits. Gideon chooses the one farthest away where fewer kids are filing out along with a thin trail of smoke.

"Hey, how come you get a cell phone?"

His teeth gleam in the dim, emergency lighting. "I'm

special that way. Do you really want to argue about a phone right now?"

No, probably not.

Along with the rest of the student body, Gideon and I find our way out one of the exits. Cool air hits my lungs. I suck in a long breath and cough it back out.

Gideon's hold on me tightens. "Are you all right?"

I lean against him. "Yeah. I hurt my hand, but I'm okay. I hope everyone else is."

Phone against his ear, Gideon makes a beeline for a stand of trees near the football stadium. "Jamis, can you take the car to the foot of the hill, under the scoreboard? I'm calling Richard. I'll be in touch tomorrow."

Wait, tomorrow? My mind spins. "How can you be in touch tomorrow if he's picking us up now?"

"We're not meeting Jamis now. The police may be watching him. However, he will wait for Dane, should he and Maggie want a ride home."

Right. "So where are we going?"

He stops short, and I stumble. When I right myself, Gideon shifts to face me. "There's a place I know not far from here where we can rest for the night. Can you walk?"

"Yes." I'm unsure what he means by a place we can 'rest,' but I'll do anything to avoid that Child Services woman and foster care.

With both hands, he gently pushes the hair from my face. His palms settle on my cheeks as his eyes search mine, but for what I don't know. A muscle in his jaw jumps in time, like a pulse. "If anything had happened to you in there, I'd ..." He drops his hands, lets his head fall back. When he speaks again he sounds more composed. "Richard is my attorney. Well, one of them. I'll have him fax the necessary papers both to the police and to Mrs. Rodriquez's office at DSS. A day or two of red tape and we're in the clear, but right now, we have to go. Understand?"

Yeah. Sure. Whatever you say. I nod. He takes me by my good hand and hauls me into the trees. My steps are wooden.

I can hardly believe I agreed to all he said with such sheep-like compliance, or maybe I can. My spirit feels brittle. I'm exhausted and confused, and for once, it feels good not to be the one in charge. The grown-up everyone else looks to for strength, to make decisions, to lead.

For tonight, I put myself in Gideon's care. Unwilling or unable to think or be strong anymore, my jailor's confidence and capable attitude is a balm to my grief-worn soul. Whatever I tell myself when I want to hate the guy, he's a complicated mix. There are plenty of bad-boy qualities to list, but he's not wholly evil either.

I came back for you ...

Maybe he's not the monster I thought.

Chapter Twenty-Two

Gideon makes several calls. I'm only half listening as he speaks with people I assume are his lawyers. We press on through the woods, spilling out onto the paved road on the far side of the school grounds. Sirens pierce the otherwise still night. We trudge down the road, past the Quick Stop located several blocks away from my high school. My shoes are not designed for long walks. They pinch my toes, and my heels are screaming. Both design issues I intend to remedy for the sake of future clients—if I ever get out of this mess, that is.

My feet sing the hallelujah chorus when Gideon points me toward the yellow cab waiting on the curb. The taxi must have been one of the calls he made while I zoned out. I could kiss both him and the driver right now.

Inside the cab, we're safe, at least for the time being. Gideon keeps a protective arm wrapped around me and examines my hand. I don't object. His calm bleeds into my body somehow, and I greedily absorb what he gives. He guesses my bone is bruised not broken, as I can wiggle all five fingers. That's good news, but it still aches.

Twenty minutes later, the taxi pulls up in front of the

Oak Winds Motel. I scan the building with a critical eye. The bushes in front are clumps of dead sticks. A broken plate glass window is taped together with silver duct tape, and there's a bald guy standing in the office doorway smoking a cigar. Few lights are on, other than a sickly neon sign hanging askew by one chain. With perhaps a total of twenty rooms facing the highway, lodging appears the type that one might rent by the hour.

Facing Gideon, I raise a brow. Not because I think I'm too good to stay here. I'm not far removed from the roach-infested floor of my old leather shop. I just don't picture a Maddox sleeping here. At all.

Gideon grins. "No one's going to search for me here, are they?"

Point taken.

We pay the cabbie and get out. Gravel crunches under our shoes as we step onto the parking lot.

"Manager here," barks the older man still watching from the doorway. "Room?"

Gideon nods and follows him into the office. I wait on the front porch while Gideon pays for our rooms in motel hell. I hope I don't have to stay here more than one night. Staying in the Maddox mansion is starting to ruin me for ordinary life.

A light breeze caresses my skin, disturbing the drooping curls around my face. The full moon casts a blue glow over the pines across the street. It must be after midnight. I hope the police haven't called Ben. A call from Child Services in the middle of the night might be just the excuse he needs to drive him back to drinking.

I'll call tomorrow. See what he knows before I blab about what happened tonight and reassure him if need be. Deep breaths leak out of me, as I resolve a plan to handle Ben. A screen door slams behind me.

"Ready?"

I shift my weight and face Gideon. "Sure." Covered in dust, the boy still looks fantastic. He seems so relaxed, so self-assured while I'm a hot mess—in both my thoughts and disheveled appearance. All I want is a shower and a long sleep. I'll have to wear my wrinkled, too-formal-for-daytime dress again, but at least my body will be clean of ash.

Gideon leads the way to room seven, fits the key in the door, and steps aside so I can enter first. Wow. The room is sparse and the bedspread appears a bit dingy. The first thing I do is pull the cheap, floral spread off the bed and place it on a nearby chair.

"What are you doing?"

My hands rest on my hips. "Haven't you seen the specials on TV about the disgusting stuff left on hotel bedspreads? Housekeeping doesn't wash them every time, you know. I'm not sleeping with that thing."

He's grinning like a chimpanzee. "What if I get cold?"

I freeze. A long pause. "You can do whatever you want in *your* room."

"This *is* my room." His tone is matter-of-fact, where mine is clearly panicked.

"We're not sleeping in here together, pal." My heels throb. I drop my bottom to the bed and pick at the laces of my boots. I have to get these suckers off before my feet need amputating.

"Sure we are. I can't afford two rooms."

Funny. He leans his cane against an old dresser. His shirt pulls up a few inches as he shrugs out of his coat, revealing a swath of golden skin. I swallow hard and ease a boot off, letting it drop to the floor.

"Raven." His voice turns serious, and I force my chin up. "I don't think the police will find us here, but I'm not leaving you alone for one second. Do you think I would ever allow them to take you away from me?" I don't know how to respond, so I don't. "Once the paperwork is sorted, we'll go home, but just in case they prove smarter than I am, which isn't possible." He pauses with a smile. "Watch ..." Gideon strolls to an exit in the far wall of our motel room. He unlatches the chain and tugs the door open.

I peek out the back. It's dark, but I can just make out a huge field that needs mowing and beyond that, trees. "Watch what?

I don't get it."

"Emergency escape hatch. Just in case."

"We make another break for it into the woods?"

"Precisely."

"Do I even want to know how you found out about this place?"

"I doubt it."

"Fine. You win."

"I love it when you talk dirty."

My tummy flutters. I'm too exhausted to argue. More than that, I don't really want to be alone, so I drop my protests. "Need the bathroom a minute or two." I take his silence as a yes. Locking myself in, I let my head rest against the door.

I run the water from the tap so Gideon won't hear me pee. *Awkward much?* Next I wash the heavy makeup off my face. My hair has taken on a life of its own. My dress comes off but I leave my short black slip on. I take my time removing the last few bobby pins and combing my fingers through the tangles. I'm stalling, knowing a beautiful guy—the enemy I swore to hate for all time that I'm also attracted to—is waiting on the other side of the door. Triple yikes face.

When I open the door, oh my stars in a blue heaven, Gideon is already lying on the bed. He's taken everything off but his pants. Ankles crossed, his hands are tucked beneath his head. He's watching the ceiling. Not me. I'm drooling over his long, chiseled torso like he's made of chocolate. Long night, anyone?

"Do you want the light on?" I hope he didn't catch the funny quiver in my voice.

"No, please turn it off."

I flip the switch. It hardly makes a difference as the neon from the sign out front shines through the cheap blinds. I lie down on my back as far from Gideon's side of the bed as I can, which isn't far, considering it's only a double. My fingers lace over my nerve-ridden tummy. I clamp my legs together until I'm more fortified than a bank vault. "Gideon?"

"Yes?"

"Why do you walk with a cane?"

Holy crap. Where did that come from? I had meant to ask him about his visits to rehab to see Ben, or maybe about how his attorney will get my custody paperwork to the police. That's so not what came out. "Sorry. Sorry, you don't have to answer that. I'm nervous. Sleeping with you is weird and ..."

Shut the hell up, Rae!

His laughter shakes the bed. "I'm not sleeping with you. I'm sleeping *next* to you. Though I'm open to any discussion you'd care to have on the former, absolutely."

"Jerk."

More laughter. Electricity shoots to my toes when he shifts, his foot brushing my calf.

"Let's drop it. I don't know why I said anything."

"It's all right." He takes a deep breath, letting his glee over my stupidity die. "I had cancer."

Shit. "I'm sorry. It's none of my business."

"No, it isn't, nor is it something I talk about ... usually." I can hear the smile in his voice. "Maybe I'm nervous, too."

Despite his teasing, my body is as rigid as death. My fingers twitch over my stomach, and I press my toes together. "You don't have to tell me."

"I want to tell you." Gideon's hand wanders over and finds mine. His fingers curl around my palm. "My mother lost four babies before me—the son my father craved, but I was a sickly child. Premature, weak, then a cancer diagnosis at four years old. As their only heir, the news devastated my parents. My father flew me to New York, Boston, even Europe, brought in specialists. I went through chemo, physical therapy, and an operation that took a third of my thigh muscle."

My throat is thick and closing fast. "I am ... I'm so sorry."

"Thank you, Raven. I believe you mean that."

I lift off my pillow to glare at him. "Of course I mean it!"

"That's very generous, coming from someone who has vowed to hate me for all time."

So he remembered. My expression falls, and I lay back down. "About that—"

"I spent most of my life in bed as a boy. And while my father sought a way to save my life, I sought relief from my pain. He brought me pets, magic tricks, and games that I practiced over and over."

I think of the coin he weaves through his fingers, the cards he's always shuffling ...

"Do you believe in magic, Raven?"

"I'm start—"

"It's very real, though most are too jaded to consider the idea."

His talking rolls over any attempt I might make to answer. Maybe this is the only way he knows to get it out. Quick and all at once, like ripping off a Band-Aid. I listen. Out of respect for what he went through. His suffering. I don't know why he's telling me all this, but it seems important to him.

"Later, the doctors declared me in remission, and then a survivor. The following year, my mother died in a car accident, and my father sent me away to school. Several private boarding schools, in fact—only the best for Nathan Maddox's boy." His voice carries a bitter edge, and my heart goes out to him. "A kid with a limp wears a bull's-eye on his back. I was different, so I was bullied.

"I never told my father. I didn't want him to see me as weak, but naturally he found out. There wasn't anything my father didn't know. He hired private tutors to educate me, personal trainers to make my body strong. Instructors taught me to fight and defend myself."

Tears blur my eyes. I've seen enough of the world's cruelty to imagine all he doesn't say. My heart breaks for the little boy who wasn't enough. Not for his father, not enough to win a single friend ... never enough, even for himself.

"We have a special brand of justice in the Maddox household." His body stiffens, and he releases my hand. "Decades of injustice birthed the Maddox way of thinking. It's my responsibility to carry on the legacy of my ancestors. We're called Artisans ... judges who blend law and poetic justice with a kind of magic in our sentencing.

"It's my heritage, and my calling, and my curse."

His words scare me. Gideon sounds just like Ben did with his vigilante talk after my mother's remains were found. "I don't understand."

"It doesn't matter. The point is, I agreed with all my father taught me, unquestioningly, until recently. Until you."

Faster than my next breath, Gideon's face hovers above me. Highlighted in glorious relief from the red neon outside, his brow, nose, and cheekbones catch the fierce glow, as though he's on fire. The rest is cast in shadow, like secrets. His body presses against me. I can't slow my heart rate. My chest rises and falls, pushing against his forearm as he traces the outline of my cheek with his fingers.

He catches my tears as they escape, then brushes them across his lips. The act is personal, sensual. I think he might kiss me. Press those lips, salty and wet with the proof of my compassion, against mine. And I want him to. My pulse races, as I slide a hand up his chest. All at once, I feel the reality of my age and inexperience. Unsure, I shift beneath his touch. "Gideon ..."

My voice breaks the spell. He drops his hand and pulls away, but he's breathing as hard as I am. My brow creases in confusion. I still have no clue what he's been talking about, but whatever it is, he seems absolutely tortured by it. Or by me. I don't know which.

"You're different. And that's changing everything." He rolls over on his back with a grunt.

The guy who has it all together suddenly seems as baffled by life as the rest of us Schmoes. "You didn't go to law school when you graduated, Gideon. Maybe it's more than me that's different. Maybe, deep down, you've known all along you were the one to change things in your family."

He says nothing more, and after a few minutes, his breathing slows.

I squirm, trying to calm down. Trying not to think about what his words might mean, what an Artisan is, or how close I came to kissing my enemy. When he still doesn't answer, I push a bit harder. "Listen, Gideon, if you'd just—"

"Go to sleep, Raven. We'll be home in forty-eight hours."

And that, it appears, is that. I don't know whether to feel rejected or relieved. Until somewhere in the night, I'm conscious Gideon's hand inches over to reclaim mine.

***

The song "Lawyer Up" from rap artist Keebo plays like it's coming from a tin can. My eyes open a slit. Oh, no. Focusing on the open bathroom door in our Oak Winds Motel room, I remember where I am. Gideon's chest expands against my back. His legs readjust, tangling with mine, and my eyelids snap wide. His arm hangs heavy and satisfying over my waist. I hold my breath as he flexes, arms tightening their hold on me. For the love of all things green, when did we decide spooning was kosher?

I, for one, remember no such conversation.

Gideon's nose parts the hair at the back of my head. His exhale sends a deep, warm breath against my neck. The moths in my stomach alight in a riot of fluttering. Though I'm lying perfectly still, I must do something to disturb him, because he stops midway on the third breath. "Rae? You awake?"

I don't think he's ever called me Rae before, but I don't correct him. It doesn't seem right considering we just pretzel-slept together.

"Mm hmm."

His fingers lift, one by one, off my arm, then his hand, his forearm ... I'm sad to lose the warmth. His chest rumbles as he clears his throat. Wow. Sleeping in the room with Dane was never *this* nice.

I wiggle away. My heel bumps him as I slide my legs from between his. "Sorry."

"Don't apologize. I rather enjoyed that."

Me, too, but I'm not going to say so. One swipe pushes the

hair from my face. "Was that your phone?"

"Yes."

I scoot to the end of the bed and let my feet dangle over the edge. "Nice ringtone. You want the bathroom first?"

"My, how thoughtful we are in the morning." Though I don't turn, I hear the smirk in his voice. "You go ahead, roomie. I'll return my call."

"Shut it, Gideon."

He hollers after me as I close the door. "The motel furnished us with disposable toothbrushes, if you dare."

"I dare." Anything is better than morning breath.

A few minutes of private time and Gideon is pounding on the door like a grizzly bear. I open the door, a scowl on my face. "You rang?"

"I did." He's beaming. "Richard's got us fixed up. The cops and Mrs. Rodriquez with DSS are satisfied that they have the correct paperwork. They've even squared their mistake with Principal Myers."

My brow crumbles. "What about Ben, did the police contact him? I don't want him upset."

"I called him."

My eyebrows do a one-eighty. "You did? When?"

He nods. "Last night. To make sure they didn't alarm him."

My throat constricts. Do I get mad at his interference or thank him for his consideration? I'd thought to call Pops today, but Gideon had acted on the impulse sooner than I had.

"You're going to see Ben this afternoon. Hurry, Jamis will be here any minute." Gideon holds his shirt in the air, poised to put an arm through the sleeve but stops. "What's wrong?" His face crumbles like I kicked his puppy. He's done all this for me, I realize, every thoughtful act, every possible care and precaution—all for my benefit.

I bolt toward him. With a running jump, I fling myself into his arms, wrapping my legs around his waist. "Thank you!" I choke down the sudden urge to cry.

"Whoa, whoa." His hand strokes my hair. His other arm tightens about my waist. "Shhh. It's okay. Raven, I told you.

I won't let anyone hurt you. No one's taking you from me."

Afraid speaking will lead to a full-on sob fest, I nod into his neck. I squeeze my eyes shut as he continues to hold me. *So beautiful,* I think I hear. I lose track of how long we stay like this before I come to my senses. Slowly, I unwrap my legs from his body, and let my feet slide to the floor. My hand is ridiculously sore, but I ignore the pain.

"Ben told me the two of you talked. Twice. But what I don't understand is why, about what? Me?"

He runs his thumb along my cheek as I stare into his eyes. "Yes, among other things."

"Like … ?" The word is little more than a whisper.

"He wants to be the one to tell you, Rae." There's my nickname again. The word melts like butter on his tongue and makes my knees do the same. "Jamis will drive you. You'll be with him in a few hours. You and I can talk after that. Remember the place I told you about? The one I want to show you?"

"Yes." I can't keep the tremble from my lip.

His hand slides beneath the curtain of my hair to caress my neck. "Visit with your stepfather, it will do you both some good. Get your answers. Everything between you and me will keep until then."

I glance up, my gaze locking on his mysterious, mismatched irises. Gold flecks catch the light in his green eye, turquoise in the blue. I reconsider my earlier thought. The mystery has always been his mind, what goes on behind those remarkable orbs. "Will you drive me to see Ben?"

His stunning eyes widen. "Of course. Anything. All you have to do is ask." He leans forward. His breath warms my skin, sending delicious jolts of nervous energy throughout my body. "Then you and me. Tomorrow. All right?"

I nod one last time. His fingers continue to stroke the stiff muscles of my neck. His touch is soothing … and foreign, making my legs as shaky as a newborn calf's. He's waiting for an answer, but I fear my voice will break. When I can't stall any longer, I take a deep breath, managing only one word. "Done."

Chapter Twenty-Three

Ben and I sit together in silence. Not in the Palm Room this time. I wish. We're in his dorm room. The place smells of antiseptic and bad air freshener. He lies in bed, smacking his dry lips together. I cringe at the pasty sound but don't let my aversion show. Instead, I offer my stepfather another glass of water, his third since my arrival.

His hand trembles as he accepts the cup. Small, red spider-like veins spread under his skin. I can't remember if I saw those on my last visit. His color is off, too. A shiver goes through me, like someone walking over a grave. My gaze travels over his face. His skin has an orange tint, as though he rubbed himself with cheap self-tanner.

"Don't fuss over me, Raven. Sit with your old man and tell me more about your doin's at that fancy-pants mansion."

My rump hits the seat of the straight-backed chair near his bed. I cross my arms. "I'd rather talk about you and Mr. Maddox getting all chatty down here and me knowing nothing about it." With my tough-girl voice locked and loaded, my feigned anger is pretty convincing. Until a smile breaks through, giving me away.

"Now girl, don't get riled." He scratches his elbow and fidgets. A sure sign he's guilty of something. "I was angry at the boy and needed to speak my mind. I'll get to that, but looky here; I got some other stuff to say first." He pulls some papers out from beneath his sheets. *What the heck is that?* "I wrote it all out, so the words will come out how I want 'em to. You just sit there, and listen, and let me say this my way, all right?"

"You're the man." It's sort of cute, how bossy he's being when he's never been able to take charge of anything before.

"First, I need to tell you about your dad. Your real one. And if I ain't too tuckered, I'll tell you more. Otherwise, well, it'll have to keep." He leans over, takes his reading glasses off the table, and pops them on his big, red nose. With a cough to clear his throat, he readjusts the paperwork in his hands. "Here we go.

"This is the story of your birth, as your mother told it to me. Your granddaddy, your mama's father, was a Cordwainer."

"A what?"

"A fine maker of hand-sewn shoes." He glares at me over his glasses. "Don't interrupt. Anyway, he worked hard and was honest, but he wasn't earning enough to support his family. One night a man came to the house. Tired and half-starved, he asked for any odd chores he might do to earn some money. Your granddaddy explained he couldn't pay him, but he'd be glad to share a meal and give him the garage apartment to sleep in for the night.

"Early the next day, your granddaddy went to finish the work he'd started the day before. When he went into his shop, and found the shoes already made and sitting on the table. Seems your father had done it to repay the old man for his charity. As your granddaddy studied the shoes, there was not one false stitch in the whole job. He'd never seen such craftsmanship, and done so quickly.

"The same day a customer came in, and he willingly paid a higher price than usual for them. With the money, your granddaddy hired your father and bought extra supplies. Soon more buyers came, paying high prices for his goods. And so it went on for some time, and your granddaddy soon became thriving and well-off again."

I squirm in my chair, dying to ask about a hundred questions, but I keep mute.

Ben squints, focusing on the next typed words. The vocabulary isn't his. I wonder who helped him write his speech. "Your mama used to sit up nights with your father, assisting him, watching him work. He was charming, and talented, and ...well, Ida was an innocent. He seduced her right under her daddy's own roof."

"What the hell?" My eyes narrow. "How could he do that?"

Ben's head falls back, and he stares at the ceiling. "I'm never going to get through this with your infernal question asking. And don't swear." A long pause. "They sort of fell in together, but kept it secret on account of your dad being so much older and an employee and all."

"Seriously?"

He frowns. "So I was told. Your father was a clever man, gifted even. It's where you get your talents, but unlike you, he was selfish, and conceited. Seems he was caught messing around with another girl in town, younger even than your mama, but she wouldn't believe it."

"That lowdown son of a—"

"Raven!"

"Sorry." I hunch down and shut up.

"To continue ... When your mama found out she was pregnant with you, she was overjoyed. She thought he'd settle down and quit cheating. They'd get married. Have a big church wedding. She told him that night she was carrying his child. You. The next day, he disappeared.

"His leaving devastated your mama. Living in the Bible Belt invites as much judgment as it does compassion. Her parents only wanted to shield her from shame, and hoped she might marry someone else. Not long afterward, I came to work in their shop as a new hire. Though I was older, too, I was madly in love with Ida and she had little choice but to accept my proposal. Never wanting you to feel you was any less than the other kids, your mama made sure you knew nothing of your real father."

I blink. Hard. And shake my head. "She *lied* to me?"

"She protected you. All you need to know is that you're special. Can't you see that?"

With a surge of anger, I lean forward. "Oh, I'm special all right. On top of everything else, I'm the bastard daughter of a—"

"No, child." The hurt in Ben's eyes makes me want to punch myself in the face. I never meant to slight him.

"I'm sorry. It's the shock. I didn't mean it, and —"

"You have every right to be upset. I don't blame you."

My head falls into my hands, and I groan. The floor is spotless. My gaze follows the joining seams of shiny linoleum as my frustration leaks away. "I'm not angry, not really. I can't judge Mother, and you know I love you, it's just ..." I always thought I was wanted. "I'm surprised is all."

"I'm sorry, about your father, honey, but you was loved. You think on what I've said, and try to forgive me and your mama for keeping the truth from you for so long." My head lifts and meets his glassy-eyed gaze.

"There's nothing to forgive, Ben. All right? Forget about him. He has nothing to do with us. I just don't understand why God lets bad things happen."

"What bad things? You mean her dying, my drinking ... you talking about you?"

"All of it, I guess."

"You, listen to me, gal. Your mama always said if God were small enough for her to understand, he wouldn't be big enough for her to worship. Remember Isaiah 61:3, 'God brings beauty from ashes.' It was her favorite, because of you."

Throat tight, I swallow. "I'll remember."

"Good." His smile is weak as he nods. "There's something else needs saying."

"Okay." My neck stiffens, bracing for whatever he'll say next.

"Here's the thing. The first time I called Maddox, I wanted

him to come down here, so I could take his head off. I was angry, blamed him for taking you away from me, and putting me in here. He stood there, saying nothing, while I yelled at him until I collapsed in my chair. I'd worn myself out in a passion. And you know what that boy did?"

My chin digs into the palm of my hand as I speak. "No idea."

"He thanked me. Actually *thanked* me for allowing you to stay with him. Called it 'the privilege' of knowing you." Ben makes quote marks in the air with his fingers as he'd seen me do a thousand times growing up. "Promised he'd care for you, that no harm would come to you, and then he left. That surprised the hound out of me. And later on, it got me to thinking."

My head tilts. "About what, Pops?"

"That's why I called Maddox a second time. See, he really seems to genuinely admire your abilities. He's rich, right?" I lower my hands and straighten, not at all happy about where his train of thought is heading. "I wondered if his company gives college scholarships or if he might have a place for you after high school, in one of his fancy clothing stores ..."

"Oh, Ben you didn't. I'm not going begging to the likes of Gideon Maddox for a job or school. Not for anything." I stand. "We don't need him."

He drops his papers on his lap. "We might."

I walk to the bed and ease myself down next to him, taking care not to jostle his IV. My voice lowers to a whisper. "What are you saying?"

"After my stay in the hospital, the doctors ran some tests. Seems all my hard living has caught up to me. Liver's shot, sweetie. I talked to Maddox because I want you to have something to hang on to."

"We have each other. You just focus on getting well. We'll figure the rest out later, once you're out of here."

"No." He takes my hand, gripping stronger than I thought him capable. "No." His voice softens. "You'll need a place to go, sweetheart. After I'm gone."

Chapter Twenty-Four

When I roll over, two eyes stare back at me, one sky blue, the other sea green. Soft morning light lifts the gloom off the night in my bedroom, like a blotter lifts ink from a page. An odd peace fills my spirit.

"You're here," I say.

"I'm here." Gideon lies on his side, facing me. The scarring around his eye shows silver in this light. He wears no shirt. Red, drawstring flannel hugs his waist.

My hand slides across his smooth chest. I close my eyes. Sinewy cords roll under soft skin. "I'm dreaming."

"Yes, you are," he murmurs. There's a smile in his voice. He leans closer, pressing against my palm. He grasps my fingers in his, pinning me with his stare. I feel the ridged muscles in his torso flex as he moves. The breath I release is quick and sharp.

"We can't be together. You get that, right?"

He lifts a lock of my hair off my cheek. "No."

"I'm damaged."

"You're beautiful." The raw look in his eyes hollows my stomach.

"I'm broken."

His fingers trace the outline of my mouth. "Not to me."

"But I can't love anyone, not anymore."

"Oh, you love. Deeply." His eyes flare. "You won me with a love that binds my heart to yours—irrevocably." He kisses my forehead, my nose. The muscles in my stomach tighten. "Chains softer than silk, stronger than iron."

My gaze drops to my fingers on his chest.

"Don't do that. Don't dismiss me. I love you, Raven. Do you hear me? I *love* you."

"Raven ..."

Light floods my room, forcing me awake. I growl and roll over, bumping Edgar. "Get thee behind me Satan, or whoever you are. If you don't close those blinds, I will kick you in the shins." The heavy scent of hickory-smoked bacon assaults my nose. While the sweet aroma softens morning grumpiness, my pride hangs on with all ten fingers.

"We really are going to have to do something with that mouth of yours," Gideon remarks. "I have a few ideas, but I'm willing to wait until after breakfast."

"Go away." I reach under Edgar's chin and scratch until he purrs.

"Tsk, tsk. Not happening." I hear him push the drapes open. "Besides, I'll not allow you to toy with my affections. Not after the way you clung to me all yesterday on our ride home, and then last night ... While I hate the underlying reason, I can't deny the effects for me were rather nice."

It's true. The news of Ben's declining health, after telling me I was illegitimate finished me off. Gideon gently led me to the car. He wrapped an arm around my shoulder while I lay my head on his chest and wept quietly all the way home. Once there, he followed me up to my room, and asked Jenny to bring a light supper upstairs. My mysterious benefactor sat reading me poetry in 'his chair' until he left without a word around midnight. I'm not sure I'll ever understand the guy.

"Don't coddle me, Gideon," I mumble into my pillow. "And be sure to say what you really think while you're at it."

"I will."

I roll over and rub my eyes. Edgar steps on top of my chest, but he's too heavy. With a sigh, I sit up and plop him in my lap for some kitty ear scratching. Gideon stops what he's doing, stares at us, and it hits me. I'm not in my bed. "What the …" The room is enormous. There's a brick fireplace across from the black, four-poster bed I'm sitting on. Rich, dark furnishings, sage-green bedding … "This is your room?"

He nods, unable to hide his smile. "Thanks for visiting. Again. I really deserve some sort of sainthood for this. Is there a Nobel prize given for restraint?"

Heat scalds my face as I glance down. I'm wearing a black lace top and gray flannel shorts. Could be worse I guess, but part of me wants to curl up and die. Suicide seems a perfectly viable option, considering I woke up in Gideon's *bed!* When I glance up, he's still, openly staring. "What?"

"It's unfair to the rest of the women at large for anyone to be so gorgeous first thing in the morning."

I keep my focus riveted on Edgar. "Thanks." His deep laugh sets off another blush, which I ignore as I kiss my cat's head. "And I'm sorry about the night visiting thing. I don't know what's wrong with me."

"There's nothing wrong with you," he snaps. Confused, I raise my eyes in time to see his expression soften. "People sleepwalk, Raven. If you need to go somewhere, I'm glad you feel you can come to me, even subconsciously."

Mid-sentence, his tone turns tender, and has a blitzkrieg effect on my senses. I blurt out the first thing I think to change the subject. "Why are you here?"

He crosses the room and takes a seat on the end of the bed. "See, now that hurts." He holds up two fingers. "First, though I enjoying seeing you in those pajamas, it's my room you keep invading." He folds one finger down. "Second, you've already forgotten we were supposed to have a very special outing today, to one of my most favorite haunts."

"Please don't say haunt."

Another laugh. "Get up, girl. Eat the delicious breakfast

Jenny made, or you'll crush her Irish pride. Then get dressed. I have to leave tomorrow morning for New York. I tried to move the meeting, but it's damned impossible. That gives us today." His brows wing up. "Well? You're not moving. Hurry up. We leave in an hour."

"Bossy."

"Stubborn." He takes a piece of bacon off the plate sitting on his end table and bites the end off with a growl.

"Fine." I don't feel like going, but it's not worth arguing over. I don't have the heart. "You win again."

He grins like a fiend.

***

I unclench my jaw and slide off the back of Gideon's four-wheeler. With a gentle tug, I ease my fingerless gloves off my hands. The bruised knuckles on my left hand throb as I press my fingers to my face. The skin is ice cold. My lips tingle from racing through the cool, crisp air. I'm not sure all-terrain vehicles are my cup of tea, but there you are.

The spot he's taken me to borders the edge of his property. A small meadow nestled alongside the Coosaw River. The water is a wide, silver snake meandering through mossy green countryside and the canopy of oaks is a slightly darker hue. The sky is brilliant, as bright as Gideon's blue eye.

He stands with his hands on his hips, taking in the view of the river. When he twists toward me, he points to our vehicle. "Will you grab those blankets?"

I release the Velcro straps securing dual rolls of plaid fabric and toss one to Gideon. He smiles. "What, no sharing?"

Ignoring his question, I walk right past him. Choosing a level spot by the river, I spread my pallet on the ground and relax. A chilly breeze tosses my hair across my face. The air smells fresh and clean with a hint of salt. Nearby, a heron stabs at a fish with his sharp bill. "It's like a painting out here."

Gideon follows me to the water's edge. His chest rises with his inhalation. "My mother and I used to come here when I was little. Jamis would haul my wheelchair outside. Jenny would make us a picnic lunch, and we'd stay for hours in the spring and late summer." His brow creases. "Before the fall winds came. I was sick a lot in the winter months. *Always* on holidays."

"Well, I can see why she brought you," I say, with an attempt to distract him from bad memories. "It's a stunning view."

His blanket hits the grass and he drops down next to me. His curls stir in the wind, gleam in the sunlight. The skin on his face is smooth and golden, until it meets the slightly darker shadow of his jaw line. "I wanted to show you this spot. I thought it might inspire something in you, the way it does me."

Of course. He brought me here for designing ideas, so I would make more clothing for him. I nod, strangely let down. When I face him, his expression remains an unreadable mask. I wonder what he was inspired to do. "Gideon?" It may not be the right time, but I have to ask.

"Hmm."

"Why didn't you go to college? Don't you want to be a lawyer?"

He shrugs. "After my father's death, I worked harder than ever to attain his goals for my life." His eyes narrow on the gentle current of the river. "I graduated high school at sixteen, took a few college classes online. My father's V.P. tutored me in business, board meetings, supervised projects, travel. Law is expected, what my father would have wanted, but I stalled on attending a university."

"Why, what do you want to do?"

He's quiet a moment, as if he's weighing his words. "You were right, about me, Raven. I was changing, but I didn't know why myself. I've been restless, confused. As an Artisan, and Maddox heir, I'm responsible for a tradition of acts committed long before my time. I'm a … keeper of those deeds."

This house has more secrets than Hogwarts. Gideon is

trying to tell me something while doing his darndest not to tell me. It reminds me of Cole, and my patience crumbles. "You can be whatever you want to be. In New York, you said when you want something you just take it. Where is that guy?"

He shakes his head. "You don't understand."

I stand, brushing away the grass stuck to my jeans. "Ugh. Explain it! People make me insane. Ben drinks because my mother is dead. Dane wants Maggie, but he won't take her because he thinks he's not good enough, and—"

"Dane wants Maggie?"

I feel the scowl creasing my forehead. "Yeah, what? You didn't know that?"

"I thought he ... never mind."

"Fine." I stare at the riverbank. "All I've ever wanted was ..." I can't finish. With Ben ill, what I wanted doesn't matter now. "Dane could go for what he wants and won't, and you ... you will become a lawyer because your father wanted a son to take his place. Grow a pair, people!"

"Raven." He rises. There's a warning in his tone that I don't heed.

"No. No! There's something strange, cursed about your house. I can feel it in my bones. Don't let it have you, Gideon."

Something flashes in his eyes. Pain? Worry? When I look again, it's gone. I must have imagined it.

I throw a blade of grass to the ground. "I don't know what to do anymore. Ben is dying. My prospects are pretty grim. I'm not feeling sorry for myself." Okay, maybe a little, yes I am. "It's just *you* ... it drives me crazy because you have all the freedom in the world. Every advantage to follow your dreams, and I'm so jealous. You are rich, smart. Capable of amazing things, and at times, you've been so nice to me ..." I throw my hands up. "All I'm saying is that you have the potential to do good instead of hurt people. It's up to you to decide what you want."

His eyes narrow dangerously. "You're right." Four determined steps closes the distance between us. His hand wraps my neck, gentle force behind his grip. I take a shallow breath as his eyes blaze a trail to my soul. With the softest touch imaginable, his fingers brush my skin. His nostrils flare, his jaw sets like concrete.

"What is it?" I whisper, both terrified and curious over the conflicting emotions evident in his shining eyes.

"You've ruined me, Raven. Broken me down, and destroyed whatever I was. Whoever I might have been." His hand stays at my throat. With the other, he runs his three middle fingers over my trembling lips. My heart beats erratically.

I take step back. I can't control my breathing and my legs have gone to sleep. I'm pretty sure I know where this discussion is leading, but I can't go forward until he answers one question. The one that's tortured me for days on end. "What about your ... that girl?"

"Who?"

"The girl. The model in New York. I saw you together in the hallway of our hotel."

"You saw that?" His head falls back, and he laughs without humor. "And how long did you watch us, sweet Raven? Not long enough, I think."

"I don't understand."

"Hmm, no, you don't. She came to my room, and I sent her away."

"You did? But ..."

Taking a step back, he pulls the gold coin from his pocket and rolls it back and forth between his fingers at a dizzying speed. "Did you know crows collect reflective objects?"

What a what? Okay, that's so not where I thought this was heading. I ease to the ground to keep from embarrassing myself with a fall. "No, I didn't."

Gideon's pacing makes my head ache. "Tinfoil, beads, coins, the male collects anything shiny to decorate his nest." He stops and faces me. "That's the way I felt about you. I wanted to own you, like a shiny, new toy. Don't deny the connection between us the first time we met."

I didn't.

"And then. When you marched into the library, so angry,

so passionate—"

"You wanted to kill me?"

"No. I wanted to possess you."

The moths in my stomach take flight. I swallow as he kneels in front of me, *almost* on top of me. I count the stitching where his golden skin meets the fabric at his chest. I want to touch him, and hit him, and scream all at once. Then he's lifting my hips, tugging me forward until his knees bump mine. "Gideon." I'm powerless against him, and I know he knows it.

"Let me get this out."

I nod, wanting to both know the truth and run the opposite direction as fast as I can.

"When you came here, in defense of Ben, I'd never seen such loyalty. You challenged me, insulted the name of Maddox. No one does that. *No one.*" His fingers thread my hair. "That took a great deal of courage, but you didn't stop there, did you?" The words come out like a curse. "No. You sacrificed yourself, gave yourself up for him, a drunk who had hurt you in every conceivable way. I was enthralled, captivated by the idea of a girl who could do something so ... unselfish for someone that undeserving. I wanted you, in every way a man might want to possess a woman, but how to hold you?" A frown pulls at his lips. "So, I came up with the idea of using your abilities as seamstress as a ruse to keep you here, with me. It was lust and envy, greed and jealousy—all acts of my dominance and will. At first."

"Oh, Gideon." A tear escapes, dropping from my lashes. He curses under his breath. When I shift, he grabs my wrist like a drowning man. I glance down, and as if he fears he'll hurt me, he loosens his grip but doesn't let go.

He lifts my hand to his mouth and speaks against the skin. "Hear me to the end? You promised ... No that's wrong isn't it?" He tries for a smile and botches it. "Will you please hear me to the end?

His earnestness slices deeper into my already aching soul. "Yes," I answer simply, needing to hear his words as much as he wants to say them.

"Days went by, weeks. Watching you was torture. As an Artisan, I'm taught to make hard decisions and distance myself from the fallout, but you ... you were never about justice. You were sent to punish me, I think." He runs his thumb from the pulse at my throat to my chest and presses his hand against my heartbeat. "The more I watched you, the more my fascination turned to concern, my attitude transformed from master to servant. You make me want to be better.

"I'm sorry, Raven. No. That's not true. I can't honestly say I'm sorry I took you. Not yet, but I'm sorry for the pain I caused you. The worry Ben felt. I need to be honest if there is any hope of having a relationship with you. In New York, the girl at my door ... I turned her down because by that point, I already belonged to someone else."

Tears flowing freely now, I sniff and wipe my nose on my sleeve.

"Stop it," Gideon orders, tone teasing. "That's just not sexy." But his eyes glitter, and he's smiling.

I shrug and sniff again. "Your fault. And who says we're in a relationship? When did that happen?"

"Raven, you and I have been in a relationship from the minute we spoke. I'm just not sure how to define it."

Neither am I. I'm not sure what he's asking for. I don't know what I can give. What's real? What's safe? It's all happening too fast and I don't know how to slow it down. "I guess there's a lot to sort out."

"Hmm, true. I expected you might say that, but while you're sorting it out ..."

He leans forward. I lean away. When he edges further toward me, I see the pattern, but it's too late. I fall on my back in the tall grass, and he's hovering above me.

"There's something else I want you to think about."

The muscles in my stomach tighten as he lowers his head, his lips capturing mine. One hand travels up my thigh. The other is lost in my hair, kneading the roots at my nape. I feel his heart pound out a rhythm against my chest and mine races to catch up. He nips at my jaw. Tongue teases my mouth, demanding entry. My lips part under increasing pressure, and we explore each other, tasting, caressing. Mind blown, colors explode behind my eyelids as he kisses me breathless. My hands slide up his shoulders to lose themselves in his glorious curls. I squeeze handfuls between my fists, push against him. He moans, sending chills through me.

"You'll kill me, I swear it," he growls in my ear. "I've wanted, *needed* this for so long."

"How long?" I pant.

His breath tickles my neck. "Forever?" He moves to my mouth and speaks against my lips. "The whole time you stood in my library yelling your head off, I wanted you." Gently, he bites at my lower lip with his teeth. My eyes roll back as he leaves a trail of burning kisses along my cheek to my ear. "And last night, while I watched you sleep for hours in my bed, then too. And now."

My heart squeezes at the vulnerability in his admission. He kisses me long and hard until I'm dizzy, and boneless. When he finally lets me breathe I whisper, "We should talk."

"We should," he says, and then bites my earlobe.

I shake my head. Pushing on his chest is like pushing a semi. "Gideon. Stop."

Gideon lifts his head. The mismatched eyes always so wary and shuttered are open and unguarded. His smile appears lopsided and a little drunk. It's a heady feeling knowing my kisses did that to him, but it scares me a little too.

My hesitation must show because he rolls off me and sits up, yet he keeps my hand firmly in his. "I'm sorry. I got carried away." He half laughs. "Damn, girl, I've never … damn."

I know exactly what he means. It's been a long time since I've kissed a boy, but no one's ever kissed me in the atom-exploding way he just did.

Gideon's lashes rise. In the time we've been out here, the sky has darkened. Winds kick up, blowing my hair across my neck like a scarf. "Let's head back to the house and warm up. We can eat our lunch in the kitchen and talk all night if we want to, all right?"

My shoulders relax. "Okay." I don't know if I can handle this guy much longer if we stay. Or if I can trust myself.

He stands, pulling me up with him. I fall into his arms, which is, I suspect, exactly what he wanted. He kisses me hungrily one last time until my mind flies apart. I'm weak and warm and breathing like a sprinter. When he finally releases me to stagger back toward our vehicle, I hear him mutter. "Magic."

Chapter Twenty-Five

Once our bellies are full of Jenny's chicken salad, potato chips, and chocolate chip muffins, Gideon and I sink into the overstuffed chairs in his library. Earlier, he pulled the drapes open, so we could watch the sun set out a long row of windows. We ate in silence, due in part to our hunger, but now, as we stare at the stars highlighted in an inky sky, his shoulders tense. He leans toward the window, away from me. A shadow fills the space left between us, and for a moment, I worry the distance is more than geography. Does he regret our talk earlier, sharing the personal details of his life with me? Doesn't seem likely, but then Gideon isn't easy to know either.

He crosses his ankles. His legs stretch out forever on the Persian rug. "Tell me what you're thinking."

"Only if you promise to stay over there." Everything's moving so fast between us, I have to slow it down.

A smile. "Why?"

I answer with mock seriousness. "You know why, I can't think when you're doing ..."

"What?"

"Stuff. To me." I brush imaginary crumbs from my jeans.

"I'm not used to it."

He crosses his arms, a satisfied smirk twisting his mouth. "I am hard to ignore."

I fight a grin. "Conceited much?"

"Just honest. Now. Tell me what you're thinking?"

The way he looks at me muddles my thoughts. I don't know what I want, yet, so it seems safer to talk about something other than *us*. "Tell me about your conversations with Ben."

"Ah." He nods. "All right. The first time, I think he wanted to find out what kind of guy his little girl was staying with, what my intentions were, and basically chew my ass out for putting the both of you into my various prison cells." Another small smile. "He was so angry, he yelled until a coughing fit made him quit. I answered his questions, asking a few of my own."

"Such as?"

"By the time Ben called me to meet with him I was so obsessively curious about you I could hardly sleep." He picks up his chair, scooting it over until his legs are near mine. "I asked him a series of pointed questions about his drinking, your living conditions, and your schooling." Gideon fiddles with the nail heads on the arm of his chair. "His attitude got humble pretty quick. He saw, by his own admission, how badly he's treated you."

Gideon Maddox is a master at getting people to see things his way. Considering Ben's stubborn streak, his change in attitude says a lot about Gideon's power of persuasion. I glance at the floor. Neither of us is wearing shoes at this point. His blue-socked feet rub against my toes.

"Why are you doing that?"

"Because you're letting me. Because I find you irresistible and intoxicating … I'm not sure it's wise for you to know how hard it is for me to sit in my chair and not kiss you." He grabs the seat of my chair and tugs it closer. "I won't touch you. I just want to stare at you until you blush again." The look he gives me can only be described as wolfish.

What have I gotten myself into? I try to focus. "I still don't get it. Why would you travel all that way to talk to Ben?"

"To make him see that you were in a better place than the one he had provided. That what was happening was due to his neglect." I bristle in defense of Ben. Sure, I can say crap like that, but I won't hear it from anyone else. "Raven, by that point, I was invested in you. I didn't understand my feelings yet. Hell, I'm not sure I do now, but when I think of that roach-infested hovel I found you in … Let's just say he's not the only one who was pissed about the way you'd been treated."

"So, you set him straight."

"Yes." No remorse. No apologies, that's a Maddox. He slides from his chair to the thick rug at my feet. Stretching out like a cat, his eyes invite me to join him, but I stay put.

"And the second time?"

"Come here to me." Before I know what's happening, Gideon lunges, grabs my wrist, and pulls me to the floor. I squeal, sure my skull will smack the ground, but he cradles my head in his hand, cushioning my fall.

I lie on my back looking into his eyes a foot above me. "Are you insane? You almost split my head like a melon!" My heart thunders in my chest. I'm only half kidding, but his face is somber, and that scares me.

"Never. And I need you close to me before I tell you this next part." His nose brushes my cheek before his mouth covers mine. The pressure increases and I let him in. His tongue sweeps mine, turning my brain to mush, melting all reason until I forget why I'm here, what we were saying. All the pain and confusion washes away, and for a few, sweet minutes, there is only him and me, and how we lose ourselves in one another.

He lifts his head and smiles down at me. His expression smug, as though he knows he's responsible for my gasping breaths and rubber muscles. Curls encircle his face like a golden halo. He is the sun.

"You broke your promise," I accuse.

His chin lowers. "What promise?"

"The one to stay on your side and not touch or kiss me."

"Sue me."

I smirk. "I just might."

"Listen, I have something difficult to tell you. I don't want to ruin this day, or hurt you, but you asked me a question, and I owe you the truth."

Fear beckons like a familiar friend. My emotions retreat. I'm the turtle inching back into her shell. I'm not sure I want to hear this, but I can't avoid it either. "Okay."

He takes my face in both hands, capturing my gaze. "Ben only mattered to me because he's important to you. When the doctors explained the seriousness of his condition, he called me. The man understands what's ahead. They're releasing him in a week. I told him he can live here, be with you for whatever time he has left."

His gaze penetrates mine. The intensity is my undoing, and a lump forms in my throat. It's not like I haven't known Ben was sick. He's been declining steadily for years, buried in drink and depression, but I wouldn't face it. Somehow, Gideon's speaking the truth out loud makes it more real. I have no choice. I close my eyes as he leans forward to kiss my forehead. "He's only got maybe a month or two. I'm so sorry, Rae."

I roll to my side and sit up. Gideon moves aside, allowing me my freedom. With a heavy sigh, I say, "I know you are."

"Ben wanted to talk to me about you and your future. Actually, I couldn't shut him up. He talked for over half an hour, before the doctors interrupted. He spoke of your gifts, character, who you are. As if I didn't already know."

I think of Gideon's background. His education and wealth compared to mine, and I fall woefully short. Has he even considered what those differences may mean if he's with me? Have I? My scaredy-cat heart retreats a little more. "I don't think you do."

"We're more alike than you'll admit. Don't hide from me, Raven."

Hiding is what I do. Panic rises like a wave inside my chest. What of my vow to avoid getting my heart trampled, like my mother? He's getting too close too fast. I'm still not certain I can trust Gideon, so I turn the discussion around and test him. "Tell me more about the Artisans. Explain how you know magic is real. Because I've seen some strange things since I've come to live here."

His eyes narrow. "Seen? You mean heard. I know. Jenny told me about the slamming doors."

"No. I mean yes, I heard the doors slam, but there's a hell of a lot more going on in this house than a door closing. Talk to me."

He stiffens and leans away. A veil of thick lash falls over Gideon's eyes, obscuring my ability to read him. "There's nothing to say. Foolish ghost stories fueled by creaking ancient architecture and odd cross ventilation." He's lying. His tone grows curt and impatient. "Don't borrow more trouble, Rae." His jaw tightens, and it's clear I'm not the only one hiding. A day that started with clearing the air between us ends up foggier than ever. Suddenly, the need to be alone and think overwhelms me.

"Look," I say. "I think we're both just tired. It's been a long day." His eyes flash, and I hold up a hand. "Maybe we should turn in. Get some sleep, all right?"

He nods, turning from me. "If that's what you want." Lost in his thoughts, I can feel him withdrawing from me, too. Closing the shutters on the windows of his heart and shutting me out again.

His face is shrouded in shadow. The edge of his profile catches in the soft light from the desk lamp. The outline shines like a crescent moon and is just as stunning. His beauty never ceases to amaze me, but the truth is I barely know him. Yeah, I let him kiss me. I wanted his kiss every bit as much as he wanted mine, but do I forgive and forget all that's happened? How he brought me here and why?

We can't be in a relationship if I can't trust him. I can't trust him if he lies and keeps secrets from me. And since he won't talk, I'll drag Dane and Mags to the attic and find out for myself.

Without another word, I rise and head for the hallway, wondering how things fell apart so fast between us tonight. In fourth-grade art class, I glued two pieces of construction paper together for a project. Unhappy with the result, I tried to separate the pages, but the glue had dried and the paper tore. I tear that way now. Uneven and ragged, bits of him are permanently attached, embedded in my skin, and pieces of me stick to him.

My thoughts are all over the road. Go. Stay. I want Gideon to stop me from leaving, fight for me. For us—if there even is such a thing. If he comes after me, claims me, maybe he won't leave like everyone I've ever cared about. My hands fist at my sides as I will him to take my arm, pull me against his chest, and kiss me the way he did earlier.

He doesn't.

My tread falls lightly over the carpet, the hardwood floors, through the door.

Like everyone else in my life, he just lets me go.

***

By the time I'd made my way downstairs this morning, Gideon had left for the airport. It stung a little he left without seeing me, and I wonder if we made a mistake. Caught up in something that should never have happened, does he regret the things he said; regret kissing me? I push the thoughts away. My plan takes precedence over my hormones and ego right now.

Dane and Mags have been here all day. We made a big, public show of our visit, eating Jenny's food, playing Nerf football in the dining room where Jamis was attempting to polish silver. Dane especially enjoyed that.

We made an equally big deal of my friends' exit, making sure both Jamis and Jenny saw them go. A half hour later, I'm sneaking to the side door of the veranda to let them back in. Gideon's only gone overnight, so we'll have to work fast.

Cole needs my help. I'm committed to do what I can for him, and he's waited long enough. I'm convinced Gideon knows more than he's telling about his role as an Artisan—whatever the hell that is—about what goes on in this house, and according to Cole, the answer lies in the attic.

"Hurry up," I stage whisper to my friends. If anyone sees us, they'll be out and I'll be hoofing it to the attic alone. A shudder rolls through me at the thought.

"Ouch!" Maggie complains.

I touch her on the shoulder. "What?"

"Dane stepped on my foot."

"Sorry, but will you please be quiet!"

"Let him crush your foot and see how quiet you are."

Dane snorts. "It's not my fault you're a midget."

I roll my eyes, starting to doubt the wisdom of my plan. I pick up Edgar to keep him from darting away and head for my room. No way is kitty in on my plan to explore the rooms upstairs. I've got enough problems, and this is DEFCON 4.

A quick stop to lock 'meow face' in my room, and we three amigos stalk upstairs to the third floor. I pinched a couple of small flashlights from the stash Jamis keeps in his tool closet before my friends got here this morning. Easy enough.

I'm first to climb the narrow flight of stairs to a small landing on the top floor. As I shine a light into the gloom, thick cobwebs hang in matted clusters from the beams and doorframes. It's hella creepy up in here. Spiders dot the webs here and there. Their *globulous* bodies hang like ebony eight balls. Dozens of spiny legs skitter from the harsh light. The sight sends prickles of fear dancing down each vertebra. I guess Jenny's cleaning duties are confined to downstairs, but if I had to kill these creatures, the job would stay last on my list, too.

Behind me, the old steps creak like a dying cow. I glare over my shoulder, expecting the heavy tread of Dane, but it's not him. Apparently, my tiny friend walks like a gladiator. I never noticed before, and knowing her temper, I decide to say nothing now.

A closed door looms at the end of the empty hallway. We creep along. Nothing but the sound of anxious breathing and shuffling footsteps says we're here. As I turn to face my friends, a dark spot appears on the side of Maggie's head. My eyes widen, and I gulp a breath.

Spider, spider, spi-der!

Dane catches my anxious gaze, and I jerk my chin toward Mags. Thankfully, she isn't watching us. Her flashlight is tracking the walls covered with webs to my right. I wriggle my fingers and Dane nods. Two ... three ... four ...

Before she can see what's happening, Dane grabs Maggie, draws her against his chest, and covers her mouth with his palm. My turn. I pull my hand inside my flannel sleeve and brush at the spider in her hair. The little bastard decides to scuttle up her head. My stomach lurches. I don't want to *smush* him in her hair, but the arachnid isn't cooperating.

Wide-eyed and bucking like a bronco, Maggie wrenches herself against Dane's hefty arms, and I thank the Lord the boy is as strong as he is. I train my flashlight on her hair and swipe again. The spider falls to the floor, and I start my bug-killing dance on its head. Dane releases Maggie who spins and pummels him in the chest. A string of cursing streams from her lips.

By this time, we probably have the whole house awake, but I can't blame anyone. When bugs and girls collide, all bets are off.

I put my hand on the door handle. "Shhh. Maggie," I warn. She ignores me, still shouting at Dane. "Maggie!" She faces me as I turn the handle. "I'm sorry about the spider, but let's get on with this before we're caught."

As I open the door, someone grabs my arm and pulls me into the black. Maggie's mouth opens in a silent scream. Dane yanks her aside and charges the doorway. His look of determined fury is the last thing I see before the attic door slams shut in his face.

Chapter Twenty-Six

The grip on my arm disappears. My flashlight drops to the ground and rolls away under some furniture. Pounding on the other side of the door begs a response, but my brain's gone numb.

Think, damn it.

I sink to the floor and crawl toward my flashlight. "Cole? Who's in here?" I ask, unsure I want an answer to whose hand I felt on my skin.

Dane pummels the door again. "Raven, if you don't open this door right now, I swear I'll break it down and kill you."

"Hang on." Flashlight in hand, I whip the beam in every direction. Shadows run before the light, regrouping in odd corners. The space is stuffed with junk, but there's no one near me. I stand on rubbery legs before bolting for the door. I hear someone breathing but can't see who. With a stifled cry, I twist the knob. Locked. Peering down, I shine a light on the handle. There's no key in the lock, no latch or bolt. "It won't open!" My hand curls into a fist, and I bang on the door. "Get me out of here!"

"I'm trying," Dane growls.

"What happened, Rae? Why did you shut us out?" This from Mags. The panic in her voice matches mine.

"I didn't."

"She didn't!" Dane and Mags answer in unison. The door shudders with what I assume is my friends' renewed attempt to release me.

With a deep breath, I whirl to face the room. My back presses against the door for support because my muscles betray me and violently shake. I feel at any moment as though I might faint, and I'm no fainter. The beam of my flashlight scours every nook and cranny, but I see no one. I'm not fooled for a minute. Someone pulled me inside this room. Or something. And they wanted me alone. *Get me out, get me out, get me out* ... I whimper. I know damn well this is the part where the guy with a chainsaw pops up from behind an old trunk and slices me in little pieces. Slowly, feet first, working his way up.

"Little Rae?" Dane's voice. He must be scared if he's calling me by my pet name. "I can't get it open. I need something to jimmy the lock. Maggie will stay with you. I'll be back as soon as I can."

"I will?" says Maggie. I hear the word 'spider' and low mumbling from Dane in return, then retreating footsteps.

A long pause follows. I heave a breath to try and slow my climbing hysteria. My pulse is racing so fast I can hardly think. Something scrapes the floor and I jump. A cold sweat breaks out all over my body.

"Tell me what you see," comes Maggie's small, still voice.

Good Maggie, make me focus. With an inch or more of dust on the floor, I make out my footprints on the wood planks. It smells cold up here, of age, and decay, and mold. The old, headless manikins in the corner are headlining the creep show. They are surrounded by furniture, crates, an ancient bicycle, and plastic Christmas trees.

"There's a lot of antiques and boxes and disintegrating crap." I finally manage.

"Is Cole with you? Do you know what he wants you to find?"

No, but excellent point, my friend. Since we have time, I might as well get what I came for. "I'll look. Will you just keep talking? Your voice is keeping me from losing it."

"Sure." Her tone is a bit more relaxed. "Well, let's see ... Crap! Spider." A stomp and squeak travels through the walls.

"Maggie?"

"Nope, we're all good here, Rae." She speaks as though nothing happened, but I hear the tremor in her voice. "Okay, there was a pop quiz in Spanish on Monday that no one passed. Kayla Harbinger broke up with Lance because he's a man-whore. We all tried to warn her, but you know how that goes ..."

While Maggie gossips, I rise and start my search. I have no idea what I'm looking for, so I snoop through box after box. Old pictures, books, and vinyl records fill the first few containers. In a far corner, I tear the lid off another crate and find a jewelry box. Inside, costume pieces encrusted with rhinestones glitter and shine. I'd love to raid these for my collection. Reluctantly, I set them aside. Another time. Keep looking.

"Did you hear me?" Maggie asks. "What, in the name of spray cheese and crackers, is going on in there?"

"What?" I stop exploring for a glimpse of the door.

An exasperated huff blasts from the other side. "I *said* did you know that Nathan Campbell won the talent contest?"

"Sorry, a little distracted, and no I didn't." I bend to search the next box.

"Very nice," she sighs. "I'm doing my best song and dance routine out here in arachnophobia land—to keep you entertained—I might add. The least you could do is pay attention."

"Right," I call. A stack of leather bound ledgers catches my eye. They appear to be the same brand I saw in Gideon's office. When I lift a few off the top, I view a smaller brown diary, near the bottom. That's interesting. I add the diary to my stack.

"Hey, I might have found something." As I shift, my butt swipes against the old highchair behind me. The dolls stacked on the tray tumble to the floor with a thud.

"Maaaaa ... maaaaa ..."

I jump as a doll sings out. Ledgers fly from my hands and litter the ground at my feet. The doll's anemic whining sends a chill up the back of my neck. I shine the flashlight on her sickly porcelain face. Tiny hairs on my body rise as her lifeless black eyes fix on me like an accusation.

The doll blinks. She smiles and I scream.

"Raven!" Maggie pounds on the door.

I open my mouth to answer, but a laugh, low and feminine, floats down from the rafters.

I know that laugh.

Without thinking, I point my flashlight straight up. There, body pressed flat against the ceiling, is Desiree. Her arms and legs are splayed in an unnatural position. I don't know by what magic the woman has defied gravity and Velcroed herself to the wooden beams above, but she looks more spider than those hanging in the webs nearby.

Her glowing white gown is splattered with crimson stains. Long, platinum hair drips red on the ends, as though she soaked them in blood. Her smile twists her features into something evil and cruel.

"Raven, are you dead?" Maggie shrieks. "Just answer and tell me if you're dead!"

Gideon, I mouth. Where are you? I take a step back and trip. Pain shoots up my hip and bum.

Another laugh filters down from Desiree. She descends as though hung from a trick wire until her toes touch the wooden floor. My heart beats wildly in my chest. Throat tightens painfully, until it feels as dry as scorched earth. I wonder whose blood she's wearing, and if I'm next.

"Why?" I can't help my question. "What do you want from me?"

Her pale face darkens. Black eyes flash as though a lightning storm explodes within her head. In the time it takes my heart to beat, she's on top of my legs. More lizard than woman, she slithers all the way up my body pressing me to the floor. Slow and seductive, she slides forward until we're face to face. I want to vomit but nothing comes up.

"Dane!" Maggie's yelling her head off in the hallway. The door handle jiggles again. Soft thuds land on the doorframe.

"Gideon!" He's not here, but even so, his name fills my throat.

"How delightful," Desiree says, her voice soft and eager. As I tripped, my flannel shirt fell open revealing the tank top underneath. Her fingers caress the skin on my chest "I wanted my freedom, but this is better. At the last, you cry out for *him.* My betrayer. I didn't think him capable of love." She giggles. The warped sound underlines her insanity. "But his newly discovered devotion makes your death all the sweeter. For you are lovely, are you not? And he loves you with a passion I've not seen since … well, mine."

Her eyes travel down my face and beyond. She strokes the flesh on my cheek and neck like a lover, making me nauseous. "What is it about you, little one?" Her eyes narrow. "Why does he want you and not me, eh? You're feebleminded and weak. A word or two whispered in your ear has you dreaming all sorts of nastiness."

I ignore the fact that she's the one sending me nightmares. All I can think is how Gideon was pursued by this witch. My heart cracks open. I didn't know. "You were his stepmother, married to his father!"

Her mouth draws into a pout. "An old man. I was young and Gideon was young …"

My stomach lurches again.

Something hammers at the door from outside. The walls shake. Dane.

I struggle under Desiree, claw at her ghostly hands, but it's no use. She's a thousand-pound apparition weighing me down. I'm held by an unseen force, helpless, doomed, and without knowing why. "Gideon doesn't love me," I say. "I'm his prisoner. We hate each other."

A wicked smile. "You're a poor liar, little one." Her hand closes around my neck with light pressure. "He stole something from me, now I return the deed with what he holds most dear."

Her glance flits up and down me once more. "Pity." Her fingers tighten, narrowing my airway. She brings her face nearer and I buck. "Shh. Don't resist me, it will be easier for you."

Blow after blow thunders against the heavy wooden door. My vision grows darker. Blood whooshes in my ears as I fight for breath. How do you fight a spirit? I think of Gideon, the risk I took to help Cole. All for nothing. My eyelids flutter.

I love you, Gideon, I do. Did he guess? *I wish I had told you.*

My vision swims, but I make out a shadow just to the right of Desiree's head. The pressure on my throat eases. Her grip loosens. A shrill curse echoes in my head. *Is it mine?*

The weight on my chest is gone. I cough; roll on my side. My hands clutch at my neck as I struggle to draw breath. Scratching. Scuffling sounds mar the air. Between banging on the door and the heartbeats in my ears, the din is deafening. A crate crashes to the ground.

"I won't let you do this!"

Cole? Thank you. Oh, God, thank you.

"Why are you protecting her?" Desiree asks. "Killing her wounds Gideon. The Artisans, they did this to you, to all of us!"

I curl around enough to view Cole. He stands at an angle between Desiree and me. "You want out?" he cries. "We all want out, but I'm not helping with your private revenge." Desiree's gaze drops to where I lie on the floor. "If you kill her, you kill our chance for breaking the ..." Cole's sentence stops as he dissolves into a fit of choking. After a moment he recovers, straightening his spine. "The girl's got nothing to do with Maddox. She's good. I won't let you hurt her because Maddox rejected you."

Desiree's glare melts a pathway of hate toward Cole. "Well, well, well. Bitch got to you, too, has she?"

With a thunderous crash, the door to the room bursts open.

Desiree vanishes. Cole looks to me where I lay gasping on the floor. His eyes dart to the ledgers scattered at my head and back to me. He nods once and is gone.

Air burns my throat as I drag in breath after breath. Maggie drops to her knees beside me. Her arms wrap around my shoulders, lift me up. Dane paces the floor. He flies from corner to corner, peering behind boxes and draperies, knocking over the manikins. I want to tell him there's no one to fight, but my mouth won't work.

Once Dane satisfies himself there's no one here to pummel, he squats next to his girls. "Is she okay?"

"I think so," Mags answers. "But what the hell?" She whispers, as though she thinks I can't hear her.

"I don't know." He flips his dreads behind his back. "Let's get her downstairs." He pauses, his face twisting with worry. When Mags raises her face to his, he reaches for her, cups her cheek in his palm. "I love you," he says. His eyes widen, as if it's just hitting him he told the girl of his dreams his true feelings. "You two, I mean."

Maggie's head angles, eyebrows bunching.

I squeeze my eyes shut. If I could scream, I would. They're lucky I don't have the strength to knock their stupid heads together.

"I mean, I love you two guys," Dane says, and then he tugs us both tightly against him.

Chapter Twenty-Seven

At first I'm shocked when neither Jenny nor Jamis show up in their pj's demanding an explanation. Then I remember they're old, half-deaf, and the place is huge. I guess it's not that surprising after all.

Maggie and I lie sprawled out on my bed. Three cups of warm chamomile tea and honey soothe my battered throat. I can whisper, but the muscles in my neck hurt like the blue blazes.

Dane rests in 'Gideon's chair,' his feet propped up on the bed. His head tips back against the headrest. He's been asleep for the last hour. I guess rummaging through ledgers dating back one hundred years isn't the most exciting task. More than that, I think the adrenaline he used busting down the attic door wore him out. I've never seen him so scared. Not that I can't relate.

After relaying what happened with Desiree and Cole upstairs, there's no question to the reality of my situation, or my sanity. Neither Dane nor Maggie saw the ghosts, but their doubts are gone, and with the bruising on my neck, I'm more convinced than ever.

Maggie shifts toward me. The mattress gives under her elbow. "All I see here are lists of court cases. Names of what judge presided, the defendants, and rulings and sentences, but nothing about anyone named Desiree or Cole. This is boring as hell, and not really telling us what we need to know. I think you should rest."

"Can't."

"Why not? You can't stay here anymore, sweetie. Dane was right all along, it isn't safe."

"I let Gideon kiss me yesterday, Mags."

"Holy crap. That's a fine thing to keep to yourself."

"Yeah. Well, there hasn't been a lot of time to tell you, what with my being stalked by murderous ghosts and all."

"True enough. You're forgiven. So, details, please. The boy is so very hot. Is he a good kisser? Because I'm betting he is."

I allow a small smile. "He's light-your-toes-on-fire good."

"Hot damn, I knew it."

"He told me Ben can stay here, until …you know. I might be in love with him, Mags."

"Well … shit."

"Yeah, but I didn't tell him."

"Does he, you know, feel the same?"

"I don't know. It's weird between us. We're not exactly normal couple material, are we?"

"Guess not, but what's normal?" Maggie's wistful tone pulls my attention from the ledger on my lap. I glance at Dane and shrug. "Yeah," she says with a grin. "I caught that whole 'I love you' confession from him upstairs, by the way."

My heart leaps into my throat. "What are you saying?"

She shakes the hair from her face. "That when Dane said he loved *us*, he meant *me*."

"Halleluiah!" I shout-whisper, then regret it. Dane stirs and Maggie smacks my arm.

"Shut up. I'm going to help you find what you need, and tomorrow, Dane and I are going to have a big sit-down that ends with some serious making out. I hope."

"You really didn't know?"

"Nope, but I'm happy." She glances at the sleeping giant next to us. "Really happy. I think it's going to be okay—if we don't kill each other."

The heaviness around my heart lightens a bit, and I beam at her. Then another thought hits me, and my smile droops. "Do you ... don't hurt him, Mags."

"Really?"

I flinch at her indignant expression. "Sorry. It's just, you aren't exactly—"

"A one-man woman?"

"Well, yeah." I feel like a dog, but her track record for dumping guys out of boredom is one hundred percent. "Sorry."

"Stop apologizing, Weathersby." She readjusts the book lying open on her legs. "You love him, so do I. Always have, I just didn't realize it until now. The guy's been through hell with his family, yet he's always been there for us." Eyes shining, she nods, as though confirming her own thoughts. "He's the best, sweetest, smartest, most decent guy I know. Hurting him would be like kicking a kitten off a cliff. He needs someone ..." With a huff, her bangs fly up, settling again over her forehead. "I know what he needs. He needs me."

"Yeah," I say. A slow smile spreads across my face. "He does." I wonder how Dane would react with being compared to a kitten. I think I'll keep that tidbit to myself. I'm so relieved I'm almost giddy.

"All right, then. Now that that's out of the way, what about you and Maddox?"

"We have some stuff to work out. First off, he's in trouble. I think it has something to do with Desiree and Cole. Gideon mentioned magic along with his being an Artisan—whatever that even means. Initially, I thought he was joking or being poetic, but it's more than that. I know it is, and he won't talk to me. According to Cole, the answer is in these books. I won't quit until I know the truth."

"Gonna save him, too, are you? I'm going to start calling you Joan."

"Who?"

"Joan of Arc."

I smack her arm. "Stop it."

Her smile fades. "No, really, I'm afraid for you, Rae. Enough is enough. If you don't back down, you're going to get hurt."

"I won't if we can get rid of Desiree. Cole says I can free them. I'm hoping that means Gideon, too. He's mixed up in this and he's almost as stubborn as I am. I know I don't have much time. We need to keep reading."

"Okay. But I'm doing this for you, not for them." Maggie squeezes my arm. I thread my fingers through hers, and turn my attention back to the dusty ledgers.

***

Maggie sleeps at my side. It's four in the morning, and both my friends are out cold. My eyes water with fatigue and my throat is raw and swollen, as though someone scrubbed it with steel wool. I set the ledgers down and stretch. My foot bumps Edgar at the end of the bed. He gives me a grouchy meow and shifts, revealing the diary I'd found in the bottom of the crate upstairs. I'd forgotten about that one. With a groan, I reach for it. Edgar complains as he slides off the end of the leather bound book. Too bad, dude.

I open to the first page and start reading.

```
Spring, 1865

     Today, Gordon confided, while dressing
me for dinner, that he overheard the cook
and deliveryman discussing the death of
Mrs. Lawrence. Her bruises apparently so
plentiful, she was rarely seen in public
this season. Having missed her presence at
```

both the Sales Hollow Christmas Ball and the Johnson's cotillion, I believe it must be true. My poor, sweet Emma.

I honored her right to choose Jonathan over me, but I will not stand idly by and see her murderer go free. That dog of a husband killed her, truth plain as day, and all because she could not carry a child to term. Pushing her around in her delicate condition, Jonathan Lawrence be the cause of the unborn deaths, too. I know Judge Patterson, the scoundrel. It's rumored he accepted a bribe that let Jonathan go free.

I traveled to The Grey Horse Saloon again two weeks prior to this entry and met with one Professor Pan, the magician. No price is too high. He will give me the means to avenge her death, though the path gives me pause. It's a clever plan, to send Jonathan through the rabbit hole where no one may follow. Were I to make a bargain with this devil, Pan, I'll trade one evil for another. Even risk my soul. Yet your blood calls to me from the ground, dearest Emma, and I cannot bear the sound. Take heart, beloved. Jonathan is as vain as a peacock. The whole of Colleton County knows he cares more for his white gelding than you, my darling. Let them rot together, then.

I will stand in the graveyard of Pan's ancestors and speak the words he gave me. Those with power enough to unlock the door between worlds. To bring justice. To be together again.

One simple photograph with the enchanted camera traps him for an eternity. A gilded frame will be his cell, the walls of my

house, his jail. He will spend his prison
sentence ruing the day he hurt you and
crossed the man who truly loved you. The
one whose heart you hold for all time.

Mathias Maddox

My pulse races. Mathias Maddox, I remember you. His
portrait hangs in Gideon's office along with all his other great,
great, great, whatever grandfathers. What did you do, old
Mathias? Who was this Pan and what did he sell you? The
Judge mentions a camera. Gideon has a camera. An old one.
I've seen it once in his office and downstairs, too. The day I
met him, it was set up and pointed right at the door.

And he was expecting Ben.

Anger roils in my belly. What did you have in mind,
Gideon?

My fingers tremble as I thumb forward and find an entry
made by Judge Nathan Maddox, Gideon's father.

2011

As decreed by my ancestors, I hereby
record another use of the Camera.

Professor Gamble called. The boy Cole
Wynter insists the accident wasn't malicious,
a prank gone awry, but this isn't the first
time. He's been expelled for his crimes,
but it's not enough. Expulsion will not
erase the humiliation my son experienced
at Wynter's hands all year, not to mention
mine. Plans are set in motion to get the boy
here. As an Artisan, I simply cannot allow
the deed to go unpunished. The ruthlessness
of his crimes is shocking, as he is a youth,
but my actions are naturally warranted and
necessary nonetheless.

Gideon's come home, of course. I've promised he need not return to school. All I feel is anger and shame. Imagine my disgust, hearing my sniveling son admit that he has no friends. His weakness must invite such continuous abuse from other children. This time, an explosion in his locker burnt a third of the skin on his face.

The medical expenses I incur are nothing. I can't have people staring at Gideon's scars in addition to his loathsome limp. He is fragile, but he won't stay that way. I've already employed the necessary people to toughen my gentle son. His mother's influence, no doubt, God rest her soul.

My father would roll in his grave if he saw what I saw today. A Maddox male returned home from abroad, hung his head in my presence and cried.

It will never, ever happen again.

Nathan Maddox

Tears splash the page, my sheets, the back of my hand. The truth rolls across me like a gigantic wave, bowling me over. Artisans, Cole, Gideon, it's like I see them all clearly for the first time. I can't quite wrap my head around the forces drawing us all here, to converge at this one point in time.

I haven't figured out how Desiree fits into the story yet, but I have a pretty good idea who to ask. She's sweet, makes fantastic cookies, and knows a hella lot more than she's admitted. Considering Desiree's creepy confession in the attic about being into her own stepson, it's not a stretch to think someone caught on to her less-than-motherly affections and took her picture. Sicko.

The anger I felt for Gideon drains, leaving me hollow and dry. Nathan Maddox was a monster. No pity. No compassion.

How can a father hate the sight of his own child? Cole, a vicious kid who tortured Gideon at school, yet saved me, helping me on more than one occasion. I'm unsure of my feelings. There's little time to process them either. Gideon will be home today, Desiree wants to kill me, and Ben is supposed to move here in a few days.

I shake Maggie and push Dane's feet off the bed. "Wake up, you guys. I need your help."

"Again?" Dane moans. His head lifts, one eye opening to a slit. It's not a friendly slit.

"We've got some things to talk about. Then you and Maggie need to leave, go home, shower, and meet up again. You have things to talk about."

"We do?" His other eyelid rises.

"Yes," Maggie agrees, stretching. "We most definitely do." There's a sexy edge to her voice when she addresses Dane I've never heard before. Her tone is teasing, tantalizing. At least, she affects Dane that way because he hasn't once shut his gaping mouth. He rubs his unshaven jaw against his shoulder, as if he's developing a tic.

Overjoyed for my friends, I can't help my grin. I know what's coming for Dane later, and it's going to knock his socks clean off.

His gaze darts from me to Mags and back. "What are you guys plotting, and why do I feel like I'm being set up?"

"Because you are." Dane opens his mouth, but I talk over him. "Zip it, you're in good hands. Before all that though, I have something to read to you. Trust me. You're not going to believe this."

"Should you be reading?" Dane's eyebrows arc. "You sound like a hundred-year-old smoker with a Godzilla complex."

Nice.

"Shut up, Dane. You're always saying crap like that," Maggie scolds. "You'll make her feel bad."

"I already feel bad." I shove the diary into Maggie's lap, flip to the first page, and point. "Read."

Chapter Twenty-Eight

After thirty minutes spent convincing my friends I wasn't leaving the Maddox mansion, I watch them drive off. Maggie scoots across the passenger seat and lays her head on Dane's shoulder. I can imagine his raised eyebrows, the hitch in his breath, the hope in his widening eyes, and I smile.

How one mind can hold so many thoughts, one heart so many emotions, I'll never know. I tiptoe back into the house, wondering how much I can take before mine blows apart. As I head upstairs, I organize my goals for the day. I'm happy for Dane and Mags, but I'll be happier for them later. Right now, I have to focus on my plan, and number one on that list is a bath followed by finding Jenny.

Hot water runs in the copper, claw-foot tub in my bathroom. I pour in a capful of lavender oil. The scent permeates the room as I lower myself into the frothy mix. I breathe deeply, already feeling more relaxed. My head rests against the rim of the tub. The water is chin deep. My muscles unknot under the effects of the heat, and I blow out a long breath.

A faint hiss answers. Something slick bumps my knee that I assume is a floating bar of soap. Another hiss and I crack one eye open. There, at the other end of the tub is a dark object. Black body, black and white striped belly, but the hood is unmistakable, a cobra. I tense, muscles petrify. A woman's deep laugh reverberates against the white tile. Panic grips my brain, telling me to run. My skin tingles. I fight the impulse to splash the thing and get the hell out of here, but I'm frozen in place. Logic says I won't be fast enough to avoid its deadly bite.

The snake rises, head bobbing, hood fully opened. I swallow my scream and will myself to hold still. Releasing a shaky breath through my nose, I pray for help.

A gurgle under my feet signals the water draining, though I did nothing to cause it. I stare at the snake, trying to decide if it's real. The hard tub under my butt, the heat of the water, the intricate pattern of overlapping scales on the cobra's body, all seem real enough.

Another swish against my leg has me doubting my bar of soap theory. I stifle a cry as the water recedes, and the culprit shows himself. A second snake emerges, this one a ball python. Dane had one for a while, so I recognize the ornate pattern on his skin. Not that the snake and I were close, mind you. Mostly, he scared the crap out of me. At least he's not venomous, but the idea of his scales on my skin is loosening the sanity-screws in my head.

A tickle on my foot and the head of a smaller, lime-green snake appears. His head rests on my big toe and God help me, my limbs tremble. He might be a garden snake except for his arrow shaped head. I think that means he's a viper. When the python sees the green snake, he rears up and lunges across my shins. The last of the tub water drains with a final slurp.

The viper's fangs emerge as he bites into the python's neck, but the larger snake is determined. He coils his body around his victim, muscles convulsing and undulating on my skin as he rolls. I bite the inside of my cheek until my mouth fills with blood. The rusty, iron taste slides down my throat. My eyes squeeze shut forcing salty tears down my face.

When I open my eyes, I blink, clearing my vision. More snakes slither up from the drain and over my feet. The cobra moves up the rim of the tub toward me. I glance at the python. His jaws unhinge, ready to feed on the smaller snake in his grasp. The viper's eyes roll white; his struggle is in vain as the air is crushed from his lungs. As the python devours his prey, I feel his muscles convulsing in a repugnant steady rhythm, and I gag.

The cobra reaches my shoulder. His tongue slips out as he tests the air, tastes my scent. Sweat drips from my temple, down my jaw, smacking the skin on my breast. The cobra must be seven feet long. My hair parts as he forces his way through the damp strands. His body winds around my shoulders, my neck. I wait for a prick. Any second, his fangs will pierce my skin, injecting liquid death into my bloodstream, and then I think ... is this happening?

The cockroaches weren't real, though I felt the fear and pain. I *feel* the snakes, but what if I'm dreaming? If I move I'm dead, but I see no other way out. It's worth the hope.

Wake up, Raven. Wake up ...

The snake slithers down my arm and across my stomach. All the muscles in my abdomen go rigid under the slick, moving scales of the animal. He turns to face me. His head stops between my breasts, though I'm not Cleopatra, and I'm not committing suicide. Am I? The cobra hisses. His pupils mere slivers inside deadly yellow eyes. Jaws lined with white fangs in a membranous, pink mouth gape. He rears back, darts forward.

Wake up. Wake up, Raven, now!

I jolt, sending a gallon of water over the edge of the tub. Steam rises from the skin on my arms. "Leave me the hell alone, Desiree!"

No laughter. No snakes, just the echo of my demand and me alone in my bathroom.

***

I hear Jenny in the kitchen, banging pots and pans around on the cook stove. "Good morning."

She whirls to face me, saucepot in hand. "Lord bless me, child. You gave me such a start!"

"I'm sorry, but I need to talk to you. Can you sit with me a minute?"

"Now?" Her eyebrow twitches. "I've got breakfast to cook, and quite a lot of chores waiting." Impatient, I toss my hair back. Still wet from this morning's unfortunate bathtub drama, it sticks to my shoulders. "Saints preserve us, what happened to your neck, girl?"

Bingo. "Sit, Jenny. It's time for some straight talk."

Blue eyes grow as big as bubbles. She places her pot on the counter, picks up a dishcloth, and scurries to the nearest chair at the kitchen table. I sit across from her. Running a hand through my hair, I gather my thoughts. When I glance up, her round face is a mix of concern and fear. I'd give anything not to upset her, but I have no choice.

"Jenny, there are ghosts in this house." When she opens her mouth, I raise my palm. "I don't just hear them, Jenny, I *see* them. Cole Wynter, the man in uniform, a horse, a hound, Desiree, and others." Jenny frowns, but I don't stop. "Last night, Desiree attacked me. Did this …" I lift my chin and ease my damp hair away from my throat again. Jenny presses her lips together. "Please don't lie or pretend this isn't what it is. You have to tell me what you know. Everything. I've survived being pushed from a tree, near strangulation, and a bathtub full of … well, never mind." My skin still moves as though snakes crawl on it. "I think Gideon's in serious trouble, and I want to help him."

Jenny twists the towel in her lap as though she means to punish the material. "Saints preserve us, child."

"I found ledgers in the attic, and the Artisans' diary. Last night. That's when Desiree tried to strangle me." Jenny's sharp intake of air is all I allow before continuing. "In the diary, it explained that there is a magic camera, used to trap people in this house. For generations, the Maddox family has taken it upon themselves to punish people when they feel there is an injustice. Isn't that true?"

A tear rolls down Jenny's pink cheek. "You don't understand."

The wail in her voice tears at me, but I won't back down. "I'm beginning to. It's why no one was allowed in the attic. The only other place you didn't want me is in the cellar. What's he hiding down there?"

"I can't. Promised, I did. Jamis, and me, our parents, and grandparents. We've worked, loyal to the Maddox family for years. He's as dear to me as my own son."

I grip her arm. "Then help him! It's wrong, Jenny. You must feel that. Surely you don't want him involved in this ... nightmare. It's indecent. Can you help me?" My eyes plead. I send up a silent request that she's capable of seeing reason. "Tell me."

Her shoulders slump. "Very well. It is as you say. The old camera is hexed. Long ago, an ancient magician made a deal with the first Mr. Maddox of this house. By taking their picture with this special camera, one traps their essence in the photos, all kept on the walls upstairs. Their bodies are stored, separated from their owners, so they are forced to live half-lives in another world."

I shudder; amazed this nice old lady would agree to harbor such a horrific secret. "Have any been released?"

She shakes her head. "None that I know of."

"Where are the bodies?" Really? In all my life, I never thought I would utter *that* sentence. Jenny's gaze shifts to a door in the back of the kitchen. "Will you show me? Please."

A long pause. "Yes." She sniffs, dabbing her eyes with the dishtowel. "God help us, yes. I will help you." She stands, withdrawing the ring of keys she keeps in her pocket. I follow her to the pantry.

For some reason, I think of pantries as dry, dusty places but this one is as neat as a pin. The tile floor gleams, reflecting sunlight from a small, lead glass window. It smells of flour, apples, and dried goods. Against the back wall, a line of stainless steel baker's racks sits end-to-end on caster wheels. Jenny rolls out the center rack. A narrow door hides behind the rack stacked with canned vegetables. No one would ever guess the door's location. I can't help but wonder what lies beyond the slender opening, and if it means me harm.

Footsteps to our rear send my heartbeats skipping.

"Jennings? What is the meaning of this?" Jenny and I angle to face the staunch form of Jamis. His expression is a seething mass of disapproval. The old man's eyes and mouth are mere slashes in his face. "Stop this immediately. Have you completely lost your senses?"

Jenny's hands slam down on her hips, keys rattling against her apron. "Just come to them, I think, old friend. I can't be a party to the secrets any longer. The girl knows. One of them hurt her last night, an innocent. It's time to right the wrongs been done to them people. And for Gideon's sake, too."

"It is precisely *for* Mr. Maddox that we remember our place and honor our heritage, our employer's wishes. I must insist you go no further."

"Or what? You arrogant little beanpole of a man. Insist all you want to. Help or don't, it's all the same to me. I'm doing this!" She spins and places the key in the lock.

"Mr. Maddox shall hear of this immediately." His voice shakes with anger. He storms from the pantry, I assume to fulfill his role as tattletale supreme.

The housekeeper's hands tremble as she twists the key. Despite her bold words, it's clear she's scared witless. She's not alone.

Hinges creak as Jenny swings the door open. There's a light switch on the wall and Jenny flips it on. "We don't go down here," she says. "No one does."

As this was my big idea, I go first. The steps are as narrow as the doorway, and covered in fine, white dust. I descend into dank air at least ten degrees cooler. My muscles tense, ready for whatever might be lurking nearby. A dusty, concrete floor waits below. There's a faint smell wafting up the stairs, a mix of chalk and ammonia.

The steps behind me groan under Jenny's weight. She breathes like a freight train, but I'm thankful for her presence. It's Spooky 101 down here. Since I've been living in one, I vow to never watch another horror movie as long as I live.

Dim light from the bulb at the top of the stairs trickles into the cellar. Like the attic, there is a lot of old junk stored in the corners. An eerie feeling of *déjà vu* washes over me. I shiver as the tiny hairs on my body stand on end. The deeper into the cellar I go, the colder the air.

"I can't go any further," Jenny whispers. Though her voice is low, it echoes around the room. "Forgive me, child. I'll wait by the stairs, but I simply can't ... look."

"It's okay. I won't be long," I say, hoping it's true.

"There," she points to the wide arch on the far side of the room. "Through there."

As I shuffle forward, my feet are as heavy as fifty-pound weights in mud. My lungs squeeze the air from my chest, and my palms sweat. I second-guess the state of my mental faculties, because a person has to be crazy to go peek inside the forbidden room. I'm not even sure what I'm hoping to accomplish. Somehow, I believe the rest of the puzzle is in this cellar. Adrenaline zings under my skin as I pass under the arch and onto a dirt floor.

I stop; hold my breath. I've been here before. In a dream, or through Desiree's eyes, I don't know. The caskets are placed as they were then. Stacked on top of one another, there must be two dozen wooden coffins. With a tremor in my step, I inch closer. Waiting, fearing some unseen force will consume me, and my fingers will shred open the first box.

God, you've got to help me out here.

I need a crowbar to pry the coffin lids up, like the one Dane used to get the door open upstairs. Glancing around, there's little in this room besides the hideous caskets, but then I see a hammer resting on the end of one box. I grab the handle. Leaning over, I hook the claw end under the lip of the first lid. My bladder gets funny when I'm nervous, and I wish I had peed before coming down here.

"Raven?"

I jerk upright. "Crap!" Jenny's voice calling from the other room nearly takes care of my need to pee. "I'm okay, just give me another minute."

When I return to my task, Cole's face looms two inches from mine. "Crap!"

"Raven?"

"Damn it, Cole, don't do that!" I lift my chin. "It's okay, Jenny. Cole Wynter is here with me."

"Jumping Jehoshaphat," she mutters. "You can see him?"

"Yes, Jenny. He's going to help me. Give us a minute, all right?" Jenny mutters again, but I can't decipher the words. My focus switches to Cole. "You are going to help me, aren't you?"

He reaches out and touches my cheek. When I cover his hand with mine, mine goes right through. His dark eyes are round and soft. His mouth tugs up one side, barely discernible, but I see it. "Thank you, Raven. You are the angel sent to free me. If I ever get out of here, you're coming home with me. I'm going to take care of you."

"What?"

"I'm not—"

A door slams upstairs. "Jennings!" Gideon's rough shout reverberates through the cellar. "How dare you."

I give Cole a hard stare. "Wait for me. This isn't over."

I turn and race for the other room. Gideon towers over Jenny, leaning heavily on his cane. His face is a mask of fury. Nostrils flaring, brows furrowed, he looks like a bull that's been stuck with barbs. "You will go upstairs, pack your bags, and leave my house immediately. Do you understand?"

Jenny faces away from me. Head bowed in front of her employer. Soft sobs reach my ears. Her shoulders shake. "I know nothing else. There's no one but you and Jamis. Please don't send me away, sir." Her gentle weeping turns to a wail. She slides to her knees and grabs Gideon around both ankles.

His shoulders square. "You know the consequences for betraying the family. What would my father say if he were here? What would he do! Just go, I release you. And for God's sake stop making a scene."

I've heard enough. "Stop it!" I say, approaching the pair but talking to him. "It's not her fault. Will you look at her? I asked Jenny to bring me here."

Gideon's eyes narrow, signaling a warning. "Stay out of this, Raven."

"I won't. This is wrong." I put my hand on Jenny's head. "Go on, Jenny, make a scene." My gaze flashes up, connecting with his. "You don't need to make this easy for him."

Gideon's chest expands. "Jennings, pack your bags. You have an hour. Jamis will drive you wherever you choose, but your position here is terminated." He reaches down and lifts Jenny to her feet with one hand. She's sniveling. I worry the old girl will hyperventilate, or have a stroke, or something.

"Don't." I shove against his shoulder. "What's the matter with you? I said this is my fault, I forced her to bring me down here."

He pulls Jenny, who still stands between us, to the side. Throwing his cane down, he glares at me. His eyes glitter with fury. His hair falls over his blue eye, leaving the green to challenge me. "This is none of your business! You have no right to interfere, no right to be here at all."

Anger fills my gut until I'm sick with it. I lift my face and stare him down. "I agree. But I am here, and who's at fault for that? Huh? The great Maddox Empire. Controlling, manipulating ... hypocrites. Self-righteous, self-serving ... ugh! You are nothing but a bully, Gideon Maddox."

He blinks as though I slapped him. He takes a step back and stares at the ground. I wrap an arm around Jenny and whisper into her ear. "Go to your room and wait there for me. Don't pack. Don't do anything yet, all right?" She nods and sets off for the staircase.

Gideon still watches the floor with a stunned expression. He rubs his jaw. "God, I ..." He raises his gaze to mine. The pain shining through eviscerates me.

"Can't we talk about this?"

He shakes his head no. With a grace that is his alone, he kneels to retrieve his cane. When I reach for him, he jerks away, following the path Jenny took up the stairs.

"Wait ... Gideon?" He ignores me, taking the steps two and three at a time. Confusion swamps my brain. I hesitate, unsure whether to return to Cole and the others trapped in their wooden prisons or pursue Gideon.

My heart, however, knows exactly what to do.

And I obey.

Chapter Twenty-Nine

Without looking back, I jog up the stairs, through the kitchen, and down the hall. Unsure how long I stood downstairs contemplating my next move, it appears it was long enough for everyone to disappear. I assume Jenny went to her room. Maybe Gideon went to his.

"Gideon!" I call, as I pound the steps to the second floor. My mind is a salad toss of anxiety and anger. I'm worried about what he's thinking, what he feels for me, and what he plans to do next. Those thoughts ping-pong with frustration over the way he treated Jenny. Gideon Maddox must be the single most pig-headed guy on the planet.

Pushing through the double doors to the west wing, I head down the wide hallway. "Gideon?" No answer. I'm running now. My breathing escalates, part exertion, part anticipation. I have to convince him to release his prisoners. I believe his emotions are somehow walled away behind this fake legacy his father left. How do I make Gideon see it's an empty inheritance, nothing but pride and guilt? He let me in for a little while. Maybe he will again.

I burst into the office where I was caught snooping weeks

ago. He's here, sitting at his desk, blond head buried between his hands. The sight stops me at the door. My heart plummets, smacking the cold floor of my stomach. "Hey ..." I can't seem to say more.

Pain isn't a stranger to me, but when Gideon lifts his head, and his shining eyes rise to meet me, it's like a kick to the gut. The wariness is evident, the protective shield back up in spades. "What do you want, Raven?" His voice is smooth, distant. It's the hardened guy I met in the library downstairs eons ago. The one who kissed me breathless in the meadow by the river is gone.

"We have to talk about this. Settle things."

His hands sink to the desktop. "No. We don't." The clock above Gideon has stopped running. It occurs to me that they always do.

I'm way too chicken to ask him about us, so I try something less scary. "Why do clocks stop when you walk in a room?"

He raises a brow. "Noticed that, did you? A side effect of anyone who becomes an Artisan. I don't know why. My father may have told me, but I have no memory of it. He died before completing my education. He died before completing many things."

The conversation isn't going as planned. I swallow and try a different subject. "What about Jenny?"

He eases back in his chair and swivels to face me, so calm, so serene. His father's training was certainly thorough. The guy's so beautiful with his quiet grace and stunning bone structure. It's all I can do not to throw myself into his arms. Not that he'd welcome that from me right now.

"You win." His smile is stiff and doesn't soften the hard glaze in his eyes. "Funny, that hurt less than I thought it would. Jenny will stay. You will go. Today. I release you, Raven. You and Ben are freed from our agreement."

You will go. Each word is a slap. The guy I vowed to hate is the one I love. The one I dreamed of leaving has ... what were his words to me? ... *won me with a love that binds my heart— irrevocably. Chains softer than silk, stronger than iron.* Right.

What a fool you are, Raven. How many girls do you think he's used that line on before you? Triple loser because I want what I can't have. He's still worth fighting to save, even if we won't end up together.

I march to the edge of his desk. "What about the others?" He arches a golden eyebrow. "You know who I mean. Cole and the others in the photos. Let them go."

"Cole?" he sneers. "Not likely."

"Why? Because your father wouldn't like it or because you're holding a grudge?" I'm torn. Cole hurt Gideon but saved me. Despite all that, it's still wrong to hold them hostage. "Your allegiance is to the wrong people. A bunch of dead guys that spread their brand of vigilante justice like a disease, infecting everyone they deemed unworthy. You worst of all. Your life is yours to live as *you* decide. Let go of your hate!"

"I can't. It's all I have left of him. Don't you see? It's all that I am."

"Ugh!" I want to scream because he's so much more than that. "No. God redeems. He forgives. You can start over and build a new legacy."

He slams his hands down on the desk. "No. I can't." The leather squeaks as he shifts in his wingback chair. With an air of impatience, he pulls drawers in his desk out and punches them shut again.

I push him harder. "Yes you can. I'll prove it to you. How do we release them?"

"No idea."

"What?"

"My father was taken from me early, Raven." His tone is sharp and merciless as a blade. "He showed me the process of incarceration, not release."

"I'm sorry. About your father, Dane told me he—"

"Killed himself? Is that what he told you?" I nod. "Of course, he would say that. That's what the coroner ruled, what the papers reported, but it's not what happened. My father didn't just die, Raven. He was murdered."

Letting out an uneven breath I say, "Oh. I'm so sorry."

"Thank you." He nods. "Desiree wanted my father's money, and she wanted me." He tosses a folder onto his desktop. "When he limited her spending allowance, they quarreled. That's when Desiree started coming on to me. Small things at first, she'd hug me a little too tightly, or for too long. When she started wearing inappropriate clothes in my presence, I avoided her, finally telling her straight out to stay the hell away." Gideon pulls out his gold coin and runs it over his fingers. "Eventually, she put antidepressants in Father's scotch. I know because she told me afterward—when I wouldn't sign my inheritance money over."

My head droops. "What …" My tongue refuses to work. "I'm sorry." My condolence sounds lame, even to my ears. I can't express what I feel. "There aren't words."

"No." His expression softens as he watches me. "She is the only person I've ever used the camera on. I couldn't let her get away with murder. After weighing my options, I contacted her, telling her I'd reconsidered her offer. She met me here, sat in that very chair." His chin jerks toward a chair opposite his desk. "I told her I'd made the biggest mistake of my life. How I couldn't live without her. I explained she could have the money, the jewelry, everything, if only she'd come back to me."

Gideon's words are calculating. I shiver at the efficiency of his plot.

"It took some time to convince her, of course, but I can be very persuasive. I fed her gluttonous ego lies until her vanity was so bloated she believed every word I said. The Maddox women knew nothing of the camera and its abilities. Desiree leaped at the chance to have her portrait taken by me."

My fingers itch to touch the bruises hidden by my hair. Desiree's face swims in my memory. Her venomous words fill my ears. Dead, doll-like eyes stare at me, wishing for my death.

Gideon's eyes darken, narrow, and I know he's not listening. "I will never release her. Them." There's violence to the quiet in his voice. The contrast turns my blood to ice.

"Then you'll spend the rest of your life alone and threatening people like Ben." I straighten. As bad as I feel for him, nothing's changed. There was never going to be any *us*. "Manipulating people like me for your own selfish gain. I'm sorry for you, Gideon. You'll never know how much because your leg is not what's twisted about you, it's your mind. You'll end up bitter and wasted, become exactly like the people who broke you."

The color drains from his face, but I won't recant. His brow creases as he refocuses on my throat. "Raven …? What the hell went on here yesterday? Tell me what happened to you."

Un-uh. You don't throw me away and then get to act all concerned and protective. Not falling for that one again. "That's none of your business now."

A muscle twitches in his cheek. "The hell you say." His tone is mostly growl.

"Goodbye, Gideon." I'll have to free the ghosts on my own. As I step away, my peripheral vision catches his movement. I need to stop underestimating him.

I bolt for the door, afraid he'll catch me, afraid of what I'll become if he doesn't. A heartbeat later, his fingers wrap my arm, digging into my flesh. "Raven, wait. I can't go through with this. I didn't mean it."

"Let me go."

"I can't. I won't lose you."

"It seems there's a lot of things you can't do, or *won't*." My heart still lies on the floor of my stomach, barely beating. Much more of this will kill it altogether. When I try and wrench my arm free, I'm knocked off balance. Gideon falls with me, and I end up on the floor, staring at the crystal chandelier on the ceiling.

His face appears, obscuring everything else. "Forgive me." His eyes focus on my exposed throat. "My God, are you all right?" He brushes my hair aside. His fingers linger on my skin, burning the memory of his touch everywhere. "What have I done …?" His fingers skim my lips. "Can we talk about this?"

Now? I wonder where the chatty side of the guy was ten minutes ago when I begged him to talk, but the fight's gone out of me to refuse him.

Gideon's fingers sink into my hair as he cups both cheeks, forcing me to look at him. "I screwed up again, I know that." His warm breath falls across my skin with his words. The tortured look in his eyes melts my liver or some other vital organ I'll probably need later on. "Every single thing you said about me is true. I didn't know … how to handle it. But you've made me question everything I knew from that first day, haven't you?" His gaze travels over my face. A storm clouds his eyes as his gaze drops to the bruises on my neck. "What happened to you? Please …"

My fingers touch my throat where Desiree choked me. "She did this because she thought it would hurt you."

He nods once before answering. "She thought right. But she won't ever hurt you again. Count on it." His gaze hardens, voice so distant the threat seems more vow than promise.

I squirm under his weight until I'm able to sit. He allows it, but won't release my hand.

"To think I almost let you leave …" His head hangs with his long breath. "I'm a complete and total ass."

"Not arguing."

His lips quirk, the humor reflected in his eyes. "You do realize it took me all of ten seconds once you walked away for me to wake up to what I'd done. I can't let you go, though I should. If I were unselfish enough I would, but you make me want to be different, better. I'm new at this. Forgive me."

"It's not about forgiving you. I've seen what you are underneath your family's influence." Dark waves of hair shield my face as I duck my head. When Gideon pushes my hair back, I turn away. "I know I'm right about the people in those pictures. When you let them go, you free yourself. I hope you will, because you could be happy." I smile but it comes out weak and tired. "I'd love to see you happy, Gideon Maddox, but …" My thighs burn as I push to a stand. "You were right about one thing. You and me … it's not going to work."

Gideon shoots to his feet. "You're wrong."

He takes a step forward as I step back. "Am I?" I laugh, the sound so cold it scares me. "That's not the message you were sending when you gave me your back in the cellar. Actually, ever since I got here. Women are disposable, something to collect and discard when you're bored." His nostrils do the bull-flaring thing again, but I'm immune. "Two days ago, we kissed. Big deal." I shrug. "There was a minute or two where I thought we had something special, different. I *was* wrong. You were right. We're better off apart."

"I see." With a head toss, he shakes the curls from his eyes. His expression is calm but calculating. I see the wheels turning in that gorgeous head of his and it's got me worried. "I'll make a deal with you. Stay. Help me release the people trapped by my forefathers. After we've done that, if you still want to leave, I won't stop you."

Gideon's good at making deals. He ought to be, he's been groomed by his father since childhood. With the instincts of a hunter, he sees what he wants and goes right for the jugular.

"I'll do it."

He's trying not to smile when he answers. "I know."

I fight not to punch him in the nose.

Chapter Thirty

Gideon turns from me and walks to the polished, antique camera sitting on a tripod in the corner of the room.

"Is that it?"

"Yes." He lifts the camera from its base and holds it over his head. His biceps bulge under the sleeves of his form-fitting T-shirt. "Here goes nothing."

Without hesitating, a downward thrust and the camera rockets toward the hard floor. Wood splits and glass shatters as it crashes. No longer a means of imprisoning people, or even a priceless heirloom, the camera is no more. It sits in a pitiful heap on the floor in ruins.

"Well?"

"Hang on." I spin around. "Cole. Cole can you hear me? Are you here?" Nothing happens as we wait. "Gideon!" I dare to hope. "We did it. We—"

Raven …

Damn. Peering over my shoulder, I watch as Cole floats into the room. "Aw, you're still here."

"You can see him?" Gideon asks.

"Yes." My voice is soft with disappointment and pity.

"Where? I don't see anything."

Cole winks at me, and I smile. "He's over here, by the door." I answer without turning. "By the way, Cole says you're as big an ass as you ever were." When I step back, I bump into a wall. Firm and steady, the wall gives, and I dare a peek up at Gideon.

"Very funny. Ask him if he's good for anything besides insulting me. Does he know how to break the curse?"

"He may, but I don't think he can tell us. He's bound by it somehow ..." Cole nods. He grins as though he's proud of me. In a fluid motion, he glides until he's right in front of me. "But anything you can tell us might help."

"Why are you whispering?" Gideon demands.

"I don't know." When Cole rubs his chin, a cocky smirk appears. I giggle. I can't help it.

You want me ... admit it. Just wait until I have my body back.

I blush.

Gideon heaves an impatient breath. "And are you looking at him? Right now?"

"Yes." I pause. Gideon obviously can't hear Cole either. "Why?"

"Because I don't like *how* you're looking at him." Seconds tick by. "Raven? Raven!" The more pissed off Gideon's voice becomes, the wider Cole's grin. "Tell him I'm going to bring him back, just so I can kick his ass all the way back to England. And tell him to stop flirting with you, or I'll kill him. And tell him—"

He can try.

"Cole can hear you, Gideon." I face him. "Destroying the camera didn't work, what about the pictures themselves?"

"Let's try."

Gideon and I race from the west to east wing in eleven point four seconds, awkward in my combat-boots, black tights, and black lace skirt. Cole floats behind us. I'll never get used to the creepy way he gets around.

When we reach the framed photos on the east wing landing,

Gideon rests his cane near a delicate side table covered with china vases. He lifts the old photos one by one from the walls and hands them down to me.

"Find the one of Cole," I say. His picture is third from the end, the handsome boy in his crisp, white shirt. Man, does he need a makeover, and I have the perfect clothes for him.

Gideon scowls as he disengages the frame wire from its hook on the wall.

Tell Gideon if he keeps making that face, it will stick like that.

"Do you have a death wish?" I ask.

"What?" Gideon says.

"Nothing, I was talking to Cole."

"Well, stop." He angles his head away, glowering into an empty space on the landing. "You don't talk to her, Wynter. Understand?" Gideon raises Cole's picture over his head. His arm muscles flex. The planes of his chest show through his snug T-shirt in a way that sucks ten points from my IQ.

I back away and hunker down against the balustrade. Gideon hurls the picture to the floor. Tiny shards of glass fly in all directions. They glitter under the glowing candles of the chandelier, hover for one promise-filled moment, and then fall with a hush onto the carpeting.

I let out the breath I didn't know I was holding. "That's it?" I ask.

"What were you expecting?" Gideon's mouth tips up at the ends.

"Purple smoke, a big bang ... something."

His eyes glint with humor. "No such luck. Is Cole finally gone, I hope?"

I face the brunette boy wavering beside me. His shoulders sag, his large eyes so full of sorrow I reach for his hand. "I'm sorry." I have no idea if he can feel my touch, but I want him to know how much I care. I whip around as another thought hits me. "What happens when you take their pictures, Gideon?"

"Not much." He kneels sifting through the wrecked picture. "A flash of light, a long hissing noise ... then there's the process of developing." He runs his fingers through his hair the way he does when he's frustrated.

"What happens to their bodies?" I ask.

Gideon's head snaps up. "What did you say?" His eyes flash wildly.

Confused, I hesitate, unsure if I've said something wrong. "Their bodies ... what happens to them afterward?"

Gideon leaps over the mangled picture and grabs me by both arms. He hauls me to my feet as his head descends.

When I open my mouth to ask what the hell he's doing, his lips crush mine. His strong arms wrap my waist. One hand moves up my back, pressing me against his hard frame, the other moves south, to my hip. My lips part, allowing him to deepen our kiss. Our breath mingles. I'm lost in his sweet scent of black licorice and spices.

"You're a genius," he says, when he finally lifts his head. The words hum against my lips. I have to agree if whatever I said causes this reaction from him. When I thread my fingers through his hair and pull him in for another kiss, he groans, sending my pulse into overdrive. He nips at my lower lip, then runs a line of kisses along my jaw to my ear. His rough breathing has my eyes rolling back.

"Tell me what I did, so I can do it again," I whisper.

Must I be subjected to this?

I startle and jerk away. "Cole! Sorry. Really. I forgot you were there."

"I didn't." Gideon grins like the Cheshire.

I face him again. "You ambushed me. That kiss doesn't change a thing between us."

Gideon smiles, grabs my hand, and tugs. "Oh, things changed, but I won't elaborate on what right now." My mouth drops. "Come on. I know what to do." He retrieves his cane off the credenza. "Let's free your little playmate and send him on his way."

I'm jogging to keep up, but Cole has no trouble.

"When you mentioned the bodies, I got an idea. My father may have given me the answer without me knowing."

"That sounds promising," I pant.

"When I was a kid, my father gave me this twenty-dollar gold piece ..." He lets go of my hand, retrieving the coin from his jean pocket to show me. "At first I thought this was just something shiny to play with. You see its size?" He tosses the coin, catching it again. "Easily lost or stolen, only my father would give a rare, antique coin to his son as a toy. When I grew older, I learned of its dual purpose. That's why it's never out of my sight."

Gideon charges forward, his cane thumping on the ground with each step. Cole and I follow. Hope mixes with curiosity, and by the time we reappear in his office, I'm out of breath and my heart is thundering.

"What now?"

"You need silver salts to develop film with this kind of camera." Gideon holds out his twenty-dollar gold piece and walks to an armoire standing innocently in the corner. "My dad made a special kind, though. A salt recipe passed down for generations from the magician who first sold us the camera. We keep the ingredients in here."

Instead of a key, a long slit in the door accepts the coin. The intricate lock whirs and clicks and Gideon pulls the door open. Inside are rows of narrow shelves covered with bottles in all shapes and sizes. He lifts a crystal cut decanter and holds it up to the light. The container is filled to the brim with a gleaming white substance, like sugar or ice crystals. A shudder runs through me as I consider the power he has.

Gideon gives the decanter a shake. "To the cellar."

Chapter Thirty-One

In the bowels of Maddox mansion, Gideon and I rearrange the coffins in two rows, a dozen in each. There's something surreal and macabre in the task. With the room awash in smoky blues and grays, it's as though I'm an extra on stage, starring in a tragedy, and none of this is real.

I brush the chalk from my hands. "What is this stuff?"

"Lime. For moisture control ... and the smell." Gideon steps over the pile of tools we stopped for on the way down.

Power of suggestion sends a crawling sensation over my skin. I don't smell anything other than lime. Do bodies frozen in time rot? I remember the wiggling maggots in Desiree's vision, and rub my hands up and down my arms to keep the chill off. "Are all of the bodies here?"

He shakes the hair from his eyes, the blond darker from sweat. "This should be everyone." He rests on an old bench near the head of the first coffin. "When I was twelve, my father told me who I was. Explained my role as an Artisan. I read the diary, poured over the accounts in the ledgers. My family has been managing people and their crimes forever, but by comparison, few were ever awarded *this* punishment." He faces the coffins. "Most we ruined financially using our power and connections. Behind the scenes, of course. The camera was reserved for those committing the worst crimes. As far as I know, only two of the photos upstairs were taken by my father. One by me. Most of the people here were photographed long before my time."

I nod believing I must be amongst the bodies of murderers and who knows what else. Cole isn't like that. He was a cruel, stupid kid, yes, but one that deserves another chance. The rest were tried by a court of law and found not guilty, until the Maddox family intervened. Life is never fair; no one knows that better than me. But it's God's job to figure this out. Not human judges. Not Gideon.

My gaze roams over the dusty room. Who knows what will happen when Gideon lets them go? I haven't spent a lot of time thinking about it until now. Some will find themselves in another era. Maybe they can start over, build a different life. The rest can take their chances with the police or with their Maker. I hardly care. I just want Gideon free of them so he can get on with his life.

Despite the cold, my clothes are damp with sweat from moving the heavy boxes. I wipe my brow with the back of my hand and sling a heavy curtain of hair over one shoulder.

"You're so beautiful."

I freeze. Gideon's words almost make me forget what we're doing here. "Don't."

"Why? I wish you could see what I see." He rises, moving toward me with the stealth of a hunter. His finger slides feather-light along my collarbone. I close my eyes, hating my weakness. "Your skin looks almost translucent in this light." I refuse to look at him, so he crooks his finger beneath my chin, drawing it up. My lids flutter open. "Thank you, Raven. I'm grateful you're here with me."

Stunned by the conversation he chose to have in the cellar of doom, I say the only thing I can. "You're welcome." Then I add, "I'm glad, too." Who knows why Gideon felt he needed to say that right now, but I'm truly proud to help him.

Self-conscious, I step out of his grasp. "Are you ready?" I'm surprised at how calm I sound, as if he didn't just set my skin on fire with his touch.

He smiles. "I'm always ready."

I roll my eyes.

He's right, you know. Cole appears on my left. *You are beautiful.*

I ignore them both. This is so not the venue. "Can I help wake them up?"

"No!" Cole and Gideon say at once.

"Do me a favor and take a seat up there." Gideon points to the stairs. "Please?" His hand disappears for a moment behind his back and materializes again with a gleaming, black gun. Where the heck did that come from? He pulls a clip from his pocket, shoves it into the bottom of the gun, and replaces the weapon in the waist of his pants.

Holy crap!

"We don't need that, do we? I can help. I want to." And I do, even though I have no idea how.

"I know, and you have." Gideon leans over retrieving a crowbar from the pile of tools he left on the chalk-covered floor. "But if this works, I don't know what might happen. Do you understand? Don't suppose everyone will be so grateful for their release that they'll march off into the night and never bother us again."

Point taken.

"More likely they will try and cut my heart out."

"Oh, don't!" My breath catches, but Gideon's expression is unwavering, confident. *I love you,* I want to say. What comes out instead is, "Be careful, please." His gentle smile and nod steady me.

"Now that I've decided, I just want the thing done and over with for good. And I need to know that you're safe." He stands erect, tilts his head until his neck cracks. "Cole?" Gideon pauses, then looks to me. "Can he hear me?"

My gaze darts between them. "Yes."

"You're up. I know we've had our … differences." His

smile is stiff. "If things go badly, I need you to get Raven out of here safely. I couldn't exactly call the police. What would I say? I'm going to wake people from the dead and we need backup in case they're pissed off? I'm not even sure this will work, and if it doesn't, how would I explain your lifeless bones in a box." Both boys laugh, but Gideon's expression quickly sobers. A palpable tension rises between them. "She's innocent of this. And she means *everything* to me. Will you help her?"

Already my plan, Cole says. He faces me. *No one will hurt you. No one.*

"Well?" Gideon barks, jolting me to attention.

I gulp a shuddery breath. "He agrees."

"Then get up those stairs, Rae. And if I say run, you run. No arguments."

It's the moment of truth. My legs tremble as I climb to the top stair and squat. Cole appears at my side. He takes my hand. "Good luck," I say, and squeeze his ghostly fingers. I hope he can feel it.

Raven, thank you. Thank you for saving me.

"I haven't done anything yet." His dark round eyes, so earnest and sad, tug on my heart.

You have. His smile is as faint as a watermark. *Whether or not I'm freed today, you already saved me.*

A bang drags my focus to the other room. Gideon starts at the far end of the first row, prying the lids off. Old nails groan and complain. Boards crack as they're loosened. I wince, afraid of what I'll see, yet unable to look away. Like eggs nestled in straw, man after man appears as Gideon tears the coffins open.

The bodies lie quiet. I recognize them from the photos I've passed for weeks on the landing upstairs. Their arms lay crossed over their breasts, faces are drawn and bloodless, but there are no maggots, no decomposition. They might be sleeping if not for their blue color. Most are wearing dark suits, the lovely Desiree in her frothy white gown, of course. I watch the years pass in the style changes of their garments, hairstyles, and facial hair.

Gideon works at a fever pitch. When the last lid is lifted,

I suck a breath as Cole's body appears. His pale blue face looks so young, no different from the guy sitting next to me, except the one in the box can't move. And the one beside me is bodiless. Yeah, except for that.

Shoving a discarded lid away, Gideon coughs as he limps out of the maze of coffins. In a corner near the back of the cellar, a black tarp covers a series of large, uneven lumps. Before I can guess what's underneath, he bends, taking hold of one end. With a swish and crackle of plastic, I'm staring at the carcass of a great white horse. The hound, Rex, I've met on at least two occasions, rests in between the stallion's legs.

"Good Lord in heaven." I shake my head. "How did they ever get him down here?" I can't even guess how many decades the animals have been here. There's no decay, no emaciated bodies to hint at their age.

Gideon wipes his hands across his red T-shirt, leaving white streaks of lime. "Times were different. The world was smaller, and men didn't question idiosyncrasies of the man who paid their salaries. Over a hundred years ago, I imagine Mathias Maddox's field hands thought him no more than eccentric."

Yeah? I imagine they thought a lot more than that, but I don't say so. "You're going to wake the horse up?" I angle my head. "And the dog?"

He blinks. "Don't you want me to? I thought … I mean, I want to do this right for you. What if it were Edgar?"

The lump in my throat is the size of a bowling ball. I clear it and answer him. "Don't do this for me. Do it for yourself."

His lips press into a grim line. "We're going to have a hell of a time getting that animal up the stairs, but he's waking up." Gideon's smooth voice is pure determination. "They all are." He lifts his head, his gaze searching mine out. I think he wants to say something, but he keeps silent. Under that intense stare, my stomach flip-flops, and before I can figure out what he wants, he steps to the coffins and holds up the decanter of salts.

I hold my breath as he starts sprinkling the substance over the bodies. I wrap my waist with both arms to quiet my nerves. My focus cuts across the people in the coffins, to the animals in the far corner and back. There's pressure, and expectation, and fear in the waiting. No sound but the hopeful beating of two hearts. Then the view changes.

Shapes fade in and out of the gray shadows around the room. They waver, finally taking semi-solid form.

"Gideon?" I whisper. "The people from the photos, they're here. Can you see them?" He doesn't answer. Cole appears at the head of the casket housing his body. I glance beside me, and just as I thought, his ghost-like image is gone from my side. My nerves tingle with anticipation. My heartbeat quickens. I press my hand to my chest to steady my rapid breathing.

Rex barks. His image stands beside that of the white stallion. The horse's neck bends as he paws the air. They both wait at the heads of their physical selves. That's when I know the silver salt is going to work. They're all here. As I scan the crowd, the flickering ghosts all pause beside their caskets, waiting to reclaim their bodies, and their lives.

One man frantically waves his arms. Something's wrong. Gripping the stair railing, I half rise from my seat on the step for a better view. The brow of a shimmering spirit creases in angry furrows; another's teeth are bared. Mouths twist in horrific violence. The prisoners raise their fists in the air, pounding, shouting over one another. They curse the Maddox name. Everyone except Cole.

"Wait!" I shriek. "They're angry. Talk to them, Gideon. Tell them *why* you're waking them up now." But it's too late. The drama I expected when Gideon shattered the photos upstairs is happening now. Shimmering, silver fog rises from the bodies in the caskets. Thin and snake-like, the mist winds itself around each individual, ascending until it bumps and curls against the ceiling. Cole meets my gaze. The ground trembles. A loud crack and Gideon shouts my name. He thrusts out a hand as the room bursts into a kaleidoscope of swirling color.

The stallion whinnies and rears. His ghost stands snorting and nickering over his prone carcass. I blink as his body and essence meld. Steam chugs from both nostrils. His mane is thrashing red fire down his arched neck. Yellow flames flicker and snap at his sides, while the animal's eyes glow white-hot. He screams. Rex howls, as his frame is encased in crackling red and blue embers.

Across the room it's the same with the other, human bodies. Cut off from the stairs by the enchanted flame, Gideon presses himself against the rough wall of the cellar. His wide eyes and incredulous expression lets me know he sees them, too. My heart thuds against my ribs. Panic climbs my throat. I scan the room for Cole but can't find him.

Rising above the coffins that housed them for so long, the corpses stand erect. I cringe, flinging myself back until my spine presses against the far wall of the staircase, but I can't stop watching. I swear the glowing men appear to grow taller. As they burn, bones bulge, pushing to break free of their ancient skin casing. The necks and heads of the men elongate. Their rib cages spread and deepen, legs grow longer, and arms bend and break at odd angles.

The group morphs into twisted, grotesque images of their former selves. Contorting the way a twig bends and curls in a fire pit. Their eyes bug from the sockets to the point of bursting. Instead, they deflate, melting from the sockets like runny egg yolks. Muscle drops from their heating bones, drips from their frames hitting the earth in sizzling plops of dying flesh. Orange and yellow, the skin pops and bubbles on the floor, incinerating before turning to black ash.

Shrieking echoes off the thick walls. I cover my ears to block the sound, but it's in my head, expanding in my chest, all around me. Sulfur burns my sinuses. My eyes water. The horse is gone, as is the little dog Rex. Under the effects of the withering curse, the men writhe and lash at each other, but their blows are ineffectual. The din rises. My head spins, and I feel incredible pressure building in my lungs. My ears pop with pressure over and over, and somewhere, above the cacophony, a clock ticks.

When the pain in my head reaches its zenith and my lungs threaten to burst, my scream joins with the others. A mushroom cloud billows against the ceiling, all red and orange and pink, promising a hot, sulfuric death. Lightning flashes. Thunder cracks, hits the cellar like a sonic boom, blowing me off the stairs. I crash against the far wall, before dropping to the floor. Gasping for breath, I roll to my side and peer back up the empty staircase. I touch my stinging forehead at the hairline, and pull my fingers back sticky with blood.

A final blast, a gush of angry wind and the room stills, growing quiet.

"Gideon?" I croak. A hand slides beneath my arm, and I'm drawn to my feet. When I raise my head, it's not Gideon I see, but Cole. And not the Cole I knew. This one is solid all the way to his shoes. He's taller, broader. His face has both filled in and sharpened. What the heck?

A deep frown covers his handsome features. "Are you all right?" His voice is lower than I remember.

"Cole. I thought I'd lost you." Weak, I lean against the wall.

The corner of his mouth lifts. "You can't lose me."

"Get. Your hands. Off of her."

We pivot together. My weight sags, and Cole's arms support me. "Gideon," I say, relief flooding my being. A crimson line runs down his left arm to his elbow. There's a gash on his cheek. "You're here. Thank you, God."

"Relax, Gideon. If I let her go, she'll fall down." As if to prove his words, Cole releases me and I stumble backward into his arms.

Gideon lunges and trips.

Perhaps he wants to avoid a fight. Whatever his reasoning, Cole eases me down onto the cold floor and backs off. My shoulder rests on the rough stone as I struggle to clear my head. Gideon's kneeling at my feet, his expression a tangle of concern and relief.

"I'm all right." I tuck my hair behind my ear. "Just need a minute."

Cole strides to the nearest coffin and inspects the contents. "Dust," he says. "Ashes and dust."

"What happened to them?" I ask.

Raising his arm, Cole stares at his hand as he flips it over. His fingers slide up his torso and neck. They run across his face, as though he's discovering himself for the first time.

Following my gaze, Gideon rises. He walks to the head of the first casket and turns. "Yes, you've aged ... around four years, I'm guessing. Though age hasn't improved your looks any."

I suppress an eye roll, actually afraid it might hurt.

Gideon scans the ankle-deep dust at his feet. "Many of these men were at least middle-aged when they were photographed. Some have been here for decades." A light goes on in my head.

Cole kneels before another coffin, peering inside. "So for the older ones, if the aging process was cumulative—"

"They were dead the minute they woke up."

A white flash darts from the shadows at the back of the room. One, dull clank later, Gideon crumples to the floor. I push off with my knees to a stand. Unsteady, my hand searches out the gritty wall for support.

Desiree stands over Gideon, a haughty grin on her lovely features. Flashlight in one hand, Gideon's shiny, black gun in the other, she faces us with a leer. "That leaves us youngsters. Only you and I made it out alive, Cole." She peeks at the unconscious form at her feet. "Sleep well, baby. You and me, we'll tango later, after I dispose of these distractions."

Ten feet away, Cole's frame straightens. "Don't do this."

"You have nothing I need anymore, little one." She laughs and points the gun at his heart. "I'm finally free." Her eyes narrow. "As you were my favorite cellmate, you will live, as long as your little girlfriend here does what I say. Now get moving, up the stairs."

"I'm not his girlfriend," I offer, as if that will help. Stupid must take over when I'm scared, because I know what she's asking. My feet won't obey, and apparently, I say the dumbest things possible.

"Shut up!"

I stall for time. "What is it you want?"

She stares at me with incredulous eyes. "Idiot! I want

my life back. I want my money, my house, and I want him." Her eyes flicker toward Gideon, face down in the ash. "I've lived abroad and lately come home to stay, haven't you heard? Clean, plausible, and to the point. It won't take more for the simpletons in this backwater town to believe. Though I can't exactly have you here, can I? He's infatuated with you, but that won't last once you're gone. Now move!"

With Gideon still out cold on the floor, Desiree keeps her gun trained on Cole. There's no arguing, pleading, or reasoning with insanity. We're on our own. I search out Cole and our eyes lock. Maybe we can make a plan once we know what she's up to. I don't know how to convey that, I just hope he's thinking the same.

I hobble up the stairs hearing two sets of footsteps climbing behind me. We're directed through the kitchen, outside and to the rear of the house. Desiree keeps her gun pressed deep into Cole's back. One wrong move and he's dead, for real this time. Whatever she wants, she'll get. I won't allow her to kill him on the birthday of his second life.

Outside, moonlight paints pictures of misty ghouls in the surrounding gloom. My head pounds and every vertebra aches like it's been bisected. My pace is slow, extracting a string of curses from Desiree. When she's done blessing me out, I ask her which way.

"Over there, by the millpond."

No blood, no body to find, I get it now.

"Desiree. Please. Let me take her away," Cole pleads. "I'll take her home, to my family in Europe. I'll keep her there. Whatever it takes, whatever you want. I promise. You'll never see us again. *Please!*"

The ground under my feet squishes at the edge of the pond. It's treacherous here, the soil sodden with the quality of quicksand. I stop with my back to the water. The mill house stands in the distance. Moonbeams silver the crumbling shingles. Blackened windows for eyes, it stands as a blind and silent witness to my murder.

"Touching, kiddo. My heart goes out to you, really, but

I can't take the chance she'll show up again. She's a bit inconvenient since I've waited so long to reclaim Gideon for my own." She shoves Cole away and takes several steps back. "And you're just so damn hard to get rid of. You wouldn't scare, so I called the authorities to take you away."

"That was you?" I couldn't exactly see her ghostly fingers dialing, but this maniac was resourceful, no doubt.

She laughs, the sound as hard and hypnotic as diamonds. Her blond hair gleams under the moonlight. Even with her dress tattered and filthy, her face smeared with ash, and the added years, she's beautiful. "I even tried a nice high school dance bonfire, just to be sure. Yet, here you stand."

Cole lifts his hands. "Listen to me—"

"Enough talk! You," she says to me, "in the water, now."

I hesitate and it's one second too long.

Desiree shifts and pulls the trigger. Cole cries out. His legs shoot out from beneath him, and he flies back, landing on the ground with a soft thud. My scream echoes through the live oaks. Limbs askew, Cole's moan assures me he's alive.

"Quiet!" Desiree orders. "Both of you." She marches toward me with dainty little steps that would be comical if she weren't so deadly. When she's two feet from me she stops short. "That shot won't kill him, but the next one will." She stretches her arm out, aiming her weapon at Cole. His knees draw into his chest. He groans and the sound wrenches my heart. "In the water."

I obey. First one foot slides in, then the other.

She smiles, her expression triumphant as I continue inching into the water. The suction takes over, pulling me down to my knees, my waist. "You almost had him, didn't you, darling. *Almost.* Well, Gideon's all mine now. I'll devour every square inch first, and then I'll kill him."

When the water reaches my chest, fear crawls up the back of my neck. Drowning. Well, I offered it freely, didn't I? A hysterical laugh boils up, and I choke it down. If it saves Cole, buys Gideon any time at all to fight her, they're worth dying for.

I raise my arms, fat lot of good it does me. It's instinct now. Cole groans my name, but I can't help him. I can't help anyone anymore. Panic wells up inside me. I know to struggle is to die faster, but my terror of suffocating is too strong.

"That's it, Raven. Good girl. Why prolong the inevitable, eh?"

A shadow looms behind Desiree's shoulder. Dark arms wrap her white dress, and a shot rings out. Moonlight reveals Gideon's face but he disappears again as Desiree struggles for control of the gun. Water covers my mouth. I tip my head back and breathe through my nose. A third blast of gunfire and I hear the bullet rip across the water near me. I pray with all my might Gideon wins.

A cry from Desiree and a heavy splash rocks the water. The ripples roll over my head, and I sink farther down. This is how I die. Panic knifes me with her icy fingers. Be brave ... God take me to my mother. I quit struggling, let go. My arms fall.

Another splash hits the water. Something rough and hard brushes my arm. I grab and miss. Reaching once more, I take hold. My fingers curl around the uneven object and I feel a tug. I grip with all my strength as the tree branch lifts me an inch.

The mud is relentless and fights for me, sucking me down. But my will is stronger. I press my lips together to keep the muck out. With my lungs near bursting, I grit my teeth; pull until my muscles shake with effort. My nose breaks the surface. Water fills my mouth. I fight like a cat as I'm hauled a bit further out. My lungs are on fire, begging for air as my head clears the pool. I cough and choke, but I don't let go of the branch.

"Raven! Oh God, baby, hold on!"

Gideon's smooth voice is like music. He's alive. As my eyes clear of water, I see someone pulling on the tree branch alongside him. Jamis? My body slides over the bank, and as my feet disengage from the deadly peat, Gideon grabs my wrists and pulls me into his arms. His hands cup my face. Despite the mud covering me, he kisses my head and cheeks, my eyelids.

While I break into another fit of coughing, he pulls his cell from his back pocket and hands it to Jamis. "Call Dave. His number is in there under 'physician.' Tell him we have a gunshot wound and near drowning. Then bring the car around."

"You hurt?" I gasp. My lungs scorch as air fills them again. "Cole."

His arm tightens around my waist. "He'll be okay. We're both okay."

Memories rewind to the heavy splash I heard just before I went under. I crane my neck, peering over my shoulder at the murky waters. "Where's Des—"

"Let's get you to the car, all right?" Gideon lifts me against his chest and stands. A girl could get used to being carried everywhere she goes, especially by this guy. My muscles go limp as his body warms me. I snuggle into his neck. The scent of ash and musk lingers on his clothes. Gideon rubs his jaw on my face; stubble scrapes my skin. "You'll be the death of me, girl."

Chapter Thirty-Two

Sales Hollow Medical Center is closed for the night, but Dr. Dave is hard at work anyway. Gideon must pay him a small fortune to drop what he's doing at four AM and see us, but that's what's happening.

Cole and I are in separate rooms. I swear we've been here ten hours, but Dave says more like two. Gideon sleeps in the chair by my bed. It's becoming a habit. I notice with some satisfaction the clock above his head keeps ticking.

I like that.

My fingers shake as I slowly pull the needle connected to my arm from the vein. I wrinkle my nose, hanging the tube over my bed rail. There's something I need to do, and it won't wait. Out the door, down the short hallway, and into Cole's room I go. It wasn't hard to find. There are only six doors on this hall.

My new friend lies in a bed hooked to an IV just as I was. He's naked from the waist up, the planes of his chest defined and lean. His shoulder is bandaged in several layers of gauze covering a wide area. Cole Wynter looks much like his picture did, but older, more mature. His eyelids blink open. I take a deep breath, but all that comes out is, "Hey."

"Hey yourself." I love his accent. An American girl is usually a sucker for a European accent, and I'm no exception.

I wrap my stupid gown tighter around me and shuffle over to the bed. "If I sit here, will it hurt you?" I nod toward the end of the mattress where his feet make two hills beneath the covers. "I think we should talk."

"Please," he says, extending a hand. "Crazy night, huh?

"Crazy life," I counter.

"Right." A long pause. "Rae, I want to tell you what happened, in my own words, okay?" Instead of answering, I pat his foot. His eyes light with amusement. "At fifteen, I was a spoiled, mean, insecure, and angry kid." He takes his time with his explanation, speaking each word carefully. "My parents were the typical, jet-setting millionaires. Pursuing their own selfish dreams and passions, they left me to my own devices to win their attention. I hurt Gideon twice. Almost killed him, as a stupid prank. On a dare. I *am* the quintessential poor, little rich kid. Or I was. Until I came to Maddox mansion. The school thought my acceptance of Gideon's family's invitation would show good will. My parents agreed only to be rid of me for spring break.

"As Gideon's father took my photograph, he fully explained what he planned to do and why. I didn't understand at first, of course. By the time I did, it was too late to fight him off."

I squeeze his toes. "I'm sorry."

"I'm not." My expression must turn skeptical. "Truly. Gideon didn't know of his father's plan until afterward. Though my experience here was extreme and almost cost me an eternity, I changed inside that house. I'm not the same guy I was and never will be again. The hardest part was when my father flew to America to search for me. I saw him enter Maddox mansion with the police. He held a newspaper up with my picture on the front page. The story claimed I was a troubled teen with a history of delinquencies, which was true. It also claimed I'd run away, which wasn't, but my father believed it easily enough.

My head falls back as I hear Cole's tale. His parents were cruel, as was he, as was Mr. Maddox, as was Gideon. People lost in a sea of bitterness and blame. "I'm sorry." There's not much more to say.

"Look at me, Raven." I do. "If this hadn't happened, there's no telling where I'd be today. I might be dead. Definitely a lost cause." When he scratches the skin near the needle in his hand, I wince. "Then you showed up."

His foot slides over and bumps my hip. I send him my best attempt at a smile.

"By the time you came along, I was already, I don't know … repentant. I watched you. Wow." He laughs. "Sorry. That sounded like a full-blown stalker. What I meant was I wondered if Gideon would take your picture. I wanted him to." When I open my mouth he talks over me. "Hang on. I only wished that for about a minute and only because I was lonely and admired you so much. Then it occurred to me I might still be with you … if I was free."

"I see."

"Do you?" His eyebrows lower with the intensity of his tone. "My family has money, Raven. A lot of it. I was born in England, but we have a home in France—the fashion mecca of the world. You could come with me. I would take care of you; spoil you rotten. Once my family knows what you've done for me, they will love you as much as … everyone else does."

"Everyone, huh?" He blushes and drops his gaze to his hands. His dark lashes fan across his cheekbones. His body has fast-forwarded to that of a nineteen-year-old, but his life experience is still stuck at fifteen. Something tells me the boy will catch up quickly. "Aw, c'mon, Raven. I think you know how I feel about you. Let me help you. Say you will leave the U.S. and come live with me."

Tears threaten as I shake my head. "Thank you for that." His shoulders droop, and I squeeze his toes again. "Really, you have no idea what your offer means to me. I may come and visit, but Ben needs me right now. Beyond that … I can't think beyond that right now."

Cole nods. "I understand. I do. The offer stands. Forever, as a matter of fact, promise you'll think about it."

"I promise." I lower my gaze, unsure what else to say. I don't want to hurt him, but I love him differently than I do Gideon. The air conditioner must be on fifty degrees, and the gown I'm in is thin as paper. I rub my arms against the chill. "What's next for you?"

Cole shifts against his pillows. "I go home. Wait for your call." His grin melts my heart. "As far as my absence? The story is apparently, shortly after I came to visit Gideon, I went for a ride on his motorbike, and crashed. I suffered blunt trauma to the head. That's the last thing I remember. The blow resulted in amnesia. I must have wandered off and gotten lost. Doctors say I have no memory of the incident or what happened in the four-year interim, post-traumatic stress or some such. What *is* known is that another injury triggered the return of my long-term memory. I'm to be reunited with my family in a few days"

"Clever. Who thought that story up, you?"

"Pfft. Who do you think?" His lips curve. "Gideon's giving me plane fare home, new clothes, whatever I want."

"Wow. That's awesome. How nice."

His smile turns wry. "It's not that nice, Raven. The guy wants me out of the way."

"I do." I twist on the bed and find Gideon leaning on the doorframe. He straightens and meanders over to the bed, cane clicking on the tile floor.

"How long have you been eavesdropping?" I face Cole again, a blush stinging both my cheeks. "Did you know he was back there?"

His smile is his answer. "There were some things Gideon needed to hear. He's not your only option, Raven." I'm not enjoying the push-pull game with me in the middle. Cole lifts his chin to Gideon. "Do you want to hit me?"

"Frankly, yes." Gideon's hand fists and he draws his elbow back. Cole's eyes widen to capacity.

"Gideon!" With one hand, I lunge for his wrist while I clutch my gown together with the other.

His arm lowers and he grins like a madman. A total psyche. "I think I'll pass on punching you, Wynter. Your time at Maddox mansion has more than served its purpose. I'm satisfied."

Cole's body relaxes and he eases into his pillow. "Sounds good."

***

Jamis drives us to the house as the sun breaks over the horizon. We're no sooner out of the car than Jenny throws the front door open and scurries down the sidewalk. "Mr. Maddox! I've been calling and calling."

Gideon frowns. He pulls his cell from his back pocket. "I had it turned off at the doctor's. What's the matter?"

Jenny's gaze flits from her employer to me. "It's Mr. Weathersby, sir. He's taken a turn for the worse." My knees falter. Gideon's hand rests on my lower back, and I press into him. "The young miss is wanted in Savannah immediately. Please, you must hurry. It's quite serious."

"No," I whisper. It's all I can manage.

"Jamis!" Gideon barks, but the old man is already getting into the driver's seat. Gideon yanks the back door of the Lexus open for me.

As I make for the car, Jenny's plump arms wrap my neck. "I'm so sorry, dearie. So very sorry."

I pat her back. "I know you are, Jenny. Thank you."

In seconds, we're back in the car and heading to Savannah. The scenery blurs as I will the miles to go faster. They've called me to say goodbye. No matter how long a person's been sick, or how prepared you think you are for this moment, you're never ready. All my plans for moving Ben into Maddox mansion, getting him well, being a healthy family are past. He won't see me go to college, or launch my first collection. I won't buy that little flat in New York for the two of us now.

We are but dust and shadow.

As Jamis drives to the front door of the rehab center, I don't wait for the car to fully stop before I'm out and running up the steps. Gideon calls to me, but I rush forward, burst through the door and shout, "Where is Benjamin Weathersby!"

A woman behind the desk wears a disgruntled expression. I'm about to tell her where to shove it, when a tiny, dark-haired woman in a white coat walks in from an adjoining hallway. I met her on my first visit here, Dr. Lee.

"Thank you, Doris," Dr. Lee says. "Miss Weathersby, will you follow me, please?"

She doesn't have to ask twice, I'm on her heels like white on rice. "What's wrong with Ben?"

"He's in advanced stages of cirrhosis. Portal hypertension, accumulated scar tissue has caused internal bleeding. He's hemorrhaging. We believe he is hanging on to see you."

Every word stabs. "Why didn't you call me sooner?"

"I am sorry, Miss Weathersby. I know this is an extremely difficult situation. I in no way am making light of your pain, but we act on the sole wishes of the patient until such time as he is unable to make decisions for himself. We called when he asked us to contact you."

Frustration builds in me like a geyser. Her explanation makes zero sense. Ben is needy, helpless, and dependent. I'm always the first one he calls when he's in trouble, and I know he wanted to leave this place, like, a dozen times.

Dr. Lee guides me down a section of the facility I've never seen before. I fight the urge to shove the little doctor aside if it will get me to Ben faster. The antiseptic smell, nurse's desk, and machinery suggest a hospital ward. She leads me to a small room. Inside is a single bed with steel rails. Since Ben is asleep, I take the opportunity to look him over. His multicolored skin is covered in brighter tangles of purple veins. Dark brown circles underline both eyes, and his flesh is downright bronze in color.

"Ben?" His eyes crack open.

"There's my sweetest girl." A hint of a smile plays on his lips.

"Why didn't you call for me?" The moment the words are out, I want to reel them back. I don't want our last minutes together spent fussing at each other.

"Time I grew up, don't you think? I had to let you go, Rae, and I have." Only now, at the end, does my stepfather decide to become independent and unselfish when all I want is to be with him. "Knew it was the end for me pretty soon after they brought me in here, but I couldn't say so. I wanted you to have a chance at a new life. Let the Maddox boy help you. Don't be stubborn like your old man." He draws a labored breath, and I glance behind me for a nurse, just in case. "Rae?"

My head snaps around. "Yeah, I'm here." I lean over and run my hand over his forehead. The skin is clammy, and I wonder again if I should call someone.

"You needed to learn to live without taking care of me. I needed to stand on my own." His hand covers mine. It's so cold, I startle.

"Does it hurt?" I grip his frail fingers. The knuckles protrude under parchment-thin skin.

"It's not so bad."

Tears stream down my face. "I love you, Pops. You know that, right?" There's a catch in my voice that I don't bother hiding.

"I've always known it, darlin'. Don't matter where you come from. You're *my* girl, and you always will be. Thank you for all you done for me." His voice grows fainter. I have to lean over to hear him. "Make me proud. I'm going to see your mama, now, Rae. Going up to heaven. But I'll see you again one day."

His eyes close, but there's a smile. The monitor goes from a steady beat to flatline. "Nurse!" I shriek, eyeing the open door. When no one appears, I throw myself on top of Ben. "Don't you leave me, damn it. Oh, God. Don't go!" Several hands grab me by the arms, pulling me off Ben. I fight, but there are too many of them. I'm deposited in a nearby chair as the staff attends my stepfather, but a sixth sense tells me it's useless. He's gone. The images of doctors and nurses blur, as

I weep for my Ben.

And the flatline screams on ...

I don't know how much time passes while they work on him. My weeping fades to quiet hiccups. Sitting numbly by, I watch detached, as if they're filming an episode of *Grey's Anatomy*. After a while, a doctor comes to me with an offer of condolence. I can hardly process his words: made him as comfortable as possible, severe toxins, too late, very sorry for your loss.

The doctors and nurses exit. They've left me here with Ben for 'closure.' Whatever the hell that means. Because the truth is part of me knew we would end here from the time I was twelve years old. Another piece of me understands I will miss him for the rest of my life.

Ben lies still and peaceful. Will I see his spirit rise? I both desire and dread to at the same time.

A nurse placed his hands together over his stomach, such a thoughtful gesture on her part. As I sit there watching his face, it looks as though he's resting. He could wake up any minute. Maybe his death is another bad dream, and when I wake up, he'll be here, snoring in his chair. I just need to wake up, or wake Ben up, whichever.

Nothing happens as I watch my stepfather's body. My mother doesn't come to meet him, nor do I view his spirit departing. Did I see Cole because he was neither alive nor dead? I decide that must be so, as I've never seen anyone's ghost before coming to the Maddox mansion.

Gideon appears in the doorway. He leans on his cane, giving me time. For what I don't know.

"Gideon," I say, as a tumble of thoughts spin in my brain. "You can fix this. Bring him back." My tone flirts with an underlying hysteria.

His eyes widen, "What?"

"How hard can it be? You know magicians, your house is magic." My voice rises as I stand. I move around the end of the bed. "Fix the camera and take his picture. Bring Ben back."

"Raven ... don't." His tone is a mix of fear and pity. A

signal I'm over the edge, but I don't care. I can't be alone. I need Ben. Gideon reaches for me, but I whirl away.

"Do it, Gideon. You're powerful, magic. I know you are! You can do anything if you want to."

He lets out a heavy breath. Not one of anger. I sense determination and strength. "No, Raven, the camera is broken, but even if it wasn't, I wouldn't do it. Not even for you. It's wrong. You taught me that."

"No!" I fly at him, pounding his chest with my fists. He stands there letting me hit him. "Your family trapped the souls of others for crimes they committed. This is *Ben,* for heaven's sake. He wouldn't hurt a fly." I gasp for breath between ranting and crying. "Do it. Do it for me!" The strength leaves my hands as I beat on him. His arms wrap me like iron bands. He curses softly, crushing me to him until I give way. Falling against him, I let the tears come freely.

"He's gone," Gideon whispers against the top of my head. "You'll never trust me if I can't be honest now." He kisses my forehead, strokes my hair. "I'm sorry, Raven." His voice catches. "My God, girl, I'd give anything for you but this. I cannot bring him back, nor would I. You were right. This is the way life is supposed to be. He's with your mother. They're together." His hand runs the length of my back. "He's with her right now."

My desperation melts. He's right. Let them go, I tell myself. "I can't breathe."

"I know." He gathers me into his arms and carries me from the room. Down the hall, out of the sick ward we go to a porch on the other side of two, heavy glass doors. Outside, the air is clean and smells of freshly mown grass. The sun is shining and I wonder how it dares to show its face on such a sad day. A chilly breeze cools the tears on my cheeks, and I shiver.

He holds me closer, as if I'll bolt if he puts me down. He's half-right. Gideon limps over to a set of rattan couches in a little cove beside the door. I lean away, but he secures me on his lap. I give up resisting, curl into a ball, and nestle against his chest. He's warm and comforting. His skin smells like salt and iron. I allow myself to feel close to him in this moment. He's different, changed somehow, and I'm proud to say I know him. My love for him swells, threatening to engulf my aching heart, but I know it can't last. Love lasts, but people don't stay, and all that's left are empty spaces in between.

Silhouettes and shadows with a chalk outline of someone that you used to love.

And what I know, what Gideon can't understand, is that hardship and pain may be what knocks you down, but it's survivable. It's the threat of hope that truly kills. Daring to stretch your fingers toward your heart's truest desire and then missing the mark—that's what finishes you off for good.

I make a vow as the door to my heart slams shut. I'm never going to feel loss like this again.

Chapter Thirty-Three

Seventy-two hours after Ben's passing, I finish my collection for Raedoxx Apparel. Curtain rods, doorframes, hooks, and vents all over my room and workspace are draped with the garments I created. I worked my little Goth butt off. Faster than I ever have before, but I was doubly inspired. The designs are a tribute to Ben, my farewell gift to Gideon, and the best work I have ever done.

Showered, packed, and organized, I sit on the end of the magnificent, winged bed Gideon loaned me and survey what I've created. Edgar jumps up on the comforter with a chirp and wanders onto my lap. "You and me, pal," I say. The confidence in my tone is meant to bolster my courage. I'm leaving. Decided the night Ben died, but that doesn't make going any easier.

I asked Jamis to bring my VW around to the front of the house. He didn't ask why, and I didn't offer an explanation. He and I have come to an understanding since the night he tattled to Gideon after finding Jenny and me in the pantry. She forgave him, and so did I. That doesn't mean he's my new BFF, though. He's old-school, and he serves Gideon faithfully.

We all do what we think is right. I can't fault the guy for that, even if he is an old cranky-butt.

Jenny is harder. I sort of love the old girl. Okay, not sort of, I do. She's awesome, and it stings like crazy I won't see her every day. But Edgar and I need to make a fresh start. I have no idea what that looks like or even how I'll get by, but I no longer doubt that I will. I have talent. I'll get a job, go to school, and work my way up. I'll be okay.

Cole's flown back home. My heart holds a big soft spot for the guy, and I hope he'll be happy. I don't know how or when, but I believe I'll see him again. One day. Desiree's gone, drowned in the millpond out back. I shudder as I relive the death that was almost mine. There was no inquiry, of course. She disappeared a long time ago, rumored to have moved to Europe. No one has any reason to look for her. Not a soul will grieve her passing. I wish I could say I was sorry, or that the way she lived and died was tragic, but I can't. Maybe there's something wrong with me. I feel zero pity for her.

Now comes the hardest part. Gideon.

His demons are gone.

Literally.

He no longer lives under the shadow of his father or his expectations. His choices are his own, whatever he decides to do. I think he'll be okay, and the thought fills me with the hope of peace. For both of us.

"Come on, fat boy." I kiss Edgar's black, furry head. "Let's say goodbye and hit the road." It won't be easy, but we can't avoid it either. Might as well get this over with. Maggie's parents have agreed to let me bunk with them until graduation, give me time to sort things out. I want to hear about her and Dane, and it will be a healthy daily distraction from the heartache that waits just off to the side, threatening to finish me if I let it in.

Ben's ceremony is Tuesday. There's no money for a funeral, though Gideon offered to cover any arrangements I wanted to make. He pressed so hard, I finally allowed him to pay the cremation fees. Maggie, Dane, and me are going up to my mother's gravesite and release Ben's ashes there. They'll finally be at rest. Together.

It's not that I don't want Gideon there, I do, but I'm not ready to be his friend. I don't know if I ever will. Seeing him is just too hard when my heart wants so much more. My head has always been smarter than my heart.

When I glance up, Gideon stands in the doorway. One hand leans on his lion-head cane, the other hangs on the doorframe above him, accentuating the cut in his bicep. He's wearing dark, stonewashed jeans, a faded brown T-shirt, and heavy leather boots. Blond rings frame his handsome face. This conversation would be so much easier if he wasn't so drop dead gorgeous.

"How are you feeling?" His gaze drops to the bags on top of my bed. A crease forms between his eyes, and I steel myself for our talk.

"Okay." I lift one shoulder in a half-hearted shrug. "I was on my way to see you. I've finished." I flap my hand in the air indicating the clothing hanging everywhere. "Your line for Raedoxx and Maddox Industries is complete—as is our contract. Everything is set for your show in Paris this spring."

"*Our* show." He saunters into the room, head swiveling to take in my newest creations. "They're incredible." He faces me with a pointed look. "You'll not be offended when I say I don't give a rat's ass about the clothes right now, though. Why are you packed?" Right to the point, that's Gideon. There's danger in his tone, but I go on as if I hadn't noticed.

I should have planned better. Mags and Dane would be the perfect buffer for this awkwardness if I had thought to arrange it. Too late now. "Maggie and Dane's numbers are on the worktable should you need to contact me, or ask questions about the collection. I have no doubt your manufacturers can work with what's here. They're competent."

"Rae." My name, soft and low on his tongue, guts me. "What are you doing?"

I look him dead in the eye. It's the only way to appear resolute with a guy like Gideon, and he deserves no less. "I'm leaving."

"Why?"

"Because my work is done. Ben's debt is paid." His eyes flash, but I can't let him see every word I speak cuts me deeper than a blade. "I learned a lot from you. It's funny, but I truly am grateful for everything that's happened. I care a lot about you, I hope you know that, but we need to be apart for—"

"You *care* a lot about me?"

I nod, the moths in my nervous stomach taking flight. "Yes."

"But we need a break?"

"Yes. It's for the best." My voice trembles.

"For who?"

I square my shoulders. "Both of us. We need distance from this …" I wave my hands, but he's already shaking his head. "…situation because it started for all the wrong reasons, can't you see that?" Tricks, manipulation, I was a game to him, a goal. Would he pursue me on my terms for once instead of his? And even if he would, I remind myself it's hopeless. I can't open my heart for someone else again after losing Ben.

I place Edgar's pet carrier on the floor and kneel to unzip the opening. After stuffing my rotund pet inside, I glance up.

Gideon stands over me, eyes blazing. "Don't do this."

"I'll see you around. Thanks again for everything you did for us." My words sound lame, even to me. "I mean that." I grab my cat and bags and rush past him. Tears sting my eyes as I hurry down the stairs. My vision smears as I pull from the driveway, blurring more with each passing mile to Maggie's house. I've done the right thing. I know I have, but then why does it hurt so much? Feel so wrong?

If Gideon is ready to love someone, it should be someone who's also ready. I had hoped that might be me, but it's selfish to try when my mind is so mixed up. He deserves someone who's less … okay, who's more … ugh! "I don't know!" Edgar meows in response. My laugh is harsh through my tears. "Sorry, boy."

The door to Maggie's house swings open and she's jogging to meet me. "Rae. Oh, honey, what happened?"

I snort as her arm comes around me. "You got any Oreos?"

"If only it were that simple."

The odd tone in her voice gets my attention. "Why? What do you mean?"

Tires screech as Gideon's Audi pulls into the driveway behind us. He gets out slamming the door shut and heads right for me.

"*That's* what I mean," she says, pointing. "He called right before you got here. Dude's loaded for bear."

As always, Gideon's limp is more pronounced without his cane, but he doesn't look worried. He looks pissed. "Are your parents' home, Maggie?" he growls.

"No."

"Good. That will make this much less awkward for them." Gideon doesn't slow. He grabs my wrist as he passes, dragging me behind him into the house before slamming the second door in as many minutes.

He turns on me. I back up.

"Stop running."

"I'm not. I told you, I've made a decision. We've been through this. I based it on facts, sound judgment, and life experience, not emotion." Gideon runs his hand over the shadowed stubble of his jaw. The habit I now recognize shows calculated thought on his part. "I ... I thought you would appreciate an intelligent, well-thought-out plan of action."

"I do, but that's not what this is." He takes another step closer. "Want to know what I see?"

"Not really, no."

"I see a girl who's been hurt so many times that she's willing to shut out any spark of love or happiness to protect herself. Understandable, but not acceptable. I won't allow it."

"Ugh. You always do this!" I lift my chin. "It's not up to you! I'm here because I need to be on my own for a while. That's what Ben said. He said I need to live by myself."

"Damn it, Raven that is *not* what he said."

My fists slam down on my hips. "How do you know?"

"Because I was there. The whole time. Do you really think

I'd leave you to face his death by yourself?" He grinds the words out through clenched teeth. "What he said was you needed to learn to live without taking care of *him.* Good God, Raven, he never meant for you to be alone."

"Yes he did. That's exactly what he said, he—"

"You've been alone for years!" He runs both hands through his hair and churns out a breath. His tone goes soft. "And you're tired. I know what that's like. I've been too selfish and self-centered to care about anyone or anything else for a long time. Let someone take care of you for a change. Me."

"You're making this harder, Gideon. Just go."

"No. Not until you hear me out." When he takes my hand, his eyes glint with careful determination. He won't be denied his chance to speak, and I can't refuse him anymore. I'm caught up in whatever spell he's casting.

He leads me to the worn, pleather sofa in Maggie's living room. The springs creak under his weight, and then mine, as he eases us onto the cushions. I'm inching away until he leans over me and I'm on my back. His face inches from mine, emits the scent of black licorice, salt, and musk.

"Listen to me, please." Three fingers run over my mouth, causing every moth in my belly to twitch. "You're worth fighting for, Rae. And though you won't admit it, I know you love me. I see it in the way you look at me, the things you say and do. That's why I won't stop until you're mine." The fire, always smoldering beneath the surface of his gaze, ignites, underlining the intensity of each word he speaks. "Do you think you can hide from me? Push me away; hurt me until I give up on you? 'Quit' is not in my vocabulary."

I cut my eyes away. "You don't get it, Gideon."

With his fingers pressing into my shoulders, he shakes me once, forcing me to look up. "Don't I? You're afraid. Terrified of what love may cost you, and I understand. I've lost people, too, but we belong together. Can't you feel that?" The heat in his gaze blasts through to my soul. "You brought me back from the dead, gave life where there was nothing but ash and decay. Trust me to do the same for you. I love you, Raven.

You're worth loving, and I'm exactly the man to prove it to you."

A hot tear slides down my cheek. Gideon bends his head to kiss it away. His lips burn my skin, and I close my eyes. I do love him. My heart thunders that truth beneath his chest, and I wonder if he feels it. I have a choice: let my heart calcify or let him love me. "People make promises," I whisper. "You can't know how scared I am of losing ..." I swallow my tears. "You can't promise you won't leave."

His lips press the ramping pulse in my neck. "I can't promise I won't die," he murmurs. "Only God chooses, I know that now. What I can promise is that I won't *leave*. Let that be enough." His fingers clamp down on my waist. With slow, purposeful torture, Gideon drops a series of kisses along my jaw. Instinctually, I raise my chin giving him greater access. His teeth graze my cheekbone. I whimper as he covers my mouth with his.

My lips part for him. Instead of the forceful kiss I expect, this one is slow, painstaking in its sweet sensuality. Gideon's fingers brush my face. The tenderness in his touch reaches into the deep recesses of my pain and bangs on the wall of my heart. My arms slide around his shoulders, and I tug him harder against me. Gideon moans. The sound, raw and primal, makes my stomach flip. When he finally lifts his head, his blue and green eyes are hooded, sleepy with his desire. "I want to own your heart the way you own mine. Choose me, Raven, freely, not because I force you, but because you need me. Because you want to."

I search his face. The sincerity in his gaze wedges itself like a crowbar between my fear and hope. "Gideon, I swore I'd never ... I can't lose you."

"You won't." His voice is respectful of my fears, careful and comforting. There's an earnestness and expectation that's contagious. Gideon's feet tangle with mine. His hand closes over my fingers and he laces them together. "Stay with Maggie if you need to. Only keep me in your life. Trust me," he urges. He kisses my cheek, my nose, my mouth. This kiss is more intense as we fight an unseen battle of wills. His confidence and my insecurity war with each other until I feel the fortress around my resolve crumble.

"I love you, girl," he whispers. "Don't take yourself from me." Whether foolish hope or some sixth sense, I believe him. When he kisses me again, all doubt fades away. Gideon's arms slide between my back and the couch cushions. He lifts my shoulders, cradling me from the waist up, crushing me within his powerful arms. His scorching lips meld with mine, rocking my world, blowing me and my worries to smithereens.

As I gasp for breath, Gideon lifts his head with a seductive smile. How long has it been since the idea of living without him felt like existing without air? I know what he's waiting for, and I offer it up with my whole being.

"I choose you."

The Happily Ever After

Dane, Maggie, Gideon, and I sit atop a hill in the Sales Hollow Cemetery. Dressed wholly in my dark creations of Goth-Steampunk, we appear as four black birds dotting the landscape, and we like that just fine.

The gray, November sky above us keeps the sun at bay, and though it's cool, there isn't any wind. Near the bottom of the knoll sits a little white chapel and the gravestones beyond. The name Ida Elizabeth Weathersby is chiseled into the marble of one. Ben's ashes now rest with hers.

Maggie leans over and grabs my hand. "We have to jet. Mom's made dinner and Dane is meeting my dad for the first time."

Dane swallows and stares at his hands. "He knows Ben's funeral is today. I'm hoping that will soften the guy up."

"Really? Oh my gosh, Dane!" Maggie punches him in the arm. "Stop saying stuff like that, you'll make her feel bad." She angles back to me. "I'm sorry, Rae. He's sorry, too." I fight to hide my smile. Gideon winks at me over her shoulder. "Are you okay, sweetie? I feel terrible about Ben." She hugs me so tightly it feels more like a headlock than an embrace.

"I will be." I glance at Gideon. "We're all going to be fine." When Maggie pulls back, her eyes shine and she sniffs.

Dane slides his hand around her waist. The gesture is natural, like he's done it a thousand times, and in his mind, he probably has. "You ready?"

Maggie's gaze locks onto mine. "No. Yes." *I love you,* she mouths. "If you need us, we're a phone call away."

"I know," I say. "Thank you. And not just for today …"

She gives my arm a squeeze then passes from Dane's grasp. My friend marches toward Gideon. On her toes, she stretches up while Gideon leans down to meet her. "Take care of our girl?"

"Always." He gives her one if his heart-ensnaring smiles.

Dane moves to stand beside me, and I hug his slim waist. He looks down from his dizzying height. His hand cups my cheek and he lowers his mouth to my ear. "If he hurts you, I'll gut him like a deer." I let my head fall back and laugh. The action feels foreign but nice. He kisses the top of my head and strolls off to retrieve his new girlfriend.

Gideon settles with his back against a tree. He motions to me with his crooked finger, and I obey, fitting myself snuggly in between his legs. Together we watch my friends as they retreat down the hill to Maggie's car. "Did you tell him?"

Our big news is that Raedoxx is offering financial aid for one student to attend Armstrong Atlantic, where Maggie's already been accepted. The newly formed scholarship will benefit a seventeen-year-old, African-American male with red dreadlocks, tattoos, and a bad attitude. Dane's a shoo-in, but first he needs to get his grades up.

I smile. "Not today, but I will." I scoot until I can see his face. "You think a scholarship will make him like you?"

Gideon's mouth pulls on one side. "Probably not, but he's important to me, because you care about him." I don't know what to say to that, so I rest my head against his shoulder. His hand rubs up and down my spine. His chest deflates with his long breath. "It's getting cold. Do you want to head back?"

"A few more minutes, is that okay?"

"As if anyone could tell you no."

I laugh. "You tell me no all the time."

"Well, I *am* the boss."

I smile against his chest. "That's not exactly true."

"Ah, but it is, you just won't admit it."

My fingers play with the buttons on his shirt. "Do you no longer aspire to be the king of Maddox Enterprises?"

"I'm happier just being your Gideon. Whatever we decide to do with our futures, we'll figure it out together."

I straighten so I can see his eyes. "I sort of like you. You know that?"

"Like?" He gives me his barely-there smile. "I didn't quite catch that. Do you want to rephrase?"

"I *really* like you?" I pluck up his hands and grip them in mine before kissing his fingers.

"Coward."

Yup. His chin lifts. His smile is cocky, self-assured as always. Maybe the loss of Ben is still too fresh. Maybe I haven't processed all we survived. I know he wants me to say I love him, but somehow I can't. Not yet.

His thumb rubs my cheek. "It's all right. I can wait. Just tell me who you belong to?"

"You." I say, without hesitation. I can't take the intensity in his gaze as he watches me. Nervous, I lean in for a kiss when a murder of crows flies overhead. They land in the tree above us cawing and flapping their wings. As I count them, my mother's rhyme comes to mind. I recite it for Gideon.

"One for sorrow

Two for mirth

Three for a funeral

Four for a birth

Five for heaven

Six for hell

Seven's the Devil his own self ...

"That's all I remember. Drives me crazy, I always get stuck after the seventh crow."

"Hm. I think I can help you." Gideon's finger trails slowly

down my arm, sending a shiver through me and not from the cold.

"Eight brings wishing
Nine brings kissing
Ten, the love my own heart's missing."

"That's it!" Excited he's heard the rhyme before; I grab at both of his arms, the solid feel of his biceps a momentary distraction. "How do you know it?"

Gideon's gaze drops to my hands still clutching his sleeves. Self-conscious, I release my hold, and he answers through a knowing smile. "My mother read to me often when I was sick in bed."

"Oh." Remembering I'm not the only one who's suffered loss, I worry I've brought up a bad memory as his focus is drawn across the cemetery. "Sorry. I didn't mean to—"

"There's nothing you can't say to me, understand? Nothing." He meets my gaze. "We'll be honest with each other and have no secrets between us ever. Deal?"

"Back to deals, are we?" He grins. I run my finger along the seam of his black leather jacket. "I wonder what your parents would have said if they had met me. We're from such different worlds, you know?"

"I really don't care. The greatest love stories are built on differences like ours."

I yank a weed from the ground, continuing on as if he hasn't spoken. "Yeah, but I'm poor, family scandalized in the news. Your dad would have shown me the door, I bet." My laugh is harsh, humorless. "Not to mention I'm the love-child of my mother and some guy who skipped out on her."

The muscles in Gideon's body coil tightly.

"Whoa!" I squeal, laughing as he twists me around, pinning me underneath him in the thick winter grass.

"Now you listen to me, woman. We're not comparing worth, remember?" His hands slide up my forearms. He holds my wrists in an unbreakable grip over my head. My chest rises and falls with my panting breaths. His eyes focus on me with fierce intensity. "You are everything I never knew I wanted. I love the way you think and create. I love your loyalty and stubborn pride. The dimple in your right cheek when you laugh, and the way your forehead creases when you challenge me. Most of all, I love when you sleepwalk into my bed late at night, and tell me how you really feel ..."

My eyes stretch, and my throat slams shut. "Uh, I what?"

"I love how you weaken in my arms, and the sexy whimper you make when I kiss you below your ear." My cheeks flame, mouth pops open.

"There will never be anyone for me but you, Raven Weathersby. I knew it from the start. And that's final." Gideon's head lowers, his mouth covering mine in a searing kiss, masterfully silencing any further discussion.

The End

ACKNOWLEDGEMENTS

No writer births a story without the help of others. God has placed the most wonderful people in my life, and I'm grateful first to Him, and to the following for making this book possible. A huge, HUGE (as in, can I make you breakfast in bed?) thank you to the talented, amazing, and all around nice people listed below:

My husband: tireless listener, flower bestower, moon hanger—you are the triple threat among men, my friend. How did I get so lucky? My girls: Blake and Madelyne, my best friends, first, and way toughest critics ever. Llama face! Love you guys.

My mom and dad, who read to me.

Brittany Booker: dog lover, wish granter, and super-talented agent. Thank you for believing in me and for working so hard. XOXOX

The folks at Month9Books have my undying gratitude for taking a chance on me. Mucho thanks to my editor and hero Georgia McBride, Allie Kincheloe for cat herding and manuscript roping, Kerry Genova, and her super-powered proofreading eyeballs, Publicity and Marketing Director extraordinaire, Jaime Arnold, *bows* you are a flipping rock star—truly, Jennifer Million for kind words and organizational skills I can only dream of, and cover artist K. Morris for her artistic vision. Thank you! These people are whip-smart and chock-full of awesome.

Early beta readers that make up the four writing chambers of my heart, Julie Belfield (plot/story detail savior), Claire Gillian (big picture girl and spotter of heroines 'too stupid to live'), Stephanie Judice (romance and feels director), and Kathleen Proa (currently holds the glittering grammar tiara). I'd like to say so much more about each of them individually, but all together? This book would be so much less interesting in about a hundred ways without their careful, spot-on advice.

Wendy Higgins and L.S. Murphy, thanks for being so great and agreeing to slog through a pre-pre-edited version and like the book anyway.

To my fans, I love you guys. No one could ask for better support than ya'll.

And for every reader out there who gives this book a try, I thank you and appreciate you more than you could ever know. ((Hugs)).

JULIE REECE

Born in Ohio, I lived next to my grandfather's horse farm until the fourth grade. Summers were about riding, fishing and make-believe, while winter brought sledding and ice-skating on frozen ponds. Most of life was magical, but not all.

I struggled with multiple learning disabilities, did not excel in school. I spent much of my time looking out windows and daydreaming. In the fourth grade (with the help of one very nice teacher) I fought dyslexia for my right to read, like a prince fights a dragon in order to free the princess locked in a tower, and I won.

Afterwards, I read like a fiend. I invented stories where I could be the princess... or a gifted heroine from another world who kicked bad guy butt to win the heart of a charismatic hero. Who wouldn't want to be a part of that? Later, I moved to Florida where I continued to fantasize about superpowers and monsters, fabricating stories (my mother called it lying) and sharing them with my friends.

Then I thought I'd write one down...

Hooked, I've been writing ever since. I write historical,

contemporary, urban fantasy, adventure, and young adult romances. I love strong heroines, sweeping tales of mystery and epic adventure… which must include a really hot guy. My writing is proof you can work hard to overcome any obstacle. Don't give up. I say, if you write, write on!

Social Media

Website: http://blog.juliereece.com/

Facebook: https://www.facebook.com/author.julieareece

Twitter: https://twitter.com/JulieAReece

Pinterest: http://www.pinterest.com/julieareece/

Goodreads: https://www.goodreads.com/author/show/5294594. Julie_Reece

OTHER MONTH9BOOKS TITLES YOU MIGHT LIKE

THE PERILOUS JOURNEY OF THE NOT-SO-INNOCUOUS GIRL
SHADOWS FALL AWAY
SUMMER OF THE OAK MOON

Find more awesome Teen books at Month9Books.com

Connect with Month9Books online:

Facebook: www.Facebook.com/Month9Books
Twitter: https://twitter.com/month9books
You Tube: www.youtube.com/user/Month9Books
Blog: www.month9booksblog.com
Request review copies via publicity@month9books.com

The Perilous Journey
of the not-so-
Innocuous Girl

LEIGH STATHAM

KIT FORBES

SHADOWS
FALL AWAY

*Falling in love with a proper Victorian girl from
1888 London may be the least of his problems.*